OCT 09

Aer.18

P9-DYY-459

ROGUE WARRIOR®

Seize
the Day

ALSO BY RICHARD MARCINKO

FICTION
Violence of Action

With John Weisman
Red Cell
Green Team
Task Force Blue
Designation Gold
Seal Force Alpha
Option Delta
The Real Team
Echo Platoon
Detachment Bravo

With Jim DeFelice
Vengeance
Holy Terror
Rogue Warrior®: Dictator's Ransom

NONFICTION
Rogue Warrior (with John Weisman)
Leadership Secrets of the Rogue Warrior:
A Commando's Guide to Success
The Rogue Warrior's Strategy for Success

ROGUE WARRIOR®

Seize the Day

RICHARD MARCINKO
AND
JIM DEFELICE

GLEN ELLYN PUBLIC LIBRARY
400 DUANE STREET
GLEN ELLYN, ILLINOIS 60137

A TOM DOHERTY ASSOCIATES BOOK
NEW YORK

This is a work of fiction. All of the characters, organizations, and events portrayed in tThis is a work of fiction. All of the characters, organizations, and events portrayed in this novel are either products of the authors' imaginations or are used fictitiously.

ROGUE WARRIOR®: SEIZE THE DAY

Copyright © 2009 by Richard Marcinko and Jim DeFelice

All rights reserved.

A Forge Book
Published by Tom Doherty Associates, LLC
175 Fifth Avenue
New York, NY 10010

www.tor-forge.com

Forge® is a registered trademark of Tom Doherty Associates, LLC.

Library of Congress Cataloging-in-Publication Data
Marcinko, Richard.
    Rogue warrior : Seize the day / Richard Marcinko and Jim DeFelice.
—1st ed.
            p.   cm.
    "A Tom Doherty Associates book."
    ISBN 978-0-7653-1794-0
    1. Rogue Warrior (Fictitious character)—Fiction. 2. Special forces
(Military science) —Fiction. 3. Cuba —Fiction. I. DeFelice, James. II.
Title.
    PS3563.A6362R644   2009
    813'.54—dc22

                                                            2009028189

First Edition: October 2009

Printed in the United States of America

0 9 8 7 6 5 4 3 2 1

PART ONE
FUN IN THE SUN

Every tyrant who has lived has believed in freedom—for himself.

—Elbert Hubbard, *The Philistine* magazine

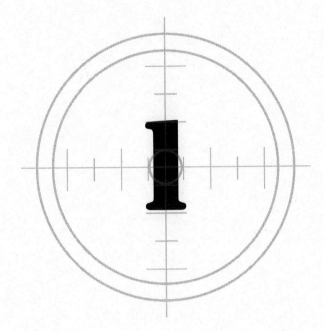

(1)

People always say it's who you know that matters.

Let me tell you, children, it's not who you know, it's who you look like.

This is especially important when you're on the roof of the tallest building on the Havana shoreline, hanging off the side by your fingernails while half the Cuban army points AK47s at you.

But we should start at the beginning.

The whys and wherefores of my arrival in Cuba would fill a few hundred pages, and just as surely cure the worst insomnia known to mankind. So let's cut through the bullshit and go to the executive version.

A recent vacation in sunny North Korea[1] had left me so refreshed that I found myself locked away in a hospital ward, in traction and in a foul mood. Unable to spring me, my main squeeze Karen Fairchild nonetheless undertook to nurse me back to health, smuggling in copious amounts of Bombay Sapphire. Thanks to the care of Dr. Bombay, I rallied and managed to leave the hospital before the billing department figured out how to spell my last name.

Karen and I planned a nice Caribbean vacation in celebration. My friend Ken Jones at the CIA had other ideas.

Ken is a former admiral who defected to the Christians in Action, the government agency known to the incredulous as the Central Intelligence Agency. In my experience, it's neither central nor intelligent, though I have to admit that I've never looked to the government to be accurate in anything, let alone naming its various parts.

Ken is the agency's DCI, an abbreviation that I believe stands for director of the Can't-Cunt Inquisitors, though most people who haven't dealt with him say it means director of the CIA.

Ken called me the day I got home from the hospital and asked how I was.

"Admiral, fuck you very much for calling," I said in my pleasant

---

[1] See: "What I did on my summer vacation," aka *Rogue Warrior: Dictator's Ransom*, available at finer bookstores and pawnshops across the land.

voice. "Doctors say I'm contagious and can't see anyone from the government for at least a decade."

"You're a card, Dick. Let's have a drink."

"Sorry, but I've got a lot of other things to do."

"I was thinking the same thing when the invoice from Red Cell International hit my desk."

It was just like the admiral to bring up money. Red Cell International is my corporate umbrella, the security company that conducts various rogue and not-so-rogue activities across the globe. The CIA owed Red Cell a considerable amount of dough-re-me, including the not insignificant expenses we'd incurred in North Korea. Cash flow being what it was, even a short delay in paying the bills would be a problem: my accountant has three kids in college, and their tuition bills were due.

"You're not trying to blackmail me, are you, Admiral?" I asked.

"Dick, I wouldn't do that. But I do have a lot of work to do. A lot on my plate, so to speak. You could lighten that load with a little favor. A tiny one, actually."

The smaller the favor, the bigger the problem. But Ken wouldn't take no for an answer, and a few hours later I found myself sipping gin with him at his favorite little bar outside of Langley.

Ken stuck to lite beer, a sure sign of trouble.

It took two rounds before he got to the point, reaching into his jacket pocket for a pair of photos that he laid on the table. One was a recent picture of yours truly snapped somewhere in what we used to call the Mysterious Orient before we all got PC religion and switched to more acceptable terms like "the asshole pit of Asia." Shot somewhere in Pyongyang, the North Korean capital, the picture showed me with my beard more kempt than normal, though from the glint in my eye I knew I must have been enjoying myself, probably by planning what I would do to one of my government escorts when I didn't have to be polite anymore.

The other photo showed me in a more relaxed moment: face flushed, eyes bugging out, teeth poised for blood. It would have made a lovely yearbook shot.

Except it wasn't me. Ken reached into his jacket for another shot, showing me that it was actually an enlargement from a group photo. The group shot revealed that the florid face belonged to a man who favored starched puke-green fatigues, a clothing choice that has never agreed with me.

"Recognize him?" asked Ken.

"We were separated at birth," I said, handing the photos back. "After the doctor dropped him on his head."

The great thing about Ken is that he has exactly no sense of humor, and it took him quite a while to figure out if I was joking or not. Which was my cue to leave, though I didn't take it.

The man in the photo was Fidel Alejandro Castro Ruz, dictator par deviance of Cuba. At the time, he was said to be ailing, though a dictator's health is never something you can count on. The favor Ken wanted was deceptively simple, as they always are: impersonate Fidel on a special tape *el Presidente* was leaving as his last will and testament. I didn't even have to talk—the words had been carefully spliced together by the CIA's technical dweebs. All I had to do was look menacing and pretend to rant for the camera.

"Do what comes naturally," said Ken. "Pretend you're talking to our accounting division about where your check is."

I suppose before going any further I should mention that I've had a warm spot in my heart and other body parts for the Cuban people. Most Cubans I know are expatriates, but I think even those still on the island are, as a general rule, happy, loving people who make loyal and open friends. They're certainly warm and gracious to strangers. The women are pretty, for sure; they're rarely demanding and are grateful for small favors and a little bit of attention.

In my experience, of course.

Fidel . . . Well, maybe at one time his heart was in the right place, but his brain and ass just couldn't provide. After he took power, rats replaced the chickens in every pot. Anyone who opposed him was imprisoned, tortured, and worse.

Before this op, I'd been to Cuba many times, but with one exception always to Gitmo—our base at Guantanamo. It may surprise you to know that a good number of Cubans work there. They were "shaken down" every night when they crossed back to go home—the government was anxious for any tiny rewards they might have reaped. Kind of a shame to watch.

The one exception I mentioned was a short stay in Havana. And then, of course . . . well, let's not get too far ahead of ourselves.

13

I taped the bit a few days after talking to Ken, reporting at 0600 to what looked like an abandoned warehouse building in northeastern Virginia. I took two of my associates with me—Trace Dahlgren and Matthew "Junior" Loring. Junior's one of our technical experts, and was along to help me pick out some gear from a vendor we use who happens to be located a few miles from the taping site. Trace was along allegedly to help make sure we got the right stuff, but really to make faces at me while I was taping.

We were met at the door by a little old gray-haired man wearing a barber's smock. He smiled when he saw me, nodded to himself, then led me across the dimly lit foyer to a thick steel door. Beyond the door was a studio that would make the folks at the *Today* show jealous. The dressing room was twice the size of my office, with thick wood paneling, a pair of overstuffed leather couches, another half-dozen chairs of various but expensive description, and—especially important to Junior and Trace—a table laden with a variety of breakfast goodies.

"What, no omelet station?" snarked Trace.

"Scrambled eggs here," said the barber, showing her the tray. "If that's not all right—"

"It's more than all right," I said. "Pay no attention to her. She has PNS."

(No, it's not a typo—Permanent Nasty Syndrome.)

Trace gave me a scowl, then started force-feeding Junior donuts in an attempt to add a little weight to his scarecrowlike frame. I left them to divvy up the goodies while I donned a slightly wrinkled set of green army fatigues for my star turn. After that, the barber took me next door to a room that looked like a 1950s version of the perfect barbershop. A makeup artist—thirty-something, blond, neck with the scent of ripe strawberries—stood next to a counter that looked to contain every cosmetic product known to woman.

"Sit, sit," the barber told me. "You are a very good likeness. You're not related, no?"

"To Fidel?"

"A good thing." The barber flipped on the television on the counter. Fidel's face filled the screen. I studied his mannerisms, watching the way he furled his eyebrows and puffed out his cheeks as he ranted about bourgeoisie Yankees trying to impose democracy on the world.

Meanwhile, the barber went to work, trimming my hair and dying it gray. One thing Ken hadn't made clear: I had to give my ponytail for my country. Seeing as how I've sacrificed just about every other part of my body, I suppose losing a little hair was no big deal.

When the barber was done, the makeup artist daubed a little bit of makeup around my eyes, adding some aging lines and liver spots. She worked for about fifteen minutes, fussing like Michelangelo finishing the Sistine Chapel.

When I looked over at the barber, he was frowning.

"You look too much like him, senor." He glanced at his razor on the counter. "If I did not know any better, I would take the razor and . . ."

The barber's name was Roberto Traba. He'd escaped from Cuba barely two years before, fleeing with his two grandchildren. He had done this even though he had an excellent job, or I should say *because* he had an excellent job—he'd been one of Fidel's barbers.

Traba had worked for years in a small shop at the western edge of Havana, well liked by his customers but unknown to the world at large. One day, *El Comandante en Jefe*—Fidel—decided he wanted his hair cut. His regular barber was sick, his backup at the wedding of a daughter.

Fidel's hair couldn't wait. One of his aides had heard of Traba . . . a bodyguard was sent to the shop, where a dozen customers were sitting, discussing the chances of the local baseball team in the island playoffs while Traba worked. The bodyguard hung a CLOSED sign in the window, shooed the half-finished customer from the chair, and brought Traba to the dictator's house a few miles away.

Traba did his work quickly and efficiently. The dictator liked him, and a few weeks later he was called back for a trim. From that point on, he worked for Fidel every other week.

Without pay, of course. For a barber should be happy to be in the presence of the world's greatest man, and not worry about the revenue he missed by having to close his shop in the middle of the week.

Had the arrangement remained the same, Traba would not have minded it very much. True, after a while the honor of being so close to the country's leader grew stale, and he had to listen to *el Jefe's* endless rants on everything from Yankee imperialism to the poor hitting of the Cuban national baseball team. But resigning such a post was not easy, and Traba would never have seriously considered doing so had the head barber not met with an untimely accident.

An accident in the home, the day after Fidel had railed about being nicked by the barber's careless razor.

The accident involved a loaded gun. Traba knew the head barber well enough to know that the man had an unnatural fear of heights, tight spaces, and guns, and would have nothing to do with any of them. What was especially curious was the fact that the previous head barber had met with a similar accident.

Traba was promoted to head barber on a Tuesday. On Wednesday, he began to look for a way to escape Cuba.

It was not simply a case of self-preservation. Three years before, his daughter had died; he and his wife had taken her two babies, aged one and three at the time. Traba's wife had passed away the following year, and now he was the girls' sole guardian.

Traba tried in vain for months to find a way to leave. He sought out boat owners, spoke to shady men who promised to get him a European passport, even studied a translation of Mark Twain's *Huck Finn* for information on how to build a raft. Then fate dropped opportunity in his lap: Fidel planned a visit to the Dominican Republic, and wanted his barber to accompany him.

Traba suggested that he go ahead of time, to survey the facilities at the television station where Fidel was to appear. Fidel agreed. The barber asked a favor—could he bring his granddaughters? It might be very educational for them.

Fidel waved his hand, signifying *yes*. Still, it took two weeks to win official approval from the bureaucrats, securing the places on the plane. Traba put the time to good use, calling in every favor and every hint of a favor he had ever earned in his forty-some years of cutting hair. Within two hours of landing in the Dominican, he and his granddaughters were in a boat halfway to Puerto Rico.

"I am very lucky," Traba told me. "I am sure that now I would be dead, and my grandchildren orphans."

"How are the kids now?"

"The best students. The best. I have only one regret . . ."

"What's that?" asked Trace.

"My brother is still in Cuba," said the barber. "They have made things very hard for him."

"They put him in jail?" asked Junior.

"No. That far, they haven't gone. They would not, I don't think, so long as he doesn't break the law. But they might as well have. In some ways, it is worse."

Traba's brother had been a baker in Havana. His job had been taken from him, and his apartment; he now lived in a small village on the south side of the island, alone. It was exceedingly difficult for Traba to contact him. Practically no one he knew in Cuba would risk carrying a message, because to do so risked angering the authorities.

"It could be worse. He could be in the mountains." Traba shook his head. "But he can't find work. Of course not. The government keeps tabs on him. The security police tell everyone not to be friends. It is a sad story."

"Why don't you get him out?" asked Junior.

Traba gave him a sad look, the sort of smile an older man gives a much younger one when he still has many painful lessons to learn.

"To get someone out of Cuba, especially one who's watched. Not easy."

Junior looked over at me, and I knew exactly what he was thinking. It was the same thing Trace was thinking. She started pumping Traba for more information about his brother, where he lived, and whether he truly wanted to get off the island.

"Are you asking these questions for a reason?" the barber said finally. "Are you in a position to help him?"

"No," I said. "She isn't. And neither am I."

Trace's eyes practically burned a hole in the side of my skull.

"That's OK," said Traba, with the barest hint of disappointment. He undid the sheet covering my clothes, snapping it in the air as he took it away. "If ever I can do anything for you, call this number," he added, slipping me his business card.

I frowned, furrowing my eyebrows as I'd seen Fidel do in the tape. "*Gracias.*"

Traba looked for a moment as if he'd seen a ghost.

"Too much like him," he said, shaking his head. "Too much."

I played Dictator Karaoke for an hour, and we were done. Traba and the makeup artist were gone when the shooting was over; I cleaned up my face, but left the gray highlights in my hair—it's always nice to see the future.

"We really should figure a way to help out Mr. Traba," said Junior as we headed toward the highway. "His brother's kinda screwed."

"Not kinda. Is," said Trace.

"Tell you what, next time you're in Cuba, you can look him up," I said.

"How about you smuggle him out?" asked Junior. "It'd be pretty easy for you."

"I'm not going to Cuba," I told him.

Junior looked like a puppy who's just been told not to pee on his water dish.

"We can't rescue every person living in Cuba," I told him.

"I wasn't talking about every person in Cuba, just the old dude's brother."

"If we *were* going to Cuba," said Trace, "it wouldn't be a bad idea."

"But we're not going to Cuba."

The video I'd made was pressed onto a pair of DVD discs. These were supposed to be smuggled into Cuba, where another courier would take them to yet another operative; none of the transporters would know what they were taking.

The smuggler was a Spanish businessman who had a well-paying sideline as a paid CIA agent. The only problem was that he had another sideline as an informant for the Cuban government—something the CIA discovered roughly twelve hours before he was supposed to pick up the discs.

The Christians in Action have never been very good at dealing with a curveball, but in this case they had a backup plan, and a backup to that, and even a backup to that.

Backup plan number two fizzled when the courier, a Canadian national, got cold feet. So the Christians went to door number three, tapping a Dominican national who'd done various odd jobs for them in the past. He was all set to pick up the discs until he got arrested and thrown in jail.

Which is what tends to happen to drug smugglers.

The CIA would have gladly sprung him from an American jail. But he was arrested in Saba, an island that is part of the Netherlands Antilles and thus under Dutch control. And while the Dutch tend to take a relatively lax view about illegal drug smuggling—even several tons of it, concealed among semifresh flowers shipped out of Colombia—they weren't willing to turn a blind eye to the fact that he had killed two Dutch police agents while resisting arrest.

Yes, those are the sorts of people we depend on to do our spying.

Three strikes, and the Christians decided to look for a new pitcher. Me.

"All I need is someone to get the DVDs to Cuba," Ken Jones told me after convening an emergency powwow at his favorite watering hole near Langley. "I have an agent there who will hand them off to someone else, who'll make the switch. It's all worked out. I just need a middleman."

"That's one position I never really liked. The middle."

"Could you do it as a personal favor?"

I laughed. That was about the *last* reason I would do anything for the CIA.

"How about for the oppressed Cubans?" suggested Ken.

"They are oppressed, and I feel very badly for them," I said. "But I've already done my bit."

"Well then, maybe you would do it because Red Cell International has several government contracts that could evaporate one day. Like tomorrow."

It was an old but effective ploy. We sealed the deal with a round of Bombay Sapphire on the rocks.

The spot for the handoff to the Cuban courier happened to be only a few miles from the town were Traba's brother lived. I'd claim it was a coincidence, but I'm the one who picked the spot.

Trace took my decision to go to Cuba as a sign that I was becoming a softie as I matured, a development that she somehow viewed as welcome. Junior puffed himself up, as if he'd had something to do with it.

The truth was, I didn't particularly want to go to Cuba. But since I *was* going, grabbing the old guy and getting him the hell out of there was the best way I could think of to give Fidel the finger. The CIA was paying three times my usual fee for the operation, and would cover the expense of taking the old guy out as well. (Not that they knew that in advance, of course.) Besides, Traba had done a hell of a job on my hair; I owed him a decent tip.

We ran the operation out of a small hamlet on the northeastern coast of Jamaica, which will remain nameless in case we need to use it again.

Following normal procedure, we arrived there in ones and twos, drifting in over the course of a weekend from a variety of directions. I came from Montego Bay, where I was happy to spend a few days of fun and frolic on an exclusive beach with Karen. It was a treat to lie on a beach without having to duck gunfire or blow something up for a change.

But all good things come to an end. On Sunday morning, she jetted back to her job at Homeland (in)Security and I ducked out a back door at the airport. A short motorbike ride later, I arrived at the small house Doc had rented as our casa away from casa.

"Cheer, cheer, the gang's all here," said Trace Dahlgren when she saw me, unleashing a stream of four-letter endearments that told me just how much she really missed me.

Let me take the opportunity to properly introduce you, since I skipped over the niceties earlier. Trace is vice president in charge of shooter development for Red Cell International. She's part Navaho, part tigress, and I can honestly say she's bailed my butt out of more hot water than a wonton skimmer in a Chinatown restaurant. There was a time in the not-too-distant past when we were more than fellow employees, but our relationship now is entirely chop-tonic—think Platonic, except that she busts my chops, and I bust hers.

The rest of the team was split between wisdom and muscle, with the usual array of talents and specialties sprinkled throughout. Al "Doc" Tremblay—aka Cockbreath and other assorted terms of endearment—had arrived on Friday to handle the logistics and play team den mother.

Those of you who have been following along at home will recall Doc was one of the original Red Cell plank owners when I was back in the navy raising a ruckus. Doc left the service as a master chief petty officer, and a good one[2] . . . good enough to have been a command master chief *several* times! In fact, the old joke may have been told with him in mind:

An old battleship admiral died and found himself at the Pearly Gates, staring up at St. Peter.

"Tell me there's no chief petty officers here," the admiral barked. "The only reason I was willing to pass was the hope that I'd never see one again."

"No chiefs," said St. Peter. "None have ever made it."

The admiral waltzed in, admiral-like. Ten minutes later, he saw a man in

---

[2] Check out Green Team, among others, for a full rundown of Doc's résumé.

khakis and a garrison cap swagger by with a girl on each arm. He had a thick cigar stuck in the middle of his cocky smile.

"What the hell?" thundered the admiral, turning back to St. Peter. "I thought you said there were no chiefs."

"Oh, that's just God. He only thinks he's a chief."

Danny Barrett arrived about the same time as Doc. Danny's a former police officer and a security specialist; he was responsible for establishing our security and coming up with a secure communications network for the trip to Cuba. He also took care of some of our contingency arrangements, making sure we could get the hell out of the country if things went sour.

Maria "Red" Ramirez was our Cuban language expert. Maria is a feisty little thing, barely five feet tall with red hair that matches her personality. (Hence the nickname. Duh.) Maria spent some time in the navy and did a little work for the DIA—Dipshits in Action, also known as the Defense Intelligence Agency—but her qualifications for the mission had to do primarily with her language and geography skills. Her father and mother came from Cuba, and she had been on the island a dozen times, legally and otherwise.

Maria was also our team medic. Everyone at Red Cell has passed through advanced lifesaving and taken a host of EMT courses; most could qualify as paramedics in the most demanding ambulance company. Maria had been a corpsman, an emergency-room nurse, and even studied to be a doctor for a year, though she didn't let that hold her back.

Rounding out the team were three young men who had done yeoman's work for me, most recently in North Korea: Paul "Shotgun" Fox, his shadow Thomas "Mongoose" Yamya, and Junior.

Shotgun and Mongoose are two special-case hard heads, inseparable but as different as night and day. They lost the FNG[3] smell in Korea, where both proved they could chew up an enemy and spit him out—and Shotgun would be laughing his fool head off as he did it. Shotgun proves that Red Cell is an equal opportunity employer: he was in the Army Rangers before seeing the light. Like Sean Mako, another of our blanket-hugger brats, his service experience has stood him in good stead at Red Cell International.

---

[3] FNG=Fucking New Guy. The smell is somewhere between the aromatic hint of a new car and the sulfurous rot of overcooked eggs.

Shotgun is six-eight, weighs at least three hundred pounds, and runs the hundred-yard dash faster than most Olympic sprinters. He runs especially fast if you tell him there's a Yankee Doodle or some other fast-food snack at the finish line. He's always eating. Always. I've seen him unwrap a Twinkie at twenty thousand feet, waiting to hit fifteen so he could pull his ripcord.

Technically, Shotgun was the team demolitions expert, though we didn't expect to be blowing many things up. He was also the unofficial morale officer. I have never seen him without a smile on his face. True, it's often a twisted smile, but it's a smile nonetheless. If there is a happier man on the planet, I don't want to meet him.

Shotgun's mirth is counteracted by Mongoose's growl. Mongoose is a former SEAL, so I don't have to say much about his abilities. He is a small guy physically: maybe five-six if he's on his tippy toes. Which puts him at the perfect height to carve his initials in your heart after he pulls it from your chest.

Actually, he only takes out your heart if you *haven't* pissed him off. If you have, his aim is somewhat lower.

Mongoose is Philippine-American, but even Red thought he looked plenty Cuban to pass as a native if necessary. His Spanish had an accent a bit more Filipino than Caribbean, but that could be finessed if circumstances demanded.

You've already met Matthew Loring—aka Junior—our technical specialist. Matt came to us to fill in for my friend and standby geek, Shunt, who has a fairly full agenda outside Red Cell. (Shunt's real name is Paul Guido Falcone. He's called Shunt because he has them in his brain. Helps him talk to Martians.)

Matthew can hack computers almost as well as Shunt, which is like comparing Mantle to Mays. As an added bonus, he's developed a taste for blowing things up. What he really wants to do is become a shooter, though he doesn't have a military background. Trace has taken him under her wing and has high hopes. For me, the jury's still out.

He's a tough kid, I'll give him that; he proved he could keep up with us in Korea. Of course, he's so damn thin he looks like he could slide under a door.

One other thing about Matt: he says he's my son.

You'll have to read *Dictator's Ransom* to get the nuances, but the bottom line is that his mother and I had a rendezvous twenty-some years before that—allegedly—resulted in Matthew's birth.

Matt is sure of it. I'm not. We haven't had a DNA test or anything that might be conclusive. Our blood types happen to match—but that could easily be random chance. How much he looks like me is a matter of opinion.

Not that I wouldn't be proud to call him my son. But the responsibilities of fatherhood have never really been my thing.

That was our team. Eight people, with a couple around the periphery, on-call as needed for specific tasks.

The operation itself was straightforward. We were to meet the Cuban courier—a Senor Fernandez—in a small town about seven miles southeast of Jobabo in Las Tunas province Wednesday morning at 0130—1:30 A.M. in civilian time.

Quick geography lesson: Cuba is directly south of the Florida Keys, ninety miles or so from American soil. The island is shaped like a spurt of water erupting from a playground fountain. Development isn't exactly rampant anywhere on Cuba, but the eastern side of the island is less populated than the west. The Sierra Maestra mountains are in the east, below and to the right of the Bahamas.

The east is also where our navy base at Guantanamo is.

Yes, it's a navy base. The prison is a tiny part of the facility, even though it's what's made the rest of the place famous.

I see a hand in the back of the class. Question?

Why do we have a navy base in the only communist country in the Western Hemisphere?

Good question, grasshopper. Save it for History. This is Geography.

Oh, all right, just this once. When we helped the Cuban people free themselves from Spain, they were so grateful they leased us the base in perpetuity. Fidel has tried denouncing the lease, but it's held up by international law—and a garrison of some of the most ornery marines you ever didn't want to meet.

Havana is on the other side of the island, on the northwest coast, 105 miles due south and a noodge west of Key West. The western end of the island is more populous than the south, though no one's about to confuse any part of Cuba with the northeastern corridor or southern California.

Much of what lies between Havana and Guantanamo is either farmland or jungle, with the occasional swamp or rocky hillside thrown in. There's no part of the island that measures a hundred miles north shore to south shore. Cuba's entire area is 42,830 square miles, which is about the size of Kentucky or roughly two-thirds the size of Florida, take your pick.

Las Tunas, the province where we were going, is on the eastern side of the island, just before the mountains. Up near the northern coast, you find a few hardy European tourists taking advantage of the pristine and nearly deserted beaches. Las Tunas, the city, is in the northern end of the province. The population is a little under two hundred thousand, making it a medium-size city for Cuba.

Jobabo is even smaller, with maybe fifty thousand people in the city and immediate area. It sits on the highway between Camagüey and Baymo in east-central Cuba roughly fourteen miles from the Gulfo de Guacanayabo and the ocean. Our rendezvous target was five miles to the east and a hair south. We could get there without going anywhere near the city, traveling through open countryside dotted with sugar fields, swamps, and the jungle.

The hamlet where Traba's brother had been exiled lay two miles northeast of the rendezvous. We'd located his address with the help of some Miami friends of Danny's. I didn't tell the barber what I was up to; I was afraid that he'd do something silly, like call his brother and tell him help was on the way. Obviously, we were taking a risk that he might not be there. But from everything the barber had said and what we could find out about inter-exiles, we knew the odds were extremely high that he'd be at his house the night we arrived.

Doc had rented us a cabin cruiser that we would use as our main transport. Along with Red, Shotgun, and Mongoose, I would take the cruiser and land on a beach in the Gulfo de Guacanayabo at 2300. We'd then bicycle along local roads north to the rendezvous point. The rendezvous was supposed to take place at 0200—2:00 A.M. That gave us roughly three hours to cover fourteen miles—five or six times what we needed, even accounting for Murphy's[4] lollygagging.

While the four of us were on the ground in Cuba, Danny would be

---

[4] You know Murphy: he's the guy with the famous laws, the most important of which dictates that whatever *can* go wrong will *go* wrong, at the most inopportune time.

sitting back in Jamaica drinking rum and monitoring transmissions from the Cuban defense forces, thanks to a hookup to an intercept station Admiral Jones had arranged. He'd also be in touch with us through an encrypted satellite telephone system.

Trace, Junior, and Doc would form a backup rescue team, orbiting a short distance from the Cuban coast aboard a Martin PBM Mariner — flying boat. They'd swoop in if things got too hot; they'd also be able to watch for Cuban patrol boats and planes.

I suspect a few graybeards among the crowd did a double take at the aircraft type, just as I did when I saw the big bird land on the water in front of our Jamaican beach house. The PBM was a World War II era patrol craft, basically a big boat with two engines mounted on a high wing over the hull. It was one of the most successful flying boats of all time, and I believe a few may have still been in the service when I was getting yelled at in boot camp for not tucking in my shirt.

This particular aircraft had a checkered history. After a brief stint in the U.S. Coast Guard, it had been mustered out of the service and used as a flying taxi in the Florida Keys and the West Indies. If you think "flying taxi" is synonymous with drug runner, you probably aren't far wrong.

Of late it had come under the ownership of one Paul M. W. Smith, a man of many talents and dubious tastes, whose main distinction as far as I was concerned was a friendship with Doc that stretched back to Doc's two-year sojourn in Egypt. M.W., as he was called, was American by birth and accent; whether there was an American passport among the dozen or so he was reputed to carry I couldn't say. Ken Jones said he was *known* to the CIA, though what exactly that meant was never exactly explained.

M.W. had invested heavily in his aircraft, updating and customizing the engines, and painted the PBM very dark blue—so dark, in fact, that the plane was invisible at night. The old-style analog gauges and gizmos on the dashboard had been replaced by a state-of-the-art glass control panel. The PBM sported the latest Russian-made military radar—not quite as good as American gear, to be sure, but entirely free of the questions the export control people at Customs liked to ask. The plane was also equipped with a number of so-called passive detectors. There was a 360-degree infrared system that could see heat sources up to twenty miles away and a radar detection unit that could pick up a leaky microwave oven five times farther. M.W. also had several radios, frequency scanning units, a full suite of satcom equipment, and a funky stereo system with MP3 plug-ins and an external blow horn.

"I use the horn every year to lead the St. Patrick's Day seaborne parade out of Port Saint Lucie," M.W. told me, showing off the plane two days before our mission. "It's got a PA attached, and sometimes I sneak up on a fishing boat and pretend to be the voice of God. Scares the piss out of them."

(Incidentally, that's just down the beach from the UDT-SEAL Museum at Fort Pierce on Route A1A—well worth a visit anytime of the year.)

Passenger and crew comfort didn't rate anywhere near as highly with him as electronics. The fabric on his seat was ripped in several places, and the copilot's seat looked as if it had come from another plane: one that had been flying when the Wright Brothers were alive.

Oh, and there were no seats for the passengers.

Doc was real pleased about that.

"Where the hell am I supposed to sit?" he demanded as we looked over the plane.

"On your tush," Trace told him. "It's padded."

"Careful, girl, or I'll bend you over my knee."

"Wouldn't you like to try."

"Pick one of those ribs on the deck and curl up," I told him.

"Bullshit on that."

"You can sit up in the cockpit with me," said M.W. "I'm not flying with a copilot."

He explained that he flew alone as a matter of "operational security," but I suspect it was just to keep the overhead down.

"Trace ought to be in the cockpit," said Doc. "She's a pilot."

Actually, Trace is a helicopter pilot, and barely past trainee level at that, but Doc was too chivalrous to let her sit on her rump in the back while he was up front.

"Here's my seat," said Junior, walking over to a bucket lodged in the ribs at the very tail end of the plane. He pulled it out, then almost fell over as he caught a whiff.

"That's not for sittin', it's for shittin'," said M.W. "It's a piss bucket. You're on a long flight and you gotta go, it's better than the alternative."

The alternative was pulling open one of the large hatches on either side of the tail and sticking your butt into the breeze. Lots of fun at two hundred knots.

We spent Sunday night going over the satellite images of the area where the team would land, planning for various contingencies, and trying to scout alternate routes and hiding places.

Monday morning saw Trace leading PT. It was a light session—broken bones the next evening would not have been welcome—so she only screamed like a drill sergeant, not the she-devil she usually is.

"My Girl Scout troop works harder than this, Mongoose," she bawled when he was doing his crunches. "Let's see some sweat."

She stopped in her tracks and glanced down at Shotgun.

"What the hell are you giggling at, asshole?" she barked.

"I can't see you as a Girl Scout leader."

"I train you pansies, don't I? After that, everything else is a breeze."

Trace really does have a Girl Scout group back on the rez, and while I've never seen it, I'm going to guess it's the toughest in the country. The only thing tougher than Chiricahua Apache males are Chiricahua Apache females.

My bones were aching and my muscles sore by the time her "light" workout was over. This encouraged a hearty round of "old man" jokes, which of course grew more and more juvenile as they progressed. Fortunately, breakfast was followed by bicycle orientation. The entire team took part in the exercise just in case the ops roster had to be shifted. We went out in two-person teams; I drew Junior.

The bikes we were using were not your normal Schwinn roadsters. Built for easy packing, they literally folded up and fit in or, in our case, on a backpack. Their wheels were small and their tires narrow; sit too long on the seat and you'd be sterile for a week. But once you got used to the pedals, you could move along at a decent clip. The gearing was so good you didn't have to strain on the hills, or not much anyway.

Junior and I pushed each other for about ten miles, trading leads. Then finally he started to pull away. In fact, he could have coasted home with a good half-hour lead if he hadn't slowed down and let me catch up.

"It's OK, Dad," he yelled back to me. "I'll wait for you."

I don't know which pissed me off more—him taking pity on me, or calling me dad.

Probably the former, but don't count out the latter.

My legs started pumping faster than a jackrabbit in heat. There was a hill directly in my face; the incline had to be close to forty-five degrees. I passed Junior about midway up and never looked back.

Oh, I heard him huffing behind me, but that only made me go faster. My heart pounded out a rap beat in my chest, and my forehead was so hot you could have fried an egg on it, but I beat him back to the house by a good hundred yards. I broke down my bike and hit the shower.

Trace was waiting when I got done.

"What got into you?" she asked.

"What's that?"

"Junior said you were mad about something."

"I ain't mad about anything."

Trace gave me the Dahlgren eye roll.

"He called you dad?" she said.

"Stick to your job and I'll stick to mine," I told her.

I walked away before she could say anything else stupid, like watching out for me was her job.

We spent the rest of the day refamiliarizing ourselves with our gear, plunked a few targets, then had a siesta. After darkness fell, we worked with the boat and airplane, practicing transfers back and forth. Then we rehearsed landings with our gear, setting up the bikes, etc. With the exception of Junior, we'd all done this a million times, but practice makes perfect, and even old farts like me have to keep the muscle memory fresh.

By the time dawn came, everybody could do their job and their backup job in their sleep. We hit the sack.

The assault team's castoff was set for 1600 that afternoon; the backup team would fly out much later at night. We had a late lunch of some Jamaican specialties—brown fish stew and curried goat. The spices were a bit strong, even with the Red Stripe beer to wash them down; I was the only one who went for the fish.

An unfortunate decision, as I discovered at 1555, when my internal organs decided they wanted to become external in a hurry.

Doc found me on my knees, worshipping the porcelain goddess.

"What the hell happened to you?" he asked.

"Stomach," I managed. Then I gave him a demonstration of my problems.

"It's 1555," said Doc, as always a paragon of compassion. "You ready to go or what?"

"I'm coming." I got up, then bent down again as a fresh load erupted from my interior. I wasn't just puking up lunch; it felt like every meal I'd had in the past thirty years was coming up. "Be there in a min-uh—"

"The hell you will," said Trace from the doorway. "You aren't going to ride in a boat for nine hours like that."

"I've been worse," I managed between retches.

"That's not the point."

"You know what, Dick? I'm going to take your place," said Doc. "There's no sense you going like this. Take your time and go with M.W. and them. If you feel better."

I growled something, then puked some more. Doc said something about how no one was indispensable and how mission integrity had to be maintained and some other such bullshit, all of which I recognized from a pep talk I had given him a few months back when I took him out of a mission. Payback's a bitch.

I probably could have gone on the boat; I was so sick a hurricane couldn't have made my insides feel any worse. I don't know how much fun it would have been for the others, though. With the top half of my digestive track scorched clean, the bottom half began doing its own spring cleaning. All manner of hazardous and noxious material was sent unceremoniously streaming from my body. I spent the next hour sitting and flushing, not necessarily in that order.

Finally, there was nothing left inside, not even mucus. I won't say I felt exactly refreshed, but I felt good enough to go on the mission. And pissed that I'd let Doc take my place, even if it had been the right thing to do.

By 1710 I was in the shower. At 1720 I was fighting off the temptation to get something to eat. I grabbed a Red Stripe, to settle my stomach and restore my fluids.

We took off as planned at 2000—8:00 P.M. Though the wind was a little over twelve knots and strong enough to kick up some decent waves, there were no clouds in the sky. Trace had told M.W. my stomach was wheezy, so he did exactly what I would have done under the circumstances—threw the plane into a seven- or eight-g power dive and turn.

Trace looked a little green as he pulled up over the waves. Behind me in the cabin, Junior eyed the piss bucket nervously.

I felt fine, of course. I had nothing left to puke.

"You're awful brave," I told M.W.

"How's that?"

"I was standing right behind you. Anything left in my stomach at this point is going to be seriously toxic."

He flew straight and level after that.

The heaviest Cuban air force and navy patrols tend to be around the northern side of the island, aimed at keeping their citizens from leaving for Yankee land. Still, we couldn't count on there being no patrols over the beach area. While the PBM could overfly it at low altitude with little risk of being seen by Cuban defense radars, the plane was fairly loud and slow. Therefore, our preferred real-time reconnaissance asset was an unmanned aircraft dubbed *Eyes 1*. Similar to the UAVs the army has been using for tactical recon in Iraq, *Eyes 1* was essentially a beefed-up hobbyist's radio-controlled plane. Doc launched it from the cabin cruiser while they were still a good distance from shore. He started the small engine, stood up, and literally threw the damn thing into the wind.

A satellite radio aboard *Eyes 1* transmitted video to both the control unit on the boat and an encrypted Web site. Junior had rigged a viewer for us on the plane with one of our laptops and a sat phone; Doc had a similar setup aboard the boat.

The plane had an infrared and a starlight camera as well as regular video, and could stay aloft for nearly eight hours. It didn't go particularly fast—I think the top speed was fifty knots, though I'm not positive—but speed wasn't what we were looking for. It was small and relatively quiet, and while not cheap, there'd be no funerals back home if one of Fidel's minions shot it down.

The trick was flying it. Doc and I had been playing with it every day for the past week or so, but Doc's curses filled my ears when I got on the satcom line.

"Problem?" I asked.

"Stinking goddamn piece of Chinese friggin' no shit-good plastic," grumbled Doc. The miniature aircraft had actually been manufactured in Utah, but I decided this wasn't the time to point that out.

"Do you need us to overfly the beach?" I asked.

"Negative. No, negative. We have an image. We have data flow. It's aloft. It's just a real bullshit pain in the back stink-ass problem steering the damn thing."

I told Doc that if he put the creativity he was using in choosing his curse words into the airplane, he'd solve the problem in no time. He cursed even more creatively, using words I'd never heard of, then managed to swing *Eyes 1* toward the target area. Ten minutes later, an image came up on the screen showing a group of palm trees and big boulders that we'd identified as one of the landmarks on the eastern end of the landing area.

Then we saw a landmark we hadn't identified at all: a Cuban defense force jeep. And six or seven soldiers, moving along the shore.

Murphy at work.

"That's what you get for taking my place," I told Doc. "Check landing area two."

Another string of curses rattled my tender ears. I hunched over the laptop and watched the coastline grow more ragged in the monitor—and then suddenly a lot bigger.

Junior pulled off his headset as Doc's curses set new decibel levels. *Eyes 1* had crashed.

Had it been shot down? Or had it just crashed? I leaned toward the latter, though there was no way to completely rule out the first. Junior tried getting some clues by rolling back the video and taking a closer look at the soldiers, but aside from the fact that they were all definitely armed, there was no clue what they were doing. It was doubtful that they were looking for us—Mr. Fernandez had no idea who his contact was or from what direction he or she would approach. But this wasn't the best way to start the night.

I went up to the cockpit to M.W. and asked if we could overfly the coast.

"It'll cost you," he said.

"Understood."

"We'll drop down real low, then pop up when we're almost there," he said. "But I have to tell you—if their MiGs show up, we're out of there. And it won't be a pretty ride home, either."

I went over the map with M.W. and Trace, who would do the actual spotting with the help of a set of Gen 3 night goggles. Then I went back to the cabin, where Junior was trying to use our Internet connection to break into the Cuban defense ministry.

Why was he doing that?

"I figure that if I can, you know, hook in there somehow," he explained, "I may be able to find out why those soldiers were on the beach."

It wasn't a bad idea—except for the dubious assumption that the Cubans were advanced enough to have a computerized message system. It kept him occupied at least.

I grabbed a pair of binoculars and sidled up to the porthole to see what I could see. The glass was thick and probably hadn't been cleaned since the plane had belonged to Uncle Sam; all I could see were reflections of my own eyes. Finally I got a better idea. I walked back to the rectangular hatch at the starboard side of the aircraft, spun the lock handle open, and pulled the door back, sliding it on its rails inside the wall of the plane.

A red light started to flash. Wind blew through the cockpit like a drunk teenager racing through a whorehouse. The plane stuttered and dropped precipitously close to the water, the engines groaning with the strain.

"What the *hell* are you doing?" yelled Trace, running into the back. "You opened the hatch?"

"I need to see outside," I told her, squatting near the opening. "Get M.W. to turn that damn red light off."

"Crap, Dick. Don't fall out."

"See about that light. It's going to give us away."

The light turned out not to have a switch. Junior came up with a perfect solution: he shot it out with his pistol.

Maybe he was a chip off the old block after all.

Landing area two was three miles farther east than our first choice. It was unoccupied. At the center of the area was a small, dilapidated wooden dock, which protruded from a soggy bog. Most of the immediate surrounding area was bog, actually; think Florida Everglades with more alligators and less retirees. The dock had probably been used by fishermen or maybe farmers during Cuba's capitalist days. Now it was a jumble of rotted timbers at the end of a dirt trail.

The satellite image had provided a much more optimistic view of the stability of those timbers than proved to be the case in person. Doc decided there was no sense tying up there. Instead, he continued up a wide stream nearby, braving the overhanging trees and silty bottom until he decided they'd gone as far as they could. They tied up in a large clump of brush, then waded across the muck to a nearby path. Doc had all he could do to keep Shotgun from stopping to make mud pies along the way.

They dried off, cleaned up, and pulled civilian clothes over their wet suits. Then they broke out the bikes and hit the road, pedaling north. Fallow sugarcane fields gave way to thick jungle within a few miles. Though they weren't hard-topped, the roads were cut straight and the team made good time, even though as a precaution they stopped before crossing intersections and were careful to follow the most deserted path possible. They spread out as they rode, keeping in touch with low-probability-of-intercept military-style radios. The limited range of the radios was one of the things that made them extremely difficult to detect, but it also meant they had a range of just over three miles. For anything farther—and to talk to us back on the plane—they had to use their sat phones.

In the days when I was first fitting my feet for frogman's flippers, SpecOp warriors had to be damn good at reading maps. Translating their squigs and squiggles to landmarks and terrain, especially in the dark, is a real skill. There's nothing that adjusts the old sphincter quicker than discovering you are up-the-shit-creek-lost as the flares explode over your head and you hear the sick sound of a hundred AK47 magazines being locked home around you.

Nowadays, even the mailman uses global positioning satellite (GPS) technology to tell him where to go. The better units have rolling maps and oversized arrows, and cute female voices to tell you when you're about to take a wrong turn off the cliff.

Doc isn't anybody's idea of an early technology adopter, but he swears by the damn things. They certainly are convenient—everyone on the landing and backup teams was outfitted with special watch-size units made by a subsidiary of Gamin just for yours truly. Not only did they show where they were on a zoomable map, but the location of each individual unit could be beamed to other units in our network.

What the GPS couldn't do, however, was tell the wearer that the bridge he hoped to cross had been closed for repairs.

Not just closed—completely removed. Which, considering that it crossed a ravine some fifty feet wide, was inconvenient.

Shotgun was riding point at the time. Eyes peeled for an ambush, he was watching everything but the road itself, and promptly found himself knee-deep in mud. This set off a round of suppressed laughter; even the normally cranky Mongoose thought it was funny. But the muck turned out to be a serious problem—trying to stand, Shotgun found the mud beneath his feet slip away. In the few seconds it took the others to get ropes, he had sunk to his chest.

Mongoose tossed him the rope from the road embankment, which was only six or seven feet away. But between the dark and the mud, Shotgun couldn't find the rope. Every move, it seemed, sank him in farther.

"Too bad you don't have Doc's nose," said Mongoose. "We could tie the rope to that."

"Ha, ha," laughed Shotgun, sinking deeper. Only his neck and head were free.

"I'm going to swim out to you," said Mongoose. "It's the only way we're going to grab you."

"You're too heavy," said Red. "Let me try."

She stripped back to her wet suit, looped the rope around her waist, and slipped into the mud. Two kicks and she reached Shotgun—who was tilting his head back in a desperate attempt to float, or at least not sink any farther. He pried one of his hands out of the mud and grabbed her.

"Pull!" yelled Red, along with a few other words not suitable for tender ears.

A mouthful of muddy sand stopped her cursing as she was dragged down by Shotgun's weight. By the time Doc and Mongoose pulled the pair from the muck, they were both covered head to toe in thick, sandy mud.

Shotgun being Shotgun, he started to laugh.

Red shut him up with a punch to the stomach so hard he nearly fell back in the ditch.

"You're lucky she hit you," said Doc. "Next time, you watch where the hell you're going."

The only workable detour was two miles to the south; they backtracked and swung east to a small hamlet and rode about a mile along a highway before doglegging to a much less traveled lane. The mud had dried and started to stink; Doc put them at the back of the pack when the wind shifted. Finally they came to a stream with enough water for them to wash in. Red shed her wet suit in favor of the pants and shirt she'd taken off earlier; Shotgun rinsed the civilian clothes as best he could, hoping the air would dry them as he rode. This was only partly successful.

The delay cost them more than an hour and a half, but they still arrived a little more than an hour ahead of the scheduled rendezvous. They dismounted a mile south of the barnyard where the meeting was to take place, then spread out so they could observe the area before moving in.

Senor Fernandez was supposed to meet them near an old tobacco barn set back behind a row of trees a hundred feet from the road. There was a ramshackle building near the barn, along with a battered and very rusted fence. They checked the area thoroughly, making sure it wasn't under surveillance.

Everything was clear. Concerned that there might be further delays on the way back, Doc decided to send Red and Mongoose north to pick up Traba's brother on their own, while he and Shotgun handled the exchange.[5]

After they'd gone over the barn a second time, Shotgun took a post in some trees at the eastern end of the farmyard, where he could cover Doc if there was trouble during the handoff. Doc stayed back by the road, using a pair of Gen 3 night-vision goggles to scan for approaching cars.

A pair of vehicles appeared a few minutes later. They were Chevy Impalas, made in the mid-eighties, probably imported originally from Canada. They rode almost bumper to bumper, kicking up a good cloud of dust as they approached the barn. Neither had its lights on.

"There's one car too many," said Shotgun, watching from the tree. "I assume this isn't him."

"Never *ass*-ume," said Doc.

"Ha!"

A few moments later the first car pulled off toward the barn; the second continued down the road.

"There's one person in the car," said Shotgun.

Doc squatted at the side of the road, watching as the car door opened. The interior light had been switched off.

"Middle-aged guy, chunky stomach and slicked-back hair, looks like the picture," reported Shotgun. "Kinda like the picture. Taking out a cigar. Big thick one."

The man began pacing.

---

[5] The exchange was supposed to be made in person because of the sensitive nature of the DVDs. It was the CIA's call, not ours.

"Is he armed?" Doc asked.

"Don't see a gun. Think it's our guy?"

"Maybe."

"What do you want to do?"

What Doc wanted to do was find out where the other car had gone. He cursed himself for sending off Red and Mongoose—if they had still been with him, he could have had them follow the other car.

The rendezvous wasn't set for another half hour. Doc decided Fernandez could wait.

"Shotgun, can you slide down from that tree without our friend seeing you?"

"Shit, yeah."

"See if that car stopped anywhere along the road past the curve. Make sure they're not trying to flank us," said Doc. He was already moving to the south, doing the same thing on his side of the road.

"That means going through the swamp," said Shotgun.

"You're afraid of getting wet?"

Shotgun stifled a laugh. "You think they're setting up an ambush?" he asked, picking his way through the muck.

"I think there's one car too many," said Doc. "Beyond that, I'm not thinking at all."

(II)

It took Red and Mongoose roughly fifteen minutes to reach the hamlet where Traba's brother lived. There were less than two dozen houses in the settlement; not one had any lights on or showed any other sign of activity. Still, they took their time checking the area out, making sure the brother's house wasn't being watched.

The hamlet was shaped like a cheez doodle, with the brother's house at the southwestern end, not easily seen from the main road or the neighbor's property. A narrow, rutted lane ran from the main road almost directly to the brother's door. A swamp backed up on the rear of the house, surrounding it on both sides. Red and Mongoose stashed their bikes near the main road—hard-packed gravel and barely wide enough for a single car to pass—then approached the house. Both had their MP5Ns[6] ready.

"Pretty small," whispered Mongoose. "Can't be more than two or three rooms."

"You go around the back," said Red. "I'll go through the front."

"You gonna knock?"

"Maybe. Let's see what we can see first."

Red squatted a few yards from the house, waiting while Mongoose worked through the soggy ground to the back. While she'd been in Cuba many times, she'd never been this far east. A million different things were going through her head, but mostly she was rehearsing what she was going to say.

Your brother sent us. Come.

We're taking you to safety now, to the north. Hurry.

Get your things and come.

But the opening was easy compared to the follow-up. Not every Cuban wanted to leave Cuba, as she well knew from her own family. Even a man in Traba's position might find dozens of reasons to stay.

Technically, Red didn't have to wake him at all. She was carrying a small pouch with a hypodermic needle and a vial of sedative strong

---

[6] 9mm Heckler & Koch submachine guns, equipped with a silencer that softens the gun's bark, but not its bite.

enough to put a man to sleep for ten to twelve hours. But Red didn't want to use the drug. Not so much because they'd have to lash the brother to the bike, but because she thought he should have a choice about his future.

"There's one window back here," said Mongoose over the radio. "I can't see much through the shade. And the dirt."

Red moved up toward the house. She hesitated outside, curling her hand into a fist to knock. Then she decided knocking might make too much noise.

The door was locked. Red moved to the window on her left. Dropping to her knees, she tried peering inside but her view was blocked by a drawn shade just as Mongoose's had been.

The window was locked. Red pulled the sleeve up on her shirt, then broke the top panel with her fist. The noise was louder than she had thought—it always is—and she froze for a fraction of a second. Then her instincts and training kicked back in. She reached inside and flipped the lock back, raising the window quickly so she could get in. Red pushed the shade aside, stepping to her right and dropping to a squat, her eyes adjusting to the dark.

"I'm inside," she whispered over the radio.

"Good. Copy," said Mongoose.

The front room was a combination kitchen and sitting area. It smelled dank and foul.

Red stayed low to the ground as she passed the window, heading toward the single doorway at the far left. She stopped at the threshold of a short hall. There was a bathroom on the right. The plumbing must be broken, she thought; the place smelled like a latrine that had overflowed.

"Mr. Traba," she said softly. "Mr. Traba. Your brother sent us to rescue you."

She stepped into the back room, used as a bedroom. The bed was on the right. Something loomed in front of her, to her left.

Red whirled toward it, gun up, finger on the trigger.

A foot touched her.

A dead foot. Traba's brother had hanged himself from the rafter in despair several days ago.

(III)

Down at the farmyard, Senor Fernandez was still waiting for Doc to make the exchange.

So were the four guys who'd been in the second car. Shotgun had spotted two of them fanned out on a rise about a hundred yards off the road; they had just enough height to see into the barnyard.

"One of 'em's got a rifle with a nightscope," Shotgun reported from their flank. "Looks like he's got it zeroed on the barnyard."

Doc didn't answer. He was too busy ducking the other two men, who were moving east across the road to set up another watchpoint. They were fairly skilled, carefully checking their flanks as they moved. Doc was just a little better, managing to slip behind them as they came back toward the barn.

"I can take these guys," Shotgun told Doc. "You want me to?"

"Negative," said Doc. Not only didn't it make sense to take the risk, but he wasn't positive they were there to ambush him—in theory, they could just be covering Fernandez in case of a double cross.

Not that it felt that way to Doc. He swung back around the two men he'd let pass him, following them from about forty yards. They ended up in the ditch where he had been earlier. He worked his way to a line of trees maybe thirty yards beyond them, shimmying up the thickest to watch what they were up to. With his night goggles, Doc could see Fernandez beyond them, pacing near the car, chewing on his cigar.

Fernandez was still smoking ten minutes after the appointed rendezvous time. The men in the ditch were still watching, as were the others to the south on the rise beyond the swamp.

Go in? Or stay.

Doc leaned toward stay.

"Looks like these guys are getting antsy," said Shotgun finally. "One of 'em is taking out a phone."

"Mmmm," mumbled Doc.

"Looks like a cell phone. Clamshell thing. Think they're cops?"

"I told you, Shotgun, don't think. Just watch."

Ordinary Cubans were forbidden to have cell phones, and all calls on the island were monitored. But Doc expected that a spy—especially one with Fernandez's connections—would have some way of communicating with his compatriots.

Still, it looked too risky. He ordered Shotgun to keep his distance.

A few minutes later, he saw another car coming south on the road. This one had its lights on. The men in the ditch tensed, leaning forward, but not bringing their AKs to bear on the car. At the last second it veered toward the barn, missing the driveway and fishtailing toward the yard beyond, where Senor Fernandez was waiting. Fernandez shook his head and turned toward the headlights.

Doc pulled himself a little higher on the tree. He checked the two men who were nearby, making sure they were still focused on the barnyard. Then he watched as a man got out of the car in the barnyard. Fernandez, standing a few feet away, took the cigar from his mouth as if to say something.

He never got a chance. A submachine gun fired from the backseat of the car, taking him down. The man who'd gotten out turned on his heel and got back in.

"What the hell just happened?" asked Shotgun.

"They just shot Fernandez," said Doc.

"Shit."

"Just sit tight."

As the car came out from behind the barn, Doc crawled toward the road and got a good look at it. It was a Ford, a little older than the Chevies. There were no tags and except for the blurry outline of the driver, he couldn't see inside.

The two men in the ditch seemed to relax.

"My guys are going back to the car," said Shotgun.

"When the car's gone, go back up to the barnyard," Doc whispered. "Be careful."

The men Shotgun had been watching got in the car. As it reached the road, the men in the ditch rose and went to the road to wait, murmuring softly as the car made its way to them. After they were gone, Doc circled around the barn, heading for Fernandez. There was no question the Cuban agent was dead; the bullets had taken off a good part of his head and blood was pooled around his body.

"I gotta tell Dick what's going on," said Doc, taking out his sat phone.

———

Up until this point, we'd been orbiting off the coast in the PBM at about fifty feet, low enough that any radars would have a tough time spotting us.

Which is another way of saying we were sitting with our thumbs up our butts, waiting for something to happen.

"Fernandez just got wasted," said Doc as soon as we connected.

"OK," I told him after he described the situation. "Get back south. Keep the discs with you. What happened to Traba's brother?"

"Red and Mongoose should be back with him any second. I'll check in with her as soon as I'm off with you—we're a little too far for the radio."

"All right. Don't screw around. Get back to the boat."

"I was thinking I'd hit a duty-free shop on the way out."

I went forward and told the pilot I wanted to see where the cars were going.

"It's dangerous, Dick."

"We wouldn't be here if it wasn't."

"Just so you know."

He hit the throttle, banked sharply, and took us over the land.

"I see the highway, Dick," said Junior, pointing through the open hatchway as I came back.

We were still a few miles south of the barn. Even with the night glasses, it was hard to sort the structures out—the small ones looked big, and vice versa. Unlike in America, where even the most remote town will give off a gentle glow of light at the darkest part of the night, Cuba was completely dark.

"There's the barn," said Junior.

I'm not sure whether he was right or not; it passed by in a flash. The pilot pulled us parallel to the road, no higher than a hundred feet, flying at a slight tilt to make it easier for us to see the ground. Junior and I gripped the bulkhead and overhead struts as tightly as we could—a slip would send us out of the plane.

"Hey, you think those are the cars?" shouted Junior.

They had pulled off the road just shy of the highway.

"Gotta be."

"Why do you think they stopped?" asked Junior.

I could think of two reasons. One was that someone had to take a whiz.

I grabbed the sat phone.

"Doc, get away from Fernandez and his car!" I shouted as the connection went through.

I'm not sure how much of my warning Doc heard, if any. The vehicle exploded before I ended the sentence, the fireball so intense we could see it easily from the plane.

There are certain points in a mission, any mission, where you feel the need to sit back and say something profoundly perceptive and even philosophical, generally along the lines of "Goddamn, that's fucked up."

You may have the need, but usually you don't have the time. And we didn't here.

Either because of my warning, his sixth sense, or his incredibly expanding karma, Doc managed to dive away from the car just before it exploded. He scrambled behind the barn as the fireball rose, escaping most of the heat and all of the shrapnel.

Shotgun, still wading through the swamp, let out a whistle. Then he did what he always does when he's impressed by something: he reached into his pocket and pulled out one of his snacks, in this case a mini-bag of Frito corn chips.

"Nice," he said, rising as the flames settled. "You OK, Doc?"

Doc gave him a status report, along with a few other adjectives relating to the lack of apparent concern in Shotgun's voice.

"Hey, I knew you were OK," replied Shotgun. "I'm just admiring the explosion. As an artist."

"They didn't use enough explosive," growled Doc, walking back over toward the car.

Maybe not by Doc's standards, but there'd been more than enough to mince Senor Fernandez's body into its component parts. The car's frame looked like a mangled paperclip, with some bits of fabric attached.

"Look at this, Doc—his cigar is intact," said Shotgun, walking over near the barn to examine the debris. "I'll bet that proves some sort of law of physics or something."

"Get those damn chips out of your mouth," said Doc. "I can't understand a word you're saying."

"Physics," said Shotgun. "Probably one of the laws of thermodynamics. For every cigar in an explosion, there is an opposite and equal explosion."

Doc examined the trail of debris until he came upon a small hunk of slightly singed plastic.

It was Senor Fernandez's cell phone, still more or less intact. I won't describe the melted skin or the shards of bone that were embedded in the cover.

At Traba's brother's house, Red and Mongoose debated whether to cut the body down. Actually, it wasn't much of a debate: Mongoose said they shouldn't; Red took out her survival knife and slit through the rope.

The dead man weighed less than a hundred pounds. He'd soiled his clothes after he died, and his body had already stiffened, bloated, and started to rot. Red carried him as gently as she could and laid him on the bed.

"We really should get out of here," said Mongoose.

Red looked for a suicide note. She found a sealed letter on the bare wood top of a table a few feet from where he'd hung himself. Hesitating a second, she opened it and began to read.

It was addressed to his brother, the barber.

In a perfect world, it would have been a sad but forgiving letter, telling Roberto Traba how much he loved him and how he knew he had to get away to save the children.

But we don't live in a perfect world.

"I hope you rot in hell," were the opening words, and then it got nasty.

Red took a lighter from her pocket and burned it. She kicked the ashes around the floor, grinding them into the wood and dirt before they left.

Exploding cars are not exactly an everyday occurrence in Cuba, and while the farm was at least a mile from the nearest house, the explosion had been spectacular enough to rouse most of the district. The police and local fire brigade were called and rushed toward the scene.

Rushed may be too strong a word. They made their way to the scene with the haste typical of a lifelong government worker secure in the knowledge that he or she will never be fired unless hell froze over. Think motor vehicle department clerks, at any time except five o'clock.

Doc and Shotgun met Red and Mongoose east of the hamlet, easily evading the responding authorities. But the missing bridge and their use of landing area two complicated their escape route, leaving them no choice but the road they had used to get here. And as decreed by Murphy's Law, this road went past the house of one of the provincial policemen.

Naturally, the four of them were approaching the house just as the man was getting into his car. He tried shouting at them, asking what was going on, but with their heads down and feet pumping furiously, none of them heard, nor would they have stopped to answer if they did.

The policeman felt this was suspicious. He jumped in his car and gave chase.

The small, sandy roads nearby favored the bicyclists, and within a few minutes the policeman's headlights were no longer behind them. But there were only a few roads here, so simply by being persistent and driving south, the policeman couldn't help but head in the right direction.

He also had a radio, which is very difficult to outrun.

One of M.W.'s scanners caught the policeman's request for help — and an answer from the local militia captain. Within a few minutes, the troops that Doc had carefully avoided when landing were scrambling eastward in his direction.

It didn't take the map Junior pulled up on his computer to realize that the soldiers would be able to cut Doc and the others off from the water. I told M.W. to swoop along the road near the shore that the soldiers were on so we could delay them. He replied with such can-do enthusiasm that for a moment I thought he was one of the air farce pilots who "helped" my guys back in Grenada.

"Are you out of your mind? They'll shoot us down."

"Not if you get close enough to the trucks," I told him.

"Close enough for what?"

"For our grenades to hit them."

If M.W. said something else, I didn't hear it; I was already back in the cabin. Junior and I took up stations on either side of the open hatchway, each of us armed with a pair of grenades.

"Now, Junior! Now!" I yelled as the lead truck appeared below.

The grenades were actually flash-bangs, designed to produce a lot of boom and light but not much damage. They do tend to get your attention, though, especially in the dark when they ignite on your windshield.

Good shot, kid.

The lead truck veered off the road, falling down the embankment and crashing into the swamp.

Despite his earlier comments—and maybe because Trace was giving him the hairy Apache eyeball—M.W. had warmed to the mission. He circled back, giving us a second chance at the troops. Instead of using more grenades—that act gets stale pretty quickly—I picked up my submachine gun and splashed a magazine's worth of nine-millimeter bullets into the front of a second truck, voiding its bumper-to-bumper warranty and taking out the radiator.

I'm not sure whether my bullets hit the cab or not. We never got a chance to go back and find out. Because just then a loud siren-type alarm rang through the aircraft.

"Missile in the air!" yelled M.W., his voice carrying over the roar of the engine and heavy whistle of the wind. "Fuck-suck-dog-cock-mother-shit-tack-whack missile in the air!"

[IV]

I have no idea why he said *tack-whack*, much less what it was supposed to mean.

The rest I got pretty much straightaway.

A Soviet-era SA-7 heat-seeking missile had been launched almost point-blank at us as we banked over the Cubans. SA-7 is the NATO designation; the Ruskies know and love it as the 9M32 STELA-2. A first-generation shoulder-launched antiaircraft missile, it has a range of about fifty-five hundred meters and can get up to about forty-five hundred meters. It'll cover almost six hundred meters a second and carries an explosive round that weighs a little more than a kilogram. That may not sound like much—it's a little less than your average bag of onions—but it's more than enough if it hits something made of very thin aluminum a few hundred feet off the ground.

M.W. had dealt with shoulder-launched missiles before, including several fired by angry creditors. His PBM was outfitted with two different antimissile systems—a high-tech laser that spun around and was supposed to blind the missile, and a rack of decoy flares that shot out from the wings and belly like a fiery shower.

Both systems were designed to scramble the missile's brain, causing it to think it had found its target and explode. This is a great idea, but it does assume you're far enough away from the warhead when it explodes that, aside from the stains in your pants, there'll be no damage.

Great in a jet. OK in a reasonably nimble prop plane. Not so wonderful in a lumbering seaplane that has taken a hard turn at low altitude and is moving with all the speed of a limp kite on a cold winter day.

Junior and I both heard the warhead explode.

The plane rocked a bit, but settled smoothly.

"That was close," said Junior, pulling himself off the deck.

Then the plane dipped hard to the left, and flames shot past the open hatch. Parts of the missile had hit the port-side engine, blowing through the crankcase and sending a piston into the fuel line.

"Stand by to ditch!" said the pilot over the interphone loudspeaker.

Our game of peek-a-boo with the Cuban army had bought Doc and company enough time for them to get past the intersection without being spotted. Abandoning the bicycles, they waded through the swamp toward the boat. Doc had point; Red was right behind him. Mongoose and Shotgun were a few strides back.

"*Jesu!*" yelled Red suddenly.

A pair of round yellow eyes stared at her from the shallow water a few feet ahead.

"Croc-a-fuckin'-dile," yelled Shotgun. "Hot shit! I've never seen one up close before."

And he didn't see one now. Before Red could pull her gun from her holster, the eyes disappeared below the surface of the water. She took a few shots where it had been, but the bullets passed into the mud without hitting anything.

"Get to the boat! *Go!*" yelled Doc, hoping that the croc-a-fuckin'-dile was a loner or maybe a vegetarian.

Red reached the boat first. Doc followed with a hurdle that would have won at least a Bronze at the Olympics. Mongoose came next, sliding over the bow with a half gainer.

"I just saw more eyes," he yelled. "Shit! Two more! They're all around us."

"Wow, where?" said Shotgun, still plodding through the swamp.

"Get your ass aboard while you still have one," barked Doc. "That is an order! *Now*, Shotgun!"

Like many of us, Shotgun has some difficulties with authority figures, but I'm sure he would have gladly complied with Doc's orders. The problem was, something had grabbed his pants leg and pulled hard in the other direction. One second he was running forward, submachine gun in one hand, Twinkies cupcake in the other; the next second he was sucking mud.

Mongoose heard the splash. He twisted upright and looked back where Shotgun had been. When he didn't see his friend, he threw his gun to the deck, grabbed his knife,[7] and dove into the water.

The croc-a-fuckin'-dile held Shotgun down, probably intending to drown him before chewing him up. The water was at most eighteen

---

[7] A Strider Rogue model, naturally.

inches deep, but the murky, muddy swamp bottom made it difficult for Shotgun to push himself up. Swallowing a mouthful of mud, he twisted around, pulling his leg and the croc-a-fuckin'-dile forward. This gave Mongoose a better target as he jumped, and the wild Filipino landed square on the croc's back.

Crocodiles don't particularly like to be ridden. This one snapped its tail ferociously but refused to let go of Shotgun's pants. Mongoose dug his knife into the croc's thick skin, carving a pattern for a wallet as he fished for a vital organ.

Obviously a lifetime member of PETA, the croc-a-fuckin'-dile objected to this crass attempt at exploitation and thrashed even more wildly. The trio spun violently in the water. Finally the animal let go of Shotgun and rolled sideways in the water, pushing Mongoose into the mud.

There was a split second of black calm. Then the water exploded, and the croc-a-fuckin'-dile shot upward.

Mongoose followed, leaping to his feet. Anyone else would have jumped into the boat, which was only a yard or two away. But Mongoose was mad—the croc had gotten mud on his hair, and like many Filipinos, 'Goose is pretty vain about his hair. Knife in hand, he waded after the croc, which had now had quite enough of the confrontation. He grabbed one of the animal's legs, twisted it over, and with one hard slash, slit its throat.

"Mongoose, get in the damn boat!" said Doc.

"Yeah. Comin'," said Mongoose.

A dozen of the croc's closest friends moved in—not for Mongoose or the others, but to sing their buddy's praises while chewing his remains.

"Are you all right?" asked Red, helping him into the boat.

"Yeah," said Mongoose, looking back. "He pissed me off."

"Man, you think you're torqued," said Shotgun, checking his ripped pockets and tattered pants. "I lost my last Twinkie out there."

Back in the PBM, Junior and I grabbed our gear and waited as the aircraft wobbled above the water. Flames no longer shot past the door, but that was small consolation as the remaining engine revved wildly, its whine something you'd expect to hear from a cat caught in a turbine.

"Brace yourself," I told Junior. "If we hit and the plane starts to sink, get out as fast as you can. I'll inflate the raft. Swim for it."

"Got it." His expression remained doubtful.

"You all right?"

"Yup."

Probably he was petrified, but I was about the last person on earth he would ever admit that to.

Up-front in the cockpit, M.W. managed to trim the controls and steady the remaining engine to the point where he could level off a few yards above the water.

The engine and a good part of the right wing had been wracked by shrapnel, but it was the float that had taken the brunt of the blast; only a stub of it remained. The float wasn't absolutely necessary to land—early model PBMs had no floats at all—but M.W. worried that not having them would make the aircraft less stable in the water when he landed.

"Let's not get too far from shore," I told him. "We may still have to pick Doc and the others up."

"They may be picking us up, Dick."

The landing party had avoided the soldiers, but the policeman was still on their tail. Doc got the cabin cruiser going and backed away from the embankment as the cop's headlights arced through the swamp. They were close enough to illuminate dozens of dull yellow globes in the murky water—more crocodiles, come to see what the fuss was.[8]

Doc cleared the mouth of the stream and headed into the open water. He checked in and I brought him up-to-date, giving him our approximate position, which was roughly four miles from the coast, almost directly due south of him.

"How's Traba's brother?" I asked.

"Not with us," said Doc.

"You lost him?"

"He was dead when we got there." Doc described what Red had found.

"That sucks."

"Yeah."

"Dick, M.W. says we have a couple of MiGs coming down from Camagüey toward us," Trace told me, breaking into the conversation. "You're going to have to shut the door and grab on to something. They're coming pretty fast."

---

[8] The publisher believes in the greening of America, and has encouraged all of his writers to include "green" themes in their novels; the crocs are my contribution. I believe in environmentalism with teeth.

We pause this fubar for a technical explanation: the MiGs in question were not those fug-ugly sixties flying banana crates, held together with glue and rubber bands that Cuba still somehow manages to fly. These were brand-new MiG-29s, outfitted with the latest avionics and radars, and at least on paper decent matches for American F-15s.[9] Generally parked on the western side of the island at San Julian, the MiG-29s are the leading edge of an air force that counts 530 aircraft—a total that overshadows everything south of the Rio Grande by a good measure.

Now back to our regularly scheduled fubar.

The fighters were coming south like the proverbial bats out of hell, and they weren't the only ones invited to the party. A pair of helicopters had been scrambled, and a Cuban border guard craft (*Tropas de Guardia Frontera*) had been alerted as well. As much as I love being the center of attention, this was a particularly inconvenient time.

"We'll be swimming soon if we stay here," M.W. told me. "Our best bet is to stay low near the water and just run toward Jamaica. We may make it. We may not."

"What are the odds?" asked Junior, who'd followed me up to the cockpit.

"Seventy-thirty theirs," M.W. said. "Unless we have to pull any evasive maneuvers."

"What are they then?"

M.W. shrugged. He didn't have to explain what that meant: if we were hit by a missile or even cannonfire at this low an altitude, we'd go into the drink real fast. There'd be no question of bailing out.

"What, are you thinking of playing the lottery, Junior?" asked Trace.

"Just want to know where I stand."

"Look at the bright side," M.W. said. "We may not even make it to Jamaica. Our fuel stores are dropping pretty fast. Something must have nicked one of the tanks."

On that note of optimism, Junior and I returned to the cabin.

Doc wasn't worried about the MiGs at first, not even as they passed almost directly over him. He was too busy calculating his course back to Jamaica and planning his fuel management.

Then one of the MiGs turned back.

---

[9] I said on paper. Don't get all hot and bothered.

"I can't say for certain that they're interested in you," Trace warned, watching on the PBM's radar. "But the plane is turning back in your direction."

The pucker factor on the boat went up exponentially. With no time to turn back and hide, Doc decided his best bet was to keep moving at flank speed. He leaned on the throttle, muttering a few affectionate and encouraging words all the while.

The MiG came back over his bow at roughly two hundred feet. This time it was easy to see—a black tornado swooping overhead. The boat shook and shuddered, pressing close to the waves as if to duck away.

"Turning back toward you," warned Trace. We'd turned our active radar off, but the MiG was close enough to be easily tracked using the passive detection gear.

"Let's try to deke the MiG slimes," Doc told Red, giving her the mike. "Send out a transmission like we're answering a call for help from the Cuban coast guard. Make it sound like they're sinking and ask for details on their last location."

Doc turned and yelled to Mongoose, who was standing guard on the bow.

"Come over here and stand by to broadcast an SOS," Doc told him. "You're a Cuban patrol boat. Garble your message up. Make it sound like you're sinking."

"Why are we sinking?"

"You're not writing a fuckin' novel—wing it."

Just then the MiG came back over the boat from the port side. This time it was under a hundred feet, with its nose tilted down at an inauspicious angle.

The better to shoot you with, my dear.

The rounds from the aircraft's 30-mm cannon splashed in the water, dead ahead of the boat's bow. Doc turned the wheel hard port, back toward land.

Shotgun was back in the open well behind the boat's cabin, munching on a Snicker's Bar to regain his strength after the ordeal with the croc-a-fuckin'-dile. Until this point, he hadn't been paying too much attention to the MiG. Doc's sudden maneuver caught him by surprise, and sent the candy bar flying into the ocean.

Which made him mad.

He grabbed his submachine gun and emptied the magazine in the direction of the Cuban plane as it flared back for another run. Whether his bullets had any effect or not, the Cuban's attack went wide right, missing the boat by a good margin.

Shotgun dropped the empty mag and reloaded, waiting for the jet to twist around for another turn.

But it didn't.

"Scared that son of a bitch away," said Shotgun.

"Everybody into the water!" Doc yelled. *"Now!"*

Shooing everyone else ahead of him, Doc was just throwing himself over the gunwale when the missile hit.

[V]

The MiG chasing us was doing about 450 knots to our one hundred and a prayer. M.W. changed course twice, pushing the aircraft as hard as he dared through the cuts, backing off when he felt the controls starting to give. The MiG seemed to miss us for a few seconds, turning eastward. But soon he was swinging back in our direction, paralleling our course, going ahead of us, and then turning almost head-on for our nose.

M.W. waited until the MiG was five miles away. Then he made us invisible.

Actually, what he did was hit the button for his electronic countermeasures, which scrambled the crap out of the MiG's radar. But it was essentially the same thing.

By itself, jamming the MiG's radar wouldn't accomplish much, since the Cuban knew we were in front of him somewhere. But M.W. had nursed the plane up to about a thousand feet, and as he hit the jammer, he pushed the nose down as hard as he dared. Then he goosed off a few flares and a small device he called the beer keg.

Fashioned from one of those small beer kegs you can pick up in the supermarket, the large aluminum can was filled with gunpowder. Armed by a simple wire that pulled out when it was ejected, the beer keg was essentially a large flash-bang grenade, exploding with a terrific flash of light in the sky a few seconds after it was released.

"Hold your breath!" yelled M.W., killing his ECMs.

The MiG driver, moving at a quick clip a few hundred feet above us, saw the flares and explosion, and assumed that the aircraft had been destroyed.

At least we hoped so.

"Toss your Mae West out the door," I told Junior, pulling the door back open. I grabbed the survival raft from my gear and snapped the handle to inflate it.

"Toss it?" asked Junior.

"Damn straight."

"Me, too?"

"You stay."

Junior, perplexed, threw the vest through the open hatchway. I shoved the raft out, kicked a few other items overboard, then jammed the hatchway shut.

The Cuban was already banking around to investigate. He must have seen the raft or something in the water, because he took several passes before deciding to give up. By that time, we were twenty-five miles away.

"He'll be bingo fuel in a minute," M.W. said. "He won't bother coming for us."

Bingo fuel meant that the pilot had reached the end of his supply and would have to return back to base.

"Are you sure?" Trace asked.

"That's the one Achilles' heel those MiGs have—they can't carry much fuel."

"Maybe somebody should tell *him* that," Trace said, pointing to the display that showed the MiG had turned in our direction.

Doc's flying leap into the water was aided and abetted by an explosion, as the missile unleashed by the MiG set off the extra fuel cans lashed to the stern. The force threw him another forty or fifty feet beyond the others, who were doing their best impression of Olympic swimmers in an effort to get away from the boat.

By the time Doc hit the water, the boat had been turned into a fiberglass flambé. He immediately started trying to gather his team. He found Red first; she was bobbing a few yards away, held up by a life jacket. A minute or two passed before he spotted another head bobbing on the water. It was Mongoose, who'd managed to grab his ruck before jumping.

"You see Shotgun?" asked Mongoose.

"Negative," said Doc.

Mongoose put one hand to his mouth and yelled for his friend. "Guns! Hey, you asshole, where are you?"

Shotgun didn't answer.

The MiG, meanwhile, had taken a turn and was coming back. Fearing the worst, Doc told Mongoose to duck under the water. Then he grabbed Red's life vest and began kicking backward from the boat.

A bright white light exploded overhead.

Damn, thought Doc; the MiG driver is going to shoot us.

He sank lower, still pulling Red along. She was kicking on her own, quiet, maybe in semishock.

Whether he saw them or not, the Cuban didn't open fire. He took two or three passes, then roared off, probably returning to a round of drinks at his base.

Though the big flames had subsided, the boat continued to glow red as it sank at the bow. Doc could hear the sound of the flames crackling against whatever flammable material was left aboard the boat.

Mongoose once again began yelling for his friend.

"Yo, jackass," he yelled, over and over. "Show your damn face! Shotgun! Shotgun!"

Doc faced the kind of decision every commander hates. He didn't know if Shotgun was alive or not. He *did* know that he had two other people in the water who wouldn't be if they didn't start for shore soon.

"Shotgun, where the hell are you?" he yelled. "You have exactly sixty seconds."

Thirty seconds went by. Nothing.

Twenty more seconds. Still nothing.

Ten. Nada.

"Sixty seconds," repeated Doc. "Then we're leaving."

Once again, there was no answer.

"Let's give him another minute," said Mongoose.

Red's breathing was getting labored—and not from anything good.

"We're gonna have to go soon," said Doc.

"Sixty friggin' seconds, Shotgun!" yelled Mongoose. "Get your idiot butt in front of my face now!"

"You ain't gonna make me kiss it, are you?" came a voice from the other side of the smoldering boat.

But it was the laugh that gave him away.

Shotgun appeared in the dim light, pushing a large hunk of foam and fiberglass that had splintered from the vessel during the explosion. There was a backpack on it.

"I figured I'd grab a few things," said Shotgun. "Saved a couple of Twinkies."

"You went back on the boat?" asked Doc.

"Just for a minute."

"Good to know you risked your life for junk food," said Mongoose.

"Gotta risk it for something," said Shotgun.

"Let's get to shore," said Doc.

Shore seemed like the promised land to us at that moment. As soon as M.W. realized the MiG-29 pilot hadn't fallen for his deception, he turned the ECMs back on, hoping to keep the Cuban's radar scrambled.

It may have worked. The problem was that the MiG was also equipped with a passive infrared system, which could pick up heat sources like warm engines from several miles away.

M.W. didn't have much of a solution.

"We just have to take our chances," he told me. "We're pretty low to the water. Maybe he misses us."

The word "maybe" isn't a word that belongs in a combat scenario. MacArthur didn't say, *Maybe I'll be back*, when he left the Philippines. *Maybe you should wait until you see the whites of their eyes* was not a rallying cry during the early stages of the American Revolution.

"Land the plane," I told him.

"Land?"

"And kill the engine. If he can only see us with his infrared, the temperature of the plane will be pretty close to the temperature of the water."

"The engine will still be hot," said M.W.

"I'll take care of that."

"I don't know if the plane's going to stand up to a landing, Dick," said M.W. "We've taken a pretty bad hit on that wing."

"We have to find out sooner or later."

"Yeah, but if we get in, maybe we can't take off—"

There was that word again.

"If I hear the word 'maybe' out of your mouth again, I'm going to wash your face in that bucket you keep in the back."

[VI]

Flp-tlpt-smack-smack-splasssshhhhh.

That's the sound a flying boat makes when it hits the water during a normal landing.

Flp-tlpt-smack—blap-smack-spill-splasssshhhhh.

That's the sound a flying boat makes when it hits the water with an engine out.

Flp-tlpt-smack—blap-shit-stink-damn-crap-smack-spill-splatspash.

That's the sound a flying boat makes when it lands at sixty or seventy knots and its damaged wing smacks against the hard-as-blacktop ocean.

I'd grabbed the bulkhead between the cockpit and cabin as we went in, but the force hurled me backward. I flew into Junior and we tumbled against the side of the plane as it dipped. Then we were thrown forward as the plane skittered like a drunk sailor across the ocean.

Not having the float made things tough on M.W., and there's no maybe about that. He slapped the damaged right wing hard against the water, overcorrected, and had trouble keeping the nose out of the drink. For a few seconds, the plane threatened to flip. Finally, the tail backed down. He got his hull flat and level in the water, then killed the engine.

"He flew past us," yelled M.W. "He'll be back."

I yanked the port-side hatch open and pulled it back. Junior was in a bit of a daze, lying against the bulkhead near the tail section.

"We need buckets," I told him. "Anything we can put water in. Start with the piss bucket."

Even in the pitch-black of the interior, I knew his face had turned green.[10]

"We're not eating out of the damn thing," I told him, grabbing it myself. "Find something else."

I leaned out of the hatch, scooped up a bucket of water, and threw it on the engine. There was a satisfying hiss.

Junior found a cardboard box and joined me; it held together for six or seven splashes, then disintegrated. I kept shoveling water onto the engine until I stopped hearing a hiss.

---

[10] More environmentalism. You can score on your own from here.

"Here comes the MiG," said M.W.

We crouched down in the hatchway, waiting. A few seconds later, M.W. announced that it had passed, but was banking to take another turn. It seemed to know we had landed nearby, but once more it shot past us. And this time it turned for home.

Because we'd made the engine cool enough that the MiG's heat sensor couldn't pick it up?

"Maybe," admitted M.W.

That was one "maybe" I could live with.

Doc and company gathered around Shotgun's "surfboard" and paddled toward shore.

Even for a former SEAL in excellent shape, a two-mile swim through rough surf at the tail end of a long mission is not exactly a lounge in the bathtub.[11] People think of the Caribbean as a warm ocean—and it is, as oceans go. But let's say that the ocean is, oh, eighty-two degrees—pretty much typical for August. Warm right?

Except when you consider that the average body temperature is 98.7 degrees, and that the laws of thermodynamics—yet to be repealed even by the U.S. congress—dictate that your body will attempt to heat the entire ocean as long as it's submerged.

You may not feel cold right away—especially if people are shooting at you and you're sweating your balls off trying not to drown. But even with a wet suit, eighty-two degrees is damn cold after you've been swimming in it for a half hour or so.

Red's teeth started chattering after a half hour. She wasn't nearly as strong a swimmer as the others, and her thin body gave up heat quickly; if it hadn't been for her life vest, she'd've sunk to the bottom.

Everyone was affected by the cold and fatigue. Doc's hands got numb with the cold, and Mongoose stopped grousing. As for Shotgun—he started singing.

Christmas songs.

"I can't get over that body, Doc," said Red, pushing her arms as best she could. "Hanging there in the dark. For days."

Doc grunted.

---

[11] A two-mile ocean swim, with fins, is required in the third phase of BUD/S. You have all of seventy-five minutes to do it. It is DAMN HARD, CHILDREN! That's why SEALs are SEALs.

"Fidel has a lot to answer for. In so many ways." Red lapsed into silence for a moment. "You think there's a heaven and hell, Doc?"

The question caught Doc by surprise. "Sure."

"If you commit suicide, you can't get into heaven."

"Given that situation, Red, I'd say it was more like murder. Fidel took everything from him. Just about put the rope around his neck."

"You think?" Her voice sounded a little less tired—but only a little.

"Sure."

"That could've been my parents. My father."

"I think we should swim, Red. As hard as we can."

"OK."

After they'd been swimming for nearly an hour, Doc spotted a light moving along the beach a half mile or so to their left. They aimed farther right. When they were still about three-fourths of a mile from the beach, the heavy whomp of a helicopter filled the air.

It was another ten minutes or so before Doc could see the helo in the night sky. It looked as if it were heading straight for them.

"Split up. Make your best way to shore. We'll rendezvous when we can." Doc took Red and pulled her with him, ducking under the waves as the chopper's searchlight approached.

He was surprised when he felt an arm tugging on his side. Red had let herself out of the jacket, dropping down with him. They swam together a few yards, then resurfaced for air and ducked back as the helo's searchlight did a zigzag through the area. They paddled together for a hundred yards or so, staying mostly under the water as the helicopter worked its search beam toward the spot where the boat had sunk.

Shotgun and Mongoose, meanwhile, were swimming silently twenty or so yards away, conserving as much energy as possible.

Well, Mongoose was. Shotgun was bemoaning the fact that he had just lost a bunch more of his goodies.

"Is everybody in the army as big a crybaby as you?" Mongoose asked when the helicopter finally headed west.

"Nah. I'm the top five percent," said Shotgun brightly.

"One of a kind, more like it," growled Doc from the distance. "You two bozos stop screwin' around and get into shore before that helo comes back."

"Right behind ya, Doc," said Shotgun. "You think there's crocodiles here, too?"

Doc decided that was a question best ignored.

With the MiG gone, M.W. decided to check the damage to the plane. He grabbed a flashlight and Mae West, then crawled out the cockpit window, climbing up onto the nose of the seaplane and back to the wing root. Junior and I pulled open the port hatch. Thinking I'd join the pilot, I reached up and pulled myself onto the good wing. But as soon as I did, the plane started to heave sharply toward the water. I scrambled up to the fuselage.

"I don't think it'll tip all the way over," said M.W. "The floats are just to stabilize things a little. They're not usually even in the water."

He didn't sound particularly reassuring. I stayed where I was as he slid out on his belly to the damaged starboard engine.

The metal cowling looked like the skin of a hot dog that had fallen into a charcoal pit. There were perforations along the underside of the wing; one or more of them must have accounted for the fuel loss. The float braces looked as if they'd been bitten off.

"It's in better shape than I thought," said M.W. He sounded almost cheerful. "I think we can take off."

He fiddled around some, sniffing the metal before crawling back inside. Trace had pinned down our location with the GPS while we were wing crawling. She'd also tried getting ahold of Doc, without success.

"Probably just an equipment failure," I told her. "Or else Doc forgot where the damn on-off switch is. You know how he is with technology."

Trace nodded, though we both knew I was full of it.

Danny's not that good a liar, so he didn't say anything when we checked in, except that he hoped to hear from Doc at any minute.

The left engine coughed a few times before spinning to life. As it did, the plane jerked forward to the left, cutting a diagonal in the water. Straightening it out wasn't as easy as you'd think; the plane slapped up and down against the waves and responded with a random assortment of jerks and gentle pulls.

Junior was curled up against the side of the plane near the hatch, which we'd closed again. He had the piss bucket next to him and wasn't complaining about the smell anymore.

"I don't feel too good," he confessed. "I think I'm seasick."

"Nah," I told him. "You're just having too much fun. Imagine we're in an amusement park."

He leaned over and started filling the bucket. Imagination wasn't his strong suit.

The engine revved, and suddenly we were airborne—moving nearly as much sideways as forward, but still airborne.

Then we heard a crack. Real loud.

Either M.W. is a damn good pilot, or we were all damn lucky, because somehow he managed to get the plane onto the water without turning it over.

I can't say the same for the wing. It had sheered off.

Junior looked up from his bucket as we coasted forward, relatively stable.

"Have we hit goat-fuck stage?" he asked. "Or is there still a ways to go?"

Actually we were well past goat fuck, riding with a wind at our backs.

It was now about 2:00 A.M. We were barely ten miles from the Cuban coast. The best we could hope for from the Cubans was that they would do the socialist thing and go back to bed until the morning. Even so, there was bound to be a patrol plane at daybreak. Not even M.W. could muster a "maybe" estimating the odds of it missing us once the sun was up.

"Can we get somebody out here to tow us back?" M.W. asked me.

"Not a chance. Not before they send daylight."

"We're screwed. We can't fly on one engine."

"We're not screwed," I said. "Rev up the engine, point us toward Jamaica, and get us there."

"What, taxi to Jamaica?" asked M.W.

"It's either that or we get out and push," I told him. "And I'm not ruling that out, either."

Mongoose was so hyped about crocodiles that when he brushed against a log a few yards from the boggy coastline, he tackled it and pounded fiercely on what he was sure was its head. Shotgun came to his rescue; when he realized Mongoose was pounding wood he naturally thought this was just the funniest thing in the world and began laughing so loud his guffaws were probably heard in Havana. Mongoose cursed him, which only stoked Shotgun's laughter.

"You two assholes are going to laugh yourselves into the grave," said Doc, paddling with Red a few yards behind them.

Shotgun stopped yucking it up long enough to grab the log Mongoose had wrestled with and push it over toward Doc, who helped Red hoist her exhausted arms over it. They all rested for a minute or so, then made their way to shore.

They were roughly two miles east of the spot where they'd landed earlier. Mongoose found a spot about a hundred yards inland where a pair of fallen trees created a natural hiding place. After scouting the area to make sure they were alone, Doc set up camp there and took stock.

All of their weapons except for Mongoose's Beretta had been lost in the ocean. They had two magazines to go with it. Shotgun's ruck—unlike Mongoose's that had been ripped by the explosion—contained a knife, most of his first-aid kit, the cell phone they had taken from Senor Fernandez, a piece of loose licorice, and a fistful of candy wrappers.

Doc took the cell phone and examined it.

"You gonna turn it on and see if it works?" Shotgun asked. "We can call Danny and tell him where we are."

"It's probably bugged," said Doc.

"You think?"

"You dumb shit, the guy was a courier for the CIA," said Mongoose. "They knew that. That's why they killed him. You don't think they're listening in on his line?"

"Maybe they stopped listening because they know he's dead," Shotgun replied.

"Your mother have any smart kids?"

"Just one. I'm an only child."

Mongoose shook his head.

"We don't need to use the phone," said Doc. "Right now we're going to rest up. Then we'll go up through the jungle here and see if we can find a town or something. We'll find a way to get hold of Danny without using Fidel's dime. Or maybe we'll just go to Havana and fly out. Right now, we're going to get some rest. Starting with you, Red."

"Uh-huh," she mumbled. She was so exhausted her eyes were nearly shut.

Doc used some dry paper from Mongoose's ruck to start a fire, then stripped off their wet gear. Red curled herself into a fetal position and fell asleep. Mongoose started to snore a few minutes later.

"I'll take the first watch," said Shotgun.

"Two hours," said Doc. "Wake me up."

"Yeah." Shotgun stared into his battered rucksack.

"Something wrong?" asked Doc.

"You think salt water will improve the taste of licorice, or ruin it?"

(1)

Recipe for a Goat Fuck:
1. Start with an "easy" mission.
2. Spice with good intentions.
3. Add real-life complications.
4. Shake hands with Mr. Murphy.

With the PBM now just an oversized swampboat, M.W. steered us toward Jamaica at a pace that a turtle would have found excruciating. Danny, meanwhile, was trying to figure out what the hell had happened to Doc.

"No answer on his sat phone, no indication where the hell he is," he told me.

"Start pumping our sources."

"Already on it. I talked to Ketchie," he added, naming a friend of ours at USSOUTHCOM (the military's Southern Command, whose interests include Cuba). "Cubans have a patrol ship going out that way. There's been radio traffic but it's all encrypted. He's going to give me updates every fifteen minutes. And I have a call in to Gene to see what he can find out."

Gene[12] works for the NSA—No Such Agency, the snoops who listen into radio transmissions across the world.

"I figure he was a mile or two from the coast when the MiGs came out," said Danny. "It's possible that they got by without a hitch and the Cubans are just jamming the sat phones."

It may have been possible, but we had spent a good amount of coin to make it very unlikely. Still, it was something.

"You want me to call Admiral Jones and see what he can do to help?" Danny asked.

"He's helped more than enough. Have a boat standing by and ready to leave as soon as we get in."

"You're going to sail back to Cuba in daylight?"

"It's faster than swimming."

---

[12] Gene isn't his real name. Duh, like I'm going to name him and get him fired.

Right about then Doc was giving up on his futile attempt to go to sleep. The dampness had cramped his legs pretty bad, and he got up to loosen his muscles by walking around. He made sure Shotgun was awake—he was—took a circuit around the camp, then decided to do some scouting. He walked about a mile through the swamp and jungle until he came to a narrow trail made of logs and dirt. A set of tire tracks cut through the mud, but it was impossible in the dim light to even guess when they had been made. Doc scouted to the east and west without seeing anyone, then headed back to the camp.

Shotgun wasn't by the fire where he'd left him. Doc's first thought was that he was in the trees taking a leak, but when he didn't appear after a couple of minutes, Doc got concerned. He started looking for him in a gradually widening circle, calling his name in a soft stage whisper.

"Shotgun, you jackass. Where are you?"

No answer.

"Shotgun? You mother-loving fat-sucking congenital doofus-of-an-imbecile—there are no snack stores around here. Where the hell are you?"

Something rustled to his left. Doc dropped to a knee, listening—and as he did, unsheathed the knife at his belt.

He knew it was Shotgun—it had to be Shotgun—it could only be Shotgun.

Unless it wasn't. His leg muscles cramped again.

The noise got closer. Doc drew a deep breath, holding it.

Then whatever or whoever was walking through the jungle stopped. All Doc could hear was his own breath, gliding between his teeth. The knife was heavy in his hand, his fingers tense. Doc readied himself to spring without actually moving. His legs were ready, his chest, left hand, right . . .

"That you, Doc?" said Shotgun.

"Damn it, Shotgun. I almost slit your throat."

Shotgun laughed and stepped out of the brush.

"Well, I almost shot you," said Shotgun. His gun was level with Doc's chest. "Wouldn't we have looked like a couple of assholes, huh, you with a hole in your chest and me with my neck slit open?"

Doc didn't find that particularly funny. Shotgun changed the subject.

"Look, I found Red's rucksack. It washed ashore."

The backpack had been ripped in half by the explosion, but the ruck containing spare magazines for her pistol remained in the bottom corner.

"There's more stuff down there," Shotgun told Doc. "The tide's turned."

"You stay here," Doc told him, though Shotgun wasn't going anywhere. "When I come back, I'll whistle so you know it's me."

"What kind of song?"

"Your funeral march."

It took Doc about ten minutes to get down to the water. That surprised him, because he thought they'd walked in farther.

His next surprise was more ominous. A ship[13] was sailing offshore, playing its spotlights all around the water. While it was far enough away that it didn't present an immediate danger, the fact that it was there meant the Cubans were still very much interested in them.

Doc waited until the ship had sailed farther east, then began walking parallel along the shore. A strong tide had whipped up, and there was a good amount of debris. Most of it was wood and useless junk from boats lost years before.

One of their plastic equipment boxes sat end-up in the surf. He waded out to it, only to find that the explosion had broken the end of the box off, and it was empty.

A few feet away he found one of our sat phones. The blast had jarred off the bottom plastic case, which was gone, along with the battery that normally sat in a slot on the casing. A few yards from that, he found a med kit and one of the team radios—probably one of the backups. The radio was intact, but lacked a headpiece. The med kit had been cracked, but the water had done little damage to the equipment and meds, since everything inside was wrapped in plastic.

Doc used the damaged gear box to collect his treasures. Working westward along the beach, he came across a tangle of debris that included an earset from an Apple iPod, probably lost by some vacationer miles away and taken by the tide. He balled it up and stuffed it into his pants. It was the only thing worth taking that he saw.

---

[13] The ship was probably a Russian Project 205EM guided-missile patrol craft, most likely Ship 262, which we were to encounter later on. Doc couldn't make out the details in the dark.

By the time he tucked back to camp, Mongoose had gotten up to spell Shotgun. He whistled back when Doc whistled, and met him, pistol in hand.

"What'd you get?"

"Sat phone. Half of one, anyway."

Not daring to relight the fire, Doc moved around until he found a spot in the clearing where the light from the moon and stars seemed strongest. The sat phone's single circuit board appeared intact. The volume control was loose, since half of it normally rested on the back of the unit, and the on-off rocker had to be held to be clicked into position. But otherwise, the phone looked as if it was in good enough shape to work.

If they could find a battery for it.

"I thought we weren't going to use Fernandez's cell phone," said Mongoose after Doc retrieved the phone from the small pile of their gear.

"We're not," said Doc. He undid the back and took out the battery.

"You gonna put that in the sat phone?"

Doc would have done that, but it didn't fit. The contacts at the edge of the radio slot seemed similar, though—four little prongs, which corresponded to four goldish-looking bars on the battery.

Doc took his knife and cut up the earphone wire he'd found earlier. Then, with the help of tape from the med kit, he wired up a crude connection from the battery to the radio.

"Ready?" he asked Mongoose.

Mongoose shrugged. "Got nothing to lose."

We were about fifty miles from shore when Doc called in to Danny. Danny called me, and patched me into the line from Jamaica.

"Doc?" I said when I heard the line click through. "Where are you, what's going on?"

"We liked Cuba so much, we decided to hang around for a while," Doc said before explaining the situation.

His handiwork with the radio solved our biggest problem: finding him. The next problem was how to get them out of Cuba.

They were way too far from Gitmo to take any chance on getting out in that direction; besides, the Cubans patrol much more heavily near the camp than elsewhere on that side of the island. While getting to Havana wasn't impossible, their lack of money and clothes added greatly to the difficulty level. The best option remained a rescue mission led by yours truly.

Picking them up during the day would have been dicey even without the ship Doc had seen; it made the most sense to wait until the following night. Because the makeshift sat phone couldn't be counted on, we arranged a series of pickup points to be checked in order of priority. Doc also said he would move inland as soon as he ended the transmission, just in case the Cubans sent someone to investigate the wreckage and the flotsam that had washed ashore.

"Did you hear what happened to Traba's brother?" Doc asked just before I was going to hang up.

"You told me he committed suicide."

"Yeah. Red's pretty broken up about it. She's mumbling in her sleep, calling his name. She was asking about whether you go to heaven if you commit suicide."

"I didn't know you were a priest now, Doc."

"Gotta do a little of everything in this business. You oughta know that, Father Dick."

[11]

I called Ken Jones at the CIA as soon as I got off the dock in Jamaica. He greeted me with the big, twenty-one-gun hello he uses when he's talking to someone who he owes a big favor to.

When he bothers talking to them at all, that is.

"Dick—*Dick*." His voice boomed over the handset. "How are we doing?"

"Fernandez is dead."

"Dead?"

"That's not the least of your trouble. He may have been a double agent."

Ken cursed. I told him briefly what had happened. I left out the part about Traba, since it didn't concern him or the agency.

"I'll get right back to you," he said.

Right back to me turned out to be two hours later—all the time I needed to nap and recharge my batteries.

"Our people are out," said Ken as soon as I picked up the sat phone. "Thank you."

"Which people?"

"The ones who were going to make the switch. They're safe. Turned out they hadn't touched down yet."

"You're welcome."

"Fernandez was just a mule in the middle. He didn't know what the discs were for, or what the plan was."

"So you told me."

"Yes, but I just wanted to reassure you."

"I'm reassured. I'm warm and fuzzy. I may even go get a drink."

"Dick, we've got a big problem here."

"I can get my people out, don't worry. I'll do it tonight."

"That wasn't the problem I was talking about," said the admiral. "Maybe we can make a deal."

Ken proposed a cooperative venture: he'd help me get Doc and the others, if I then went and swapped the DVDs out.

"I don't think so."

"You're going to need help getting your people out, Dick."

"Not really."

Ken changed tactics. "What about the people of Cuba?" he asked. "Don't they deserve a fresh start? Don't they deserve hope?"

"They deserve more than that."

"So you'll switch the discs for us?"

"I don't see how you got from A to Z there."

"We will, of course, pay at your usual inflated rate. And expenses."

"Ha."

"You're going to need our help to get your people, Dick. Without us, there's no guarantee. And let's face it—I don't think there's anyone else around who could switch the tapes, let alone live to not tell about it."

"Are you trying to butter me up, Ken? The cholesterol count of this conversation is getting pretty high here."

The conversation continued for a while before I told him I'd do it.

In truth, I'd decided before he asked.

I didn't need Ken's help to get Doc and the others out, or at least I hoped I didn't. And even if I had, it wasn't exactly a fair swap—the fact that Fernandez had been made, even if he didn't know what the discs were for, made any plot to move the discs even more dangerous than it already was.

But I was more than a little pissed at Fidel, and I did want to do something to help the people of Cuba. Traba, his brother, Red's family, the other Cubans I've known over the years—it made me mad knowing they'd all been screwed for so long. Somebody had to do something to help them.

Your heart's bleeding, I know.

If it makes you feel any better, Ken also agreed to pay triple my usual rate . . . which worked out to a lot of Bombay for Daddy and friends.

A short while later, Junior hooked one of our computers to the encrypted satellite phone, pulled up a special Web browser, and turned the back room of our vacation house into a secure video conference center. There were two other feeds. One was from CIA headquarters at Langley, where Ken and some of his Cuba hands had gathered. The other came from the infamous "location not disclosed," which by all indications was in Florida somewhere.

73

Ken started off by promising we'd have access to some real-time intel networks and other data the CIA controlled or was privy to. I guess he wanted to prove he could be generous when it didn't cost him anything. As it turned out, that access, while in some cases useful, wasn't nearly as critical as the intel that had already been gathered, most of it from humanint sources, aka real people.[14]

From what I learned later, the Agency had good intel on Fidel's taped will because one of the men who had helped make the tape had been a CIA mole. Unfortunately for us, Fidel had decided to eliminate the small team that had created the video, and within seventy-two hours of its completion the half-dozen techies were all dead. Only two copies of the video were made, both on DVD; the master was destroyed. Unfortunately for Fidel, the mole had already fully briefed his CIA handler.

In a perverse way, Fidel's decision to eliminate the team probably made things easier. Since very few people besides his brother and perhaps a handful of Communist Party big shots knew the tape existed, there was no need to put the DVDs into the Cuban equivalent of Fort Knox. Often times, the best hiding place is in plain sight. The discs weren't all in plain sight—both were locked away in safes, according to the CIA sources—but neither was directly guarded.

Which didn't mean they'd be easy to get.

Fidel kept one of the DVDs in his office at one of his Havana headquarters. The other was believed to be at a bunker/villa he'd recently built on the northeastern side of the island.[15] The bunker was part of a military base that was still under construction. The Christians in Action had gathered a large amount of information about both sites. In the case of the bunker, they had detailed blueprints, thanks to the architect in Estonia who designed the facility.

By the end of an hour and a half, we had more than enough information to sneak in and out of either complex, locate the DVDs, make the swap, and get out.

Ass-u-ming the CIA information was correct, of course.

Big assumption, I know.

---

[14] For obvious reasons, I'm going to skimp here on the precise nature and benefits of the intelligence.

[15] I'm not supposed to say where it is, but if you put your ruler on Guantanamo and drew a straight line north to the water, you wouldn't be far off.

After the briefing, Danny went to work tapping sources in Miami to see if he could round out the information the agency had given us without tipping our hand. I changed into my sweats and went for a run, during which I planned most of the operation. When I came back, I called everyone together and laid it out for them.

"Sounds kind of complicated," said Trace when I was done.

Complicated is not a compliment. As a rule, successful operations follow the KISS principle—Keep It Simple, Stupid. In outline, the plan *was* simple: we'd parachute in with supplies, hook up with the landing team, then head east. That job done, we'd go to Havana, make the second switch, and use phony IDs to fly out. It was the details along the way that added complications.

Danny made a few suggestions, which I immediately integrated. Junior, meanwhile, sat at the edge of his seat, practically salivating at the idea of a night jump into hostile territory. They're sweet when they're young and green.

"I'm ready, Dick," he said as I wrapped up. "When do we jump?"

"You're not coming, Matt," I told him. "We need you here to make sure the access to the CIA system and the intel network is smooth. You have to stay with Danny."

"A technical expert? Screw that."

He may have added a few other choice words, and possibly hinted that I should go somewhere else besides Cuba. But he had zero choice.

"You're our technical expert. That's why you're here," I reminded him.

"This is bullshit." Junior slammed his cup on the table and stormed out.

Trace and I exchanged a glance.

"You didn't expect him to be happy that you were leaving him behind," she said, picking up her coffee.

M.W.'s plane was damaged so severely there was no hope of using it to get back to the island; the next order of business was finding alternate transportation. Rather than relying on Ken, I did what all SEALs do when they run into problems: I called another SEAL.

If you were going to describe the stereotypical SEAL, Jamie Richie would fill that description. As I've said many times, the image most people have of SEALs is completely wrong. They're not all big bodybuilder types. SEALs come in all shapes and sizes, and most of the truly dangerous ones are skinny, short, and look just like the guy who does your taxes. Until they slit your throat, that is.

But Jamie Richie looks like you probably imagine a SEAL looks. Big—six-six and still growing—he has a blond buzz cut, biceps as thick as eighty-year-old oak trees, and a scar across his cheek that he got in a place he's still not allowed to talk about. A few notches past forty, he lives in Miami, primarily so he can indulge in his two favorite pastimes: working on his tan, and picking up women. Not necessarily in that order.

He also happens to be a supervisory pilot for a major European airline, whose name starts with L, though you didn't hear that from me.

"Demo Dick!" he said as soon as he heard my voice. "How are you, cockbreath?"

"Better than you, angstrom brain."

We exchanged some more terms of endearment, questioning each other's intelligence, morals, and parentage. Once that was out of the way, I told Jamie what I needed.

"And you're where now?" he asked.

"North side of Jamaica."

"Hey, you know there's some really interesting voodoo doctors out that way," said Jamie. "I've heard they have a potion that makes women strip naked as soon as they drink it."

"I can do that with a whisper."

"Still the same old Dick."

"Can you help me?"

"Stripping women? Or with the plane?"

"Let's start with the plane."

"Be at the airport at 2100," he said. "Bring your own stewardess. And drinks for the crew."

Junior was still in a stew when it came time to leave. He gave Trace a big kiss and a shoulder chuck.

I got a frown and dagger eyes.

"I'll talk to you soon," I told him, holding out my hand.

"Yup."

He kept his hands in his pocket.

"You gonna wish me luck?" I asked.

"I still want to come."

"You know why you can't."

" 'Cause I'm your kid and you don't want me getting hurt."

"Come with me," I told him sharply, and marched him out the back of the hut.

His face was red. I think he honestly thought I was going to take him over my knee and spank him. Believe me, the thought did cross my mind.

"When I give you an assignment, you do it," I told him. "That goes for everyone on this team. It has nothing to do with DNA. You're here because you can do a job. Who your father is or isn't has zero to do with it. *Capisce?*"

"I get it."

"I'm not even sure you are my son."

Junior opened his mouth to say something else, but I didn't let him.

"End of discussion. This is not a democracy. You have no freedom of speech."

"It still fucking sucks," he said.

He may have been holding back tears; it was hard to tell in the dark. I let him have the last word.

While we'd spent the day getting our proverbial shit together, Doc and the others had been moving around, trying to stay away from the Cuban troops and policemen sent into the area to look for them. The fact that the boat had been blown into so many tiny pieces took a little of the heat off; the Cubans were more than happy to believe no one had made it, and spent most of their effort looking for bodies along the shore. Still, the whole area was on alert, and every so often as Doc and the others moved through the jungle they heard sirens blaring in the distance.

They moved deeper inland and farther east as they went. The biggest problem wasn't the Cuban patrols, or the crocodiles, which Mongoose kept mentioning every time they came near a puddle. It was hunger. None of them complained, not even Shotgun, who ordinarily can't be seen without some sort of candy or cookie or something in his mouth. But their stomachs rumbled.

At three in the afternoon, Doc checked in. Danny gave him the outlines of the plan, letting him know that he would be staying in Cuba for a few days longer. Doc began scouting for trucks we could use, and found a pair parked near an open pole barn about two miles from where they'd landed the night before. Worst case, they'd get us up to Victoria de las Tunas, where we'd be able to find better transportation.

Red didn't like the idea of stealing the trucks, and told Doc that after they found a hiding spot to wait for us about a half mile from the pole barn. Their theft would cause hardship for the people at the farm, whether they owned the trucks or not.

"It won't be like they're totally lost," Doc said. "Victoria de las Tunas is only twenty-five miles away or so."

"I doubt it will work out for them. If the trucks are government-owned, it will be even worse."

Doc couldn't make much of a counterargument, so he didn't bother.

In the long run, the owner or owners of the trucks and the people on the farm would be better off, and if given the choice, were likely to freely volunteer the vehicles to the cause of freedom. But Red knew they neither had the choice nor would ever know why the trucks were taken.

It was also possible they wouldn't volunteer the trucks, or even want freedom. While Fidel was loathed by many, many Cubans, there were others who feared democracy. But you don't start debating political or philosophical issues in the middle of an operation. Once you're in, you're in. Shades of gray are fine back at the bar; once you're in the field, things are black or white. Otherwise the only color you're going to see is the bright red of fresh blood. For all her compassion for her parents' former countrymen, like the others, Red knew she had to do whatever it took to get the job done.

You've undoubtedly heard many stories about people sneaking weapons and bombs past airport security. Most of the time they're testing the security.

Those are the cases you hear about. I wouldn't worry about them. They're anomalies, few and far between.

It's the ones you *don't* hear about that should scare the shit out of you.

But no matter how lax the security in the Jamaican airport terminal was, Trace and I wouldn't have been able to beat it by going straight through the gate. Even the most ganja-happy guard would have realized something was up if we walked up with parachutes and enough weapons and ammo for a small army.

So we didn't go through the terminal, or walk up to the gate.

We drove there instead, in a truck belonging to the airline. No one even asked for ID; they just smiled and waved us on as we slowed near the hangar.

Now you can worry. Granted, this was Jamaica. But we could have done it at JFK or LAX or Dulles, you name it, with only a few slight alterations in the game plan.

When Jamie said he'd help us, I expected that he'd find us a little island jumper that could scoot in and out of Cuban airspace without too much trouble, a charter that would fly over where we wanted to jump, then land in Havana like nothing happened.

But that would have been too easy for Jamie, who has always been a bit of a showboat. He turned up with a large two-engined airliner[16] about as inconspicuous as a battleship in a bathtub.

"Couldn't get anything bigger, huh?" I asked when he met me on the tarmac.

"I would have brought a 747, but the runway here was a few feet short. As it is, I have to watch our takeoff weight."

The aircraft had been involved in some sort of test run in Mexico and had to be flown back to the States. Jamie's position as a supervisor allowed him to pull rank and take over the test, choosing as his helpers two other pilots with military backgrounds who could be counted on to keep quiet. I believe he has a don't-ask, don't-tell agreement with his boss; I know I would if he worked for me.

We were taxiing to the runway no more than ten minutes after settling into the cabin. The plan was simple. In an unusual show of good sense, Cuba follows international treaties and allows airliners to fly over the island without undue hassle. Jamie and his crew would take us up to about twenty thousand feet, then pass close to but not directly over our target area. When we were inside the drop zone, he'd flash the lights. Trace and I would then open the door and jump. Fifteen minutes later—a few minutes more or less, depending on the wind and other vagaries—we'd shake Doc's hand at the edge of the cane field where he was waiting.

High-altitude jumps are old news; you suck oxygen or hold your breath for a few thousand feet, bitch about the cold, and basically fall in the general direction of your target. When the altimeter on your wrist beeps, you pull the handle and groan from the tug on your gonads.

---

[16] After I wrote this, Jamie asked that I not ID the aircraft since it might make it obvious which airline was involved, and cost him his job. So the exact ID has been deleted. If you fly medium distances anywhere in the U.S. or Europe, you've probably been on this type of plane.

Better you should groan, though. The alternative happens a little too quickly for my taste.

With chute deployed, you steer around to the spot where you're landing. This is extremely easy in the movies, where the breeze never kicks above two knots and every light in the county is showing you where to go. Pitch-black, wind whipping past your ears so hard you figure it must be a hurricane—that's a different story.

But that's easy compared to getting gear to fall in the right spot. The U.S. Air Farce has a sophisticated set of computers and satellite communications equipment in their heavy movers that can get an M1A1 between two parked cars on a Chicago alleyway if the need arises. But that gear costs big bucks, and the taxpayers weren't about to front me the money.

Jamie couldn't steal it, either.

So Trace and I rigged the four ammo pouches—think duffel bags with extra stitching and inflatable cushions to soften the impact—with remote parachute-glide wings fashioned by a friend of mine who works as an engineer at Law Enforcement Technologies out in Colorado. His wings, which have attracted some interest from the Pentagon, are connected to a computer that calculates when to deploy the parachute and then steers it toward a pre-entered GPS spot. Very impressive—but extremely difficult to do with any kind of a conventional parachute.

But this rig didn't use a conventional chute. The wings literally were wings, made primarily of a carbon resin material that is stronger than steel and a good deal lighter. As they fell, the wings used flaps on the leading and trailing edges to adjust their steering, just like an airplane would.

Getting out of a commercial airliner at twenty or thirty thousand feet is not quite as easy as opening the door and yelling Geronimo. There's a slipstream around some airplanes that can make things a little unpredictable. As the plane moves through the air, its wings and fuselage generate different wind currents and eddies. Depending on the design of the plane, along with its speed, etc., these currents may not effect you at all. But they can also try to smack you against the fuselage or wing harder than a pro bowl linebacker.

The easiest way to deal with this is to choose the right airliner. Back in the day, that meant picking one with a rear staircase. Piece of cake. We used to do it in SEAL Team Six (ST6). So did D. B. Cooper, who left a 727 with $200,000 back in 1971. The FBI thinks he didn't survive the jump, since some of the money was found on the ground years later, but there are plenty of people who think otherwise.

Now, with changes in airline design, it can be a little trickier. You generally want to jump from the rear door, and in some cases you use a special baffle to help you get out smoothly. We did one of those.[17]

Assuming you *can* open the door, you have to be careful to make sure there's no change in pressure that will suck you out of the aircraft. That means that the cabin has to start out depressurized.

Yes, Grasshopper, that means no oxygen. Um, noooo, we did not hold our breath.

Once in flight, Trace and I sucked air from a portable rack, waiting for the signal from the cabin. When we were about thirty seconds from the jump point, Jamie pulled his flaps. This caused the plane to brake in midair, dropping like a brick with wings for a few thousand feet. While he was declaring a Mayday—he had to assume he was being tracked over Cuba—we went to work. I slid open the door (pushed and grunted was more like it), then set out a little laundry chute to make it easier to slide the gear and ourselves together.

The chute is similar to a contraption ST6 used to get large teams out together on similar jumps. It looks a little like an oversized shoehorn, and is held in place by a set of bolts and clamps once the door is open. It can be easily jettisoned or pulled inside before landing.

Ordinarily it's a peach to put down, but in this case Mr. Murphy must have made some adjustments, because when I went to get it in place, the right side wouldn't snap in correctly. The wind was so severe I was almost pulled right out of the aircraft as I worked to adjust it.

Sweat started to pour through my gloved fingers as I jerked my thumb against the oversized handle. I cursed, I snarled, I popped it with my fist, but it still wouldn't slap into place.

"Five seconds, Dick," Jamie told us over the shortwave radio.

Trace gave me the evil eye through her goggles. We had a limited window to jump out; if it took me too long to get the baffle into place, we'd end up in the Florida Keys. Or maybe Washington, D.C.

Two more hard pops with my hand and the clamps still hadn't closed right.

---

[17] Again, Jamie says that identifying the precise method might ID not just the plane but the airline. We should note that the 727's basic design was changed after Cooper's jump to make it much harder to do what he did.

"Fuck it," I said. I kept one hand on the baffle as I leaned over to grab one of the supply bags. "Get out, Trace. Come on."

Trace tossed the supply bags and tumbled into the darkness. I went out after her, pushing off from the plane and letting go of the slide at the last possible second.

Not good enough for Murphy. The slide flew completely off, bashing me on the back of the head and giving my tush a good shove toward Mother Earth.

Fortunately, I have a thick skull and an even tougher rump. The only permanent injury was to my pride.

By the time I got my bearings I'd already fallen a few thousand feet. My GPS (the units transmitted each other's position, remember) showed Trace nearly a mile to the east. I pulled my arms up, got my legs out, and slowly turned to the proper bearing. The wind whipped against the side of my body so hard it felt as if it was going to blow off my helmet; the strap tugged, and for a few seconds I thought my head would come off if the helmet didn't. Then things settled down. I tucked my head back, took a few deep breaths, and started steering myself toward the spot marked out in the GPS dial.

In ST6, we worked it so that a release at thirty thousand would get us a stable group under canopy between twenty-three thousand to twenty thousand feet. Trace and I hooked up at 21,500—well within spec, thank you very much. Meanwhile, Jamie had taken his plane back on course and declared his emergency over. Anyone who had the slightest interest was tracking him, not us—even if we hadn't looked like false returns or specs of dust on the radar, he was where the emergency was.

"You still with me?" Trace asked.

I grumbled something back.

The bags, meanwhile, were sailing downward, guided by their high-tech parasail gear. Two were exactly on course, and a third was just slightly to the north of where it should be.

The location of the fourth was a mystery. The sending unit wasn't working, though whether that was because of a problem with the electronics or the wing had screwed up was a mystery. There was nothing Trace or I could do about it anyway.

Our landing zone was the sugarcane field Doc had spotted during the day. Doc had given us the GPS readings, and we'd looked at a video image courtesy of Ken's connection before taking off. (Imagine Google

Earth, but with the resolution you could get with a good camera from the roof of your house.)

I kept waiting for Mr. Murphy to show his ugly face, maybe by spinning the numbers in the GPS display like a Las Vegas slot machine, or throwing a massive funnel cloud in my face. But apparently Murph had had his fill of fun when he shoved me out of the plane. Trace and I hit the ground within two meters of our targeted X.

Two of the bags were waiting for us ten meters away.

So was Doc.

"About time you got to Cuba," he said, grabbing my hand.

"Fuck you very much. Where are the others?"

"One of the bags fell across the road," Doc said. "Red went to fetch it. Shotgun and Mongoose are arranging transport."

"A limo, I hope," said Trace.

"For you, a horse-drawn carriage, m'lady." Doc gave her a mock bow, then dug into the equipment bag for food.

Not every vehicle in Cuba is ancient, just the best ones. The truck Shotgun and Mongoose were appropriating was a 1952 Ford pickup. The rear bed had been removed years and years ago, and replaced with what looked like an oversized Easter egg basket made of a hodgepodge of salvaged wood. Sugarcane, dirt, ground-up beets, and other assorted vegetable remains littered the planks at the back, giving it a picturesque lived-in look.

The cab, on the other hand, looked as if it had been vacuumed clean; there wasn't a crumb of dirt on the floor nor a smudge on the windshield. The original seat cover had been replaced by quilted fabric, the sort you'd find on a comforter at a fancy hotel.

The truck's door locks had been removed eons ago. In place of the ignition switch, a pair of thick wires hung down below the dashboard.

"Why would they take the switch with them?" Shotgun asked Mongoose, holding them up.

"Where'd you grow up? The suburbs?" said Mongoose. "It's hot-wired. They probably lost the key. Touch the two wires together, and the engine turns over."

"Wow. The shit you miss growing up in the suburbs."

Shotgun's first attempt showered sparks across the front seat. Mongoose grabbed the wires and slapped them together. There were more sparks, and then a groan from the engine as it started to turn over.

"Pump the gas, pump the gas," said Mongoose.

Shotgun did as he was told, but the engine didn't catch.

"Watch out." Mongoose ducked under the dashboard. They didn't have a flashlight, and he had to feel around with his hands. "There's another set of wires down here," he said. "Did you unhook them?"

"You musta kicked them."

"Hang on."

"Maybe those guys can help figure it out," said Shotgun.

"What guys?"

"The ones coming out of the house."

Two Cubans had appeared around the corner of one of the farm buildings about thirty yards away and were headed their way. It was hard to tell in the dark, but one looked to be carrying a Mossberg.

The other had an AK47.

"They're not going to fire at us," said Mongoose, hooking the wires together. "They're not going to want to ruin their truck."

"You sure?"

A barrage of buckshot ripped into the windshield before Mongoose could answer. Shotgun twisted away at the last second, but still caught a shower of glass shards in his arm and shoulder.

"Now pump the gas while I turn over the starter," said Mongoose.

"You pump the gas," said Shotgun, throwing open the door. "I've had enough of this Cuban bullshit."

I'm sure there are a few readers—one or two, maybe, including his mom—who feel *certain* that Mr. Fox—better known as Shotgun—rolled out of the vehicle onto the ground, dusted himself off, and approached the two Cuban gentlemen with a grin and silver tongue, explaining to them exactly how important their vehicle was to the grand cause of freedom and liberty, and suggested that they let it go in the interests of humanity and the future of the Cuban people. Those readers are no doubt convinced that, the world being at heart a nonviolent paradise, the two Cubans felt moved at the bottom of their hearts, and not only gave Shotgun and Mongoose the truck but their weapons and spare change. Further, one of the men ran into the farmhouse and grabbed the fifty-year-old rum he had been saving for his daughter's wedding, presenting it to the Americans as a goodwill gesture. The other gathered firewood and broke out a guitar; for the next half hour, Cuban and American voices shared the night, singing "Kumbaya," "God Bless America," and a number improvised on the spot entitled "Kick That Bastard Fidel in the Groin for Me."

Those of you who feel that way will want to skip ahead a few pages.

Shotgun flew into the dirt, tumbling over as another pack of shotgun pellets hit the hood of the truck. He scrambled to his left, grabbing the pistol from his belt. The Cubans cursed and screamed, promising that his days as a thief would soon be over.

The two Cubans were silhouetted against the background of the buildings, which made them easy targets. Shotgun squeezed off two shots, dropping the man with the AK47 even before he was able to start firing. Shotgun turned his attention to the other man, who was running toward the barn. He hit him once or twice in the leg; the man fell but managed to keep moving, crawling behind the barn.

Mongoose had hooked the wires together. As soon as the engine started, he jerked the truck into reverse and swung in Shotgun's direction. The lights came on in a house farther up the hill, maybe three hundred feet away. A woman screamed.

"Guns, come on," yelled Mongoose. "Let's go, let's go."

"I want that fucker's Mossberg," said Shotgun.

Mongoose cursed. The idea had been to steal the truck without being seen or heard, and while that was no longer possible, in his view getting the hell out of there ought to be the next highest priority.

But there was no stopping Shotgun once his mind was set. He ran to the prone Cuban, grabbed the AK47, then dropped to his knee, covering the corner of the building where the other man had retreated. He counted off to three, then threw himself up and around the corner, gun at his side, ready.

He didn't fire. The Cuban was lying, faceup, breathing hard, gun off to the side where he'd dropped it.

Besides the leg, the Cuban had been hit in the arm and the chest. Shotgun patted the man's pockets, saw he wasn't carrying spare ammo, then jumped up and backed away. He fired a quick burst from the AK toward the barn to keep the other Cuban in check, then bolted for the waiting truck.

Mongoose jammed the gas and popped the clutch, hoping for a quick takeoff—and promptly stalled the truck.

He never was very good with a stick.

Cursing, he started fumbling with the wires again.

"Yo, what are you doing?" asked Shotgun.

Too busy trying to figure out the right wire configuration again, Mongoose didn't answer.

"Shit," said Shotgun. "Where'd this asshole come from? Stay down on the floor!"

Shotgun ducked beneath the dash himself as a fresh shotgun round sailed into the cab. As the remaining shards of windshield glass rained down on them, Shotgun raised the AK47 and returned fire, emptying the mag.

By then Mongoose had the engine turning over and was desperately pumping at the gas with his other hand. Finally the engine caught; he scrambled up and got the truck moving again, slumping sideways. He left it in first gear all the way to the road, the engine whining as if it were about to explode.

We'd heard the gunfire and started in the direction of the farm buildings when the truck flew over the hill. Mongoose skidded to a stop on the road in front of us, stalling the truck again.

"What the hell happened?" Doc demanded, looking over the battered front end of the truck. "I've seen Swiss cheese with less holes."

"They didn't like the fact that we double-parked," said Shotgun.

"Jesus, Shotgun, what happened to your face?" asked Trace. It was covered with blood.

"Mama spit on it when I was born," said Shotgun. "Been breaking mirrors ever since."

Red had found the other bag in a small tumble of weeds and met us about a half mile down the road. She rode in the back with Mongoose and me, picking glass shards out of Shotgun's arm and back. The pain seemed to tickle his funny bone; he giggled practically the whole way to Victoria de las Tunas.

The truck was too battered to drive into the city. We weren't in the greatest shape ourselves. Trace and I had brought fresh civilian clothes for everyone to change into, but their trip through the swamp had left Doc and the others pretty grimy. Mud was caked in their hair; I doubt crocodiles smelled worse. Rather than heading northeast toward Castro's bunker, I decided we'd spend the day in Victoria de las Tunas. Trace and I would stand watch and find better transportation while the others slept. We had false IDs and papers, along with European credit cards, so it wouldn't be too hard to find a place to stay.

Back in Jamaica, Junior did a Web search and found a hotel on the north side of the city that advertised for European tourists. He used a phone line that routed the call through Mexico to make a reservation.

"Hot and cold water," he said. "A real deluxe place."

We abandoned the truck about two miles southwest of town, in a field a few hundred yards from the main road. Then we divvied up the gear and started walking. They were all tired—Red leaned forward as she walked, held upright only by momentum—and it took us nearly an hour to get to the city. It was still an hour before daybreak, too early to go to the hotel without raising more questions than it would be worth answering. So we scuttled around a bit. Mongoose found a spigot on the side of a *servio*—a gas station—we could use to wash up.

Red and I found a small grocery store that had just opened for the day. We went in and bought a few things for breakfast. Talking with the owner, she worked up a cover story on the fly, claiming I was a well-off and loopy German tourist and that she'd been hired as a guide to Guantanamo

Province farther east, where I was in search of an exotic bird seen only in Cuba.

This was the first time I'd met a Cuban since I'd pretended to be Castro. My hair and beard were back to being black, and to be honest, I'd more or less forgotten who I looked like. But the woman kept staring at me, and it wasn't hard to guess why. Finally I snapped out a bunch of German at Red, asking when we were leaving.

"He could be *el Jefe*'s younger brother," said the storekeeper.

"Really?" Red made a face, then pretended to look me over. "I don't know."

"He could use a younger brother—a real brother, instead of the old washed-up faggot that he has."

Red shrugged. It was the right play: criticism of Raul, especially by questioning his sexual orientation, is common in Cuba, but there was no way for Red to know whether the woman was being sincere or trying to trap her.

My part was easier: I was pretending not to understand Spanish, so I simply ignored them, picked out a loaf of bread from her meager supply, and gave it to Red to buy.

"Your German friend should think about taking over," the woman told Red as we left. "It won't be long now."

My first impression was that was a hopeful sentiment—that the Cuban people were ready for a change and would eagerly embrace it once Fidel finally kicked the bucket. But Red felt discouraged.

"She wasn't talking about an election," she explained as we walked back to the empty lot where we'd left the others. "So many of these people have lost hope for democracy. The future they see, another strongman. It plays right into their hands, into Raul's and the other communists around him."

"They're not against democracy, they're just not hoping for it yet."

"I don't know that they ever will."

"They will."

Red didn't answer. Maybe she just didn't trust herself to hope that much.

By Cuban standards, the hotel was a three-star business accommodation, which meant that you could find toilet paper in most of the bathrooms.

I left Trace to play lookout while I went and scouted some transportation for us to the northern side of the island. With a little help from Junior, who gave me some more tips thanks to his satellite view, I located the perfect vehicle: a Cuban telephone van, parked conveniently in a lot three blocks away, right behind the government telephone office. From the size of the lot, it seemed likely there would be more trucks there that night. Even better, the lot was equipped with a small gas pump. There was also a fence topped by barbed wire, but it wouldn't present much of an obstacle.

The only complication was a video camera mounted above the back door to the building. We'd have to make ourselves presentable for the camera. Or rather, make the camera presentable for us.

Transportation out of the way, I went shopping for a few things to make it easier to change my "look." A couple of shirts, a few caps: I was a new man. One or two people stared at me the way the woman in the grocery store had, but most were much more interested in the convertible pesos I flashed.

Wandering farther, I found a small toy shop that sold stuffed animals. I picked up a crow for a dozen pesos.

"Reminds me of my ex-wife," I told the elderly clerk as I checked out.

By seven o'clock, everyone was up and ready to rock. We filtered into a small restaurant a few blocks away. The restaurant was mentioned on several travel Web sites as catering to foreigners and very well-off Cubans, which meant that the food was bland and the service so-so. But it also meant that we were inconspicuous, not the novelty we would have been in a restaurant that served primarily locals.

Even so, we were the talk of the town.

The theft of the truck at the farm had not only caught the attention of the local police, but had also interested a regional newsman for *Granma* who was working on a story on the rise of banditry in the country. (*Granma* is the official party paper; it's named after a yacht that Fidel tried to use to invade Cuba. Really.) The reporter and a cameraman had spent the day touring the farm and the countryside to the south, where apparently there had been three or four different thefts over the past few months. His story would be a massive exposé, exposing the corruption caused by a society that was slipping toward decadent capitalism. The journalist had taken a blood oath to stop the decline, upholding the highest standards of the Revolution.

I knew all this because the newsman and his producer were having dinner a few tables away, loudly proclaiming their views to a pair of embarrassed local officials.

One little tidbit we picked up: both of the men Shotgun had shot had survived. Trace promised him that he would be taking a refresher course in marksmanship as soon as we got back home.

"Ah, it's all in his head," said Doc. He turned to Shotgun. "Next time, pretend you're shooting at a giant Ring Ding. You'll have no problem."

We stayed at the restaurant until just after nine, then moseyed on over to the telephone company. There were now seven trucks in the yard, including three vans. Even better, there were no watchmen on duty. Our only concern was the video camera attached to the building.

The camera covered a large swath of the lot, enough so that it was impossible to get over the fence without being seen. That meant we'd have to attack it from behind. Or above. Or both.

The telephone building was a three-story brick building painted white. It wasn't all that different than the sort of early twentieth-century structure you'd find in a Midwest town in the U.S. before what was euphemistically termed urban renewal in the sixties and seventies. Shotgun and I went around to the side, where a narrow canopy had been built over the side door. I used his back as a stepping stool to get a grip on the bottom of the canopy, then boosted myself up over the edge and clawed my way to the flat roof.

The moon was full and bright, and I had no trouble picking my way across to the back, avoiding the stickier puddles of mud as well as some toilet vents. I found a place to tie off my rope, then lowered myself a story and a half to the camera. I rested my right foot gently on the camera, then reached into my shirt for the stuffed bird I'd bought earlier.

"What are you doing with the bird?" Shotgun asked, peering over the side of the roof above me.

"Fluffy hates cameras," I told him.

I kicked the camera with my right foot so that the lens pointed to the ground. At the same time, I dropped the bird, making it look like it had collided with the video camera.

Placing my feet on the building, I pushed off and jumped into the yard, well clear of the camera's now severely limited view. A split second before I landed, I heard a low, guttural growl that I could have sworn came from a Doberman pinscher.

But I was wrong. As my feet hit the pavement and I pitched hard to my left, I realized that the noise had not come from a Doberman. Instead, it came from two Dobermans, poised to spring a few feet away from me and looking very hungry.

[IV]

The dogs had come out of a hidden door below the back steps that connected to the basement. One of them sniffed at the bird I'd thrown. Growling, she took it and ran behind one of the trucks, where she proceeded to rip it to shreds. Her friend, unfortunately, wasn't a bird fancier. She took a step toward me, spit curling back from both sides of her mouth. I tried slipping my hand toward my gun, but she growled as if she knew exactly what I was doing.

She had a look in her eyes I'd seen before. It was the same vicious glare Shotgun used when staring down a double cheeseburger with bacon. We locked eyes.

"Shotgun!" I yelled. "Throw me down some snacks."

"Snacks? Like what?"

"Anything. Just make it quick."

"Here's some licorice."

Somewhere there's a dog that loves licorice, but this wasn't the one. The candy smacked on the macadam right in front of her. She never even glanced in its direction.

"More snacks, Shotgun. Something with fat."

"Gees, Dick, I have a limited supply."

"Something the damn dog will like."

"Twinkies!"

They were actually the Cuban near equivalent of Twinkies, which Shotgun had bought on the way back from dinner. He neglected to open the package, but that didn't bother the Doberman — she wolfed it down, plastic and all.

Then she came for the main course: me.

Fortunately, the two or three seconds it had taken her to grab the Twinkies were all I needed to grab my knife. I was ready as she jumped. Her momentum carried us to the ground; by the time I rolled up to my feet, she was dead, her gut split open.

I didn't have time to celebrate. Her companion lunged at me, fangs-first. I jumped out of the way, just missing her teeth. Then something black flew down and smacked her in the head and she collapsed.

"I figured you didn't want me to shoot her," said Shotgun, climbing down the back of the building. He'd thrown his knife into her skull. "Makes too much noise, right?"

The dog lay there whimpering, blood flowing out of her mouth. I pulled the knife out, then put her out of her misery.

"I feel bad for her," said Shotgun.

"Why's that?"

"She was just doing her job."

"Let's do ours."

"Gotcha," said Shotgun, heading to the fence to open it.

Truth was, Shotgun was right. The poor mutts just happened to be in the wrong place at the wrong time. But that was the story of our Cuban vacation, from A to Z.

I pulled the dogs under one of the bucket trucks, then picked out a pair of vans for us to steal. These were almost brand-new, imported from China. Their ignition systems were all intact—and the keys were sticking in the slots.

"Mama always said, don't leave your keys in the car," said Doc, joining me inside. "You think anybody heard those dogs?"

"Sure. But dogs bark all the time. Even in Cuba."

The pump had two separate locks, one on a chain that hooked through the nozzle and secured it to the pump frame, and the other on the pump itself. Doc picked the first one without too much trouble; it was a Yale model similar to one of the locks he practices on to keep himself sharp. But the second was an older brand he'd never seen. He dropped the narrow spring tool he was using twice before he managed to get things lined up.

"Always the easiest things that give us problems," he said, finally popping it open.

We topped off the tanks and saddled up. Trace and Shotgun rode with me; Red, Doc, and Mongoose took the second van. Even though we had our radios, we stayed close together, practically driving the 150 miles bumper to bumper.

Northeastern Cuba is a beautiful place. It's far enough away from Havana to make it *almost* possible to ignore the repression, especially at night when even the most observant visitor can't see its effects in front of him. And if you're just visiting, the poverty doesn't register either. Broken-down shacks by the side of the road are picturesque. The lack of things like gas stations and convenient marts seems positively bucolic, rather than an indication of a crapped-out economy.

The countryside feels raw without being threatening, almost as if you're moving through a Disney landscape. The jungle is real enough—the trees lean over the roads, and the shells of thatch-covered huts sit amid thick clumps of quick-growing vegetation. But the glow of the moon hits the sand on the shoulders with a silvery glow that bleaches everything else away. And in the light of the first dawn, the sun seems to pull white and blue sparkles of electricity from the ocean's edge.

We reached the town where Fidel's bunker was located just as those early rays were starting to hit. The house had been dug into a hill rising over the sea, right in the middle of an army outpost. A set of heavy guns were dug into man-made caves along the rocks; as formidable as these looked, they wouldn't be a problem for us unless we tried re-creating the Bay of Pigs invasion. More problematic were the guard posts and triple fence line, which was sure to be studded with the latest Chinese electronic gizmos. The beach area was fenced off as well, with a barbed wire-topped fence that ran well into the water.

The bunker had been sited so well that finding a good place to look over the entire installation was difficult. The closest I could get to the gate area was a rocky crag nearly a mile away. Even from the top, the only way I could see anything was by leaning half my body out over a sheer cliff. The other half attached itself to a big boulder and prayed.

Hoping that Mr. Murphy wouldn't send a sudden gust my way, I surveyed the place with my binoculars. There were at least a dozen soldiers standing in knots of twos and threes near the gate to the base. Other groups were scattered just inside the fence. A half-dozen members of Fidel's elite bodyguard unit manned the gate between the base and the bunker. Every few minutes, at irregular intervals, a jeep-type vehicle drove inside the fenced perimeter circling the bunker. A fifty-caliber machine gun was mounted desert-rat style on the back. Signs warned that the strip in front of the fence had been mined.

Since sneaking onto the base area looked difficult, I decided we'd take the lazy man's approach—we'd go through the front door.

But not with the telephone company vans.

It wasn't just because I was worried that their theft would be reported across the island. Junior, with the CIA's help, was monitoring the Cuban police alert system, and would tell me when the alert went out, if it did, but the warning would be of little value if we were sitting at the gate when the bulletin went out.

The problem was that the guards seemed to be trained to carefully examine vans. As I stretched myself out for my view, two pulled up. The men inside were ordered out, and the trucks thoroughly searched.

I don't mean thoroughly searched the way the police back home or even MPs at a base entrance search a vehicle. They didn't ask pretty please may we have a look in the bomb-shaped package on the rear seat?

Hell no. They hustled the men out, put them on the side of the vehicle, and patted them down with enough vigor to make them candidates for the choir. Then, while the men were forced to lie on their bellies, hands in the air, each box in the van was removed and opened. The rug over the floor in the back was torn and lifted up. Two soldiers hopped inside and dismantled more of the vehicle, carting out the rear seat so they could have a close-up look at it.

When the van was declared clean, the two men who'd been in the cab were told to get up, show their papers, and answer questions. From the distance, I couldn't tell what they were saying—for all I knew, they were debating Cuba's chances in the World Cup. But it sure looked like they were being asked something more than whether they'd ever left their lunch boxes unattended.

Not every truck got that treatment, however. Two troop trucks passed right through with little more than a perfunctory nod and wave. They *looked* like they belonged. Hence the difference.

That's always the difference, isn't it? If you walk down the hall with the right swagger, you can stroll right through the Kremlin or White House with an MP5 in your left hand and a grenade in your right.

What we needed was a truck that looked as if it belonged on the base. My first choice was a fire engine, which can go pretty much anywhere it wants to the world over, as long as the siren is wailing. The problem would have been locating one outside the base, though I'm sure with Junior's help we could have figured something out. But as I clambered down the ridge, I noticed something just as effective.

"A cement truck?" asked Trace when I told her and the others what I had in mind. "I'm not hiding in a goddamn cement truck."

"Cool. A cement truck," said Shotgun. "Can we dump the cement out, Dick?"

A semiregular stream of the trucks was heading in and out of the facility, working on a dock complex on the southwestern side. The cement factory was about three miles south, part of a massive gravel pit carved out of the foothills. Between them was a stretch of road that looked like a pair of backward Zs on the satellite map, perfect for an ambush.

Almost perfect, at any rate. The road had been cut down the side of a hill. There was no cover for almost fifty yards on either side of the road as it cut back across the steep incline. Our first thought was to take the vans up the road, block it, and then take the trucks over. But we found a pair of soldiers stationed at the intersection of the road and the nearby highway as we approached. They presented arms—and guns—when we tried to turn up the road.

I rolled down my window.

"They're saying it's a restricted area," whispered Red under her breath from the passenger seat.

I told them there was a downed wire, repeating a phrase I'd practiced all the way up the road for this very contingency. My pronunciation was perfect, but the soldiers weren't impressed. They shouted that they were under orders not to let anyone pass, and made a show of readying their weapons to fire.

Red opened the door and walked toward them, saying that she was the shift supervisor and that it was very important that the wires be fixed. She threw a little swerve into her walk, putting her hips to their best use. But the men must've been eunuchs. They shouted at her and waved her back to the truck.

"Time to try Plan B," she whispered as she climbed back into the truck.

Red hasn't been with us all that long, but she knows me well enough that she braced herself as she pulled the door closed, sure I was going to run down the guards. But while that would have been temporarily satisfying, it would not have helped us toward our ultimate goal. So I backed up slowly, and with Doc following, made a U-turn on the highway.

"What are we doing?" Trace asked over the radio.

"We're going to take the long way around."

"Story of my life."

The double-backward-Z had been cut through the hillside for a very good reason—the long way around was *really* long. More than thirty kilometers clicked around the odometer before we arrived at the front

96

gate of the cement plant. We stopped just down the road from the plant building and cut the telephone wire. Then we hopped back in the trucks and headed toward the plant.

There were no guards at the front gate, because after all, who steals cement? Red and I peeled left toward the administration building; we got out of the truck harrumphing and shaking our heads at the horrible situation we were confronted with, no doubt a Yankee plot designed to isolate Cuba even further. We strolled inside the building and immediately began looking for the problem with the phones—something that naturally involved checking every unit in the place, no matter where it was located.

Doc and the others, meanwhile, drove their van to the plant area behind the building where a cloud of dust showed that the cement operation was in full swing. Empty cement trucks would pull up in front of a large loading area, then back in one at a time to get filled. Unlike in America, where most cement trucks have only a driver, two people worked each truck here. When the truck pulled up, the assistant would hop out and with a few hand signals wave the driver toward the rig at the rear. He'd wait while the truck was being filled—generally kibitzing with anyone else who happened to be around.

Especially if the people who were just hanging around happened to be doling out cigars.

I'm not sure where Mongoose had gotten the cigars—undoubtedly back in Victoria de las Tunas on his way to dinner, but as soon as he hopped out of the van with a fist full of puros, the assistant who was standing nearby made a beeline for him.

Mongoose's Spanish was excellent, but it had a Filipino flavor to it, which immediately roused the man's curiosity. Lighting his newfound friend's cigar, Mongoose began a long explanation of his background and the tortured path his parents had taken after arriving on the sandy beaches of the workers' paradise; he was about halfway to Havana when Shotgun lowered the boom on the Cuban.

It wasn't a boom; it was a blackjack, but you get the general idea.

Mongoose dragged the assistant into the telephone truck, pulled off his coveralls, and put them on. He was still rolling up the pants legs—they were about six sizes too big—when the now-loaded cement truck rolled up, ready to go. He hopped up and jumped into the cab. Before the driver could ask what had happened to his coworker, the door behind him flew open and Shotgun slapped him on the side of the head. Mongoose slid behind the wheel and pulled away.

Trace had an even easier time with the second truck; the driver's assistant was so smitten by her offer of a counterfeit Coke—held in front of her loosely buttoned blouse—that he surely never felt Shotgun's blackjack when it knocked him into the dirt. She took care of the driver herself, snapping her fist into the side of his head after he made the mistake of asking why a slut was getting into his vehicle.

Shotgun carried the Cuban to the van, where Doc administered a healthy dose of phenobarbital to keep him and the other assistant sleeping for a while. While Shotgun finished trussing them, Doc climbed into the driver's seat of the van and followed Trace to the work gate at the rear of the plant that the cement trucks used to exit.

Up until now, the plan had worked like the proverbial Swiss watch. But it's always what you don't know that comes back to bite you in the butt, and that's what happened here. The military base was only one of several large jobs that were being supplied with cement that day, and a different procedure had been set up for the trucks that were working there. The trucks heading for the post had special clipboards attached to the doors containing their orders and some paperwork. Neither of the trucks we had snatched had the clipboards.

I'm not positive the guards at the base would have noticed; the trucks I'd seen moved in and out at a pretty good clip. But the supervisor who was funneling the vehicles out of the plant noticed right away. He waved his arms and ran after Mongoose as he started to the right, the direction of the base. Mongoose saw him and did what anyone would do—he tried ignoring him and stepped on the gas. But the truck had a standard transmission, and Mongoose's difficulty with the clutch once again resulted in a stall.

"Where's your board?" the supervisor demanded, jumping on the running board. "And where the hell is your assistant?"

Mongoose gave him a what-the-hell-are-you-talking-about look. The Cuban pointed at the side of the truck and asked again.

"Musta fell off," mumbled Mongoose, trying to use as few words as possible.

Mongoose's accent may have aroused suspicion. Or maybe it was the lack of his assistant. Then again, the supervisor might just have naturally been a prick. He demanded to know who Mongoose thought he was, and what he thought he was doing.

"What do you mean, who am I?" answered Mongoose indignantly.

"You are a screwup, losing your paperwork and trying to get out of trouble."

"Someone took it."

"Who? Your assistant?"

Mongoose bristled—exactly the right thing to do under the circumstances, since it made it look like it was his assistant who was the screwup.

But that still didn't get him off the hook.

"Who are you?" demanded the supervisor, no longer speaking rhetorically. "What's your name?"

Red and I could hear the exchange through Mongoose's mike, which was clipped below his shirt. I knew that if he gave a false name, the supervisor was likely to realize it and there'd be an immediate problem. On the other hand, it was obvious that he wasn't going to bluff his way out.

"Trace—hit your horn. Distract them," I said over the radio. "We need a driver's name. Doc—can you get something from the two guys we took out? An ID, anything?"

"I'm working on it," said Doc. Shotgun was in the back of the van, rifling the pockets of the men he'd knocked out. But they didn't carry IDs or money in their coveralls, apparently leaving everything in their work locker room.

Fortunately, Red was already a couple of steps ahead of me—literally. She sprinted to the time clock we'd passed on the way in and pulled out some cards.

"Horatio Garcia," she said, decoding the notations and guessing at the abbreviation for driver. "Use Horatio Garcia."

Mongoose had tucked his earphone down under his shirt collar so it wouldn't be seen. Unfortunately, that also meant he couldn't hear us telling him what to do.

"Now look at the problem you've caused," said the supervisor as the horn sounded behind them. "Everyone's getting off schedule. This is going against you."

Mongoose answered with a curse. The supervisor once again demanded to know who he was.

There was now a line of three dump trucks behind them. Doc and the van were wedged in the middle.

"Hey, Red, you better find a woman driver to cover Trace," said Doc, pulling the telephone van out of line. He leaned on the horn, jammed the gas pedal, and made a beeline for the supervisor. He hit his brakes at the last minute, fishtailing to a stop as the supervisor jumped out of the way.

Shotgun, meanwhile, had jumped from the van and sprinted up the other side of the line of traffic.

"Your name is Garcia," he hissed at Mongoose through the open window on the other side of the truck. "Horatio Garcia."

"I need one of those clipboards."

"From where?"

"On the side of the truck. Then get in here like you're my assistant."

"Where do I get it?"

"Steal one, asshole."

"Asshole yourself, dickface."

Shotgun trotted back toward the end of the line, looking for a truck that had one of the clipboards. He finally spotted one behind the spot where the telephone truck had been; he walked past as nonchalantly as possible, grabbed it from the side, then circled around and ran back to Mongoose.

The supervisor meanwhile had jumped to his feet and was denouncing the idiot telephone worker, accusing him of having learned to drive in "Yankee land," apparently the most devastating slur he could think of. Doc had gotten out of the truck, and while he occasionally yelled a curse word, mostly he pounded the hood of his vehicle, implying that the supervisor was lucky that he was hitting the metal and not his flesh.

Shotgun rushed up and made a show of pulling himself back into the truck. The supervisor was still mumbling to himself when he returned to Mongoose's truck.

"Here," said Mongoose, holding out the clipboard. "It fell."

"Humph."

The supervisor gave Shotgun a scowl, and waved Mongoose through.

Trace had stolen her own placard during the commotion, grabbing one off an in-bound truck. She slowed but didn't stop as she came through the gate. The supervisor started to stop her, but then realized that was futile, and instead stopped the next vehicle and began haranguing its crew instead.

A good thing, since according to Red there were no female drivers, or at least she couldn't find a time card with a woman's name in the proper section.

Shotgun had doubled back to play Robin to Trace's Batman. She nearly ran him over before stopping to let him in.

"Thought you needed an assistant," he said, pulling himself into the cab.

"That'll be the day," she told him.

Shotgun laughed and pushed back in the seat.

"Think there's a place to stop for something to eat on the way?" he asked. "Pretending to be Cuban kind of works up my appetite."

And what had I been doing while the others were having all this fun, you ask?

Repairing the telephones, of course.

Repairing, making it worse—all a matter of semantics.

Killing the power to the facility was a little harder than killing the phones, since it turned out that the closet holding the telephone gear was not where the circuit breakers were. In fact, I never found the circuit breakers per se. What I did find was a fenced-in area behind the back of the administration building that contained several large transformers, all conveniently marked with DANGER. HIGH VOLTAGE signs.

The signs were handy as well as convenient, since they were made of metal and almost exactly the right size to cause a short between two of the poles in one of the transformers. The eighth of an inch or so difference between a perfect fit and just missing was not a drawback; the gap produced a huge spark that not only fried everything within two feet, but made a nice crackly sound as it did.

The shock also threw me into the fence, even though I was a good distance away when I tossed the sign across the open wires. The outline of my body is probably still pressed into the links.

"Quitting time," I told Red over the radio. She was still inside, near the front of the building. "Meet me in the van."

"*Madre Maria*," she said. "Mother of God."

"You OK?"

"I'm fine. I'm going to the van."

I walked back through the building, which was now in the dark. The secretaries and other office people were complaining about the power failure. One came out of her office and asked if I knew what was going on. I shrugged and shook my head.

Power interruptions are not as common as they once were in Cuba, but if we'd been anywhere else, this one would have elicited a few curses but no real surprise. Apparently the cement plant, though, had some sort of priority and was not used to being cut off in the middle of the day. The plant boss followed me out to the truck, sure that we had caused the power outage. He promised that I would end the day with a job cleaning toilets in the farthest reaches of the province.

Red leaned her head out the window and said calmly that we had nothing to do with the power failure, but couldn't work while the plant was in the dark. When the power was restored, we would come back.

A reasonable response, but the plant manager hadn't gotten his position by being reasonable. He ranted and raved, until the only thing left to do was give him the one-fingered salute and leave the way we had come.

"It should take them until tonight to get everything sorted out," I said after everyone had checked in. "We'll have to have the trucks back by then."

"I hope that's enough," said Red.

She held out a newspaper she had grabbed off one of the desks inside, and immediately I realized why she had Mother-of-Godded inside the building: according to *Granma*, Fidel had gone to the hospital the night before with a heart attack.

He was still alive, but just barely.

[V]

We parked the vans about a half mile down the road from the intersection of the highway and the rough-cut road. Then we hiked up through the woods to the others, who were waiting with the trucks. Since the legitimate vehicles all traveled with only two people, we decided two of us would have to hide. But there was no practical place to do that except the cab, which meant squeezing down in the space behind the seat.[18] I went with Shotgun and Mongoose; Trace, Doc, and Red took the other truck.

Cramped as it was behind the seat, I was completely hidden from view as Mongoose rolled up to the gate, pausing just long enough for the soldier to wave us through.

"Man, did you see that burrito he was eating?" Shotgun asked as we rumbled on.

"That wasn't a burrito. Burritos are Mexican."

"What was it?"

"Some sort of food thing."

"A food thing?"

"Yeah, a thing."

"I think it was a burrito."

"Shotgun, when this mission is over, I'm arranging an audition for you for the Food Channel," I said, squeezing myself out from the back as we cleared the gate.

"Wow. Will you?"

"Yeah, they'll call your show Dipstick and the Iron Chef," said Mongoose.

"Who's Dipstick?" asked Shotgun.

I left them cutting on each other and slipped out of the truck. Dressed like your typical Cuban day worker, I had a small fanny pack at my belt, carrying a rotozip and some other tools I needed. My pistol, a PK that has been my companion through thick and thin, sat in the belt behind it. Heavier weapons, even a submachine gun, didn't make sense; if I had to blast my way out, my mission had failed.

---

[18] I'm sure some of you would have enjoyed seeing me swimming in the cement in the back as the drum spun. To you I say, fug yourself.

The complex covered nearly two square miles, and was laid out in the shape of a giant liver. We were on the top end, near the side of the ribs. Fidel's bunker was all the way on the opposite end, where the large intestine bends down toward the anus.

Fitting, I suppose.

While the guard at the gate had let us through without a problem, he waved down Trace's truck as she reached the gate.

"What do you think this is about?" she asked Red, who was hiding behind the seat.

"Not sure."

The guard walked over and took the clipboard from the side of the truck. Then he walked over to his guardhouse.

"Must be some sort of spot check," said Doc. "Hang tough."

"If they're going to do a spot check, then Red better get out of the cab," Trace said. "Because they'll search it."

It was a good point, but Trace made it a little too late—the guard was already walking back. He put the clipboard back into its slot. Then he waved the truck forward—not down to the port where the others were dumping their loads, but to a small turnoff just a few yards away.

Trace considered ignoring him and simply driving down to the dock area, but a Russian Zil—a troop truck similar to the two-and-a-half-ton truck we used during the Cold War—came up and blocked her way.

"Now what?" whispered Trace as the guard went over and began speaking to the soldier driving the Zil.

"Distract them. Red—get out of the truck and go meet Dick," said Doc. "Slip out behind me."

Trace's Spanish isn't bad, but her accent would get her in trouble if she talked too much. So she needed to wordlessly distract everyone while Red got away from the truck.

She used an old standby—a strategically popping button. The button shot up as her boots hit the dirt. All eyes immediately stood at full attention. Red slid to the ground and slipped away as Doc walked in front of her.

Doc, conscious of his accent as well, settled for a glare rather than a harangue. This had the same effect on Cuban bureaucracy as it does on government workers in America: nothing.

In fact, Trace's distraction had worked so well that not only were the two soldiers at the gate staring at her; everyone on the base within a hundred yards was probably focused on her chest.

"*Cemento*," she said finally. "It will harden."

The man who had stopped her tore his eyes from her chest, glanced at the cab, then he told them they were good to leave.

"Leave?"

"*Sí.* Turn around and go. Go."

The crew contracted to work on the port had planned to work with twenty truckloads that day; the truck that Mongoose had driven through the gate was number twenty. The guard said he had not been too surprised by the extra truck—everyone knew that the dumb-shit *campesinos* on the eastern end of the island couldn't count.

The plan had been for Red and me to survey the site while the trucks were dumping their cement. Doc and Shotgun would then slip away and help us get into the bunker, while the others drove off site to alleviate suspicion. There was no way that was going to work now.

"Don't worry about it," I told Doc over the radio as he and Trace headed toward the exit. "Shotgun, what's your situation?"

"We got a construction foreman on our butt, yelling at Mongoose for not knowing what he's doing," whispered Shotgun. "He's tearing him a new asshole. I think Mongoose is going to pop him."

"Don't let him do that."

"Check. You want me to stay here?"

The supervisor, angry at Mongoose's obvious incompetence, had taken over in the driver's seat, shoving Mongoose aside. Shotgun had gotten out and enthusiastically directed the truck backward toward the dumping area. It was obvious that they were going to be watched fairly closely.

"Red and I will get into the bunker ourselves," I told him. "Stay with Mongoose. Get out of the installation and make sure you set up the Cubans real well before you leave them in the truck."

"Copy that, chief."

How did they set them up?

Both Trace and Mongoose drove around to the telephone trucks, where the original crewmen were still sleeping off the pokes Doc had administered. Along the way, Doc stopped at a small store and bought some rum. (Shotgun also bought some snacks, naturally.) The cement trucks were driven back into the yard and parked in the lot above the loading area, where the empty trucks were usually kept. The Cubans were untrussed, then liberally sprinkled with the alcohol.

We were never really sure whether they were all found like that, or if the drugs wore off in time for them to make a hasty escape. In any event, anyone downwind of them or the truck cabs would never believe anything they said.

Besides the fences, the only thing separating Red and me from Fidel's house bunker were a pair of barracks buildings. In contrast to everything else on the base, both were very old, with paint peeling or worn off the sides, and several of the windows either broken or replaced by boards. Since they didn't appear occupied, we ducked inside one of them, hoping to survey the fence area from cover.

But the building turned out not to be empty at all. Even though the insides were in even worse shape than the outsides—large chunks of plaster hung from the dilapidated ceiling, and the floor had more tin patches than boards—it was being used as a base hospital.

A skinny man with narrow, close-set eyes looked up from his desk as we entered, silently asking why we had come.

Red snapped into nurse mode, saying that I had a stomach ailment and needed to rest. I began to moan. The man gave me a malingerer's frown, but nodded and told me to go into the wardroom.

About a dozen men filled the large, open ward beyond the reception area. They were scattered in beds and chairs around the place, possibly to minimize the chances of each man infecting the other, though it was also possible they'd been placed that way to make it harder for them to compare notes on their treatment.

A fireplug of a nurse was working at the far corner of the room. Florence Nightingale she wasn't; she glared in my direction, then barked that I should lie down and not make any noise until she got there.

"Great bedside manner," whispered Red.

"See if you can find us some uniforms to get past the guards," I told her. "Or IDs or something."

Red spotted a large closet at the end of the room near where we'd come in and headed over toward it. Florence Nightingale, meanwhile, ambled in my direction. The floor trembled with each step.

"What is your problem?" she demanded in a tone several shades more severe than the one a hanging judge would use to deliver a death sentence.

"Ohhhh," I said, bending over and clutching my stomach.

"If you're going to throw up, don't do it on my bedsheets," she barked. "The bathroom is over there."

I waddled, bent over, in its direction.

"And what are *you* doing?" Florence Nightingale asked Red.

"My friend needs a blanket," she said, rummaging through the closet. There were several uniforms inside, with enough variety that she had hopes of actually getting something to fit us.

"We don't have blankets."

"What kind of infirmary is this?"

"One for sick people."

Red marched to her indignantly.

"My friend is a hard worker—he drives a cement truck. His father was in the Revolution, side by side with the great leader. And this is how he is treated?"

Florence Nightingale spit on the ground.

"If I had a peso for every relative who marched shoulder to shoulder with *el Comandante en Jefe*, I would have enough money to build a villa in Miami."

Florence spit again, then turned on her heel and stormed out.

"Sister Mercy is trying to give up smoking," said the man in a bed nearby. "She's off to have a smoke."

"She's pretty free with her tongue," said Red, who was amazed not that the nurse felt as she did, but that she was willing to say it so freely.

"The news says Fidel is on his deathbed," said the patient. "Though I bet he has a better room than this."

"Maybe he has three Sister Mercy's," said another patient. "One for each shift. He deserves it."

The other laughed. The men began trying to top each other with descriptions of what Sister Mercy would do to Fidel to ease his pain.

Emptying his bedpan wasn't on the list.

Red ducked back into the closet and grabbed the uniforms, tucking them under her arm. I grabbed a towel and buried my face in it, pretending that I was queasy as I came out of the restroom. As soon as I saw she was ready, I put my head down and walked toward the exit.

"Much better," I said, passing the attendant.

"Nurse usually has that effect on people," he said smugly.

The uniforms made us less conspicuous, but they couldn't get us onto Fidel's side of the complex. There were two more fences to cross, with a narrow track for a patrol vehicle but apparently no mines, since the vehicle whipped right across the track without anything exploding.

Near the water, the fence was interrupted by a double-wide gate and a freshly paved macadam apron showing where a road was intended to go. A video camera and a magnetic card-reader guarded the gate.

When setting up their security, the Cubans had undoubtedly thought of the video camera as the keystone of the system, arranging it so it could swivel and provide a wide view of the area. Naturally in their minds the view made it impossible for anyone to sneak inside. But the camera was actually their greatest weakness. It focused all of their attention exactly where it shouldn't be.

On the good-looking redhead whose magnetic card wasn't working right when she went to open the gate, for example.

"*Senorita*, you have to swipe your card with the flick of your wrist," said one of the guards over the nearby speaker.

Red shrugged, then tried again. When the gate didn't open, she looked up at the camera and pleaded that there was something wrong.

Red has perfect pleading eyes, but it was more likely that the loose buttons on her shirt and the consequent glimpse of cleavage had more of an effect on the camera monitor. He promised that he would call a supervisor to help.

"Can't you just open the gate?" she asked.

"Of course not," he said. "Your pass must be authorized."

"But it is."

"I can't tell that from here."

"No?"

Give the Cuban his due; despite the eyeful he was getting, he didn't budge. Neither did the supervisor, who didn't believe her story that she had been sent to help fix the problems in the security jeep.

"There are no problems with the jeep."

"I only do what I am told."

"Report to the barracks," said the supervisor. "We will get this straightened out."

Red threw up her hands in disgust, then stomped away from the camera.

One woman's stomp was another's sashay, and there's no doubt in my mind that Red had their full attention as she walked away. But by now her diversion was unnecessary—I'd climbed both sets of fences and was making my way to the bunker. I hiked up the hill about a hundred yards, then cut across to the left, avoiding a second camera covering the front yard and surrounding area.

A garden and a pool sat immediately below the bunker, added by the Estonian architect as an executive amenity: a patio Fidel could doze on while fantasizing about the destruction of America. *El Jefe* valued his privacy—maybe he liked to sunbathe out there in the nude—and so there were no video cameras. According to the CIA briefing, a three-foot-wide pressure-sensitive strip ran around the exterior of the garden. I moved toward the garden slowly, trying to see if the strip was marked out in any way.

A low, spiked iron fence ran around the perimeter, and it was logical to conclude that the strip was on one side or the other of the fence. But which? Jumping three feet would be easy. Six feet would be harder, especially since the uphill, rocky terrain made it hard to get much of a running start. And since the fence was barely a half foot off the ground and consisted entirely of spikes, I couldn't use it to rest on in the middle.

Whoever had disguised the strip had done an excellent job. Rocks and small bushes had been planted on both sides of the fence, in a very random pattern. Finally, I decided I had no choice but to jump the entire distance. I planned my approach, took one last look around, then took off, head down as I counted my steps. On three, I leapt forward, sailing upward.

I was just about even with the fence when I saw the pebble trail that ran around the inside perimeter, a short distance from the fence.

The three-foot-wide pebble trail, undoubtedly placed to disguise or mark the pressure-sensitive detection band.

The pebble trail I was about to land on, heavy feet first.

Doom on Dickie.

I shifted my weight backward, trying to land short of the pebbles. It was an extremely acrobatic maneuver, but it was also a severe pain in the butt, as I crashed to the ground brain-first. Somehow, I managed to keep my legs in the air, a few inches over the strip of pebbles.

Rear end throbbing, I rolled over and went to the building. A covered patio extended roughly ten feet into the mountainside; at the rear was a set of large sliding glass doors. According to the CIA informant, these were equipped with alarms. So were the windows on the second floor.

The third-story windows, however, were not. I picked out the one on the corner, which according to the plans belonged to a small study, and then climbed upward. The ample space between the blocks made this easy. The casement window was locked, but it gave way easily when I slid my knife inside. I bent around it and pulled myself into the room.

The Estonian architect had designed Castro's lair as if it were really three buildings, one inside each other. I was in the outer shell. This was used by Fidel as a kind of official vacation house, a palace where VIPs and foreign visitors could be entertained. The rooms were unimportant for anything else, sacrificial lambs in the event of a bombing attack.

The next layer in, separated from the others by thick, shock-absorbing walls, was an official workplace for Fidel's secretaries and other hangers-on when he was in residence. There were two entrances to it, both through the outer "house." In each case, they were located at the bottom of an L-shaped staircase covered by video cameras and protected by claymore mines. Though not powerful enough to damage the double doors, the claymores would make mincemeat out of anyone attempting to get in against Fidel's wishes.

Fortunately, I wasn't taking either entrance.

My path was through the utility tunnel, which ran like a tree trunk from the outer to the inner sanctum, with branches in between. The trunk had thick walls to protect it from attack. Of course, these walls could not cover the entire tunnel, since technicians needed access to make repairs: the Achilles' heel of any modern-day fortress.

The main entrance to the tunnel was a door-sized opening in the closet just off the hallway near the front entrance. This was inconvenient for a number of reasons—the most prominent that it was dangerously close to the video camera covering the entrance area—so I chose the backup, which was in the wall in the servants' wing. Eight hex-head screws held the plate to the wall. I unscrewed them with the RotoZip, slipped a set of magnetic connections against the sensors to keep from alerting the system that the panel was off, and then removed the plate. Strapping an LED miner's light on my forehead, I crawled up into the shaft, pulling myself between the conduit and the water pipes until I reached an overhead trunk that swung toward the main line.

From there, it was easy. A ladder was embedded in the wall, and once I got past the air exchange area, all I had to do was climb straight down.

A long way down.

I had to thread my way through a tangle of wires twice before I reached the access panel to Fidel's inner lair. I clipped the alarm, then pulled the RotoZip from the fanny pack, slipped in the drill bit, and went to work removing the screws from the back end.

The top lip on this panel was much narrower than the one on the panel I'd come in through, and it slipped off as I drilled through the last screw. I managed to grab it before it toppled down, but I dropped the power tool in the process; it must have hit every rung before landing in the well at the bottom of the shaft.

There was nothing I could do about the noise, except hope no one was around to hear it. I left the RotoZip where it had landed and leaned forward through the hole, sliding the panel down toward the floor gently. I watched the patched alarm cord as it stretched . . . and stretched. Until finally I had to stop, still far from the floor.

According to the plans, the panel should have only been less than a foot from the floor.

The detection system included a coded relay set on the panel, making it impossible to simply bypass. I held the panel with my left hand while I fished with my right through the fanny pack for another connecting wire. The panel wasn't all that heavy, but in my awkward position it began to feel like a piece of solid lead. I found the wire and slipped it in place, maintaining the connection while I lowered the panel to the floor.

Or rather, lowered it about a third of the way to the floor. The Cubans had decided to place the panel at the top of the utility closet rather than the bottom. And the ceilings here were twelve feet high.

I didn't have any more wire on me. So I pulled the plate back inside with me, looking for a place to stow it. But the rungs were too narrow to hold it, and the bottom of the passage was too far away. I tried wedging it into the tangle of wires and conduit that ran up the sluiceway at the side, but the panel was too heavy to stay without being secured in some way.

Pausing to rest, I noticed that a large plastic wire harness held the wires together about six feet over my head. The harness looked thick enough to hold the panel if I put it there. But it was just a little too far for the wires I'd used to patch the alarm to reach.

There were plenty of other wires in front of me. Why not cut one, use it temporarily, and then patch it back together on the way out?

Why not, Pilgrim? Why not?

Not knowing what each specific wire was for, I realized I was taking a risk that I'd cut off something that would set off an alarm. But it was either that or toss the plate down, which would bring the troops right away. I stayed away from the round wire sets that looked like they were for data links, and chose one of the two flat ribbons, hoping they were connected to television antennas or something similar. A snip here, a snip there, and my cheat wires now reached six feet.

My left arm was threatening to sheer out of its socket by the time I finally wedged the panel into the wire harness. I bent one of the cables around to snug it in, then peered back through the space into the utility closet.

Nobody there but a few inquisitive spiders.

Since they had the plans and seemed to know so much about the bunker, it wasn't hard to guess that the Christians in Action had made a play at bugging Fidel's lair while it was being built. Just in case they had, I whispered sweet nothings to Ken and company under my breath as I tiptoed down the hall. The walls were lined with paintings. And they weren't the kind you find at Wal-Mart. They were Renaissance old masters, and if they were reproductions, they were damn good ones.

Stolen?

The thought occurred to me. I took my miniature camera out and snapped a few photos, then proceeded down the hall to Fidel's office.

Fidel had made a big show of giving up smoking several years before the bunker was built; the government media had done numerous stories on how he had kissed his beloved stogies good-bye on doctor's orders.

He'd kissed them all right. And from the stench in the hall he was kissing them still—then lighting them up and puffing away, maybe three or four at a time. There was no smoke in the house, but even with what must have been a state-of-the-art ventilation system, the place smelled like slowly simmered tobacco.

It was worse inside *el Jefe*'s office. The floor was lined with thick rugs; I could practically see the smoke wafting from them as I walked across the floor.

The safe was located in the wall at the right of the console behind Fidel's desk. I dropped to my knee, took out the stethoscope,[19] and began playing doctor.

Many people with old-fashioned tumbler safes grow tired of the hassle of running the dial left and right and left again before turning the handle. They tend to leave the combination preset—doing the first two numbers, with only the last remaining. So the first thing I did was rotate the dial slowly, listening for a click. When I heard it, I leaned on the handle.

But Fidel's an anal SOB, and he'd set his lock accordingly.

I slipped off the earset and connected the stethoscope to a small machine roughly the size of an iPod Shuffle. Then I turned the dial slowly while the machine listened. The machine tracked the different clicks as I went back and forth, and presented me with a set of eight possible combinations.

The safe opened on the second set. I undid the suction cup, rolled the stethoscope up, and pulled open the door.

Nothing would please me more than to report that the Western Hemisphere's biggest communist had a store of child pornography hidden in his safe. But if it was there, I didn't see it.

I did see at least one hundred stacks of American one-hundred-dollar bills, neatly piled at the bottom of the safe. I was sorely tempted to slide a few hundreds from each stack. I doubt Fidel would have known the difference.

Some old photos sat in a beat-up old shoe box on the shelf above the money. There were also a pair of revolvers and a tin box contained a baptism certificate and some booties.

What I was looking for sat in a manila envelope at the side.

Testamento.

Inside was a DVD.

And another. And four more, making a total of six in the envelope.

Taking them all was an option, but not a very good one. I turned and looked around the office. There was a credenza catty-corner from the desk with a TV and DVD player. Very nice of Fidel to be so helpful.

The first DVD I slipped in was a collection of old home movies

---

[19] Did I explain that the stethoscope was digitally enhanced? To give you an idea of how powerful it is, a doctor using it to hear a heartbeat would blow his eardrums out if the volume was cranked to high.

showing Fidel as a child. I watched thirty seconds' worth, then tried the second.

The lights came on in an office exactly like the one I'd shot my video in. And there he was, looking just like me.

I slapped the TV off, swapped discs, and tucked the real one into my fanny pack. Then I put everything else in the safe.

A bookshelf took up one side of the room. Naturally I had to look over his collection before leaving. And wouldn't you know, down at the very bottom, in the right-hand corner next to some old dictionaries, was a copy of *Rogue Warrior*, the beginning of the franchise.

First edition, too.

A better man would have resisted the impulse to pick the book up and inscribe it: *Fuck you very much*, el Jefe.

I had just put away my pen when the light went on in the hallway outside.

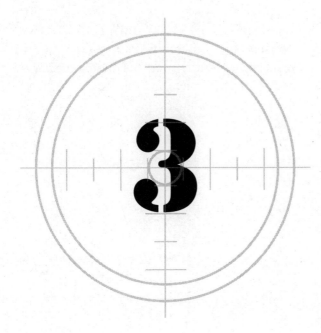

Ideally when you're doing a sneak and peak, you have someone watching the command post or security people, ready to warn you if they're coming. In the old days, this was done with a set of binoculars and Mark-1 eyeballs: a member of the team would be strategically placed, watching to sound the alarm. The new school approach substitutes high-tech toys—audio and video bugs, for example—in place of the human eyes.

But that's in an ideal world, and few ops are ideal. In this case, placing sensors would have been more trouble than they were worth. Red was watching, but it was impossible for her to cover all angles. She'd settled on making sure no one approached from the base; there was no sense covering the security kiosk at the front of the house, since guards could pass from the kiosk into the inner parts of Fidel's house without showing themselves.

And the truth is, it was my own fault the guards had come. The wire I had cut in the shaft was not connected to an antenna but a motion sensor in the foyer. My cutting the wire had apparently lit a button on the panel in the security office, and two of the guards had come down to figure out what the hell was wrong with it.

But first they had to search the entire suite, part of their security protocol.

Smart protocol.

Damn.

On the bright side, if I hadn't stopped to autograph the book for Fidel, they probably would have seen me in the hallway, since they had an unobstructed view when they came in. But that unobstructed view now meant I couldn't leave the office: one man stayed at the foyer, covering the other as he went through the rooms.

Smart. Damn again.

I edged close to the door. Taking out the men wouldn't be hard—I could knock out the first when he came in, grab his gun and eliminate the second.

If I did that, I'd probably escape—with the emphasis on "probably," a word that I still don't like, even when I'm using it. But the mission would definitely be blown to hell.

Better than dying in Cuba, though.

I slipped my hand to the blackjack in my back pocket. The soldier finished looking in Fidel's kitchen, then crossed the hallway to the bedroom. He started laughing about something—for all I know there was an inflatable doll on the bed—and came out haw-hawing so merrily even Shotgun would have been outlaughed.

He ducked his head into the office. I raised my arm . . .

Then he ducked back, still laughing, and continued down the hall.

The soldiers were perfect examples of how you can have the best set of security protocols in the world, do a decent job training your men, and still get blindsided by expectations. The men came downstairs expecting that there was a short or some other malfunction that had messed up the systems and set off the alert. Though they had been trained and were fearful enough of their supervisors to check the suite before doing anything else—something the supervisors had no real way of checking—their search was perfunctory at best. They believed there was a problem with the sensor, and that's how they acted. After all, they'd been in the security booth and knew no one had come past them. While they weren't stupid enough to disregard standing orders, they weren't smart enough to think outside the box, either.

Not that I was complaining.

I was too busy holding my breath as Tweedledum checked the rest of the suite. Tweedledee remained in the foyer, scraping his feet and apparently poking the device he thought had failed.

The men had clearly been in the suite before—which was a break for me, since if they hadn't they probably would have spent more time there, maybe even pretended to be *el Jefe*. They also wanted to get back upstairs, where one of the early World Cup qualifying matches was on TV. The guard searching the place walked right by the closet where the panel was off without bothering to open the door, then returned to his companion in the hallway.

"Clear," said Tweedledee. "What are you doing?"

"It's probably a loose wire."

"It's not going to help if you fiddle with it. You'll make it worse."

"Not necessarily."

"The technician will just have to come."

"It won't be cleared then until next week. We'll have to stay inside the suite every shift. No TV."

More rules. Good ones, too. But rather than increasing security, they decreased it—the guards didn't want to hang around without some diversion.

"Maybe there is something we can do," said Tweedledee.

"The sergeant is a jackass."

They bitched and moaned a bit more, the way soldiers do when talking about an unfair—in their eyes—superior. They also monkeyed with the microphone system. Finally, Tweedledum told Tweedledee to go back upstairs and check to see if it was OK.

"Just call Jorge."

"Then he'll report we reset the circuit. Make sure no one sees you. Be quiet. We'll say it was a fluke."

Silence. Then the question soldiers have asked since time began.

"Why me?" asked Tweedledum.

"Because I have to take a dump," said Tweedledee.

"It's against the rules."

"Should I do it in the hall."

"Upstairs—"

"I'll never make it." He was already walking toward it.

"You're always in the bathroom."

The lavatory door closed. Tweedledum left the suite. I gave the office a quick glance, making sure everything was back in place, then hightailed it to the closet.

The first order of business was replacing the wire so the motion detector would work. But I couldn't undo the alarm wire until I got the shaft cover back into place. And I couldn't do that until I recovered my RotoZip, which was lying somewhere down at the bottom of the shaft.

Putting the access plate back into place would make a fair bit of noise; there was no way to do that with my two friends in the suite. I decided, therefore, to try patching the broken wire first, in hopes that they would go back to their game. Since I couldn't take the wire off the cover until it was back in place, I picked out another wire, spliced it, and made my repairs. Only then did I clamber down to fetch the RotoZip.

The toilet flushed just as I returned. I stuck my head through the opening, listening as Tweedledee emerged from the bathroom a new man. Five or ten minutes later, his compatriot called down on the radio, telling him that the detector was working.

And that the Cubans had just scored.

"On my way," said Tweedledee, hustling to catch the replay.

I drilled new holes for the panel's screws, then replaced the originals with my own. Each had to be glued in place—a tedious process, since it meant pressing each one against the hole in the panel and counting to two hundred while the glue set.

With everything finally set, I eased the panel down the ladder, balancing it against my shoulder. Getting it through the opening wasn't difficult, but turning it around and pulling it into the exact right spot so that each screw would go into the right hole was a serious bitch.

Where have you heard that before?

The lip at the top of the panel was so narrow it was almost impossible to grip as I pulled it back toward me. Finally I reached into the bottom of my fanny pack and took out one of the suction cups I'd brought along in case I needed assistance climbing. I attached it to the back of the panel, and used it to hold the panel in place. The top screws went in easily, but the holes on the side were slightly off, and I finally had to snap off two of the screws I'd inserted to get it in place.

Tweedledee and Tweedledum chose that moment to open the closet.

II

There can't possibly be anything wrong with the air-conditioning," complained Tweedledee.

"I'm telling you, the light was on."

"In your dreams."

"It wasn't the sensor?"

"That one was off. Should I have told Jorge?"

"No."

"I tried resetting it and that didn't work. It has to be something with the thermostat—maybe from the fumes."

"What fumes?"

"Your fumes."

"One of these days I'm going to strangle you."

"Not here. It will make a mess."

"Get the tools and come on. If there really is a problem, it will be something for the technicians to handle."

"Staying on guard here without air-conditioning—easier to sneak over the American fence."

I heard one of them clattering around for the toolbox in the corner of the closet. He grabbed it and went back into the hall.

Maybe it was a good thing the Cubans had placed it near the ceiling after all.

I grabbed two nuts from my pack and threaded them quickly onto the top screws to hold the plate in place. Then I fixed the wire I had cut earlier. I was about halfway through securing the rest of the bolts when Tweedledee and Tweedledum came back to replace the tool kit.

"I told you it was working. Your eyes are useless."

"I know what I saw."

"You didn't feel the breeze from the vent?"

"I hope you cleaned your crap out of the toilet."

"Too bad I did. I would make you eat it."

The door closed. I finished securing the panel, cleaned up some of the metal shavings, then went back up the ladder.

———

Red was watching the compound from a cluster of trees not far from the water. She'd recovered her gear and had her radio on, listening for my signal when I came up onto the interior patio.

"I'm here, Red. How's it looking?"

"Not the best, Dick. They added another set of soldiers around the raceway."

I glanced at my watch. It was five minutes past three.

"It might just be the shift change," I told her. "Hang on for a little bit, then set the fire."

"Not a problem."

Red had hooked up an incendiary device in some big tree branches nearby. She would set them off by remote control, and I would sneak out during the commotion—a basic but effective misdirection play.

Having to get around two patrols rather than one added to the chances that Murphy might interfere. I moved out to the edge of the interior patio, looking for the soldiers in the hope of timing their routine. One of the jeeps they were using was idling on the east side of the track, the soldiers scanning the exterior fenceline. The second was moving toward it, going at a pretty good clip. Then suddenly the driver hit the brakes, pulled a three-point turn, and proceeded back the way he had come, moving very slowly.

Again, whoever had designed the security protocol had done an excellent job, telling the patrols that they must move in a random pattern, changing their directions and pacing constantly. Shifting the number of patrols was also an excellent move, making it harder to find vulnerabilities.

But since the actual work was being done by humans, I knew there had to be plenty of vulnerabilities. I also knew that if I watched long enough, I'd discover what they were.

One thing was obvious right away—the guards' attention was focused outside the wire. I could have walked naked through the yard, past the swimming pool, all the way to the ocean and they wouldn't notice me.

Duh!

I hailed Red on the radio and told her what I was doing.

"How do I get out?" she asked. "Shotgun and Mongoose had to leave because the supervisor was watching them."

I was about to suggest she swim out herself, when she beat me to it.

"The only problem is getting past the guards without them seeing me," she said.

"So let them see you."

122

Fidel kept a pair of twenty-foot speedboats tied to a small dock at the far east side of his bunker area. The cockpits of both were covered with canvas, but I was more interested in the rope holding them to the dock—thick, old-fashioned hemp.

The Rogue Strider would have cut nicely through both, but then it would have been obvious that someone had been there. So instead, I put the knife to a different use—unscrewing the hitch holding the line, then prying it off as if the boat had naturally pulled the faulty screw from its mooring.

The little boats were surprisingly heavy to tow through the surf. I hadn't gone more than fifty yards before starting to pray that someone would spot them "drifting," even though I knew the farther from land they were the better for both me and Red. By one hundred yards, I had moved beyond prayer and had begun to curse. At 150 yards, I said to myself that enough was enough and let go of the rope.

One of the eagle-eyed lookouts finally spotted it a few minutes later. A woman ran out after them, paused to take off her work clothes, and joined them.

Red, of course. She carried a small rucksack with her into the water, though I doubt anyone who saw her noticed.

Red swam west, going with the tide as the others struggled to the east as they attempted to corral the boat. Much farther from shore, I swam as quickly as I could, mostly below the waves, in Red's direction.

"You OK?" I asked as I caught up.

"Uh-huh."

"Need help."

"Fine. I'm fine."

We swam another three hundred yards or so before I found a spot where I thought it was safe to land. She crawled up out of the surf and collapsed, too exhausted to move.

"You know, Dick," said Red finally, "this could be considered sexual harassment."

"What's that?"

"I think you just wanted to see me without my top on."

"I love to see you without a top on," I told her. "But I'm an equal opportunity employer. Take off your bottom and I'll strip, too."

(III)

I don't know whether the video camera at the telephone company hadn't been fixed because of basic inertia, incompetence, or simply a lack of funds. Whatever the reason, it made things a lot easier for us when we returned the trucks to Victoria de las Tunas around four the next morning. Mongoose took another page out of his early childhood, rolling the odometers on both vehicles back, making it look as if they hadn't traveled at all. I'd love to have seen the face of the manager or whoever it was who discovered them in the lot when he reported for work at 8:00 A.M. that morning.

At roughly that moment I was pulling into Guáimaro, a city roughly thirty miles by car to the east of Victoria de las Tunas. I'd gotten there by a method of travel particularly popular in Cuba, especially at night—I'd gone up to the main road and stuck my thumb out.

Hitchhiking is so big in Cuba that, like everything else in the country, the government has tried to stick its hand in it. It seems every town near a highway has its own *el punto amarillo*, named after the yellow-uniformed government worker who's supposed to facilitate hitchhiking. The worker collects a few pesos from you for blessing the deal. But this being Cuba, the government's "help" is something most people try to avoid when possible. Hitchhiking at night or in the early morning can be easier than during the day, since at night you end up giving your money to the driver instead.

Red and I rode in the cab of a delivery truck. The driver gave me a few sidelong glances, but he was much more interested in Red's breasts, even though they were well ensconced in a sweater and a fresh change of clothes we'd liberated along the way. Red didn't seem to mind much; then again, that might have been because she spent most of the short ride sleeping.

Guáimaro won't top the list of any European tourist looking for a romantic if cheap Cuban getaway. It is cheap, but it's anything but romantic, a poor town in a poor country. Most of the roads in the city are dirt; the morning we were there a strong wind whipped up a fine grit storm.

The city is important historically—it was here that the Assembly of 1869 met, approving a constitutional government and calling for the end of slavery. But our interests were strictly directed toward finding a place to sleep. Doc, who'd gotten to the city a half hour before Red and me, had found a small guesthouse or casa willing to rent to European visitors, no questions asked, even though it was very early in the morning.

The extra euros he slipped the proprietor may have helped.

Trace took the first watch. Within a few minutes, everyone else was snoring. Feeling a little too restless to sleep, I went out on the second-story porch Trace was using as a lookout.

She gave me a funny look as I sat down.

"Any trouble getting here?" I asked.

"Easy."

"No complications?"

"No complications."

"Something wrong?"

She frowned, but didn't say anything.

"Worried about Havana?" I asked.

"No."

"How'd Shotgun and Mongoose do?"

"Same old, same old. Like a married couple. How's Red?"

"She did good."

"How are her boobs?"

"Not as pert as yours."

Trace frowned. "She's not that good a shot."

"No one's as good as you, Trace."

Clearly she was a little jealous about my spending time with Red, though she'd never admit it. And of course if I brought it up she'd pretend she didn't care. The interesting thing—to me, anyway—was that she wasn't jealous of Karen Fairchild. But then I never pretended to entirely understand women, just to love 'em.

"What's the next move?" Trace asked finally.

"We get over to Havana."

"I know that. I don't want to ride in the back of another pickup. Especially with Shotgun and Mongoose."

"We're not going to. We're going to take a train."

"They have trains in Cuba?"

Not very many, and most of the ones that they do have are about as dependable as a 1972 Ford Pinto and half as safe. The one notable exception to this is the *Tren Francès*, aka the French Train, which runs between Havana and Santiago de Cuba.

Our ticket west.

The only problem with taking the *Tren Francès* was the fact that the nearest station was in Camagüey, roughly fifty miles farther west. The easiest way to Camagüey was by one of the intra-city buses, but these are usually sold out days if not weeks in advance, and are generally only available to Cubans.

Theoretically, the buses are never completely sold out, as two seats are left open to "anyone" who shows up at the station, but reality and theory are often at odds in Cuba, and a conversation with the hotel owner made it clear that there'd be little chance of getting a seat.

On the other hand, the owner told Red, she knew someone who could take us there for a small fee. The someone turned out to be her son, who for a hundred pesos apiece was willing to drive Red and I to the center of Camagüey.

A hundred pesos apiece was considerably more than what the bus would have cost, but I agreed to pay it when I saw that he owned a station wagon. Not twenty yards down the road, we "happened" to come upon Doc and Trace.

"There are some guests we met at the hotel," said Red, pointing. "Stop and let's give them a ride."

The driver protested only long enough for Red to suggest that she would tell them to kick in another twenty pesos. She didn't even have to make that suggestion when we saw Shotgun and Mongoose a short while later. It was a tight squeeze, but we made the trip in just over an hour and a half, which included avoiding a checkpoint the driver knew would give us trouble. Overpaying for basic services, especially quasi-legal ones, can have some advantages.

Tren Francès is about on par with the older, nonexpress Amtrak trains that run up and down the northeast coast. The bathrooms don't have toilet paper, but otherwise the trip was no worse than the ride I took last fall from Rogue Manor to my publisher's.

We rolled into Havana Estación Central at 0215, and made our way to the Parque Central, a large hotel in the middle of the city where Junior had made reservations for us.

After we checked in—all separately of course—we rendezvoused down at the bar, where Sean Mako was waiting.

Sean is another one of the young bucks we've been lucky to recruit to Red Cell International over the last few years. As I believe I mentioned earlier, he's also proof of our nondiscrimination policies: Sean is a former blanket hugger, an Army Ranger who realized SEALs have more fun, at least once they're out of the service, and came over to the dark side.

Sean had been in Havana for the past two days, getting the place ready for us. He'd been at the train station when we arrived, making sure we weren't watched, then shadowed us back to the hotel.

I bought a drink and went over to his table.

"Anyone ever tell you you look like Fidel's long-lost younger brother?" Sean asked.

"Fuck you very much."

"His picture's all over the place," said Sean. He took a sip of his drink, a local rum concoction. "What's with the 'Socialism or Morte' shit? Those freakin' billboards are everywhere. Man, these people are nuts to put up with this crap."

"You prefer Pepsi ads?" said Doc, pulling up a chair.

"Women in tight jeans would suit me just fine."

"Heathen," said Trace, grinning as she sat down.

"If communism worked, you think they'd need slogans like that? We don't go around putting up billboards that say, 'Capitalism or die.'"

"Maybe we should," said Doc.

"It's fucked up, man. Why don't they just, like, kick the asshole out?"

"It is more difficult than that," said Red. "You see, at first, Fidel seemed to many people a hero. The old government was no good. Batista . . ."

She stopped speaking for a moment, looking around. Despite the hour, the bar was a little more than half full. No one was paying attention to us, though, and Sean had already swept it for bugs.

"He was a terrible dictator," continued Red. "Corrupt. Worse. He put many people in jail, destroyed many lives. Fidel was just one of many who opposed him. This was in the early 1950s and Fidel, he was a lawyer. His family was very rich, and he ran for a seat in the Chamber."

Red grew up in America, and ordinarily she sounds pretty midwestern, since that's where she came from. But her tongue had taken on a slightly Cuban rhythm since we'd come to the island, and tonight she sounded positively Cuban, her accent thick.

"When Batista suspended elections, Fidel filed a legal challenge. When he saw that the challenge would go nowhere, he turned to violence," said Red. "He led an attack on the Moncada Barracks, far in the east, near Santiago de Cuba. It failed. He was thrown in prison. He was to be executed, but the Catholic fathers pleaded with Batista, and the death penalty was suspended."

"Another argument in favor of the electric chair," said Doc.

"He was at the Isle of Pines, the most notorious prison in all Cuba," said Red. "In 1955, the Cuban congress passed a resolution giving all political prisoners amnesty. Castro was freed. He fled to Mexico. But the real trouble was just beginning."

Castro returned in another abortion of an attack on government forces in 1956, landing in the *Granma* at Playa Las Coloradas. The landing was an attempt at an invasion, and it was a real fiasco. Government troops played "how many rebels can you kill before reloading" from easily held positions near the beach. Most of the men with him were killed or captured, but Fidel, his brother, and some others made it to the Sierra Maestra mountains where they slowly built a guerrilla force.

Castro was far from the only one opposed to Batista; even members of the navy eventually mutinied. Batista was a real slime, so bad that the U.S. not only opposed him but eventually cut off weapons sales to him. By that time—1958—Fidel's ragtag army in the west had been organized into a pretty damn effective raiding force, specializing in hit-and-run tactics.

By the time Batista left Havana on January 1, 1959, Fidel was not only leader of the largest and most effective guerrilla group, but he was famous as an opponent to the regime, and when he stepped into power it seemed preordained to many Cubans. The U.S. wasted little time recognizing his government. President Eisenhower—yes it was Ike who "lost" Cuba, not Kennedy—sent a new ambassador.

Actually, Ike didn't so much lose Cuba as think he'd found it. Like most Americans—and Cubans for that matter—Ike didn't realize that Fidel actually hated the U.S. He didn't just want to get rid of Batista; he was out to create a socialist paradise in Cuba, with him as its permanent protector. After gaining power, he did what all good dictators do—he killed or jailed not just his enemies, but anyone he saw as a potential threat to his rule.

That included Red's grandfather.

"My grandfather had been with Fidel in the mountains in 1957, just after Playa Las Coloradas," she told Sean, referring to Fidel's disastrous invasion.

Her grandfather had come to the mountains as a schoolteacher in 1955. The conditions in the small village were terrible, and it was no surprise that his sympathies were with the local people and not the absentee landowners. When Castro came east after the disaster at Playa Las Coloradas, Red's grandfather was one of the people who helped shelter him and his small band of rebels.

"He gave them food, helped find a place for them to stay," Red told Sean. "Fidel was a powerful speaker. Few people who heard him would not join his movement. He promised a better way for the poor farmers. My grandfather joined immediately."

Red's grandfather became the captain of a group of *escopeteros*, rough partisans in the mountains. (Not all the *escopeteros* were aligned with Fidel, but the grandfather's group was.) After Batista was ousted, he became an important government official in the village where he had been born.

Even though the country was not yet officially communist, it was clear within six or seven months after Batista fled that Fidel was headed in that direction. Red's grandfather was against this, and apparently had no problem speaking his mind.[20] In the summer of 1959, he was jailed on trumped-up charges that he had denounced Fidel personally.

It was a lie, since her grandfather still somehow revered Fidel, thinking the new government's actions were merely mistakes perpetrated by ignorant comrades. He was sent to the notorious Isle of Pines prison, where he died in the mid-1960s.

"They killed him?" Sean asked.

"They fed them maggots in handfuls of sugar swept from the mill floors. The amount of flour and corn for one man each week would not feed a baby for one day. They did not put a gun to his head, no," said Red. "But they killed him as surely as if they had put two hands around his neck and choked him."

"I'm sorry," said Sean. "I didn't know."

"Most Americans don't," said Red. "They hear of Fidel and they think he was a hero. They don't know the rest."

"Don't go by Sean," said Doc. "He's just a dumb shit."

---

[20] Red's grandfather's family owned a small plot of land, but it was smaller than the limit Castro's government imposed. Though compensation was promised to those whose land was seized, the amount was small and in many cases it was never paid. Red's grandfather spoke out about this, and many other issues.

Sean turned red.

"No, it's not your fault, Sean." Red touched his hand, which made him turn even redder, though for a different reason. "Cuba is not important to most Americans. Why should it be? Just a small island, yes? But with great suffering."

And with that, she got up and went to the bar for another drink.

Our lesson in Cuban history complete, we set our plans for the next day. Sean briefed us on the security arrangements around our target area, ran down some of the preparations he'd already made—renting cars, bicycles, some safe rooms at hotels and a house outside of town—then gave me some DVDs with photos and videos of the area where Fidel's office was.

"Your Spanish must be improving," said Doc when he finished. "You've done pretty damn well."

"There's only one word you need to know here: *Cuánto?* As in: How many *dinero* are you going to take from me?"

Sean wasn't just being cynical. The country was poor, and money talked loudly enough to get many things done. In most cases overtly bribing someone was completely unnecessary; the business arrangement was itself a bribe.

The government was often in on it. Rental car companies, for example, were all owned by the same government agency. It charged a fixed rate, payable in convertible pesos, the official government money for travelers. (Fifty-five a day for a Hyundai Athos, when we were there.) But in some instances—the house, for example—payments on the side in "real" pesos, the money regular Cubans spent, definitely helped things along, even though in theory it was illegal. Euros, though in theory worth much more than either, were not always accepted, because of the hassle some folks had using them. But everyone needed money, even the best-off government workers.

Sean had picked up a variety of information in his travels. There was a veritable army of Chinese businessmen in town, trying to arrange different deals. There were even more pickpockets around; Sean had grabbed one fellow the day before just as he was about to take off with his wallet.

"But that turned out to be my lucky day," said Sean, taking out a pair of cigars from his pocket. "Right after that, I ran into this guy whose brother worked at a Partagas factory. I got 'em cheap."

Red glanced at the cigars and laughed.

"What's so funny?" asked Sean.

"Those aren't Partagas. Someone rolled them at home."

"You sure?"

She took one, running her fingers over it quickly. "The roll is good, but the leaf has too many veins. It would never be used at the factory."

"They smell good," said Sean.

"Well, they *are* Cuban." She got up and went over to the bar.

"I also found this great place for breakfast," Sean told us. "I'll take you there in the morning."

"You'll be out of here before then," I told him.

"What?"

"I need you to get this back to the States," I told him, sliding Fidel's last will and testament DVD to him. "I want you to bring it directly to the admiral."

Sean looked like I punched him in the gut.

"Make us a copy, too," I added, ignoring the hurt-puppy look. "I'll have Junior rig some sort of copy thing up."

"Can't he take it?" Sean glanced toward the bar, where Red was getting her drink. "Cuba was just getting interesting."

"History lover, huh?" Doc chuckled, then drained his glass.

[IV]

Getting into Fidel's office was about as hard as getting into an American submarine complete with nuclear missiles.

No wait, I'm wrong. The submarine was a little tougher. Not much, though.

Getting out was a different story.

Our hotel was near the Capitolio, the fancy former government building that looks somewhat similar to our Capitol building in D.C. The building is now a museum, Internet café, and tourist attraction. The Cuban national congress, called the National Assembly,[21] meets to rubber-stamp everything Fidel, or lately his brother Raul, tells it to in a big building a few miles to the southeast called the Havana Convention Center. The real seat of government is at the Communist Party Headquarters, or *Comité Central del Partido Comunista de Cuba*, the large, pretentious, but fitfully air-conditioned building at the south end of the Plaza de la Revolución at the center of town.

But I digress.

The Capitolio dome looks out over the harbor area, the old part of Havana, and by far the prettiest part of the city. It's a must-stroll for tourists; if you don't like the old buildings, you'll at least appreciate the old cars you can see here. Like all of Havana, there are pockets of poverty and plenty of disrepair a block or two away, but I wasn't on the island to institute social justice, and neither are most tourists.

Fidel has a number of homes spread out in Havana and across the island, and even more offices. In fact, if you want to get a glimpse of one of his houses, open up Google Earth on your computer and go to these coordinates:

23°04'48.99" N
82°29'07.07" W

---

[21] Technically, the *Asamblea Nacional del Poder Popular*, National Assembly of People's Power.

That one is on the west side of Havana, on the outskirts of town. Note the tanks parked about a half mile away. And the armored personnel carriers.

According to the admiral's intelligence, Fidel's favored working office of late—along with a small apartment for him to rest in—was located in the Miramar area of Havana, west of the Old City near the water. Prior to the Revolution, this was the exclusive area of Havana, the place where well-off families would build their dream homes. A few large apartment buildings dot the edges now, and there are traces of the steady dilapidation that you see throughout the rest of the city because of the country's extreme poverty. But most of Miramar remains an exclusive area. It's where most countries locate their embassies, and where the highest-ranking Communist Party members have their homes. When the windows break here, they replace them with glass, not cinder blocks like they do in much of the rest of the city.

According to the information Ken's people had given me, Fidel's "secret" working office was a five thousand square foot modernistic house overlooking the beach (though not on it). Sean's initial recee showed the information was very likely correct; he had spotted six guards in the vicinity, along with at least two video cameras. The house also matched with the general description the barber had given me.

Our first order of business was site surveillance. Driving through the immediate area was impossible unless you had an extremely good reason to be there, but the front of the building could be seen from the roof of an apartment complex about a mile and a half away. Shotgun and Mongoose went there an hour before daybreak, lugging a bird-watcher's telescope that Sean had purchased two days before.

The apartments had been informally subdivided so that several families could live in each unit. This is common in Cuba, especially in the cities. If there were three bedrooms, there would generally be three families sharing everything. While the building itself was in need of repair—the cement at the front entrance was crumbling, and there were rust stains all along the windows—Sean had reported that the halls and stairway were clean enough to eat off.

The reason became apparent as my two shooters were met by a sudden flood of warm water and a scent somewhere between ammonia and fresh pine needles.

"What!! Ruining my floor with your big, muddy shoes?" bellowed a Cuban grandmother from down the hall as they walked in.

Mongoose started to apologize, but the woman would have none of it. She scooped up two rags from the pail and walked over to them.

"You will clean it," she demanded. "And take off your shoes before you go any farther. Where are you going?"

Sean had given them the names of some of the people who lived in the building. Mongoose, forgetting momentarily which family was on the top floor, rattled them all off together.

The woman looked at him suspiciously, but before she could ask exactly what he was up to, Shotgun intervened.

"Fame?" he asked, trying to say "hungry" in Spanish.

His pronunciation was off, but the package of Twinkies he held up in his right hand made his meaning crystal clear. The woman glared at him, but cast a friendlier eye toward the snack.

"Here you go." Shotgun tossed her the pack.

The woman snagged it with the prowess of a Pro Bowl free safety. Mongoose explained that he and his friend were bird-watchers from Canada, and were here hoping to catch a glimpse of the very rare red-breasted black heron, which they had heard could only be seen from certain roofs in the vicinity.

"You have any more of these?" asked the woman, finishing the cake.

Two Twinkies and ten minutes later—they had to wipe up and re-mop the part of the floor they'd walked on—Shotgun and Mongoose set up their telescope on the roof. The rare red-breasted black heron declined to put in an appearance, but the security team at Fidel's offices made very punctual rounds, sweeping around the outer perimeter of the property at precisely ten minutes past every hour. They did this in two-man teams. One man carried a long wand, presumably a device to detect electronic surveillance equipment; the other had an Uzi. The sweeps were always preceded by the appearance of a third guard on the roof, whose expression indicated either that he was bored or jealous of the other guard, who after all got to play with a real submachine gun instead of the AK47 he was assigned.

The Cubans spent almost precisely seven minutes surveying the perimeter of the property—something Trace calculated by watching from a small sailboat to the east of the house a mile and a half out to sea.

The CIA intelligence, including the satellite data Junior surveyed, failed to turn up any reserve security force, but we knew from Fidel's other sites in the city that there must be one. It took a while, but Trace—who was sailing the rented boat with Red and Doc—finally doped out their location in a second building about a block away. A pair of armored cars were kept in a garage there, hidden from the satellite. A dozen or so security people came and went in a little more than an hour's time. We estimated that there were no less than eighteen people assigned to Fidel's security, and very possibly more.

Six against eighteen? We had them outnumbered by a mile.

And where was *moi* while my employees were bird-watching and sailing?

I had the glamorous part of the operation: I was scouting garbage trucks.

The local television news had a big update that night on Fidel's health. Except for some stock footage, there were no pictures of Fidel; the station made do with some pictures of the outside of the hospital where he was.

But according to the reports, Fidel was in good shape. Excellent, even. The heart attack had been a false alarm. He'd had angina, heartburn, agita—but no heart attack.

You'd think a crack medical team would know the difference between a coronary and eating too much spicy food. There certainly were enough doctors to make the call: the commentator listed the doctors taking care of him, going on for several minutes.

"What's he doing, reading from the phone book?" said Doc sarcastically.

After the health update—and with no apparent irony—the newsman said that Raul had scheduled a special meeting in two weeks for a vote on the possible succession.

"Gee, I wonder who's going to get chosen," said Doc. His irony, or rather sarcasm, *was* apparent.

I smelled a rat. Fidel might not have had a heart attack, but the report had not been released without some sort of thought. Undoubtedly, the government was trying to prepare the people for Fidel's demise.

Red agreed.

"Nothing happens on the news by accident," she said. "We may not have all that long to get this done."

She was right, but there wasn't much we could do about it. If Fidel had the bad grace to die that night—well, that would just be Mr. Murphy's way of pulling down his pants and mooning us all.

Garbage trucks are beautiful in their ugliness. They are perfect creations, absolutely Zen-like in their perfection. Their form is at one with their function. A large box, a convenient crusher, and enough horsepower to pull a battleship up Mount Rushmore.

They do stink, however. At least the one I drove through Miramar the next morning did. Mongoose and I had borrowed it from the yard about a half hour before.

That's another good thing about garbage trucks. Most people never expect them to be stolen, and don't do much to prevent thieves.

Mongoose drove. I worked in the back, lifting cans from the curb and dumping them into the truck. I dragged a garbage can across the pavement and waited a second before hoisting it. Then I sighed heavily, placed it once more on the curb, and checked my watch.

Five minutes to seven. We were running three minutes ahead of schedule.

A Cuban yuppie down the street gave me a dirty look. I watched as he got in his brand-new Chinese rice box of a car and drove toward us. Since we were blocking the street, he had to wait until Mongoose moved forward. Which Mongoose wouldn't do until I knocked on the side of the truck. Just before I was about to, the driver rolled down his window and began telling me that I was a pimple on the ass of progress, and that in the war between socialism and death, I had chosen the side of death.

I wrinkled my nose and grinned. Then I walked—slowly—to the side of the street and dumped the can I had already tossed into the back. Only then did I pat the side of the truck.

Mongoose lurched forward, barely out of the way. The Cuban (clearly a very high-ranking government or party official, for otherwise he wouldn't have lived here) stepped on the gas and sped around us, no doubt considering whether the egalitarian society was the ideal it was cracked up to be.

We proceeded up the hill until we came to Fidel's house. A single plastic can of garbage had been placed at the curb. I picked it up, dumped the contents in the back of the truck, then returned it to the curb. I was just about to give Mongoose the double tap when a plainclothes security officer emerged from the house and whistled at me to stop.

"You! Wait! Wait! Do you hear me?"

I stopped.

"The lady needs you to help her. Come. Now."

I took a few steps out from the back of the truck and glanced at Mongoose. He shrugged. I shrugged back.

The lady in question—one of Fidel's personal cleaning women—appeared behind the security officer and began haranguing him.

He rolled his eyes, then turned to me and whistled again.

"Let's go, come on. *Christo*—today, before she chews my ear off. She's worse than my wife."

Probably he meant to say these last few words under his breath, but his breath was a little too strong. The lady told him that it was quite incredible that he was married at all, and she would remember to say a prayer for his poor wife, because obviously she had to put up with incredible suffering and pain far beyond what any woman had to endure, and women as a general rule had a great deal to endure, since they had to live with men, especially beastly imbeciles of which the man was specimen number one, the very worst of all time.

This went on for the sixty seconds or so it took for me to reach the steps, whereupon the critique was turned from the security guard to yours truly.

"Look at your shoes! You wipe those shoes before you come into this building. Do you understand? Those hands! Those hands touch anything except for the bags I have for you, and I shall break them. What is this country coming to?"

The cleaning lady was Red, who had arrived with Trace a few minutes before. The guards had proven more conscientious than most, not only checking the IDs—obtained from the real cleaners—but also calling over to the public works department headquarters to make sure that the women were legitimate. Anticipating that this might happen, we'd finessed the problem by intercepting the guard's telephone's radio signal, transferring it to our satcom line, and having Junior reroute it to one of Ken's people in Miami.

(You'll remember that the sweeps for electric devices were conducted at ten minutes past the hour. The guards believed that the checks made them safe from eavesdropping or any sort of electronic surveillance the rest of the time as well—a very natural assumption. The device we used to intercept the call worked by blocking all transmissions in and out, and then transferring our line for the legitimate one. Doc, who had it in his rental car, simply moved on once the call was made.)

I was about to follow Red up the steps into the building when the guard ordered me to stop and empty my pockets.

I turned them inside out for him, and held up my hands to allow him to pat me down, which he did. Then he ordered me to take off my cap.

"What is the delay?" demanded Red.

"We have procedures, miss."

"The hell with your procedures. You come and help me with the garbage."

The guard ignored her.

"Your cap," he told me.

I lifted it.

"Hey, José," he said, calling to his companion inside the doorway. "Come here."

The other guard walked over, being sure to give Red a wide berth. The two men began talking together quietly, glancing in my direction every so often.

"What is the delay?" demanded Red.

"Doesn't he look familiar to you?" said the guard finally.

"Familiar? He's the garbage man. You think I know all of the garbage men?"

"He could be Fidel's cousin," said the one who had just come out. "Change the hair a bit, some age marks . . ."

Red pulled her eyes deep into their sockets. She drew herself up to her full height—all sixty inches.

She looked almost as fierce as Trace.

"I have never, never heard of such a thing," she spit. "Such—blasphemy! Infamy! Blasphemy!"

She disappeared into the house.

The guard who had just come out started to laugh.

The other did not.

"Get the hell in there and do what she wants," he told me. "Be quick. She'll have us all fired. And we'll feel lucky that that's all she does."

I don't think being fired is the worst thing that can happen to a garbage man, even in Cuba, but I complied anyway.

Red and Trace had located Fidel's office on the first floor in the center of the building. While it wasn't as elaborately protected as the one in the bunker was, it was still isolated from the outside by thick walls, making it relatively safe from a bombing attack. The hallway outside was also under constant video surveillance. The door was locked, and the keys that the cleaning ladies had did not include one for the office.

A minor problem.

Red called to me as I shuffled down the two steps to the hallway.

"In here. You must empty these bags for us," she said, pointing to the conference room diagonally across the hall from Fidel's office.

Trace was down at the other end of the hall with her vacuum, right under the video camera. As I entered the room, I slipped my hand under my belt and took out my lock picks. The vacuum suddenly revved. Rather than sucking in air, it began spitting it out. A huge plume of dust filled the hall—and a small cloud, shot out of one of Trace's spray bottles, completely obscured the camera lens.

I trotted to Fidel's door, lock picks in hand, trying not to cough. Dropping to one knee, I inserted the pick and spring and then worked the lock as quickly as I could.

Red, who'd gone to the top of the steps, started coughing uncontrollably—the warning that someone was coming.

The lock finally gave way. I swept inside so quickly I dropped the spring on the floor. There was no time to pick it up, however. I closed the door as quietly as I could, leaning back and listening to what was going on behind me in the hall.

Red had begun screaming at Trace in extremely loud and heated Spanish that she was a fool and an imbecile, and would have to clean up all of the dirt with her tongue. The guard who'd come down to find out what was going on didn't say a word; he just turned and walked back upstairs.

Fidel's office was laid out roughly the way his office in the bunker was, with the safe behind his desk. I hunched down, tried the lock to see if it would open (it didn't), then slowly worked the dial through the combination I had used out east, hoping to shortcut the process.

That didn't work either.

I reached for my stethoscope, then realized I hadn't worn my fanny pack—too much risk of being searched on the way in.

Duh. Trace and Red had carried the safecracking gear in with their equipment. They hadn't had a chance to hand it off.

I went back to the door and knocked twice. Red was nearby, ready to open if the coast was clear. But with the vacuum still going, she couldn't hear my signal.

She didn't answer the second time I knocked, and I assumed the coast wasn't clear. Rather than waiting, I went back to the desk and started looking for a spot where Fidel might have written down the combination. I couldn't find anything that looked even vaguely like a set of numbers.

I tried knocking again. Still nothing.

The combination *had* to be some sort of sequence that had something to do with Fidel or the Revolution, didn't it?

Dates jumped in my head. 7/26/1953 — the date of Fidel's attack on Moncada Barracks.

I tried every combination. Nada.

1/8/1959 — the date Fidel entered Havana.

Nothing.

Fidel's birthday?

Zilch.

I even tried the address of the house.

Then I remembered something one of the CIA instructors who'd taught me how to open safes had said at our very first lesson. Safes come with what he called "tryout combos." These are the company-issued combinations that are supposed to be changed by the safe owners. Most, however, don't.

He'd made us memorize the tryout combinations for a number of safes. It wasn't actually that hard, since they generally fell into predictable patterns—the numbers, after all, were meant to be easily remembered by salesmen.

The safe in front of me had been made by the Chicago Safe Company in the 1950s. Very useful information, if I could remember the tryout combo.

I'd aced the exam, but that was years ago. I stared at the dial, trying to will my brain cells to give me the proper combination.

40-70-50-30.

No.

40-50-60-70.

Click.

Score one for memory. The safe opened, its door swinging easily on well-oiled hinges.

Unlike the safe out in the bunker, this one was almost bare. A single DVD in a white envelope sat on the side. The only other item was a pearl-handled revolver.

I zipped open my garbage man's coverall and pulled the DVD out from its sleeve beneath my shirt. I made the switch and then, resisting the temptation to see if the gun was loaded, closed the safe, gave the area a quick once-over to make sure it was clear, then went back to the door.

I was still two or three feet away when it flew open.

I expected to see Red, gesturing at me to get the hell out of there.

But instead I saw Raul Castro, face red, stunned into utter silence.

[V]

Brother!" said Raul.

I took half a breath before I responded.

"Raul!"

"Cocksucker!"

"Motherfucker!"

He broke into a smile. "Why are you here? Why are you dressed in coveralls?"

The truth is, Raul was several sheets beyond drunk. The smell of rum was so strong a single whiff was enough to give me a buzz. I'm not sure how he was able to walk, unsteady as he was.

If he'd been sober, there's no question he would have realized at first glance I wasn't Fidel. But he wasn't, and you go with what works. If the brother of the Western Hemisphere's biggest scumbag is going to collapse in front of you, you grab him and make a run for it.

Or at least you slide him onto the couch, which is what I did as Raul began a nosedive toward the floor.

"Chavez, Chavez, all I ever hear is Chavez," he said drunkenly, spinning around and plopping onto the couch. "That Venezuelan pig. Believe me, brother, he is a curse on us. The Yankees are calling him Enemy Number One! Enemy One! Hugo. *Huuuu-go.*"

Raul shook his head. Clearly he thought his brother should be enemy number one; being displaced as top world slime was disheartening.

"How does he threaten them?" continued Raul rhetorically. "Oil. Oil! We had nuclear weapons. Nuclear weapons, Fidel. Russian weapons, yes, so who knew if they would work? But compared to oil? Oil? A bourgeoisie luxury. That is Huuuu-go's claim to fame. A bourgeoisie fat pig who pretends he is the keeper of the Revolution!"

Raul looked up at me and squinted.

"You don't look so good, Fidel." He wriggled his nose. "And you smell."

"Mmmmm."

"I thought you were in the hospital."

I shrugged.

"I don't blame you for leaving," added Raul. "What idiots! Their heads come off at the slightest provocation. If I find who put the rumor out that you had a heart attack . . . They are all vampires and witch doctors. They told me to give up smoking! Eh, like you."

He winked, then reached into his jacket pocket for a cigar. Except that he wasn't wearing a jacket, and so came up empty. This puzzled the crap out of him, and he sat dumbfounded on the sofa, opening and closing the imaginary jacket.

Red hissed at me from the door, signaling with her head that it was time to go—beyond time to go, really. I agreed. But as I took a step, Raul grabbed my arm.

"How about one of your secret stash, brother?" said Raul. "Eh? I know you have some. I know you sneak a smoke here. Eh? Yes?"

I frowned at him.

"Ah, Fidelisimo, holding out on your brother. I think you secretly like Huuu-go Chavez, yes? Huuu-go, scumbag pig."

Raul lurched forward. I thought he was about to decorate the rug with whatever he'd been drinking all night, but instead he glided, head down, behind Fidel's desk. With one hand on the desktop, he reached to the bottom drawer and pulled out two cigars, then laughed.

"There are no secrets between brothers, eh, Fidelisimo? Heh, heh, heh."

He reached into his pocket and took out a cigar cutter. He had a little trouble lining up the cigar and razor blades, and for a second I thought he would snip off his finger and bleed to death.

Not a bad idea, actually.

Instead, he snapped the crown off the cigar, then snipped the other one and held it out to me. I stepped toward him and took it.

If I popped him on the forehead, it would look like he had simply collapsed and knocked himself out. Then I could take the cutter and snap off part of his finger. Lock the door and leave—by the time he was discovered, he'd have bled to death.

Not part of my assignment, but I don't think Ken would have minded. Not too much anyway.

And who cared if he did?

Red cleared her throat behind me. I looked over and saw that there were two plainclothes men and one uniformed guard in the hall behind her—Raul's bodyguards and one of the men from upstairs.

"Have a light, Fidelisimo."

Raul held out a flame so high I thought he was going to burn the ceiling. I took the cigar and puffed a few times.

"Eh, just like the Fidel of old!" Raul laughed. "The hell with the doctors, yes? The hell with this talk of death."

He stopped speaking and stared at me for a few moments.

"You're not dead, are you, Fidel? Is that why you smell?"

"Sir, we would like to clean the room," said Red.

"Yes, yes, the room. Eh." Raul stepped out from behind the desk, then veered drunkenly toward the door. "I don't feel too well, Fidel-isimo. I am going to bed."

The two bodyguards followed him down the hall toward the stairs. The uniformed guard, however, glared at me.

"Let's go, let's go," barked Red. "We don't have all day. Take the trash."

She'd managed to sneak a bag near the door. I grabbed it and started out.

"Wait," said the guard.

He stepped up close to me. He had a rifle slung over his shoulder, an AK47 whose folding stock had been removed. Grabbing it and killing him wouldn't be too hard—but then I'd have to get past the others.

"Let me see the garbage," he said.

I handed it to him. He stepped back and opened it, then riffled through the collection of crumpled papers. He frowned when he was done, and handed it back.

"Go."

I took the bag and started up the stairs, fighting against the adrenaline rush that was pushing me to run. I was just going through the outer door when someone yelled to me to halt.

It was one of Raul's bodyguards, double-timing down the steps. He looked me up and down. For a second I thought he was going to frisk me, and I considered what I would do if he found the DVD stuffed into my shorts.

But that wasn't what he wanted. He looked me in the eye.

"If you tell anyone of this, you will be shot."

I nodded. He reached over and slipped his hand into my pocket.

"Discretion pays," he told me. "Now get the hell out of here. Quickly. And remember, we know who you are."

[VI]

Y ou were in there a long time," said Mongoose when I finally reached the truck.

I tapped the side of the cab without answering, then hopped on the back. My pulse rate was still well into triple digits, I'm sure.

We finished picking up the garbage on the rest of the block, then took the truck over to the garbage scow in the harbor, completing the regular run so that no one would suspect anything. By the time we got rid of the truck, Red and Trace had finished at Fidel's office and gone to one of our safe rooms at a different hotel. There Red became brunette; Trace did her hair so that she now had bangs.

Mongoose and I changed at the garbage compound, then went to yet a different hotel where we showered and got pretty. Doc and Shotgun, meanwhile, were rolling up the operation, making sure we hadn't been shadowed and tying up a few loose ends that needed knotting. By 3:00 P.M., the entire team was in the lounge at the Santa Clara hotel, sitting at the far end of the room, tall rum *libres* in front of them.

Except for yours truly. I stuck with Bombay Sapphire.

"A toast to sunny commie Cuba," said Doc, raising his glass.

Red frowned at him. But then she relented. Slightly.

"I'll drink to the people of Cuba," she said. "And to the future."

Shotgun chugged his drink. "This stuff really hits the spot," he said. "I didn't know they had a liquid version."

"What are you talking about?" asked Mongoose.

"Rum cake. This is the liquid version."

We were all a bit cocky. We figured we had a right to be. We'd just pulled off an almost impossible mission. The only thing we had to do now was act like tourists and catch our flights out. The first, Doc's and Trace's, left for Canada at six. Shotgun and Mongoose would head out to Mexico at six-thirty, and Red and I would board a similar flight a half-hour later. We had our exit euros ready and all our gear was packed. I would check us out of our rooms at the hotel, dropping the keys off at the desk as I went out the door. Checking out wasn't an absolute necessity, but the less strings left untied the better.

I had Fidel's DVD with me. Since we'd already smuggled one out, I had the option of destroying this one, but I knew Sean had gotten through the airport without any problems. Before we left I'd hit a tourist rip-off joint and buy a CD player and some discs, stuffing it in with them.

Why a CD player when it was a DVD? Because if anyone at the airport asked me to demonstrate that it worked, it wouldn't—and they wouldn't see what was on it.

We ordered some food. If there had been any bad blood or jealousy between Trace and Red, it wasn't evident now. Trace can be absurdly professional; if she doesn't want you to know she's got a problem with you, you won't know it.

Red, on the other hand, keeps all her emotions very close to the surface. That's one way you can tell she's Cuban.

A television was playing at the other end of the bar. There was another health bulletin on Fidel. His doctors said he was doing much better.

"If he keeps getting better and better, he'll be immortal soon," said Doc.

"He already is," said Red.

My satellite phone began to vibrate.

Not a good sign, I thought.

I didn't want to talk in the bar, even though we'd already checked it for bugs. So I let it buzz and took a few sips from my drink before going outside. I glanced at Doc, who immediately realized what was up and sent Mongoose out to trail me and make sure no one was eavesdropping. Then, just to be doubly safe, he sent Red after him.

I walked a couple of blocks, doubled back to make sure I wasn't being followed, then headed in the general direction of the Malecón as Mongoose took up my tail.

Danny had placed the call. He didn't leave a message—he knew I'd realized he'd been trying to get me and would call him back.

"This is Dick," I said when he picked up. "What can I do you for?"

"Junior has something," he said. "Hold on."

Junior was in Florida, where he had met Sean and copied the DVD. It took a second for Danny to make the connection.

"Get a tan yet?" I asked him.

"Um, did you get a chance to, uh, look at that movie. Closely?"

"Just the opening credits."

Damn, I thought, *did I grab the wrong one?*

"It's real interesting," he said.

"And?"

"Well—"

"Out with it, Junior."

"Can you talk?"

"Damn it, tell me what's up. Is it the wrong video?"

"No, it's the right one. But um, there's a coded number on the disc. Stamped into the plastic. You got to look at it under a black light."

"What sort of code?"

"Real basic—three of three. Numerals."

Three of three?

As in, copy number three? Of three?

Ken and his sources had said there were only two copies.

Doom on Dickie.

"Dick? Are you still there?"

"Yeah, I'm here."

"You should watch the video if you get a chance," he added. "There's a lot more on it than you think."

"Are there porn shots?"

"Just threats. I'm in a bad spot here, Dick. The connection's not that good."

"Find a better spot and call me back."

It took Junior a half hour to find a place where he could talk. By then, I'd gone into a club not far from the hotel and borrowed one of the lights that bouncers used to check the stamps they gave people at the door. Sure enough, there was a code on the DVD—1/3.

After that good bit of news, I headed over to La Epoca, an expensive hard currency department store in downtown Havana. Four stories high and stocked with goods most Cubans can only dream about, La Epoca is open only to party members and rich tourists. It has a two-tiered price system: party members get their goods cheap; tourists pay through the nose. My Chinese-made DVD player cost five hundred euros—which worked out to something like a thousand percent markup at the time.

It hurt, even though my pesos were counterfeit.

I checked the DVD back at the hotel. Fidel's florid face filled the screen. There he was, bushy beard and overgrown eyebrows.

"Man, you guys could be brothers," said Shotgun.

"Who says we're not?"

Fidel started talking. The Revolution was continuing, etc., etc. Red turned away.

I would have too, except that suddenly Fidel's threats and predictions grew very specific.

". . . And I guarantee you, fellow Cubans, fellow members of the glorious generation of socialist men and women, that the Yankee bourgeoisie decadent capitalists will feel my death even more strongly than you will. And that within twenty-four hours, they will begin dropping like flies of the most horrible disease imaginable. This is my last gift to you . . ."

PART TWO
DEATHBED SURPRISE

Never strike a king unless you are sure you shall kill him.

—RALPH WALDO EMERSON, *JOURNALS*

〔 I 〕

Technically, the existence of another disc was not my problem. My job was done—I'd been retained, under somewhat difficult circumstances I might add, to swap two DVDs, and I had done so. I'd also gotten my people and we were on our way out.

But the admiral didn't see it that way. In his view, I'd been hired to swap the discs, whether there were two or three or twenty-three hundred.

I argued, though not very hard. I've never been one to live by technicalities. And I was starting to like Cuba.

"We're pumping our sources," Ken told me when we talked by secure sat phone. I'd taken the precaution of using one of our rentals and driving a good distance from the city, far away from eavesdroppers and signal stealers. "We should have the definitive location in twenty-four hours."

"That's nice."

"Dick, you're not thinking of leaving Cuba, are you?"

"Thinking? No. On my way? Yes."

"Dick—it's not like you to leave a job half finished." Ken never was very good at math.

"I'm sorry, Ken. I've already done more than I signed up for."

"Dick, I'm counting on you. You know you're the only person in a position to carry this out quickly. We don't know what Fidel's real health is. He could go at any minute."

I'll spare you the rest of his wheedling. I agreed to stay for twenty-four hours while the Christians in Action did their best to figure out where the missing disc was.

"And what about this plague?" I asked. "What's that about?"

"You've seen the video?"

"No, it came to me in a dream."

"It's all bullshit, Dick. Fidel doesn't have the capacity for any sort of biological weapon. It's all a load of crap."

"I doubt he'd make a boast like that if he didn't think it was true. He doesn't want to be remembered as a liar."

A mass murderer, maybe. Just not a liar.

"Our people don't think it's real," said Ken. "It doesn't jibe with the intelligence we have."

We don't know it, so it can't be true. Classic Christians in Action thinking.

"Twenty-four hours," added Ken. "We'll have the information for you by then."

"I'll call you," I promised.

"Where will you be?"

"Disney World."

Havana, Orlando—almost the same thing.

We spent the next twelve hours reloading.

Doc and Trace had already checked in for their flight. I decided not to pull them off. If we did go after the disc, we'd need to get more gear into the country, and it would be easier to arrange things with them starting offshore.

The rest of us headed for an unlicensed—aka illegal—guesthouse about twenty miles from the city that Sean had said always had vacancies. I figured we'd spend the night and next day resting up and waiting to see if the admiral bucked usual CIA procedure and came back with useful information.

Everyone was antsy the next morning. Mongoose had gotten up early and was practically tearing the walls down, treading back and forth in his room, waiting for first light, breakfast, and something to do. Red was a bit calmer, chatting with the owner, but I could tell from her knitted brow when she glanced across the room that there was no way she was spending the day hanging out.

Thank God for Shotgun. He was his merry, hungry self when he came down to breakfast, laughing as Mongoose grumbled, and helping himself to a full plate of sugar-drenched cakes the matron had made, charming her with his appetite. He helped himself to more coffee, insisting that her cooking was the best he'd ever had. If the paperwork hadn't been so onerous, I'm sure she would have adopted him right there.

In Canada, Doc and Trace arranged some new finances and credit cards, funding bank accounts we could tap into from Cuba. They found a "facilitator" who was able to provide them with some European identity documents to go along with the accounts and some new identities.

And then they went shopping, buying clothes and some other items to make a lengthy stay in Cuba comfortable.

Junior returned to Jamaica—grousing, of course—and took over for Danny as our main contact. That let Danny fly over to Miami, where he went to work looking up some friends and near friends and near near friends to see if they might have any information about Fidel's deathbed surprise.

Did I mention Junior was grousing?

I'm being generous. He wasn't happy with the assignment, and didn't mind telling me about it. He wanted to join Doc and Trace, and he tried arguing his way into that part of the mission.

"I can speak Spanish," he said.

"Not as well as they can. Besides, that's irrelevant to their cover and not what we need right now."

"You won't let me go because I'm your son."

"That's a crock of shit," I told him.

"That I'm your son, or that's the reason you won't let me go?"

"Both."

"I am."

"Your DNA doesn't matter, Junior. One way or the other. You have a job. Now do it."

"Why don't you love me, Dick?" he blurted.

"Love's got nothing to do with it. Stop whining, or I'll kick your butt into next week."

I may not have been his dad, but I sure sounded like it. Matt grit his teeth and kept them clamped shut.

I really can't blame him for wanting to be where the action was. Support people and backbenchers are critical to a successful operation, but it's hard to see that when you're young and full of spit. Been there myself, and I definitely got a case of red ass trying to keep myself on the bench.

Frankly, if the four of us had had to stay at that guesthouse all day, red asses would have been the least of my troubles. Fortunately, the lady who owned the place supplied us with an excellent diversion.

We'd given her a cover story about coming to Cuba from Spain to fish. Just after breakfast, she recommended a local guide who had a boat. She helped us make the arrangements—undoubtedly with a small commission—then sent us off with some food. Mongoose's mood brightened;

as we walked down the pier he started talking about how all Filipinos were great fishermen, and how his great-grandfather had once caught a shark with his bare hands.

"What did he do, hold the bait in one hand and knife him with the other?" said Shotgun.

"No, he fell in the water while they were fishing, and the next thing he knew, the fin was right there," said Mongoose. "So, he had no knife. He had nothing but his bare hands and feet. The shark came, he gave it a chop on the snout. As it went past, he grabbed the top fin. Instantly, they were underwater."

Mongoose has a way of saying instantly that makes you feel like your heart just skipped two beats. Bullshit or not, everyone hung on every word he said.

"They went underwater. My grandfather started pounding on the fish's head. The shark snapped, but it stayed underwater. Finally, my grandfather realized what the solution was. He leaned forward, and jabbed his right eye in the shark's eye. Like this."

Mongoose went to demonstrate on Shotgun, but he was not quite quick enough. His friend intercepted him, and the pair grappled, rolling to the dock laughing hysterically.

Red shook her head. "All a joke. And I believed him."

The words she added in Spanish were somewhat less generous.

"You all right there, Red?" I asked.

"I don't like fishing, Dick."

"What else you want to do?"

She shrugged.

"Listen, I'm not going to play headshrink," I told her. "If there is something you want to do, tell me. We have a few hours today. Tomorrow, we're back to business."

"I would like to go to Cayos Verona,"[22] she blurted. "But I don't want to go alone."

It took about three hours for Red and I to drive down to Cayos Verona, the small town on the southern coast of the island where her grandfather had lived before becoming a schoolteacher in the western mountains.

---

[22] You can look for it, but you won't find it. The name is a pseudonym. The description is accurate, except for the parts that aren't.

While Red had been in Cuba many times, she had never come here, only to Havana and two other cities to the west where relatives still lived.

The area was famous for its tobacco, and we passed barns and tobacco sheds that looked like they were brand-new, shining in the sun as they waited for a new crop to be grown. Most of the houses, though, looked like they'd been plucked from the edge of hell. A good number were tin-roofed shacks that had been battered in a hurricane months before and not yet been repaired. We drove on, following a route too obscure to host any checkpoints, until we finally reached Cayos Verona on the coast.

The village consisted of perhaps a hundred houses, clustered on streets that spread from a tiny town square like spider legs. A small church sat across from the square, and that was our first stop.

When I say the church was small, I mean it was barely bigger than your average school bus. As a matter of fact I'm not sure a school bus could have fit inside if the doors were removed. The front doors of the church were open, and we went in.

Rather than stepping up, we went down two steps into the nave. The place felt cool and damp; very little light came in through the windows, and it was so quiet I could hear Red breathing heavily as she walked up the aisle toward the altar.

I stood in the back and watched as she went up and knelt near the cross, praying as she imagined her grandfather did as a boy. The church didn't have any pews, but it had everything else that made it a church — the altar, a beaten-to-hell (literally) Christ on the cross at the front, a lit candle on the side.

Red crossed herself and came back down the aisle, deep in thought.

"Can we see the town?" she asked.

"Sure."

We walked down a packed-dirt street to the right, playing friendly tourist.

Not *too* friendly — I had my pistol under my shirt and my eyes were roaming back and forth, looking for trouble. If things got hairy, we had a pair of MP5s and some flash-bangs in the car. But the only trouble I spotted was in the form of two kids, maybe seven or eight years old, who ran up to Red and started calling her aunt. It was probably a semi-scam — other strangers had probably given them candy or money when flattered — but Red was touched, and she bent down and started talking to them, asking them about the village.

Within seconds, an older woman appeared in the doorway of the nearest house. She came out and scolded the boys, who bolted down the block. Red went over and introduced herself, explaining that she had had a relative who lived in the village many years before.

Both women were suspicious of each other: the older woman because Red might be a government spy, and Red for obvious reasons. But within a few minutes they had reached some sort of unspoken agreement to trust each other—and not to ask certain questions, like who exactly Red's relative was. If asked, Red would have stuck to the cover story that we were from Canada, but she wasn't asked. Instead, we were escorted through the village, introduced to whoever passed by, and treated to a running commentary of life on the southwestern shore of Cuba.

It was a hardscrabble life, not something you could romanticize. These people were very poor. But they were also generous with what they had, and much more open with strangers than even the friendliest town in South Carolina, which in my experience has been among the friendliest places in America.

The village fishermen—all three of them—were out on their boats, but our guide took us down to the dock, very proud of all eighteen wobbly feet of it. Then she went back to the center of town and rounded up a few of her neighbors. We had lunch in the backyard of the village's grandest house, a one-story brick building on the highest ground (by about three feet) above the town square. There was a seemingly bottomless pot of rice and chicken, with tiny little peppers that sparked in your mouth and made the homemade liquor they served taste even better. The fact that I didn't smoke scandalized the locals; even the women smoked fat cigars here.

"Thank you," said Red as we drove back toward our guesthouse. "I appreciate it more than I can say."

"You're welcome."

She had her head back on the seat, eyes almost closed. The day seemed to have tired her out ten times more than any of the operations we'd pulled already.

None of the last names of the people Red had met were familiar. But she hadn't come to see anyone specific. She was more visiting her grandfather, or to be more specific her memory of him.

We were a few miles from the house when suddenly she sprang forward. Hand on the dash, she turned to me.

"You think things will be better when Fidel goes?"

The easy answer would have been sure. But it wouldn't have been honest.

"No way of knowing."

"I think it will be," she said. "Definitely."

Shotgun and Mongoose were sitting in the parlor when we got back, watching the news with the woman who owned the place. We sat down and joined them. A few minutes later, the announcer said with great portent that freedom fighter Imad Mughniyah had been killed by a car bomb in Damascus.

The Israeli government was being blamed for his death, apparently triggered by a car bomb.

Remind me never to double-park in Damascus.

We all observed a moment of silence for the dead bastard . . . a moment of silent jubilation. Imad Mughniyah was a Hezbollah slime who'd planned at least one hijacking, numerous kidnappings, and a number of suicide bombings, starting in the 1980s. Our paths had crossed once or twice, and not very pleasantly.

I did feel a twinge of regret at his passing: it meant I'd never have the chance to get the bastard myself.

(II)

Ken was in a cheery mood when I checked back in.

That was a very bad sign.

"We have two possible locations," he said, as if he were checking off the options for lunch. "One's in Communist Party Headquarters. Fidel has an office there. The other is out east—way out east, where he first set up his guerrilla command."

"These are guesses, right?"

"Hell no."

"Ken, you're a lousy poker player. How good is your intel on this?"

"Good. Not the best, but good."

There was no point in pressing him any further. Instead, I asked if there was anything new on the other matter—Fidel's deathbed surprise.

"We're working on it. How long before you have this wrapped up?"

That was the end of our conversation.

"WAG planning," said Doc, when I spoke to him by sat phone a little while later. "My favorite kind."

WAG = Wild Ass Guess. WAG planning is a specific version of wishful thinking generally practiced by Can't-Cunt officers seeking to justify their existence. Having been a chief for a number of years, Doc had a great deal of experience dealing with such plans, and their fallout.

"We'll start in Havana," I told him. "Party Headquarters is worth a sneak and peak."

"Matter of opinion."

"Getting tired of Cuba, Doc?"

"Tired of Fidel. You see what happened to Mughniyah?"

"Yup."

"Real shame if that happened to Fidel."

"For the moment, we have every incentive to keep him alive."

"Maybe that's the idea."

The thought had crossed my mind—that Fidel had actually set the plan up as some sort of twisted insurance against an American plot to assassinate him. But it was a little too convoluted for that.

I gave Doc the option of taking a pass on the project.

"No, I'm in. And Trace is chomping at the bit to get back. What sort of goodies should we bring?"

We spent the next day in Havana, touring Plaza de la Revolución, the big square in front of Communist Party Headquarters that's ground zero for the Cuban government. The center of the park features a monument to José Martí, the late nineteenth-century Cuban patriot and freedom fighter who must roll over in his grave every night.

Even though Fidel has co-opted him, Martí's a guy anyone who really thinks they value freedom ought to study. Among other things, he's the fellow who said, "It's better to die standing up than to live kneeling down."

You're not going to find a better statement of first principles than that.

Across from the monument is a bland box of an office building that on its side features a wire sculpture of Che Guevara. That's the interior ministry, home to any number of Cuban bureaucrats and worse. Then there's the National Theater, which among other things hosts Fidel's show-stopping speeches. My understanding is that they used to lock the doors before he started talking; no potty breaks when the commander in chief is onstage.

Communist Party Headquarters—our target—sat at the south end of the square. The CIA had copious maps and photos of the area, along with real-time satellite imaging, which made it easy to run our surveillance checks and map out the neighborhood. Then with the help of some makeup, I underwent an ethnic-transplant, becoming an old Chinese gentleman, complete with Asian eyebrows, a deeply respectful bow, and business cards promising everlasting prosperity and fortune. Taking a break from selling bourgeoisie goods to the old-line pinkos—that was my cover—I joined a tour of the building escorted by a member of the Cuban chamber of commerce.

(Junior's magic fingers had wormed a way into the organization's computers, discovering the tour and securing me a place in it. One more reason he was where he was.)

There were ten of us, and I was the only one not from Europe, which made it easy to play the inscrutable oriental as the tour guide extolled the virtues of Cuba's "open" economy. He took us into the legislative chambers and then into the office area behind the scenes.

Communist functionaries in Cuba undoubtedly work as hard as government workers anywhere, which explained why the place was nearly empty in the middle of the day. The guards were mostly older men—the youngest I saw was on the far side of sixty-five. There was the usual assortment of wired alarms, a few motion detectors, and a security monitoring station filled with red lights and a Chinese-made radio.

Chinese-made to U.S. specifications, I should say. Very convenient.

The tour led us through several ceremonial rooms on the first floor, and even a few where people worked, though these did not include the cabinet secretary's office, who after Fidel and Raul was the most important person in the government. Ken thought the DVD might be in any of their offices, though pride of place belonged to the dictator.

The tour leader then took us to the third floor, where Fidel's and Raul's offices were located, showing us both. I ruled both out immediately.

It was obvious from how neat they were and how sparsely they were furnished that the offices were used for ceremonial purposes only. That's why we could be taken there in the first place. Neither Fidel nor his brother used them to get any real work done.

The work offices were in the basement—not because it was cooler down there, but because the ceiling and surrounding walls were reinforced against a bomb strike, something Fidel and his people still feared some forty years after the Bay of Pigs. While I couldn't slip away to get down there, I did get a good look at the doors to the stairs, opening one and making sure it didn't have an alarm.

Our guide gave me a funny look, then directed me down the hall to the men's room.

Junior got Shotgun hooked up with another tour for European travel agents, assigning him a cover as an Estonian. We scrambled to concoct a passport for him; ironically, it turned out not to be needed, and Shotgun had a grand time pretending not to understand a word anyone else said to him, while helping himself to a myriad of snacks offered by the host. He managed to focus on his job long enough to assess the locks used on the doors, look over the phone system, and locate the utility conduits. That evening, Mongoose and I examined the exterior and surrounding park and neighborhood, looking for good access and egress points. Red searched out the places staff members hung out, gathering information and three ID tags as she went.

Doc and Trace flew in from Canada around seven. They were covered as an independent video team working on a documentary on the Cuban governmental system. We needed a story to smuggle the high-tech gear in, and this cover also gave us an excuse to go to Party Headquarters and other government buildings if we needed it. (We needed a little help arranging the cover story on such short notice; fortunately, I had a few outstanding IOUs from some friends in Ottawa and Toronto, who smoothed the way.)

Doc and Trace were met at the airport by a member of the Communist Party's Revolutionary Orientation Department—in other words, a high-level security type trained in PR and bullshit. She helped whisk the bags of video equipment through customs after a cursory check.

And fee. That was in cash. Unspecified in any of the formal documentation, for some reason.

Shotgun trailed them to their hotel and subsequent "orientation," just in case something went wrong; Mongoose joined up with him after finishing with me. In the meantime, I met Red and went to borrow a car from a party member in northwestern Havana.

We may have forgotten to ask permission, but I'm sure he didn't mind. He'd even filled up the gas tank earlier in the day.

Leaving the keys would have been even better, but you can't have everything.

We needed the car because we were on our way to the outskirts of Havana to meet with a man who called himself José Martí. Unlike the original patriot, this José was a black marketeer specializing in ammunition, a highly prized and difficult-to-find commodity in Cuba. We'd been turned on to him by one of Danny's contacts, who described him as a cross between Darth Vader and a carny hawker: as likely to kill you as sell you something. Heck of a way to enforce a no-refund, no-return policy.

Whatever statistics are cited about how safe Havana is didn't apply to the area where José did his business. It was edging midnight by the time we got there, but there were knots of people on the street corners, young males mostly, standing with the universal posture of wannabe thugs. In my experience, wannabes are considerably more dangerous than the real thing; they're too stupid to know when to walk away.

"You can get anything here," muttered Red under her breath, and I'm sure she was right. Illegal drugs were big sellers, but the streets in

José's neighborhood featured a veritable department-store selection of items ranging from illegal anywhere to simply inconvenient to obtain in Cuba. On one street corner, someone had set up a display of toilet paper and books on a stand made from a coat rack.

We were clearly outsiders. While I had an MP5 on my lap, the real thing that protected us was the fact that we were obviously customers, and shooting us would be bad for business.

Red took a left down a narrow street, heading in the direction of the ally where Danny's contact had told us we could meet José. The street was so narrow, only one car could pass—a very easy place for an ambush. The buildings on either side were three and four stories tall, with their windows blocked out by cement blocks. This is common in Havana, where glass is considered a luxury, but it added to the short hair factor.

As in, my short hairs were all standing at attention, tightened by the knot in my stomach.

"You sure about this?" Red asked.

"Think of it this way. We're seeing a part of Havana most tourists never see."

"Mmmm," said Red, unenthusiastically.

Three garbage cans sat in the middle of the alley fifty feet from the intersection, blocking it off. We couldn't see anyone nearby. There were no windows on the buildings on either side of us.

"There'll be lookouts on the roof," I told Red as she turned into the alley.

"And snipers."

"And snipers."

She stopped in front of the garbage cans.

"Leave the car running," I told her.

"No shit."

She took a deep breath, then checked her .45. It was an old Colt, a military model older than she was. "Let's do it."

We got out of the car at the same time. We passed the garbage cans, walking toward the back of a building about seventy-five feet from the car. A set of steps led to a basement door; the stairwell had a thick iron pipe railing. A few metal spikes stood out from the bricks where a fire escape had been. Otherwise the wall was blank, all of its windows in its four stories filled in by bricks.

We walked slowly until a pair of spotlights flicked on from the stairwell. The lights were surprisingly powerful, strong enough to nearly blind us. I resisted the urge to raise the submachine gun, holding it down by my side—visible, though not immediately threatening.

"Who are you?" asked a voice near the light at the left.

"A friend sent us. Christo," said Red in Cuban Spanish, using the password Danny had supplied. "We're looking for José Martí."

"He died long ago."

"Yes, but now he sells things of interest to people in need."

There was no answer. I could see someone or something moving near the edge of the searchlight. Finally he stepped out from the shadow, just at the edge of the light.

"I am José Martí," he said. "What do you want?"

"To make a deal."

"And who sent you?"

"Christo."

"Christo is dead many years."

As far as we knew, Christo wasn't a real person, just the name used to initiate a contact. Neither Red nor I knew what the answer was supposed to be.

"Maybe he came back to life, like José Martí," I said in Spanish. I put a growl into my voice, trying to disguise my accent.

The man by the light laughed.

"Yes, yes, all the great heroes return. They walk among us every day. Every day. What is it you want to buy, Christo?"

"Hunting rifles," said Red.

"What sort?"

"The best you have."

"AK47. Very expensive," said José.

Red shrugged.

"I can get you four. With a hundred bullets apiece. Three thousand euros each."

Three thousand euros—at the time somewhere in the area of $4,500 American—was several times what the guns would have cost in any other black market in the world. Hell, you can practically get them for free in some places.

"I can pay a thousand each," said Red.

"For a thousand I can get you some bullets."

"Five thousand for the lot."

"Five thousand will buy you two," said José Martí.

Red looked at me. We had only taken ten thousand euros with us, and there were some other things we wanted to buy. I showed her three fingers, signaling that we could settle for that many guns.

"I can give you seventy-five hundred for all four," said Red.

"Seven for three," replied José Martí.

"Bullets—"

"A hundred rounds apiece."

"We need more."

"Two hundred."

"A thousand."

Martí scowled. "A hundred Euros extra."

"Fine. Grenades?"

Our friend shifted, but said nothing.

"We're fishing," Red told him. "We need an easy way to catch the fish."

José Martí shook his head. Asking for the grenades had crossed whatever line he was comfortable with. Red told him it was fine, but the damage had been done.

"Where do we pick up the guns?" she asked.

"Tomorrow it will be arranged."

"Tomorrow is too late. I am taking them now, or there is no deal."

José Martí tried to renegotiate.

"No," I told him.

We stared at each other for a few seconds. He had the advantage—the spotlight made it difficult to see.

"Problem, Dick," whispered Red.

"You take the guys on the roof. I have José," I told her.

A second later, the bullets started to fly.

(III)

It's not that easy to shoot down from a roof at someone in an alley. First of all, if the alley is very narrow, you have to get close to the edge to see your target. Most shooters don't like that, especially in the dark. Then there's the problem of hitting a moving target—never easy under any circumstance, but especially when you're standing on an uneven, slippery surface, like the edge of a roof. Finally, you usually overcompensate for your height advantage by aiming a bit low.

Don't buy it?

Neither did the people shooting at us, who did a damn good job of covering the alley with lead. If it wasn't for the fact that I shot out the spotlights before they got sighted, we'd be buried in that alley right now. Assuming they went to the trouble.

We ducked against the wall on opposite sides of the car, where the shadows and height of the vehicle gave us a bit of protection. Frustrated, the gunmen concentrated on the car. Glass, metal, and bits of brick and mortar from the buildings filled the air as the gunmen gave an impromptu demonstration of how quickly the AK47 can run through a full magazine.

When the gunmen paused to reload, I raised my head, looking for a shot. But I quickly lowered it as they began firing again.

I heard Red whistle. Figuring that she was signaling a move, I raised my gun and fired off a burst, then hurled myself forward, still in the shadows as the gunmen tried to nail me down. I'd like to say that I nailed at least one of them with my shots. But then I'd like to say I'm a billionaire.

I did get their attention, at least. Their bullets dug a few feet from my head.

When the hail of bullets lifted, I began moving backward in the direction of the stairwell where José had been. I figured I had two choices: I could go down the stairs and face José Martí directly in his lair, where undoubtedly he was prepared for me, or I could *really* tempt fate by climbing up the wall in full view of the gunmen on the roofs, hope to find a roof entrance or skylight on the building, and pop down into José Martí's lair from above—where, of course, he'd still be waiting for me.

Under ordinary circumstances, I'd've chosen Door Number Three—none of the above. But that door had been replaced with cinder blocks. So I went with option two.

Red and I had divvied up our last flash-bang grenades between us, two each. I took one out, kissed it for good luck, and threw it over the car, toward the intersection with the street.

One thousand one, one thousand two . . .

As soon as it exploded, I leapt up and grabbed the lowest iron spike, pulling myself upward. The gunmen began firing furiously—down toward the end of the alley where the grenade had exploded, thinking that I had tossed it to clear the way for a breakout.

At some point, they realized their mistake, stopped firing, and started looking for me. By then, I was scrambling onto the slightly pitched roof of the building, trying desperately to find something to grab on to so I wouldn't fall on my ass. The roof seemed to be made of a coat of very loose pebbles over a slippery coat of tar or maybe rubber cement; every time I grabbed something I started to slip toward the edge.

My lack of forward progress became an acute problem when the gunmen realized where I was and started plinking the roof. Desperation increased the amount of friction between my soles and the roof, and I managed to toss myself over the peak—only to find I couldn't stop, sliding forward on my belly toward the front of the building and, presumably, the ground. I snagged a roof vent with my right arm, curling around it to a stop, my feet dangling over the edge. I caught my breath, then pulled my feet up one at a time, still clinging to the vent.

I was just about to take stock of my options when I suddenly started falling again—this time straight down, as the roof around the vent collapsed.

After making it to the end of the block, Red tucked her pistol into her jeans and started to scale the facade of the building on the left of the alley. The concrete blocks that covered the first-floor windows made this relatively easy. It was a different story on the second and third floors, however. She was able to get up on the cornice above the blocked-up window, but then found the rest of the wall too smooth to get a grip. She worked herself all the way to the corner, hoping to get a grip up there, but found none. Finally she spotted a fire escape on the next building over, which was separated by an alley nearly eight feet wide. She climbed down and was just climbing the fire escape when my flash-bang went off.

The boom surprised her as much as it did the Cubans. She froze, thinking the building had exploded. By now the gun blasts had done a job on her ears, and her head had a slight fuzz to it, a sort of mental smoke that mixed adrenaline with shock and sensory overload. She collected herself, then started climbing again. There was enough light to see the rungs and a bit beyond, but the roof itself was a collection of shadows. Unlike the roof I was on, hers and the others were flat; she crawled to the middle until she could see the men on the next building taking their potshots at me.

If they heard her pistol over the growl of their own weapons, those were the last sounds they heard—Red took out both men in quick succession with shots to the head.

That left two men on the far roof, neither of whom she could see. She crawled out to the edge of the building she was on, gauging the distance she'd have to jump. Then she rose, took a few steps back, and jumped.

She cleared the alley, but as she landed, her right toe clipped the top of the low wall that ran around the roof. Red crumbled—a good thing since the men on the other roof had seen her and began firing in her direction. Bullets whizzing above her head, she crawled over to one of the gunmen she'd killed, using his body for a shield until the shooters ran through their magazines. Then she jumped up, fired two shots into what she thought was one of the gunmen, and rolled against the low wall at the edge of the roof.

It's one thing to turn a blind eye to black marketeering, and quite another to let thugs threaten the state monopoly on violence. As soon as the first gunshots went off, it was inevitable that the Havana police would respond, and in serious force. They turned out every car with a siren, and more than a few without.

I was thankful for the sirens—they woke me up.

The roof deposited me, briefly, into a small attic. The attic seemed to be home to fully half of Havana's pigeon population, and a deep bed of guano broke my fall. But if the roof was weak, the attic floorboards were even weaker. After straining for perhaps a half second, they gave way and I hurtled down to the building's fourth floor. I lay stretched out in dust and bird shit for somewhere between a few seconds and several minutes until the sirens shook me from my slumber.

I rolled to my right, nearly retching from the stench of bird crap as I struggled to my feet. The room was so dark I couldn't see my gun lying in the boards and debris next to me; I had to feel around for it and was ready to give up two or three times before I found it.

Expecting the floor to give way any second, I walked forward slowly, hand out until I touched a wall. Then I felt my way around to the door. The good news was, there was enough light in the hallway for me to see. The bad news was, it came from the bubblegum machines on the police cars, shining through the upper windows at the front of the building, where there was still glass.

I found the stairs and started down, still trying to clear the cobwebs from my brain. As I reached the second floor, I heard someone running up the steps from the basement. One hand on the banister, I leapt over the side to the first-floor landing, crashing into José Martí's back as I came down.

It's not every day you flatten a national hero. I would have savored the memory if the circumstances were different.

"I think it's time to renegotiate our price," I told José, picking him up by the scruff of the neck. "I think free is good."

Apparently he didn't agree, and began screaming as I pulled him back down the steps with me. I slammed him against the side of the wall a few times, but that only made him angrier, and finally I had to pitch him ahead of me into the dimly lit basement.

Though poorly lit, the basement was dry and clean—or at least the parts that I could see were. Crates were stacked at least chest high nearly wall to wall. José had enough gear to equip half of Cuba's army.

Which was only fair, since that was probably the source of most of his stash.

I picked him up by the scruff of his neck and asked where the explosives were.

"You idiot! The police are surrounding the building. We'll never get out."

"Where are the explosives?" I said. I pushed the MP5 into his chest. "I'm not asking again."

He pointed to the corner. I dragged him with me. There were boxes marked for plastique, nitro, and dynamite.

There were also grenades. I helped myself to four.

"Open the dynamite," I told him.

"The police are going to arrest us."

"You maybe. Not me."

Reluctantly, José Martí pulled down one of the crates marked dynamite and opened it.

"Blaster caps?" I asked.

"Caps?"

"I want to blow the fucking stuff up."

"Fuses — there."

The box at the left had a collection of old-fashioned blasting fuses, the kind you may have seen in the movies with a braided fuse similar to what you'd see on a firecracker.

I love firecrackers, but using them to set off dynamite is not my idea of fun. But it was my only option.

"Stand against the wall," I told José Martí.

"You're an American," he said, finally figuring out my accent.

"And you're going to be dead if you don't stand against the wall."

José Martí raised his chest. "I'm not going to aid Yankee aggression."

I raised the submachine gun. His patriotism evaporated and he stepped back against the wall.

I pulled a wick off one of the fuses and tied it into another fuse. I made a quick arrangement of the fuses and dynamite, then lit the rat's tail in the middle. The fire sparked, then slowly began working its way toward the sticks.

Not slowly enough, in my opinion.

"Let's go, José," I yelled.

He was happy to comply, beating me to the steps.

Just as he had predicted, the police were surrounding the building; we could see the lights of their cars revolving through the windows at the front.

"Which way is out?" I asked José as we got to the first floor.

He didn't answer. I grabbed his back and pushed him down.

"No problem waiting here until the dynamite explodes," I said.

"The side," he managed, pointing. "I'll show you."

I followed into a side room. He ran to the corner, then began clawing at a stack of boxes.

"Help me get them out of the way," he said.

I grabbed a few and tossed them down. I expected to see a hole in the wall, but there was none.

With the boxes gone, José Martí put his hand up against the wall and started pounding it with the side of his fist. The wallboard cracked.

"Like this," I told him, reaching up and booting through with my heel. The board gave way, revealing a hole just large enough for us to crawl through. But it wasn't to the outside — it was to the building next door.

I pushed him through, then grabbed his leg and pulled myself over him into the next room.

"The dynamite, the dynamite!" he whined.

"Now where do we go?"

"We won't make it!"

"Sure we will," I told him.

But he was right — at that moment, there was a tremendous explosion below us, and a good portion of the building shot upward like lava bursting from a volcano.

[IV]

The force of the explosion threw Red backward on the roof, and she tumbled toward the edge that faced the street we'd taken to get there. By the time she stopped rolling, the secondary explosions had begun. Crate after crate of ammo and other goodies began cooking off in the fire. Yellow and red flames shot upward, towering high into the night. Havana hasn't seen such fireworks since the Spanish blew up the *Maine* in 1898.

The police scrambled for cover, called for backup, and ordered coffee, donuts, and marshmallows. Red scrambled back the way she'd come, climbing down to the ground and then circling around toward the front of the building, hoping that I had somehow managed to escape the explosion.

She wasn't very hopeful, actually. She was literally praying for a miracle, rattling off Hail Mary's like the old Italian ladies at six o'clock mass.

I was on my knees at that moment myself, though I was crawling rather than praying.

The basement walls of José Martí's building had channeled the main force of the explosion upward, reducing the shock on the neighboring buildings. Even so, the corner of the building we were in collapsed, sending two walls tumbling together. Jose led the way to a set of steps that went downward. Going down didn't strike me as a particularly bright idea, but I followed him anyway. The steps led to a steel door with a number combination lock. He pressed a few numbers, got it open, and pushed into a narrow, dank passage.

I had to move my shoulders sideways to get through. Something had hit José Martí when the building exploded, and he was limping heavily. If it weren't for that, he probably would have been able to slip away from me. Even so, I had to summon a burst of speed when we came to a set of stairs going upward. I grabbed the back of his shirt as he hit the street, halting him.

"We can't stay here. The police will block off the entire area," he said. "They will make arrests. Everyone will be arrested. Americans especially."

"This way," I told him, pulling him toward what I thought was the street Red and I had come down.

"This is behind the building."

"I want the alley where I met you."

"The explosion surely demolished it."

"The alley," I told him.

He put his head down and turned to the right. As we started to walk, I heard more sirens.

"I'll kill you if you try to get away," I told him, sliding the gun against his back as a reminder. "Don't try anything."

He started walking. The MP5 is a small gun, but it's still large enough to be noticed on the street. I kept it down by my side, staying close to the buildings as we walked. We walked in a big circle toward the alley. Red, meanwhile, had gone as close as she could to the building. Blocked off by the police, she came around in the other direction. We met about two blocks from the alley, fifty yards from a police checkpoint.

She broke into a trot when she saw us.

"Thank God. I thought you were dead," she told me, hugging me.

"Not yet."

Jose Marti looked at us. I think he thought I was going to let him go. Fool.

"You owe us some guns," I told him. "I want them now."

He shook his head. "My guns, all of my guns, were in that basement. You blew it up."

"Then take me to one of your competitors."

Unlike José Martí, Peiro Garcia lived outside the city, in a large (for Cuba) detached house protected by six or seven guards and two Dobermans. He wasn't much for conversation, or for haggling. Even with José Martí's professional discount, Garcia still wanted seven hundred euros per gun.

He did, at least, throw in six mags per gun, and a thousand loose rounds each.

With the purchase complete, José Martí had gone from asset to liability. I couldn't just let him go. Even if he didn't want revenge—ha, ha—he'd have no problem trying to cut a deal at my expense if the police picked him up. He might have known only that I was an American, but that was more than enough to get the security apparatus very hot and bothered.

José undoubtedly did the math and realized what his likely fate was, so he tried to head it off as we drove away from Peiro. We were in one of the rentals, picked up from its stashing point behind a church about a mile and a half from the center of town.

"Get me to America. Get me to America and we'll call it all even."

"Why? So you can spy for Fidel?"

"I hate Fidel." He spit on the floor of the car. "Take me to America. I have a network of suppliers—they can be useful. I hate Fidel."

"You're a bullshit liar," said Red.

"I am a liar, yes, when I have to be. But you'll have no trouble from me if you take me to America. I can help you. Tell me what you are planning—only take me out with you."

I had no intention of telling José Martí what we were doing, of course. But Ken might welcome him. He'd send him to some out of the way army base in the Midwest, debrief him, then persuade him to return to Cuba as a "friend." Bankrolled by the CIA, he could be an even bigger player in the underground economy.

I was just mulling how we might get him back when Red grabbed my arm.

"That's a checkpoint," she warned, pointing ahead to a small line of cars on the road ahead. "They must have set it up after the explosion."

We were nowhere near the explosion, but her guess was probably on the money.

"If they stop us, we'll all hang," said José Martí.

"Hang tight," I told them, cranking the wheel hard to the left.

My choice of escape routes was deeply flawed: the police had blocked off the road with a large truck. When I saw it, I turned down a second road to my right. This one wasn't blocked off, but it was filled with police conducting follow-up checks of people they'd stopped at the roadblock and in the immediate area.

One of the officers tried waving me down. I waved back—with the rear end of the car, fishtailing it against his side and sending him airborne into a parked police van nearby.

That may have made his friends mad. They began shooting at us. I cranked the wheel sharply and sideswiped another car. I reached the end of the block, then turned left onto a wider street and headed toward the water.

It was a little before dawn, and Havana was just waking up. A number of early risers were out, but the traffic was light enough on the Malecón that I managed to get a good head start before the first police car appeared behind us. We had a four-block lead.

I'd stretched it to six blocks when the bus appeared in front of me, leering slowly from a side street like a dazed circus elephant looking for its bath. I hit the brakes and cranked the wheel to the right, broadsiding the bus. Somehow still moving, I twisted the car around and got it down the street the bus had just come out of. But a truck was stopped halfway down, and when I veered away from it, I found myself moving head-on for a black Russian Lada. I tried to pass him on the right, running up for the sidewalk, but there wasn't enough space or time. We crashed together, the impact twisting the Lada into the truck and wedging us against the side of the building.

Red threw off her seat belt as soon as the car stopped moving. She took her gun and batted out the shattered windshield, climbing onto the hood. I followed her.

"Get the guns from the trunk," I told her. "And as much of the ammo as you can carry. I'll take José."

But when I slid back into the car, I saw that José Martí wasn't coming to America, at least not in this life. He hadn't been wearing his seat belt, and had been tossed so hard against the side window that his head had gone through. His neck was now impaled on part of the glass and twisted metal; the entire back of the car was washed in his blood.

That was one way to solve the problem of what to do with him, I guess.

[V]

Escaping the police wasn't hard. The bus had stalled in the middle of the intersection on the main road, and by the time the cops who'd been chasing us got through the traffic and avoided the other victims, we were long gone.

More difficult was finding a place to hide the weapons.

We took a zigzag course away from the accident, walking through a drowsy residential area. After walking for four or five blocks, I spotted a set of steps that led to a courtyard behind a row of apartments. We ran down the steps, went into the courtyard, and stuck the rifles behind some bushes at the edge of the wall.

It was a lousy hiding place. I knew as soon as we put the guns there that we'd never come back for them; it would be way too dangerous. But we couldn't walk through Havana with them. All of the trouble we'd gone through to get them, all of the money we'd spent, the bruises—had all been a waste. Worse, they cost us my submachine gun, as well as several dozen bullets.

I wished I'd spent the night at the bar, communing with the good Dr. Bombay. I would have been way ahead.

The far side of the courtyard opened into another underpass leading to the neighboring street. Red and I paused in the middle to regroup, straightening our clothes before going back out on the street. Some of José Martí's blood had splattered on my shirt. I took it off, balled it up, and threw it down. My black T-shirt reeked of sweat, but at least there was no blood on it.

Red looked a little worse for wear herself. She'd torn both knees of her jeans, and sported a black eye.

"If we run into the police, we'll tell them we're lovers and just had a quarrel," Red said as we walked. "They'll believe it."

I'm not so sure they would have, but fortunately her theory was never tested. We hopped on the first bus that passed.

It was only after it began moving again that I realized it was going the wrong way—back in the direction of the accident. We held our breaths as the damaged bus came into view. But the police waved the driver past the tangled remains. We stayed on for four more stops, then got out and found another bus that took us right to our hotel.

The newspapers didn't carry any stories about the explosion in the heart of Havana's black market, nor did Doc and Trace's minder mention it when she showed up to take them to breakfast that morning.

The minder's name was Margaret "Maggy" MacKenzie. She gave a cock and bull story about how her great-grandparents had come to Cuba as immigrants from Ireland around the turn of the century, had settled there and done relatively well for themselves. Their descendants had worked hard and become, as she put it, "privileged." But their consciences bothered them greatly, and when the Revolution came they had wholeheartedly welcomed Fidel and the party.

Not a word of the story was true. We'd put Junior to work checking Maggy MacKenzie's background with our Christians in Action friends, and had found, surprise, surprise, that they had a fat dossier on her—and not just because she "escorted" a large number of journalists on their visits to the country.

Maggy MacKenzie had gone to Cuba in the 1980s from the U.S., by some accounts an idealistic college girl and by others simply a young woman looking for a little excitement and danger. Instead, she had found romance, at least long enough to get pregnant. But the father abandoned her; then her baby died in childbirth. Either convinced that socialism was the best blueprint for mankind, or too ashamed or depressed to go home, MacKenzie eventually got a job with the government as a low-level clerk.

The Christians in Action weren't sure exactly when she got involved with the Cuban security apparatus; they would have known about her from the very beginning, but at what point they took a real interest in her wasn't clear. In any event, she had become a translator, then a media specialist, gradually winning more important assignments. She was now a party member and highly trusted, or she wouldn't have been ushering documentary makers and newspeople around Havana.

The fact that the Agency had that much detail on Maggy MacKenzie indicated that they had probably tried turning her into a spy at some point. We don't talk about things like that, though. Presumably, it didn't work, or her file would not have been available.

Presumably.

Breakfast at the hotel featured an array of Danishes that would have made Shotgun weep. Trace doesn't have much of a sweet tooth and stuck to coffee. Even Doc passed on all but a single rum cake.

"Not hungry?" asked MacKenzie.

"Gotta watch my weight," he said.

"You? On a diet?"

There was a certain twinkle in her eye. As breakfast went on, it became obvious that she had a bit of a crush on him. Doc and Trace began using that to their advantage. The original plan had been for Doc to plant a series of small surveillance bugs as they went. When it became obvious that MacKenzie was going to spend a lot of time talking to him, Doc handed the bugs off to Trace, and she began placing them,[23] leaning against a wall here, a loose shoelace there. She could have taken a video camera from her purse and nailed it to the wall opposite the main entrance of the building, and MacKenzie wouldn't have noticed. Doc took great pleasure in explaining how his camera worked—an explanation I would have loved to hear, since he typically can't explain how a razor works, let alone something complicated.

What Doc can do is talk your ear off, and he talked MacKenzie's into his pocket.

Just for the record, I should note that his wife—Donna—is absolutely a saint . . . unless someone messes with her man. Let me put it this way. Donna, who retired as a navy senior chief, would cut the heart out of anyone who put their hands on her husband. And she would do it with *great* precision, as she was a corpsman . . . or *corpse*man, as the case may be. You don't mess with Ms. Donna.

Doc knows this, of course, and even in the name of duty he's careful where to draw the line. But even Picasso would have been jealous of the line he drew with MacKenzie; in short order, she was leading them through the building, discoursing on the alleged virtues of the island's supposed democratic-socialist system. Trying to keep herself from gagging, Trace asked if she could interview the cabinet secretary.

MacKenzie's voice betrayed more than a little doubt when she said it might be arranged, but Doc ignored that.

---

[23] If you've ever been on a tour of the Christians in Action HQ at Langley, you'll remember the display case in the main corridor with actual "bugs" used during the Cold War. A couple of them are the size of pencil erasers. The new generation bugs are even smaller.

Ours are better.

"We should check the lighting then," he said. "To make sure I can shoot. I wouldn't want to waste your time."

"My time is your time," answered MacKenzie.

"Great," said Doc.

God help me, thought Trace, but she kept her mouth shut as MacKenzie took them down the hall to the cabinet secretary's office on the first floor. The secretary's office consisted of two rooms. The outer room, generally occupied by an aide, was used as a waiting area, with a couch at one end of the aide's desk and some files at the other. There was a simple key tumbler in the doorknob not much more sophisticated than what's found in the average home in the States. There were no alarms.

The aide seemed to have gone out for a cigarette or was on some errand, because the outer office was empty. The door to the secretary's room was closed.

"Lighting's not that good here," said Doc, shaking his head regretfully. "Maybe in the inner office?"

"I'm afraid the secretary can't be disturbed," said MacKenzie.

"He's in there?" said Trace, starting for the door.

"I'm sorry, no," said MacKenzie, her voice halfway between command and alarm.

She touched Trace's shoulder, trying to stop her; Trace flashed a look so venomous that Doc was sure she was going to belt her.

"I'm just knocking," said Trace. "No harm in asking."

MacKenzie gave her a dirty look, but Trace is the queen of dirty looks, and the glare was hardly enough to keep her from trying to get into the room. But the cabinet secretary was not in.

"What about Provisional President Castro?" said Trace, using what was then Raul Castro's official title. "Are we going to have a chance to interview him?"

"He's a very busy man."

"Maybe we could see his office," said Trace. "To check the light."

"We'll worry about that if he agrees to an interview," said MacKenzie. Her tone made it clear she wasn't going to even ask.

After a medicinal session with Dr. Bombay, I had a brief but refreshing nap, then got up and strolled around the neighborhood surrounding our two-star hotel, which was located on the outskirts of Havana's tourist area near the Old City. After a brief constitutional—during which I determined we were not under surveillance—I bought a few newspapers and ordered a coffee at a small café next to the hotel.

José Martí's death in the car accident had been ignored by *Granma*, the party's official paper, but it hadn't been entirely kept from the press. A small item appeared on page five in the *Hoy, Havana*. (The name means *Today, Havana*. Like, *get a move on*.) The destruction of the bus was tied into the explosion in Havana's black market shadowland the night before. According to the police, a dispute between different bourgeoisie criminal elements had erupted in an all-out war. José Martí represented one faction; the story ended before naming the other.

Inquiries were being made, said the reporter. At least one arrest was imminent. My money was on the public official whose car we had stolen, which of course had been found at the scene. He might have an ironclad alibi, but you'd expect that from a wily criminal.

"Hey, don't I know you?" Shotgun asked, walking up to my table.

I gave him a frown and gestured for him to sit down. I hate being interrupted when I'm reading the paper.

"I'll have like the biggest cola you got. And what sort of, like, cupcakes do you have?" said Shotgun to the waiter when he arrived.

I helped with the translation.

"Mongoose just checked in," Shotgun said when we were alone. "Doc and Trace are still on tour. Nothing exciting going on."

I put down the paper and leaned back in my seat. My sixth sense—the trouble alert that goes off when something is screwed up—was bothering me. I couldn't pin it down though. I definitely trust my instincts—you don't get a scarred carcass without learning a few things you can't explain, even to yourself. But I couldn't get my unconscious to cough up the problem.

I tried focusing my mind on the problem of weapons, which we still lacked. Assuming we couldn't pick up the AKs and my MP5—and that was a *good* assumption—we were down to four submachine guns, the ammo in them, and three spare magazines. We had six pistols, and enough spare bullets for a dozen magazine changes, give or take a loose bullet or two.

Resupply through the black market was out of the question; the area would be under a virtual lockdown that night.

In theory, we wouldn't need weapons for the op at Party Headquarters; it would be a finesse operation from the get-go. But they would be nice if and when Mr. Murphy intervened and the shit hit the fan.

"Penny for your thoughts," said Red, strolling over. She looked almost demure, wearing a sleek blue dress that clung to her curved but trim hips. She slid into the seat across from me looking as fresh as if she'd spent the last two weeks alternating bubble baths with downtime on the beach.

"His thoughts are worth a dollar," said Shotgun. "Probably more. They're always costing someone somewhere something."

"You're very profound, Shotgun."

He laughed and looked up at the waiter, who was just approaching with rum cakes so soaked with liquor that they smelled as if they would spontaneously combust. Shotgun's eyes opened wide, and a grin grew on his face.

"Better bring more," he told the waiter.

"What else did we use that credit card for?" I asked Red. "The one Sean used for the rental?"

"Should have been just the rental," she said.

"Mmmm."

That was standard operating procedure, but there was always a possibility that there'd been a slipup somewhere along the way. It was the sort of detail Mr. Murphy loved to take advantage of.

"How else can they trace that car to us?" I was talking out loud, but I was really asking myself.

"They can't," said Shotgun. "We didn't even get gas."

"Worst case, they can trace it to Sean, and he's out of the country," said Red.

I mentally ticked down all of the other possibilities I could think of. Not finding one that positively linked us, I let it go. I had to trust that the gears in my brain would turn up whatever was bothering me eventually.

Experience showed that they would. Though whether they would do so in time for me to deal with the problem rather than react to it was an open question.

(1)

The external doors and windows in the Party Headquarters Building were protected by a standard burglar alarm system, which would sound as soon as a connection was broken. Backing those up were motion detectors in some of the hallways and rooms. Getting around the system wouldn't have been too difficult, but it would have taken considerable time, and still left the surveillance cameras and guards.

So I decided we'd get in through the bathroom.

More specifically, through a small exhaust fan above a washroom at the rear of the auxiliary building attached to the back of the main structure.

The fan was somewhat similar to those used in American homes, except that the fan vented directly to the flat roof above it. Trace had confirmed this fact during a break on her tour, even noting that there were only four bolts holding it in place. She'd also placed video bugs both inside and outside the lavatory that we could watch to make sure the way was clear. There were stairs a short distance down the hall; as an extra bonus, this portion of the hallway was not protected by a motion detector or any other sort of security device.

In short, the fan was the perfect entry point.

Almost.

Bathroom exhaust fans tend to be on the small side. The ones here at Rogue Manor—put to good use daily—measure just over a foot diagonally. The fan in Communist Party Headquarters was industrial-sized, but even when it was removed, the housing was barely big enough for a person to squeeze through.

Red could make it. Trace, if she squeezed her assets together, would just fit. None of the rest of us had a chance.

And that's how it became ladies night at Communist Party Headquarters.

Doc and Trace began the evening at the Parade Room, a corrupt bourgeoisie restaurant owned by the Cuban government in the heart of the business district. Since it was owned by the government, naturally prices were triple what they might have been anywhere else in the universe. A hundred and twenty euros for a piece of strip steak? That's a rip-off even if it's called Steak *Libre*.

Trace excused herself just before dessert, claiming woman problems and saying she'd prefer to skip the night's worth of bar-hopping they'd already planned. MacKenzie gave her a sympathetic nod, then turned and smiled at Doc.

"But we can go on, no?"

"Absolutely. We're going to see Hemingway's hangout, yes?"

"The Bodeguita del Medio, first. Then La Floridita for daiquiris."

She mentioned a couple of the other bars.

"Join us if you feel better," Doc told Trace.

"Tomorrow, maybe," she said.

Trace bent forward a little as she walked from the table, hamming it up just a bit. She walked down the block, certain she was being followed—not just by Mongoose, who was her protective shadow, but by a plainclothes Cuban security officer as well. That was good—we wanted him to follow her all the way to the hotel room. Trace adjusted her speed to make sure he had no trouble.

The hotel room was bugged—again, something we put to work in our favor. Trace moaned and groaned, got some aspirin from the desk, drew a bath, turned on the television, and fell asleep.

Maybe not sleep-sleep. It only sounded like sleep, thanks to the small digital recorder she left playing on the bed, right next to the bug. Meanwhile, Trace went out the window and climbed up to the roof above. While the plainclothes shadow pulled up a seat in the lobby—he would stay there for another two hours before heading home—she met Mongoose around the block.

Red and I had already completed a recee of the Headquarters Building. It turned out that the disturbance in the black-market district the night before played in our favor. The Cuban authorities were determined to stamp out what they perceived as a turf war, and flooded the area with police. Most of the patrols that ordinarily sat on their thumbs outside the Party Building and in the nearby streets were assigned to sit on their thumbs near the black marketeers. A single uniformed car was parked near the front of the building, its driver fast asleep.

Inside, there were only two security men, who took turns making hourly patrols of the entire building, starting in the basement. They followed a strict pattern and walked very slowly, making it easy for us to use our video bugs to track them.

The bugs that Trace and Doc had planted transmitted a very weak signal that was collected and amplified by a device the size of a paperback book, which in turn relayed them to a receiver station.

If we'd been in the States, I would have put the monitoring station in a van, staying mobile a few blocks from the building. Unlike what you've seen on TV and in the movies, I didn't need much space. The monitoring equipment was a battle-hardened laptop that weighed all of eight pounds; the receiver was even smaller. The laptop screen could show me several images at once, and software in the unit could be set to alert me to sudden noises or different shapes in the video stream.

But while vans are pretty common in the States, they're not nearly as common or readily available in Havana. Given all of the complications of the night before, I decided that instead of going through the hassle of obtaining one, I'd simply locate my tactical headquarters in a nearby building. The one I selected had the added bonus of providing a clear view of the rear grounds of the Party Building. It did this because the building had no back wall.[24] We rendezvoused there just before midnight.

Trace changed on the way over and like Red was dressed in classic black. She rouged her face with some burnt cork, dulling the highlights.

"Takes ten years off," I told her.

"Fuck you very much." She turned to Red, who was similarly attired. Both had their gear in black body-hugging rucks and belly packs. "You ready?"

"Yup."

The ladies went off and I settled down in my new *palacio*, clearing off enough of the crumbling cement and debris on the floor to sit without putting a permanent pimple in my delicate derriere.

"Dark eyes, this is Spider," said Shotgun, who was driving a scooter on the street. He would make the rounds while I was helping the others, making sure no one jumped on my back while I was doing the same for them. "Snow White and Evil Stepsister just passed by."

---

[24] A photo of a similar building was recently posted on Google Earth, if you're interested. Search "Rooms with a view of Plaza de la Revolución" in *Habana*.

"Good. Copy, Spider."

Trace had picked the code names. She called herself Snow White, saying she liked to work against type.

The park behind the Party Building provided cover for all but about ten yards of the approach. The final ten yards were lit by spotlights at the top of the building. After crossing through this space, Trace and Red would hug the building for no more than twenty-five feet until they reached a low set of trees at the southeastern side of the auxiliary building. From there, the shadows as well as the angle of the main building and the nearby trees would give them plenty of cover.

I lost sight of them after they cleared the open space, but I could hear Trace's hard breath over the radio as she ran. They made their way to a low roof at the rear of the auxiliary building, then climbed rungs installed in the masonry by workers who needed access to the air conditioners on the roof.

Their first order of business was to visit the air-conditioning unit that served the main part of the building. They pulled out the fuses, then went over to the smaller wing at the rear where the fan was located. Red put a lighter to the tar covering the connectors holding the assembly to the flashing and roof as she isolated the screws.

"Phillips head," she told Trace. "The tops are pretty beat."

"We better drill them."

Trace took the RotoZip and went to work. But halfway through the second screw, the tool began making the noise your car battery makes two weeks out of warranty on the coldest morning of the year.

"Fug," said Red.

Either Mr. Murphy had used the tool for an all-night battery-draining house-building party, or I had broken it when it fell at Fidel's bunker. They tried to use a standard Phillips head, but the screws were too stripped for that. So they went to their backup, a folding hand-cranked drill. Someone who was really skilled with it might get through wood reasonably fast, but going through metal with it was a different story, even with the finely polished bits they'd brought along. They drilled, hacked, and pulled, spending more than ten minutes per screw—not exactly the way we'd planned.

Red had just dropped into the restroom when the guard started his round.

Which wouldn't have been a problem, if he hadn't decided to start at the back of the building, breaking the pattern he'd used every other time we'd watched.

And on the second floor, which was the top of the annex where Trace and Red were.

"Snow White, the Big Bad Wolf is in the stairwell. I'm not sure where he's going," I warned, watching him on the monitor.

"Is he coming here?"

"Affirmative. He's walking pretty quick. He's at the corner."

That was less than ten feet from the restroom. Trace flattened herself on the roof and waited.

The reason he'd started here became clear a moment later, when he pushed into the women's room. Apparently he'd decided the men's room was too far, and he needed a seat for what he had to do anyway.

Red slipped into the stall, one foot on the toilet seat, the other bracing the door as the lights turned on. She held her breath, praying silently that the guard wouldn't choose her commode.

He didn't—but he did go into the one just next to hers. He sat down and went to work.

The fan apparatus was too heavy to put back quietly. Fortunately, the hole was out of eyeshot from the guard's stall.

Red practically gagged as the guard grunted and hissed. Job finally done, he started humming. He flushed twice, washed his hands, and went out.

"Better put your oxygen mask on before you come down," she whispered to Trace.

While the ladies were engaged in chemical warfare, Doc and his date hoisted a few in the name of Ernest Hemingway. Hemingway—his connection to Cuba predated the Revolution—was as much a drinker as a writer, and the two devoted fans of literature followed closely in his footsteps as they surveyed the slightly dowdy though well-preserved bar where he had allegedly completed many of his drinking masterpieces.

Doc spiked his Scotch with large amounts of water and ice, but made sure to ply MacKenzie with rum and Cokes that were very heavy on rum, getting her as sloshed as possible.

"Can you dance?" she asked as the waiter brought another round.

Where most Cubans' English deteriorates in inverse proportions to the amount of liquor they drink, MacKenzie's got better. Her Cuban accent faded and a distinct midwestern twang entered her tongue.

"I'm not much of a dancer," said Doc.

"We should dance." MacKenzie got up and took his hand.

"There's no dance floor," said Doc.

"We can make our own, come." She wrapped herself around him and began rocking back and forth.

"Maybe we should go somewhere else," suggested Doc.

"A wonderful idea!" MacKenzie let go, raising her hands excitedly. "Your hotel is only a few blocks away."

"I meant a better place to dance."

"We can dance there, no?"

She flashed her best bedroom eyes. Doc didn't want to go back to the hotel, since Trace wasn't there, and he was worried that MacKenzie might somehow find out.

He also didn't want to go back because he valued his marriage . . . and his life. Some lines can't be crossed, even in the name of duty.

"There'll be plenty of time for that," he said. "First. Show me the sights."

MacKenzie frowned, but quickly regained her enthusiasm.

"The sights! Yes!" She pulled him from the table toward the door. "Let's get a taxi. We'll see the nights. The *sights*. At night. Night sights."

"Why don't we take a walk around?" said Doc.

"We'll walk on the beach! Come on."

MacKenzie sobered up as they walked out of the bar, and Doc went on his guard. He thought she was being genuine—but it had been quite a while since anyone had tried to pick him up, and now he wasn't sure whether he was being played. He didn't have his radio and wasn't wearing a bug. Mongoose was watching him somewhere but he wasn't sure how close he was.

"Let me check on my boss," he said as they came out of the hotel. "I want to make sure she's OK."

MacKenzie clapped his clamshell phone closed as he opened it.

"Don't use your cell," she told him. "It goes through the Cuban phone company. They make up dummy charges. The socialists ripping off the idiot capitalists."

"I don't mind," said Doc, growing more suspicious. "I'm not the one paying."

"No, no, no. *No.* She's fine. Look, there's a taxi. Come on."

Mongoose had followed them out of the bar and got close enough to see Doc's worried expression as they got into the taxi. He grabbed his bike, then called me to tell me what was going on.

"I'm not sure where I'm going. I'm on the bike—we're heading down toward the old harbor. I'm about a half block from them. I don't know what's going on. Humpty Dumpty had a funny look on his face."

"Maybe something he ate didn't agree with him," I told Mongoose.

"It looked more serious than that."

"Shotgun, you awake down there?" I asked.

Shotgun being Shotgun, he answered with a mock snore.

"What's up, Dick? Why'd you wake me up?"

"Real funny, asshole. Get on your scooter and go back Mongoose up."

"You sure?"

"Get your ass in gear."

"Halfway there."

The guard took a quick turn around the rest of the addition, then headed upstairs. Trace and Red made their way downstairs to the maze of offices used by the elected officials and their staff. Trace led the way, their path guided by my miner's flashlight. Avoiding the main corridor, which was covered by a motion detector, they threaded their way through the narrow passages until they came to the cabinet secretary's office.

Trace made quick work of the locks. She checked the door at the inner office for electric current—a telltale sign of a burglar alarm. When she saw it was clear, she nudged the door open, not entirely trusting the electronic gear. But the room wasn't wired at all.

They checked the desk. The bottom drawer was locked by a combination lock similar to a safe's. With the help of the stethoscope, Trace had it open inside of three minutes. Aside from some papers and certificates, the drawer was empty.

Red had stopped riffling the drawers on the other side, examining a paper instead.

"What are you doing?" Trace asked.

"This is a list of criminals of the state," said Red. "They're all politicians.[25] They're going to be arrested and executed when Castro dies. Look at what it says—*eliminate*."

"We don't have time."

"This is important."

"It's not what we're here for."

Red was wearing a miner's-style flashlight on her head. When she looked into Trace's eyes, she nearly blinded her. "This is important. This is valuable."

"Watch your light, for christsakes."

"I'm sorry."

"Take pictures," Trace told Red.

"I can use the copy machine. It'll be better."

"Go."

Trace, annoyed, went through the rest of the desk. The DVD wasn't there. Nor was it in the two file cabinets nearby. The document of state enemies to be killed was nearly fifty pages long, and Red was still copying it when Trace finished.

"Come on, let's go," said Trace.

"Don't be so testy."

"Fuck yourself, testy," said Trace. "We have to finish before the guard makes his next round. Kick butt and let's go."

Red continued to copy the pages.

"Let's go!" hissed Trace.

"Relax. I'm almost done."

"Forget almost."

"What's bothering you?"

"We're running late."

"Something else is bothering you."

"You're just slow. Come on."

Downstairs, the guard had returned after his rounds. He and his companion got into an argument about one of the local baseball teams, and within a few minutes the second guard grew so animated he rose and started cursing his companion. Then he turned and began walking away.

"Where are you going?" demanded the first guard.

---

[25] The list referred to political officials and aides connected to the Cuban national congress only. I'm not sure how many names were on it, but the type was small and the pages full.

"Doing the rounds."

"It's too early."

The Cuban shrugged.

"Snow White, the guard is starting his rounds," I warned. "Looks like the standard—"

That was the last word I got out of my mouth. Just at that moment, I caught the shadow of something running across the yard toward the building. I rose, but I was too late to see who'd entered.

"Trace, Red, sit tight," I told them, pulling off my headphones. "I'll get back to you."

I slid the laptop against the wall, closing the lid almost all the way to reduce the amount of light. Then I grabbed the submachine gun and hopped to the doorway.

Was the person whose shadow I'd seen the only one who'd come in, or was he simply the only one I'd seen?

I edged out into the hall, trying to hear any sounds below. Most likely, whoever had come into the building was a vagrant. But it could also be the police.

Shotgun was already halfway to Old Havana to back up Mongoose and Doc. I was on my own.

Something fell to the floor of the first floor, a rock, maybe, slapping against the concrete with a muffled crack.

I eased over to the staircase and lowered myself to my haunches, trying to see below. The angle was too steep, so I started down the stairs, moving slowly but steadily, twisting my neck over the rail.

Whoever had entered the building was moving toward the stairs. His feet began shuffling upward, moving quickly.

A second set of footsteps fell in behind him.

I reached the floor below the one where I'd been sitting. Slipping from the stairwell, I tiptoed through the hall to the nearest room, then went down on one knee, the staircase just in view. A faint shadow appeared, bobbing upward. It had something in its hand, a pistol, I thought.

Raising the MP5N, I waited.

Faithful readers as well as devout practitioners know the MP5N as a relatively quiet weapon. The sound that comes from it is more a metallic *shush-shush* than the loud bang traditionally associated with a rifle or other gun. Still, it's not whisper-quiet. Someone on the street below might not hear it, but anyone in the building would.

I'd have to grab his gun. I had only one spare mag of ammo with me.

Whoever was coming had stopped trotting and was now trudging slowly. The shadow grew, and then a face in the darkness.

It was a kid, eleven or maybe twelve.

With a gun in his hand.

(II)

The kid stepped off the stairs onto the landing. For a second, he looked as if he was going to grab the banister and head on up to the third floor. But instead he stopped and turned, looking right at me.

"Okay, son," I said, in slow, curse-free Spanish. "Put the gun down. Now."

The kid froze, but only for a second. Then he started to lift the weapon.

The right thing to do in that situation, the only thing to do, is to shoot the little bastard, even if he is only eleven or twelve years old. Because he has a gun, and it's either kill or be killed. Shoot first, ask questions—never.

And that's what I should have done. That's what you should do if you find yourself in a similar situation.

But instead of doing the smart thing, instinct took over and I threw myself forward, flying across the ten or twelve feet between us like a rocket leaving a launch pad. I hit the kid square in the chest. The gun went flying, and so did we, falling down the stairs into the kid's friend, a girl nine or ten. We tumbled down the stairs together, smacking our heads against the wall and steps.

The gun tumbled down with us, landing right next to the boy. Fortunately, he was so stunned that by the time he went to grab for it, I had it.

No, it wasn't fake. That would put a nice little bow on the story, but this isn't a story with a lot of ribbons.

The gun was a .38 caliber revolver older than me, let alone the kid. But it was clean, freshly oiled, and the bullets I took out would have put very nice holes in my carcass.

Trace and Red had just closed the door to the auxiliary staircase when the door above opened and the stairwell flooded with light. Trace pulled Red under the stairs with her and pulled out her pistol. The guard mumbled to himself as he clambered down the steps, complaining about his companion's lack of baseball knowledge.

Both women held their breaths as he came down and walked right past them. As the door swung closed, Trace started to get up, but Red grabbed her, some sixth sense telling her it wasn't safe.

Sure enough, the door swung back open a second later; the guard had decided that a precursory glance up and down the darkened corridor—there hadn't even been enough time for him to locate the light switch—was all that was necessary. He shuffled back up the steps, his grumble becoming less severe as he rose.

Mongoose had done his best to keep up with the taxi with Doc and MacKenzie, but the driver had stomped on the gas as he reached Malecón, the wide street that ran around the seashore. The street was as wide and smooth as a superhighway, and with almost no traffic on the road he shot so far ahead that Mongoose lost him.

Shotgun, approaching from the other direction, cut down a cross street, aiming to cut him off.

"What color is the car?" Shotgun asked as he reached the inter-section.

"It's a white cab, a legal one," answered Mongoose. "It was moving like a bat out of hell."

"Don't see it."

"Maybe he got past you already. He was *moving*."

"Yeah."

Shotgun gunned his scooter westward, the direction the cab was taking. The coast was lined with large buildings and a scattering of houses, nearly all luxurious. Shotgun followed all the way to *5ta Avenida Tunel de Malecón*, a tunnel that ran under a finger of water where the sea pierced Havana's west end.

"Man, don't you have a clue where they went?" Shotgun asked. "I don't see him anywhere."

Worried that Doc was in serious trouble, Mongoose pedaled down near the seawall, found a place to stop, and after checking to make sure no one was nearby, took out his sat phone and called him.

"What the hell are you doing with this gun, kid?" I asked, holding the weapon up.

The kid made a face, then tried to duck past me and get away. I grabbed him and threw him against the wall. I like spunk in a kid—I was a pretty lively brat myself—but this was way over the line.

"What's with the gun?" I asked again.

"Please, senor, don't hurt us," said the girl, still back in the stairway. "We were only going to kill rats."

"Why?"

"For dinner."

It took a few minutes and some candy bars to get to the full story. The kids were cousins, not precocious lovers. The girl had found the gun in her father's bureau and told the boy; the boy thought they should use it to kill the rats they had seen in the nearby building.

For fun or food, I wasn't exactly sure which. They were skinny enough for it to be the latter.

"What's you father do?" I asked the girl.

"He is a policeman."

"You think you could shoot off a bunch of his bullets and he wouldn't notice?"

The kids gave me the blank look kids give every adult when confronted with their stupidity.

"Do you have any more bullets?" I asked.

The girl shook her head.

"Turn your pockets inside out," I told them.

I'm not sure whether to blame Murphy or bad parenting, but the kids were a complication that was hard to deal with. I didn't want to let them go, since there was a good chance they'd run home and tell the girl's father what had happened. On the other hand, if I kept them here, there was always the possibility that their parents would wake up, realize they weren't home, and come looking for them.

"Where do you live?" I asked.

The boy gave me an address so quickly it was clear that he was lying.

"What would happen if I take you there right now?" I asked. "And told your father what you did?"

"Please don't, senor. Please," said the girl.

I looked at the boy.

"Or maybe I'll just take you down to the police station," I said to him.

His lip quivered a little, then he got control of himself and put the tough-shit look back on his face.

"So?"

"If I stole a gun out of my father's drawer, my backside would have hurt for a week." I gave them the gun back, but kept the bullets. "Get the hell out of here."

"What about the bullets?" said the boy.

I threw them out of the open part of the building. "Go find them."

Doc may have been in trouble, but it wasn't the kind of danger Mongoose was worried about.

MacKenzie had the driver take them out to Laguna Salinas, a suburb of the city about fifteen miles to the west. She knew a beach there complete with palm trees and everything except for salsa music.

They weren't quite halfway there when Doc's phone rang. Their agreed protocol was to act as if it was a wrong number; Doc would give his location as best he could.

"Carlo, where are you?" asked Mongoose in Spanish when Doc clicked on.

"Excuse me?" said Doc in English. "Who is this?"

"Carlo?"

"You want directions for where? Malecón?"

"Where on the Malecón?" said Mongoose.

"I don't understand what you're saying, OK? Who are you? You're looking for directions to the Malecón?"

"Is that your producer?" asked MacKenzie.

"No, it's some drunk Cuban asking where the Malecón is."

"Give me the phone," said MacKenzie.

"No, no, let me practice my Spanish," said Doc. *"Donde esta?"*

"Havana," replied Mongoose cautiously. He'd heard MacKenzie in the background, though the tone of her voice confused him.

Or maybe it was just the slur of her words.

"You go west," said Doc, trying to give hints without being too obvious. "Then you will find the beach. I mean, Malecón. Shit, I said that in English, didn't I?"

Doc was stalling, trying to think of a way to give him the control words that indicated he was OK, when MacKenzie suddenly grabbed the phone from his hand.

"Don't bother with him," she said drunkenly. "We should be alone tonight."

Then she threw the phone out the car window.

———

The kids ran down to retrieve the bullets. I trotted upstairs to the laptop, flicking through the images to find the guards in the building. Trace gave me an earful when she was finally able to answer my radio call. I didn't bother explaining.

"You have a clear path up to King's Castle," I told her, using the code word for Raul's office.

"No shit."

"I wouldn't shit you, Snow White. You're my favorite turd."

"Hah, hah."

Trace appeared on the screen, edging around the corner in a crouch, then striding quickly in the direction of the hall that led down to Raul's hideaway. Red was right behind her.

"Listen, I have to move," I told Trace when they reached the building. "I'm going to be off the air for about five minutes. Don't move until I'm back. You have fifty minutes before the next round."

"Are you personally guaranteeing that?" asked Trace.

I didn't answer. No sense giving Mr. Murphy another excuse to kick me in the butt.

Mongoose and Shotgun worked their way down the Malecón, hunting for the taxi that had taken Doc. But there were so many places to check, and so many crossroads, that they soon realized it was hopeless. After roughly a half hour, Mongoose tried calling Doc again. But all he got was Doc's voice mail.

Doc, meanwhile, was facing one of the most perilous situations he'd ever faced, a life or death situation.

Or maybe just lust or death.

MacKenzie slipped the taxi driver twenty euros to wait, then got out of the car and led Doc down to the shoreline.

"Isn't the night perfect?" she said. Then she dropped all pretense, along with her skirt.

"I'm happily married," said Doc.

"No problem." MacKenzie wrapped herself around him.

Doc did what came naturally . . . to him, anyway. He started talking . . . and talking and talking and talking, until MacKenzie passed out, either from inebriation or exhaustion.

At least that's the story Doc tells, and for the sake of his marriage, I won't question it. Once MacKenzie was slumbering peacefully, he put her over his shoulder and packed her into the cab. When they got back to Havana, Doc told the driver to deposit her at Villa Marista—state security headquarters.

"Villa Marista?" The driver was more than a little apprehensive.

"That's where she works."

"At this hour?"

"They're expecting her. Just leave her with the guard at the gate," said Doc.

"But . . ."

"They'll know what to do."[26]

Shotgun and Mongoose were about ready to go over to Villa Marista themselves and tear the place apart looking for him. But after being dropped off at the hotel, Doc used the phone to call one of the Canadian phone numbers we'd arranged to forward to Junior. The Cubans were undoubtedly eavesdropping, so the message he left was short and sweet.

"Busy day today, honey. Going to bed."

Junior snickered, then called Mongoose.

"He's all right," he told him.

"He's all right where?"

"Back at the hotel."

"You sure?"

"I'm looking at the number."

"What was he doing?"

"You can't figure it out?"

"Doc? No way."

Junior changed the subject. "How are you guys doing out there? Do you need help?"

"We're fine, Junior. Just fine."

"Work on Dick, for me, would you? I need to get out in the field."

"Uh-huh."

Mongoose had seen Junior in action in China and Korea, but he thought he still needed some seasoning.

Shotgun needed seasoning as well, but of a totally different kind.

"Cool," said Shotgun, when Mongoose told him that Doc was OK.

---

[26] There is a completely different possibility—that Doc did partake of the minder's charms. But saying that would get him in trouble with his wife.

"Come meet me over here near the Malecón. There's an all-night stand selling roasted peanuts. They smell great."

I'd told Red and Trace to wait until I relocated to our backup lookout spot, but that had about as much effect as telling the wind to stop blowing. They slipped down to the basement and found Raul's hideaway office. Getting past the magnetic switch on the door was simply a matter of jumping the foil contacts; Red found the contact by tracing the current, then slipped a thin metal and wire jumper into the jamb. Picking the lock was nearly as easy.

The motion detector was more difficult. The first problem was finding it without setting it off. Red knelt by the door, poking a telescoping optical wand inside to look for it. The scope had a very narrow viewing range, and it took quite a while for Red to find the detector in the opposite corner of the room, even though it was roughly where she expected to find it.

Like most motion detectors, the one guarding the basement offices was actually a heat sensor. Depending on how good the alarm is, it's often possible to defeat a motion sensor by moving toward it very, very slowly. But that takes Zen-like patience, a quality neither Trace nor Red had in abundance.

Another way to defeat them is to slowly warm the room until it's close to body temperature. We had killed the AC on the way in to make things easier, but the building had only reached eighty-two degrees, not nearly warm enough to fool a mediocre sensor, let alone the pretty good ones I figured Fidel would use. Warming the entire room another sixteen degrees would take quite a lot of oil. And the detector was too far from the door to use a device that would slowly heat the air around it, Bunsen-burner style.

So the next best option was to cool down. Way down.

Once she found the unit, Red donned what looked like a puffy chem suit, then pulled the lanyards on two canisters of compressed gas, turning herself into a walking ice cube.

Ice cubes aren't seventy-eight degrees, but you get the basic idea. With the suit inflated, Red walked slowly toward the detector. Once she was underneath it, she reached up and undid the shield protecting the infrared detector. A piece of clay did the rest.

Past experience had shown that with all that effort expended protecting the outer office, it was highly unlikely that there would be anything guarding the inner door. Still, they couldn't take that for granted. Trace checked for a circuit running along the doorjamb. Before putting her pick into the lock, she tried turning it gently.

It wasn't locked.

That didn't mean there wasn't a motion detector inside, though. Red and her cold suit eased into the room.

"No detector," she said. "Lord, I'm freezing. And I gotta piss."

"There's a soda bottle right there," said Trace.

There were several soda bottles, as a matter of fact. The room was a mess. There wasn't much furniture: a pair of couches, both covered with thick Spanish red leather, flanked the small room, and a single desk stood at the side. A stereo and a television were propped on a table in the corner. Official papers were scattered around the desk, and piled high on one of the couches. The floor was littered with empty bottles, coffee cups, and newspapers.

The first thing they checked was the television, but there was no DVD player there. While Red sorted through the papers on the couch—mostly routine legislation and proclamations designed to reinforce the Communist Party's rule—Trace went through the desk. The drawers on the right side were all locked with individual locks. After checking to make sure they weren't wired with an alarm system, she slipped her pick and spring tools into the bottom drawer. It stuck a bit, testing her patience as well as her technique. When she finally got it, she found it was filled with cigars.

The next drawer had some envelopes and stationery. The top drawer had an appointment book in it. She put it on the floor and started snapping photos.

"It's not a total loss," said Trace when she was done. "We know he's a slob."

They backed out of the office, hitting the detector with a blast of cold CO_2 to cover their retreat. Down the hall they followed essentially the same routine at Fidel's office, getting past the alarms and rifling everything they could find to rifle.

Meanwhile, I'd relocated to the roof of an apartment building two blocks from the first. This one was taller and had a slightly better view of the Party Headquarters Building, but was occupied; I had to be quiet as

I snuck up the back stairs. Once I had everything set up, I checked back in with them.

"You have ten minutes until the next rounds," I told them over the radio. "Assuming they stay on schedule."

"Thanks," said Trace. "We're in *el Jefe*'s office. Still looking."

Fidel's office was the exact opposite of his brother's, without a paper out of place. Its only furniture was a thickly padded leather chair. There was no safe, no television, and definitely no DVD.

"Maybe it's hidden in the upholstery," suggested Trace.

"No, it'll be easy to get," said Red.

"How do you know?"

"I know."

"There's only one way to find out." Trace took her knife, picked the chair up, and cut the bottom out. The disc wasn't there.

"How are we going to fix it now?" asked Red.

Trace walked out to the small secretary's office without answering, then returned with a stapler. She stapled the bottom back together, then put the chair back where it had been.

"Let's get the hard drive," said Trace.

"Are you sure?" asked Red. "Dick said the guard's going to make his rounds soon."

"I know what Dick said."

Trace relocked Fidel's door and went to the secretary's desk. We'd discussed the possibility of stealing the hard drive, even though we weren't sure what sort of intelligence it would provide. Naturally, it would be discovered missing as soon as the secretary came in the morning. But since the DVD hadn't been in the building, alerting them to the break-in wouldn't compromise the overall mission.

Besides, it was too good to pass up.

The computer at the side of Fidel's secretary's desk was a Lenovo—once made by IBM, now a Chinese owned and controlled conglomerate. Trace got down on her knees, put the computer on its side, and unfolded the unit like a book.

Just about then, the guard started his rounds. He was a few minutes early, but the growing heat in the building annoyed him. I heard him tell his companion to check the thermostat again, and if it didn't work, to go out and check the AC units.

"Snow White, Stepsister, time to move," I said. "The wolf is on the prowl."

The computer was open on the floor, but the hard drive was still attached to its rail.

"How much longer?" Red asked.

"The screw is stripped," said Trace. "I'll have to drill it out."

"The battery in the drill is dead."

"Then I'll just rip the damn thing apart. Give me a screwdriver," said Trace.

The guard, meanwhile, passed our last video bug and headed down the stairs.

"Snow White, Stepsister, he's huffing and puffing," I warned.

"Damn," said Trace.

She may have said something else, but if so it was drowned out by the siren below.

III

When I'd let the kids go, I figured that they would spend a little time looking for the bullets, then sneak back home, replace the gun, and tough out whatever inquisition the father put to them when he discovered the bullets were gone—two or three days from now.

I was counting on the kids being devious. Those who steal guns out of their parent's bureau drawers usually are.

What happened, apparently, is that one of the kids ran home and spilled the beans. And then instead of thrashing the kids to within an inch of their young lives, the man who owned the weapon called up his comrades at the force to go out and look for me.

Yes, I will shoot them next time.

Three police cars sped past my building, pulling up near the one I'd left. I could hear more sirens in the distance.

My options were limited. I was already at the far end of the range of the system supplying the feed from the video bugs; if I relocated, I'd be useless to either Trace or Red.

Of course, getting arrested wouldn't particularly help them either.

I decided to sit tight for a while. It was the right thing to do, even though lights were flashing all over the street below.

In Fidel's office, Red doused the light and froze near the door. Trace crouched behind the desk, the computer open next to her.

They assumed that the guard would try the door and then move on. Otherwise he'd set off the alarm, something we hadn't seen or heard him do.

But we all know what happens when we ass-u-me something.

Red nearly fell over when she heard the guard's key turning in the lock. Then, either out of brilliant inspiration or just because she didn't know what else to do, she grabbed the small knob of the lock with one hand and the handle with the other.

The guard couldn't turn the key. Thinking he'd picked the wrong key, he pulled it out from the lock and examined the others on his chain.

In the ten or twelve seconds it took him to get another key and try it, Red reached down and grabbed the foil tape that jumped the alarm, then bolted from the door and on her tiptoes raced to the desk, tapped Trace to follow, and together they hid in Fidel's inner office. They closed the door, locked it from the inside, and crouched by the couch.

The guard tried several keys before settling on the right one. He opened the door to the outside office, stuck his head in, and flicked the light on. Trace, her MP5 ready, went over the route she'd memorized as the quickest way out.

The guard hesitated a moment, then flicked the light out and left.

"Thank God for lazy guards," whispered Red, collapsing against the wall.

Trace jumped up, listening at the door to make sure the guard had actually left. She gave him a full minute, then eased back out. Red collected herself, then followed.

"Just tear the damn thing out," she told Trace.

"Relax. Now we have plenty of time. We can't move until he gets back."

Red sighed.

"That was smart of you, jamming the lock," said Trace.

Red wasn't sure how to take that. It was the first time Trace had actually offered her a compliment.

Our video bugs didn't show the panel at the security desk, so there was no way to know if the security system was actually working or not. That wasn't a problem for the door alarm—the women could easily jump it on the way out—but what about the motion detector?

What about it?

It wouldn't be a problem, unless the guard at the front desk was watching very carefully.

"You didn't check the president's office," he said over the radio, scolding the guard making the rounds. "You're supposed to go inside."

"I did."

"Don't lie to me."

"I'm not lying."

"You are a liar and a lazy bastard."

The two men argued for a few seconds more. The guard making the rounds wasn't pleased—but he still turned around and retraced his steps.

Trace pulled the last screw from the rail and removed the drive, then pried the wire connections loose. She pushed the computer back together carefully, then rose to go.

"Snow White, the wolf's on his way," I told her over the radio, seeing the guard passing on his way back to the basement. "He's coming back into Fidel's office because the motion detector didn't go off."

Red was already at the motion detector.

"Hit it with the CO_2 and let's move," Trace told her. "*Come on.*"

Red sprayed the sensor, then put the cover back. But her hand was cold, and it slipped out of her fingers to the ground. She hopped down—she needed a chair to reach comfortably—grabbed it, and tried again.

"Come on, come on," said Trace.

Red snapped in the cover. She left the chair in the corner and bolted to the door. They slipped out and got around the corner just as the guard came down the steps.

"I thought you'd go back," radioed the Cuban covering the security station.

"Not because of your threats," said the guard, continuing toward the office.

Yes, gentle reader, the alarm *did* go off before the guard went inside. Congratulate yourself on being a step ahead of the security detail.

But only a step ahead.

"Get the hell out of there. Now!" I told Trace and Red as soon as I overheard the guard. "Go. Go!"

"We're going," said Trace.

"Watch out when you come out the back," I added, warning them about the police in the area.

"Are you in trouble, Dark Eyes?" Trace asked.

"Always," I said. "But I'm OK at the moment. Head east when you're out."

"Copy. We're on our way."

Red and Trace were climbing onto the roof when the guard opened the door to Fidel's office. It must have been just about then that he realized what his comrade had said earlier. He picked up his radio and called the desk.

"I'm at Fidel's office."

"Why'd you go back?"

"Is the alarm on now?"

"Yes."

"Did it just go on?"

"A minute ago. When you radioed."

"Something's wrong. Very wrong."

On the roof, Red replaced the fan and slathered roofing tar on the screws, making it look as if it hadn't been disturbed. Then she joined Trace, who was scouting an escape route from the side of the roof.

"The police are right up that street there," said Trace, pointing about a block and a half away. "We'll have to cut across this way. Take the face paint off. Try to look normal."

Red took out her Handi Wipes and swabbed the black off her face. But there wasn't time for them to change into civilian clothes—two of the police cars were heading in their direction.

"Snow White, Stepsister, get off the roof now," I warned, watching as the patrols moved toward the northern end of the square. Another car came up—the police had decided to search the woods behind the building for the pervert who'd bothered the kids.

Trace and Red got off the roof, but they were barely a dozen steps away from the building when a pair of headlights arced in their direction. They threw themselves behind a low wall, hiding as first one and then two more service trucks rolled up not six feet away.

But it wasn't the police. They were the air-conditioner mechanics, called to look at the HVAC system.

That sound you heard was me, being hoisted by my own petard.

Sixty seconds later, a security response team and the shift supervisor arrived at the front of the building, called out by the security guards because of the motion detector.

Trace radioed me and said they were stuck.

She didn't know the half of it. The supervisor had just called in a full alert. Following their standard paranoid procedure, the building and its grounds were about to be locked down and searched, inch by inch.

"What should we do?" Trace asked me. "Can we go back the way we came?"

"Negative," I told her. "Hang tight until I think of something."

"Start thinking real fast," said Trace. "They're all around us."

[IV]

Even if Trace and Red hadn't been virtually surrounded, it would have been time for me to leave my post anyway. The police were going door to door, looking for anyone who had seen a bearded child pervert who looked vaguely like Fidel, and sooner or later they were bound to come to the apartment building.

Sooner, actually—I could hear people below looking out their windows and asking what was going on.

I got Shotgun on the horn and told him to get back up here on the double.

"Sure thing, boss."

That wasn't exactly what Shotgun said. His mouth was full of food, so what he said sounded more like, "Mrumphg gaw cutsuck." But that was close enough.

I made it down one flight of steps when I heard a door opening below. People flooded out from the apartment, heading for the front. I did a one-eighty, slipping down the hallway. But it turned out to be a dead end, blocked off by two apartments.

If you can't beat the police, join them.

I knocked loudly.

"*Poliza!*" I yelled, in the threatening guttural tone that works so well on the highway patrol. "Open up!"

There was no answer. That was even better—I put my shoulder to it and thumped.

All I got was a bruised shoulder. Breaking doors down is a lot harder in real life than it looks in the movies.

I'll hit my head against a wall all night, but not the rest of my body. I turned and began knocking on the next door.

"Police! Quickly!" I yelled.

This time, I heard the rumble of footsteps. A large, fairly rotund man pulled open the door.

"They're escaping!" I yelled, dashing into the apartment. "The fire escape! Where's the fire escape?"

A woman about the same age as the man but rail-thin pointed a trembling white hand toward a window at the right, just past the kitchen.

I ran to it, threw up the sash, then bolted onto the fire escape outside. I ran down two floors, then went over the rail, jumping to the sidewalk and running up the street.

Two blocks away, I found a house with a garage very close to the road. Ducking behind the bushes, I pulled out the radio and went back online.

Shotgun was two blocks south. I gave him directions.

"Take me just a minute, Dick. Gotta duck some of these police cars."

"Well get moving. Trace and Red need us."

"Too bad we can't take a cop over there, huh?"

"Hold that thought, Shotgun. Hold that thought."

Police cars are absurdly easy to steal. For one thing, cops almost always leave their keys in them, especially when responding to a possible crime scene. For another, put three or four of them together in a bunch, and no one will notice that another is missing.

After Shotgun picked me up, we circled around to the far side of the police activity, then closed in on their exposed flank—a pair of police cars parked a few feet at the northeastern end of the block.

"Hot shit!" said Shotgun, slipping from the scooter. He ran to the car, hit the button for lights and sirens, then laid some rubber as he accelerated away.

It took a few seconds for the police to react. Then there was a mad scramble for the remaining cars.

"Snow White, Prince Charming has just kissed the frog," I told Trace and Red. "Get the hell out of the castle."

Meanwhile, Shotgun was re-creating the classic sixties movie *Bullet*. He took the car down the wide boulevard, feinted toward the cemetery—the gates were locked or I'm sure he would have driven through—then made a beeline for the Malecón. Thirty yards after reaching the highway, he slammed the brakes on and jumped out.

He was still laughing his head off as I sped up on the scooter. It's nice to see someone who really enjoys his work. He hopped on the back and we took off west, leaving the scene just as the light of the first police car began flickering at the bottom of my rearview mirrors.

As soon as Trace and Red saw the cars zipping by, they ran south through the park, crossed Avenida de La Independencia, and then worked their way through to Calzada de Ayestarán. There they got into one of the rental cars we had stashed for an emergency, and after a sufficient series of switchbacks and a quick change of clothes, rendezvoused with Shotgun, Mongoose, and me in a tiny after-hours café overlooking the harbor.

"Wow, where the hell have you been?" said Mongoose as they walked in. "You look like shit."

Trace gave him the evil eye. Red collapsed in the chair next to me. Shotgun laughed, then went and got another round of drinks.

When the girls revived, we compared notes. Despite all the fun we'd had, the mission had been a bust. The missing DVD was still missing.

"Not entirely a bust," said Red. She took out the list of people to be arrested when Fidel died. "This may be useful."

Not to be outdone, Trace pulled the hard drive she'd stolen from her pocketbook. "Fidel's secretary may have trouble using his machine tomorrow."

I slid the hard drive into the pocket of my tourist-issue sport coat—yes, I'd changed, too—and ordered another Sapphire.

"Maybe the drive will tell us where the DVD is," said Red. "If we could put it into another computer."

"Good thinking, Red. We'll get it to Junior and see what he can come up with."

"Ya oughta have him come to us," said Mongoose. "He's going stir crazy in Jamaica."

"Shotgun will take it to him on the first flight out we can find," I said.

"Why me?"

"Because your Spanish is the worst of the bunch," I told him. "And besides, they'll never find it in all the food you carry."

Shotgun grumbled a bit, but made the 6:15 A.M. plane to Mexico, transferring to another aircraft that flew him over to Jamaica. The hard drive was encrypted, but defeating the encryption was as easy as blowing a little cold air on it.

Nitrogen oxide, actually.

The encryption in most computers, especially personal computers, uses a set of chips to apply complicated mathematical equations that scramble the data. Basically, the chips act like translators. If you could peek into the chip as it's working, you could figure out the equation that's being used to conduct the translation. Once you know that, you can unscramble the data.

That's the layman's explanation. Junior—and Shunt, who taught him how to do it—make it seem a lot more complicated, talking about nanos and micro-heads and all kinds of crap, but I've watched them do it and it's easier than making ice cream. They freeze the chips involved in reading and encrypting the data, put in a piece of software that Shunt wrote, punch a few buttons, and download the data to a fresh drive. Add a few fancy words to the process and you can make a mint as a consultant to the NSA, affectionately known (or not known, as the case may be) as No Such Agency.

While Red and I took Shotgun to the airport, Mongoose dropped Trace off at her hotel.

She was just about to go through the revolving door at the front when she spotted MacKenzie walking toward the reception desk. Trace quickly turned around and headed for the back door. But as she turned the corner, she noticed someone watching it. Rather than risk being seen, and realizing that by now MacKenzie would have called up to her room anyway, Trace went down the block to another tourist hotel, this one with a retail shop in the lobby. She bought a tracksuit, and after dumping her clothes in a waste can, jogged back to her hotel.

MacKenzie was waiting for her, face red and lips sputtering.

"Where have you been?" demanded the Cuban minder.

"I went out for a jog."

"A jog?"

"What's the big deal?"

MacKenzie began sputtering to the effect that Trace and Doc were guests of the Cuban government and every breath they took had to be pre-approved, stamped, and OK'd. Trace frowned, but didn't say anything. MacKenzie had a hangover of major proportions, but the broomstick that was bothering her undoubtedly belonged to whichever superior had found out about her date the night before.

Doc was sitting on a couch a few feet away, sipping a coffee and doing his best not to laugh. He'd already received an apology from Ms. MacKenzie for "whatever may have happened the night before" as well as a series of embarrassed sighs.

"So, did we get the interview with the president?" Trace asked as the minder ran out of wind.

"There will be no interview with the president," said MacKenzie. "Or the cabinet secretary."

"Maybe we can go over to the Party Building," started Trace, "and find someone to talk—"

"We will not be going over there. The building is off-limits until further notice."

Trace glanced over at Doc. "What will we do?"

"There will be something better." MacKenzie pressed her lips together. "A press conference."

Doc got up and ambled over.

"As a general rule, I miss press conferences," said Trace. "They're pretty boring."

"This one is very important for the future of Cuba," said MacKenzie. "President Castro will attend. And acting President Castro. You will be glad you were there."

An hour or so later, Doc and Trace found themselves in an auditorium with several hundred other journalists, at least a portion of whom were legitimate, though a sizable minority were probably spies. Raul, considerably more sober than the last time Trace had seen him, opened the session with a speech so long and boring that even Fidel would have been bored. And in fact, *el Comandante en Jefe* might have fallen asleep behind stage, since he didn't come out for more than an hour after the press conference began. By then, his brother had ruined his grand opening, and the surprise: *el Jefe* was announcing his retirement as Cuba's dictator.

Journalists are cynical by nature, but not one person in the entire audience snickered. A few may have snored, at least a dozen yawned, but most dutifully noted that this was an historic moment for Cuba.

Fidel's retirement ranked right up with John Gotti's announcement that he was getting out of the gangster business, or better yet, Putin's stepping down as head of Russia. True, something changed, but no one seriously believed that Fidel was letting go. Once you've been king of the hill, no matter how small the hill, you don't go back to being a peon. Even the way Raul kept glancing over at his brother every few seconds while they were together onstage made it clear who was really going to be in charge.

The questions were mostly planted, the answers about what you'd expect. It sounded more than a little like a Nobel Prize ceremony honoring

one of history's all-time great leaders, not the man who took a belea-
guered nation and turned it into one of the poorest in the hemisphere.

The only consolation was that Fidel looked sick as hell. He'd come
straight from the hospital, and according to the rumors Doc heard while
waiting with the other camera crews, was due to go back via ambulance
as soon as the dog and pony show was over. He didn't take any questions,
leaving everything to Raul. He left before the food.

While Doc and Trace pretended to be titillated at seeing the great dictator and his brother in the flesh, Red, Mongoose, and I bumped our way
eastward on a tag team of buses. With each new bus we boarded, the notion that vehicles should ride on shock absorbers and springs became
more and more theoretical. Fortunately, I can sleep just about anywhere
when I have to, and as far as I was concerned the trip was a succession of
twenty- and thirty-minute snoozes punctuated by the occasional poke in
the ribs by a Cuban matron who found my snoring annoying. It reminded me what it was like trying to catch some rest with my first wife.

We arrived in Holguín around five the next morning. After shuffling
to the nearest open restaurant for breakfast, we went our various ways.
Mongoose and I played tourist, renting a quartet of hotel rooms—always
good to have backups—and then checked out the Natural Science Museum and points of more immediate interest, such as the nondescript
shop two blocks from the bus depot where we could get authentic-
looking official documents at a very reasonable price.

Red scoured the city in search of a vehicle she could buy without too
much hassle. She ended up getting a deal on a 1960s-era Triumph motorcycle. It looked like an old Bonneville, though so many of the parts
had been replaced and reworked that its exact vintage was hard to dis-
cern. A new bike called for new clothes, and she spent the rest of the day
outfitting herself before gassing up at the local *servicentro* and taking off
for Baracoa. Using only her GPS and instincts, she navigated muddy,
rutted, and unmarked roads up and down the Sierra Maestra mountains,
until she reached *La Farola*, the Cuban equivalent of a superhighway
connecting Baracoa with Guantanamo province and the rest of the
world.

Yes, superhighway is meant sarcastically.

Twice Red ran off the road, once into a ditch and the other time into
the jungle brush. She got into the city around sunrise the next day, found

an illegal boardinghouse to stay at, and after a quick nap went to survey the town.

By that time Mongoose and I were on our way to Frank Pais Airport, south of Holguín, where we boarded a flight for Baracoa. Cuba's airlines are on a par with Red China's—circa 1958. We flew in a Cubana de Aviación "Aerotaxi" An-2. I can't blame you if you've never heard of the aircraft. It's a Russian-made biplane that would look right at home in the original *King Kong* movie. The cabin is actually spacious—if you're a midget. The plane's single propeller engine—well it is a big propeller—sounded like a washing machine trying to walk its way up the basement steps. My teeth vibrated in sympathy with it as it started, and by the time we were in the air every bone in my body was humming.

Mongoose spent the entire flight with his fingers digging into the seat.

I will say the scenery was interesting. The mountains were spectacular, though generally when I'm flying in an airplane I like to fly *above* the landscape, not below it.

Mongoose knelt and kissed the dirt as soon as we got off the plane. We found our bags, then hired a pair of *campesinos* who offered their truck as a taxi into town.

You wouldn't know it to look at it now, but Baracoa has played a critical role in Western history. Columbus landed here in 1492. Things went downhill for the Taino natives from there. Spanish real estate barons swept in and established the town in 1511, making it the oldest European settlement in the country.

I wouldn't be completely surprised to find that there are still some buildings from then. The town isn't all that much bigger than it was in the sixteenth century. It's certainly poorer. Take away the handful of hotels, and the place would look like a Spanish city circa 1700 or so. That and the crystal-blue water on its beaches are its main attractions these days. The few tourists who come here are searching not so much for old Cuba or to re-create fantasies about the conquistadores or to walk in the surf Columbus and his sailors peed in, but for cheap, rustic isolation.

Which told me that Ken's so-called intelligence on where the missing copy of Fidel's last tape was kept was probably as accurate as the CIA briefings I used to get in Vietnam . . . not worth the paper they weren't written on.

The museum was easy to find. It was right in the center of town, a one-story metal-roofed building whose clay bricks had been aged to make it look just as old as its neighbors. It wasn't quite finished yet, or at least not open. I played dumb tourist and went up, knocked, hanging around for a while before a local woman came up and told me the place was closed. She directed me toward the tourist office. She stopped mid-sentence, wrinkled her nose, and then told me in very thick Cuban Spanish that I looked very much like Fidel.

"Are you his son?"

"Excuse me?" I asked. "I don't really speak Spanish."

"Son, boy—you look like *el Jefe*, the president. Fidel Castro."

"I'm not him."

"Well, you look like him. Be careful."

"I try."

Mongoose and Red had done a complete survey of the area while I was playing tourist. The local police department was small, and looked like it closed up shop when the sun went down. But strangers clearly stood out here, and we'd have to figure that we'd be noticed and probably remembered anywhere we were seen.

"So we go in after midnight," said Mongoose after we met up at the Revolution Hotel on the beach just before dinner. The bar looked better than the one at our hotel—it was actually a bar, rather than a desk with a few chairs in the corner of the lobby.

"How do we get in?" asked Red.

"We sneak in the basement door at the back, assuming Dick's right that there's no burglar alarm."

"What if he's wrong?"

"Dick's never wrong."

Mongoose was so sincere I was tempted to give him a big wet one on the forehead—then kick him in the behind for being either naive or an ass-licker.

Red displayed the proper cynicism, giving a snort even Trace would have admired.

I picked up my rum and Coke. The place was so isolated the only gin available was Polish antifreeze, not worth jilting the Doctor over.

Mongoose continued to lay out the mission, doing a reasonable job sketching a straightforward sneak and peek of an unoccupied and unguarded building.

Just the sort Murphy likes to hide in, I thought several hours later as

I checked around for signs of a watchman. I didn't spot one on my first pass, nor on my second, so I snuck around to the back of a feed store across an alley from the rear of the museum. Then I watched patiently for more than an hour before concluding that the building really wasn't being watched.

Another bad sign, but now that we were here, there was no sense not having some fun.

"I'm on my way," I told Mongoose.

He was watching my back from a roof one block over. Red was sitting at a café across from the police station, which had in fact closed for the night.

I slipped through the shadows and threw myself against the wall of the building. Easing toward the door sideways, I kept expecting something, someone, to walk by on the street or pop out from somewhere I didn't expect. This was all just too damn easy.

No alarm wires on the door. No infrared motion detectors in the hall or upstairs. No alarm. Not even, it appeared, any electricity.

The basement was divided into two large spaces by an L-shaped partition. The outside door led into the inner room inside the L. I flipped on the LED light on my miner's flashlight and started looking around.

A pair of folded workmen's ladders leaned up against the wall next to the door; otherwise, the room was empty. So was the outer room, except for some boxes containing pamphlets and educational material about the museum and its exhibits.

The upstairs front room, which I'd seen from the sidewalk, was nearly as bare. The smell of fresh paint hit me as I came up the steps; it mixed with a musty, stale smell, as if the place had been painted and then forgotten for weeks or maybe months. After checking for alarms—nothing—I walked quickly and on my tiptoes to the hall that ran down the right side of the building all the way to the back. There was just enough light from the windows for me to see, and I continued my cat burglar routine as I walked through.

The front room was devoted to a history of the Cuban Revolution, starring Fidel, of course. The wall opposite the door was covered with a large map of the island, stars and balloons commemorating where different events of the rebellion had occurred. There was a mural on the right, and a diorama on the left showing a guerrilla attack on a group of ill-trained regular army soldiers in 1958.

Fidel definitely deserves some credit for his generalship during the Revolution. He wasn't exactly a quick learner, but he *did* learn. When he started in 1953, he knew as much about small unit combat tactics as your average lawyer-politician. Which is to say, he knew nada.

His first few encounters, including the idiotic attack on the Moncada Barracks in 1953 and the equally disastrous return to Cuba aboard the *Granma* in 1956, demonstrate just how inept he and those around him were. But he gradually learned how to be effective as well as ruthless, perfecting hit-and-run tactics that, while not as sophisticated or as fanatical as those the Viet Cong used, worked a hell of a lot better than anything the Cuban army tried.

Granted, a good portion of Fidel's success had to do with the even more pathetic tactics of the Cuban army, as well as the general ineptness and cruelty of Batista. Still, give the devil his due—he only had to be a *little* better than his enemy, and he was.

What Fidel really excelled at was getting rid of rivals. After the fall of Batista, he consolidated power effectively and brutally. As Red's family could attest, many of those who had fought against Batista found themselves fighting Castro as well. Or rather, would have fought Castro, except that he never gave them the chance.

None of that was in the display devoted to the Revolution. Nor did the diorama note that a lot of the weapons Fidel's men used had come from the Alabama National Guard. And there wasn't room on the mockup of the battle between the revolutionaries and the army to show that the revolutionaries made use of M4 Shermans that had very recently been part of the American National Guard.

Yes, class, the United States played an important role in the Cuban Revolution, though that's an inconvenient fact as far as both the U.S. and Castro are concerned. It's also inconvenient to note that political pressure from foreign governments—including the U.S.—and the Catholic Church forced Batista to release Castro from jail in 1955, arguably the most critical decision if not for the Revolution, then for the Communist takeover that followed.

Castro paid back his debt to the Church by seizing its property in 1961. But I digress.

The back room on the first floor was outfitted as an office. It didn't look as if anyone had done more than arrange the furniture. Two desks, chairs, and empty file cabinets were covered with a fine layer of dust. I searched for hidden doors and compartments, and even went back to the room with the diorama and checked under the table to see if something was hidden there. But clearly it wasn't.

The DVD wasn't the only thing missing. My friend Murphy seemed to be AWOL as well. That bothered me more than the fact that Ken had apparently sent me on a wild goose chase.

Two hours later, we toasted the pointless op with a nightcap back in my room, where I broke into my personal medical kit and partook of some of the Doctor's finest. We'd checked the room for bugs but found none; apparently the eastern tip of Cuba is so isolated from Havana that no one feels it's worth eavesdropping on the tourists here.

"Maybe there is no third copy," said Mongoose. "Maybe Fidel can't count."

"He's not Shotgun," I said.

"Maybe it's a trick though. To throw off anyone who got it."

"I doubt it."

"It could be anywhere, Dick," said Red. She was sitting cross-legged and sideways in the upholstered chair opposite the bed. "Maybe he gave it to one of his children, or maybe Raul's family has it."

I didn't answer. Mongoose and Red started exchanging theories on where the video would be. I wasn't actually thinking about that—I was wondering whether we'd been sent out here because Ken wanted me out of Havana.

It seemed far-fetched, but his intelligence on the other DVDs had been impeccable.

Maybe *too* impeccable?

I was overthinking the situation, but the CIA's history in Cuba made it difficult to trust anyone, especially my old friend the admiral.

About the only person you could truly count on was Fidel—he was consistently a liar and a slime.

"Dick's got it figured out," said Mongoose finally. "He's got that look."

"Do you, Dick?" asked Red. "You know where it is?"

"No," I said, getting off the bed to refill my glass. "But I know someone who does. And it's about time we asked him."

[V]

While we were studying history out east, Trace and Doc were dabbling in the arts in Havana.

The fine arts of eavesdropping and trading information, to be exact.

After the press conference, Trace returned to the hotel to rest up. Doc went down to the hotel club to sample some of their bourgeoisie cognacs.

He was about two sips into a Gautier cognac when he heard a familiar foreign voice at the other end of the bar. It took him a few seconds to identify the language—Russian—but once he did that the rest was easy. The big loud bass belonged to a good friend of his we'll call Ivan.

Ivan is a member of the Russian FSB—that's the *Federal'naya Sluzhba Bezopasnosti*, the foreign spy service once known as the KGB. Among his different portfolios, he's an expert on the Chinese and, as far as we knew, worked out of Tokyo. (We knew that because he had met me there during my Korean adventure, and even helped me out. Kind of.) So the fact that Ivan was here not only surprised Doc but piqued his interest.

Even if Doc had been a Russian language specialist, he was sitting a bit too far away to really hear much of what Ivan was talking about. It was pretty obvious he wasn't happy though—the words Doc could hear were almost all curse words, the one area of any language where Doc might be considered an expert.

Doc suspected he was being watched at the bar by one of MacKenzie's compatriots, but he couldn't figure out who it was. He wracked his brain trying to come up with a way to contact Ivan without tipping off the minder. Passing a note was out of the question; even if it wasn't seen, the waiters were surely on the payroll of the political police. He thought about using that golden oldie of following him into the men's room, but knew they were probably bugged.

So instead he sipped his cognac, quietly biding his time to see if an opportunity presented itself. Doc tried following nonchalantly out of the bar when Ivan left, but the Russian moved too fast for Doc's ambling nonchalance, and the door to the elevator had already closed when Doc got there.

The car stopped at two floors, fourteen and seventeen. Doc made a note of it, then went back to the bar. A few sips into a fresh drink, he got a hankering for a cigar and some fresh air. The bartender sold him a cigar out of the humidor, and Doc decided it was a nice night for a stroll.

A few blocks away, he finally identified his trail, a mouse of a fellow who looked to weigh 110 in a rainstorm. But his slim size made it easy to duck between the shadows, and Doc found him extremely hard to shake. He wandered toward the Malecón, mingling with a knot of Spanish tourists on a cigar tour, but the shadow stayed well within earshot. Doc finally decided to give it a rest—literally, as he went back to his room and pretended to go to sleep.

The Cubans had bugged his room in five different places, including the bathroom. Doc began his usual noisy routine, turning on the television and running the water. Then, he told himself out loud that he was hungry, and needed a snack before going to bed. So he called room service, and had them deliver a cart of french fries and hamburgers. He met the server at the door in his pajamas, made a good fuss, then ate and returned the tray to the hall—leaving the door slightly ajar thanks to a piece of gum wedged into the lock plate. When Doc got ready for bed, he discovered that the door was open and closed it.

Of course, he was in the hall by then. He'd taken the precaution of leaving a voice recorder with some of his mumbles and snores set to run in a half hour to add to the illusion.

Doc tiptoed down the hall to the stairs, then made his way to the roof. From there, he started calling every room on the two floors he thought Ivan might be on until he found him.

Doc got him on the third call.

"The Italian place, for a drink," said Doc, using English since he couldn't trust either his Russian or Ivan's Spanish. "Fifteen minutes."

Doc guessed that Ivan was being watched just as he was. So Doc found a girl[27] a few blocks away, described the Russian to her, and paid her to kiss Ivan on the street and, as she did, tell him to go over to the Renaissance Hotel bar instead.

Ivan had a big grin on his face when he spotted Doc in the far corner of the bar twenty minutes later.

"I thought it might be you, *Americanski*."

---

[27] Yes, that is a euphemism.

He clapped him on the back. When Ivan claps somebody, they generally can't breathe for a few minutes. It's also good to check and make sure your wallet is still there.

"What the hell are you doing in Cuba?" Doc said, signaling for some vodka. "Smuggling in more missiles?"

"No, no, no," said Ivan. "Business is off-limits tonight. We no talk business. Vacation."

Ivan's English tends to deteriorate when he doesn't feel like talking about something.

"Bullshit it's vacation. What the hell are you doing here?" asked Doc.

"I shit you, *Americanski*? You favorite turd. Ha-ha-ha."

Doc stayed with it, gently coaxing, moving off the subject, sharing old war stories—Ivan had been in Egypt for a while—and plying the Russian with vodka. Lots of vodka. Finally, a chance comment broke loose a torrent of abuse.

"Now that Fidel's out of the picture, you think Hugo Chavez is the dictator to beat in the Western Hemisphere?"

Ivan practically spit up his vodka.

"What makes you think that Fidel is really out of the picture, *Americanski*?" he said. (The terms of endearment have been withheld to protect tender ears.) "You believe a man who has been king all his life can walk away from being king? You are foolish. Everyone wants to be king. Today we call president. Same *thing*."

"Even Ivan."

"Ivan especially." He clapped his chest. "Ivan would make great king."

"You're too short," said Doc. "Kings are at least six-eight."

"If I am king, I kill everyone over six foot tall."

"You'll rule a land of midgets."

"Like Fidel, no?" Ivan laughed. "Except that he can't do that with Chavez. Now the student has become the teacher. With his oil, he causes many problems."

"I thought Chavez was a friend of yours."

Ivan practically spit. "Chavez. Venezuela. Do you think this is 1960 all over again? This is the twenty-first century, *Americanski*. Oil. Gas. Energy. He is a competitor. Putin doesn't like him," added Ivan. "That is good enough for me."

Had the conversation ended there, Doc probably would have taken it all at face value. In fact, he was about to change the subject when Ivan continued.

"It's the Chinese who are trying to make a deal with Chavez. The Chinese are the ones starting mischief."

Ah, thought Doc. That's why Ivan was in town. He tried not to show too much interest.

"What are they up to?" Doc asked.

Ivan winked.

"Well?" asked Doc.

Ivan ordered another round. On Doc of course.

"I hate the Chinese," said Doc.

"We drink to that."

"So what are they up to?"

The Russian responded with a saying in Russian that means, basically, go have sex with a barnyard animal, preferably in a blizzard.

"Why is it a secret?"

"You're not so naive, *Americanski*. Tell me about Korea. What did your boss do there?"

"I'll tell you everything if you tell me why you're here."

"Vacation. Ha-ha-ha."

That was all Doc managed to get out of Ivan. He snuck back into his room with the help of a call to room service for coffee, caught a quick nap, then met Trace and MacKenzie for breakfast. They spent the day talking to a half-dozen minor officials willing to walk the tightrope between praising Raul and lamenting that his brother was no longer able to lead the country.

Since their date had gone awry, MacKenzie had grown somewhat chilly, which was just fine by Doc. The big sunglasses she'd donned to hide her hangover remained in place, and Doc suspected she was still feeling a bit queasy. He suggested they knock off early and go for drinks; she begged out.

Operation Wild Goose Chase over, Mongoose and I left Baracoa and made our way back to Havana via plane and bus to Santiago, where we caught the night train east. Red took the train as well, abandoning the motorcycle at the station.

Doc checked in with Junior while we were on the train, and Junior patched us into a conference call. Ivan's interest in what the Chinese were up to didn't surprise me. The Chinese have done a lot in the Western Hemisphere over the past decade besides buying American computer companies. It was also the sort of information that Ken undoubtedly already had, though of course we'd pass it along.

More interesting was Doc's description of the press conference.

"Fidel looked like a ghost," he said. "A pasty ghost, straight out of *A Christmas Carol.*"

"The ghost of commies past, or to come?" asked Junior.

"Both," said Doc.

He was more right than he knew.

Charles Dickens's *A Christmas Carol* has always been one my favorite Christmas stories. The Ghost of Christmas Yet to Come is a bit of a Rogue Warrior himself—fearless and relentless.

Still, it's a story, not something that happened in real life or was ever likely to happen in real life. Not because of the ghosts. There are ghosts all around us, whether we choose to see them or not.

It's the part where Scrooge changes and becomes a nice person. Most people would say *piss off* five minutes after the ghosts were out the door.

Red found us a new place to stay in the southeast corner of Havana, an illegal hotel used almost exclusively by expatriate Cubans visiting relatives. (You can do that, as long as you bring the regime cash and don't make trouble.) The location suggested easy cover stories; Red and Mongoose became brother and sister visiting Pop while I was a family friend along for the ride. It was a good story, but we never used it: the owner asked no questions and stayed far out of our way.

What I had in mind was simple: I'd locate Fidel and ask him where the DVD was. I'd do this by making him think I was him—that he was having a conversation with himself in a dream. To do this, we needed two things: a dose of Demerol or some other sedative, and definitive information on where he was.

The intelligence came first.

Doc said that Fidel had left the press conference in an ambulance. Our first night in Havana, when we were planning on driving around to all the hospitals in the city, the local television station broadcast an exclusive interview with *el Jefe* on the transition of power. They opened the show with a covering shot of the hospital where the interview had taken place. Bingo.

That left the drugs.

During the Cold War, the Western media used to run stories about the miracle of Cuban health care, focusing especially on the wide availability of cheap prescription drugs. The stories were limited to the point of being bogus; you could find aspirin, certainly, but Cuba was about the last place in the world you could get expensive medicines, for free or otherwise. It's not much better today, out in the rural areas especially. Fortunately, our needs could be fulfilled by generics, and we were willing to use any number of substitutes. The most important quality was that they be available at a small clinic, the sort with a friendly staff and almost nonexistent security procedures.

Especially the latter.

I was going to have Trace and Doc ask their minder for a tour of some medical clinics so we could scout some likely targets when a pain in the side of one of our fellow guests at our hotel saved me the trouble. The landlady made an immediate appointment with a clinic a mile away. Now *that* you have trouble doing in America, and I was duly impressed. So was Red, who was in the kitchen getting some tea when the guest came in with his complaint. She volunteered her services as a nurse and shoulder to lean on, and accompanied the man to the doctor.

The clinic was a small building at the edge of a residential area, with a visiting area about the size of a couch. It was clean, smelling more like flowers than medicine, and staffed by two overworked but amazingly friendly nurses and one doctor who looked older than Fidel and mumbled to himself in the hall. Red went into the examining room with the patient but couldn't locate the drug cabinet. But that was a minor concern: there were no alarms and only simple locks on the building's doors and windows.

"It'll take me ten minutes," said Red.

I winced, but it was too late. Mr. Murphy had already heard.

Let me update the status of the rest of our crew:

Junior had taken the disc to the States to get a decrypted copy and then deliver the original to the CIA. Shotgun was en route to Mexico, where he would stand by in case we needed him. Danny had returned to Jamaica, mixing piña coladas and lining up resources for any new contingencies that came up. With the PBM still out of action—repairs were proceeding with the help of our Christians in Action brethren—he'd arranged for an Agusta 109 helicopter based in Havana to be leased to a very wealthy European tourist for sightseeing on the island.

The Augusta was tempting, but we could only use it as a last-ditch backup. The pilot would almost certainly be a former military man, and the few helos on Cuba were all owned by a government company and generally under close control. Those were not insurmountable problems—Trace could fly the aircraft if a gun in the ribs didn't convince the pilot—but it meant our first flight would definitely be our last. And more importantly, we wouldn't be able to count on the chopper arriving with enough fuel to get us back to the States.

Hitting the clinic looked like such an easy job that I decided to let Red and Mongoose handle it alone that evening while I went over and checked the security around Fidel's hospital. If I liked what I saw, we'd go in later that night, just as soon as Red and Mongoose got the drugs.

That meant I had to conduct my research in character. So I spent the day practicing my Fidelisms while watching the recent video of *el Jefe*, courtesy of a download Junior arranged through the sat phone and a borrowed PC. Then with Red's help I made myself up, dying my hair and beard, adding some liver spots, playing with makeup to add the weight of nearly fifty years of communism to my face.

"Don't let the landlady see you," said Red when we were done. "She'll have a heart attack."

The finishing touch was pretend-army fatigues just like Fidel himself favored, purchased by Mongoose at a tourist-only department store. I looked more like Fidel than Fidel himself.

Renting a car wasn't practical, so I borrowed one from a few blocks away. It was an old fellow—a '58 Chevy to be exact—in showroom shape with a church's worth of Santeria statues and icons scattered throughout the interior. It was like driving a Catholic church to the local sock hop, except that the radio seemed only capable of playing salsa.

Fidel's hospital was located in a ritzy area northeast of the city. A bit smaller than most hospitals in the States, it was a brick building eight stories high with a meticulous lawn and a discreet sign that made it clear only the crème of society got sick here.

There were guards just inside the gate, along with an armored car behind them blocking the road to the building. Two more armored cars were parked opposite at the driveway, though I only spotted one soldier near it, and he seemed to be dozing. The entire property was walled off, and there were video cameras at the top.

Perched over the sea, the hospital had its own beach area. Barbed wire ran along the back wall, and I had to assume that there were video cameras there as well.

Obviously the best option was to go in the front door.

Red and Mongoose left the guesthouse about the same time I did, walking and then trotting to a wooded lot a few blocks away. There they changed into their working clothes—basic black—and continued to the clinic.

A jimmy of the window to the rear examining room proved unnecessary—it had been left unlocked. Red went in; Mongoose stepped over to the bushes and played lookout.

Red went immediately to the doctor's office and began poking around. She spent a lot of time unlocking drawers and filing cabinets, but couldn't find so much as an aspirin. She got excited when she found the closet in the hall locked, but the lock turned out to be protecting a vacuum cleaner. She couldn't even find a hypo needle.

With no place else left to look, she went to the receptionist's cubicle and sat down, trying to psych out where the drugs would be kept. An American doctor's office would be awash in samples and all sorts of medications. She knew not to expect that here, but still was convinced there would be *some* medicine somewhere.

While she was thinking inside, Mongoose was watching a set of headlights approaching down the road. He thought at first it was me: the roads had been empty until that point, and I'd said that I'd loop back to pick them up when I was done if I hadn't heard from them. But the car went directly into the lot without stopping.

"Somebody's coming in," he warned Red. "I think it's the doctor. Shit. There's a woman with him. Shit. Shit."

There were about five more shits. By the last, Red had hidden herself in the closet with the vacuum cleaner.

The lights flipped on. The doctor walked to the back, apparently to get something out of his office. He whistled as he went, clearly in a good mood. Whatever he wanted wasn't hard to find, and he quickly returned to the front.

There he stopped whistling. Other sounds of pleasure ensued.

"What's going on?" asked Mongoose over the radio.

"He's examining a patient," answered Red. "It'll be a while."

Not as long as the doctor's friend wished, apparently, and she soon started protesting.

"Another car coming," warned Mongoose as a second car pulled into the parking lot.

A man and two women, all mildly high, got out.

"This ought to be interesting," Mongoose told Red as they walked up the path.

That turned out to be an understatement. The newcomers were apparently expected, and within a few minutes the doctor's friend had absolutely nothing to complain about.

Who says Mr. Murphy doesn't have a sense of humor?

(II)

There were no drugs in the clinic at all, a fact that Red wasn't in a position to determine until close to two in the morning. By then I was back in the hotel, makeup off, sipping a little Bombay Sapphire in anticipation of their return. Even without the orgy and with a sedative, I would have waited until the next night to get into Fidel's room; my plan required a little preparation and I didn't want to rush it.

Though doping Fidel might not be absolutely necessary, dulling the old bastard's senses was desirable. So I decided to take a shot at procuring some drugs myself the next morning when my trick knee began acting up.

A very trick knee, as it only acts up on command.

It did this while I happened to be right across from a small suburban hospital.

I believe the nurse at the desk said something along the lines of, "Get the old coot a cane," and tried to shoo us out. But Red insisted that her gray-haired uncle (my hair was still dyed to look like Fidel's) needed care, and eventually we were shown seats and told the doctor would be with me shortly.

Same thing you hear in America, where it translates loosely into "don't hold your breath."

It meant roughly the same thing in Cuba. After a few minutes, the old coot got up to visit the facilities. Being an old coot, he walked right by the men's room, past a few examining rooms, and into a pharmacy.

Or rather the back room of a pharmacy, which was a hell of a lot more convenient. The narcotics were kept in a screened-in cabinet at the back of the room maybe six feet from the door — close enough so that you could hear someone walking down the hall, but far enough away that you could duck back in time before they saw you.

It was a busy hospital. I ducked back twice before I was able to pick the lock, and three times more before I was able to locate the right shelf.

Because of shortages and bourgeoisie drug company policies like actually demanding money for their wares, the pharmacy was not as well stocked as an American hospital would be. There were a lot of off-brands and substitutions. I never did find the Demerol. But at least part of the reason was the fact that I found something a hell of a lot better, at least for my purposes: $C_{11}H_{17}N_2NaO_2S$, also known as thiopentone sodium, aka Trapanal, aka sodium thiopental, aka sodium pentathol.

That's right, truth serum.

Famous for its ability to elicit information from targets in Cold War-era movies, sodium pentathol is actually just a very fast-working sedative. Whether it has any real ability to get the truth from people is a matter of debate—though it was used to extract information from a confessed serial killer in Nithari not too long ago. I pocketed a bottle, closed the cabinet, and backed out to the hallway, mumbling to myself as I continued my wanderings back in the direction of the waiting area.

"The doctor's ready for you," said Red as I came in.

"Good, let's go."

"You actually want to see him?"

"I'm hoping I can steal a syringe," I told her, passing the serum off.

I didn't get a syringe, but Red did, pilfering it from a tray outside the examining room. Just as importantly, she found two sets of doctors' scrubs. She couldn't fit them both into the large pocketbook she'd brought, and had to make two trips to get them out, by which time I'd received not only a cane and a bandage for my knee, but a fistful of Robaxacet: codeine-flavored aspirin substitute.

I prefer Dr. Bombay's finest myself. But in my line of work, stockpiling painkillers is never a bad idea.

Trace and Doc were booked on a flight to leave Havana for Canada at four o'clock that afternoon. I decided that it would be a better idea if they could delay their departure until midnight or later, just in case I needed Trace to grab the helicopter. Danny found a 2:00 A.M. red-eye back to Toronto, perfect for our purposes. Then Doc went back to the well with Maggy MacKenzie, telling her that he wanted to treat her to a nice dinner as a good-bye gesture.

MacKenzie was wary, but even Cuban thought police don't get to eat out in fancy restaurants all that often, and eventually she agreed that they should have one last meal on Doc's television station.

Playing the imp, Trace asked if they wanted her to get sick again.

"No," said MacKenzie, looking a little pale. "No."

What is the vehicle that never gets turned away from a hospital?

If you guessed ambulance, you've never had an emergency in New

York City or some other place where Medicaid reimbursement rates make treating the sick a losing proposition. The vehicle you're looking for is a hearse.

The beauty of using a hearse to get past a security post is that even the most anal inspector feels uneasy taking a look at the furniture. None of us like to look too closely at our future.

Our hearse was parked at the back of a very fancy funeral home in the Miramar section of the city, at a funeral parlor I'd noted during our garbage run a few days before. Red and I paid them a visit at noon—a few minutes *after* the two proprietors went to dinner.

Red made a show of going up to the door and knocking, just in case we were wrong about the place being empty. I went around back, popped the hood on the ancient Cadillac, and had it started inside of thirty seconds, probably quicker than if I'd had the key.

I picked up Red a block away. We headed over to a building on the outskirts of town where we'd stashed our clothes and gear before boarding the bus to get there. Mongoose was waiting.

There was a coffin in the back. Red went around to the tailgate to take it out; bodies are generally removed from hospitals in a gurney and body bag.

"Holy Mary, Mother of God!" said Red, pulling open the lid on the coffin. "There's a corpse in the box, Dick."

She wasn't kidding. An elder Cuban dressed in a fine suit complete with a slightly wrinkled rose lay in the coffin, waiting to meet his maker.

He looked too comfortable to disturb, so we put the lid back on and gently set the coffin down against the back wall. For all I know, he's still there.

A half hour later, we pulled up to the gate in front of the hospital. The guards gave us a perfunctory search, then waved us through.[28]

We backed the hearse into a spot near the loading zone at the rear of the hospital, then got out and very deliberately took out the body bag and our gear. My makeup kit was inside one of the doctor bags; if anyone asked, we'd say it was to make the corpse look lifelike.

---

[28] I should probably mention that we timed our arrival to hit about ten minutes before the shift change. This way, the next set of guards who came on duty wouldn't realize there was a hearse at the loading dock, and wouldn't be looking for us to leave at any specific time.

The video camera covering the back swiveled twice while we were taking the cases out; whoever was working the security desk had a thing for morticians, or at least short cute ones like Red.

Inside, though, it was a different story. The security guard at the door nodded but said nothing as we walked in. My black suit was a bit tight across the shoulders, and a size and a half too small in the thighs; it made me look extraordinarily stiff—appropriate under the circumstances. Red wore a similar suit, though hers was loose where mine was tight. Her hair was tucked up beneath her cap, and her chest had been restrained so that she looked more boy than girl—a precaution since we weren't sure how common women funeral attendants were on the island.

The entrance fed into a hall that ran to our left and right; elevators were located about midway down each side. The set on our left featured a pair of soldiers in full combat regalia, along with an officious-looking young man with thick rimmed glasses and a clipboard.

We turned to our left, passed the elevator there, and ducked into the stairwell. I leaned against the door, resisting the urge to hum the stripper song as Red quickly pulled her funeral suit off to reveal her nurse's uniform.

"Top floor, let's go," I told her as she slipped on her sneakers and put her dress shoes in one of the suitcases. We double-timed up the steps to the sixth floor. Trace's routine of wind sprints paid off; we reached the top landing without losing our breath. Red adjusted her makeup, glanced at me, then slipped out into the hall.

Our first order of business was to locate Fidel and scout the defenses. We'd guessed that Fidel was staying on the top floor, since it had the best view of the ocean and would be easier to guard, but we'd guessed wrong. Only one of the rooms was occupied. A pale old woman lay in the middle of her bed, covers off, talking nonstop at the ceiling as Red passed by her door.

The only other person on the floor was a bored nurse reading a magazine at a station at the far end of the hall. She gave Red an odd look as she walked down it.

"Wrong floor," muttered Red after going all the way to the end of the hall and turning back around. "I'm such a bird brain."

"Why are you taking the stairs?" asked the nurse as Red started to open the door.

"Exercise."

Red pushed through, shaking her head. A moment later, the door opened behind her.

"You know you're not supposed to take the stairs," hissed the nurse. "If the soldiers see you, you will be fired like Debra."

Fortunately, I'd been waiting at the next landing and was just out of her view. I ducked back beneath the stairs, listening as Red turned and went back.

"God, I forgot," said Red, going back. "I'm trying to lose weight. So I walk everywhere."

"You? Lose weight? You'll be a scarecrow," said the other nurse. "You need some meat to grow boobs. That's how you get the men. And where is your tag?"

Red patted her hip, as if expecting to find the ID tag there.

"It must have fallen off downstairs," she said.

"Now you're *really* going to be in trouble."

"I can't be fired," blurted Red. "What would Papa do?"

"It must be on the stairs somewhere," said the older nurse. "Go look. Be quick and quiet—if you hear someone coming, hide."

Solid advice, under any circumstances.

"Remember—stay away from the fourth floor," added the nurse.

"Of course. I'm not a fool," answered Red, closing the door. She winked at me. "He's on the fourth floor."

I told Red to stay put while I went back down to the first floor and took the elevator up to scout around. There were three other people in the elevator when I got in, all going to the third floor.

I pressed five, then waited. As soon as the others got out, I pressed four, only to find it didn't work.

An elevator key fixed that. More difficult were the two soldiers standing directly in front of the doors when they opened.

"Who are you?" said the one on the left roughly. The other just glared. Both had AK47s in their fists—the cuddly paratrooper model with its folding stock and cute banana clip. "How did you get onto this floor?"

"Here for the body," I said.

"Out, out, you're on the wrong floor."

I glanced around, pretending to be lost. Another pair of guards stood at the nurses' station in the center of the ward. The second elevator was located just beyond them. This was set up as a checkpoint, with a small table and a functionary who was apparently reviewing potential visitors to see if they were on Fidel's must-see list. A small group of these lucky duckies stood in a line behind the table, apparently queued up to enter Fidel's room, which appeared to be the second from the end on the right.

"I asked you, how did you get here?" repeated the guard. The men from the nurses' station began approaching, and I decided it was time to go. I stepped back into the elevator, letting the doors close. The soldier hit the elevator button to reopen them, but I had left the key in the control panel and quickly overrode his command. They slapped shut and I dropped to the first floor, where Red was waiting when I stepped out.

"Someone's coming down the stairwell from the fourth floor," she whispered.

"They're looking for me," I told her. "Let's go down to the morgue."

The elevator had already begun to ascend, so I walked down the hall toward a second stairwell. When we reached the basement, we spotted a pair of bored soldiers at a card table across from the elevator. They were paying considerably more attention to their game of dominoes than anything else, but we'd taken only two steps from the stairs when one of the soldiers rose and barked after me.

"Where the hell do you think you're going?" he said.

I heard him get up. Then I heard the much more distinctive sound of an AK47 being locked into firing position.

Funny how certain sounds stay with you.

I turned around, pointing to myself. My cap was pulled down over my face, and I kept my eyes focused on the floor. Red kept walking.

"Yeah, you, jackass," said the soldier, obviously a very sensitive type. "You're not supposed to use the stairs. Who the hell are you?"

There are several words for undertaker in Spanish, many with quite an elegant ring to them: *dueño de una funeraria, empresario de pompas funebres*—anything along those lines would have done. Unfortunately, I couldn't remember any of them.

"I said who the *hell* are you?" demanded the Cuban, as patient as he was polite.

"I'm here for the dead," I told him.

"Dead? You are here for your own funeral."

It took an act of sheer willpower not to tell him I was here for his or, more to the point, reach to the back of my waistband, pull out my PK, and deliver the oratory.

"What the hell are you doing?" said Red, stomping back to retrieve me. "Do you think we can keep bodies lying around all night and day until you decided to show up? Do you understand what an important hospital this is? This is the most important hospital in all of Cuba! And what are you? You are an ant, a bug, a cockroach."

I turned toward her, mumbling an apology.

"You're not even dressed properly," Red scolded. "Your shirt is not buttoned. You are a slob!"

"I was just telling him that myself," said the soldier.

Red scowled at him, glancing up and down. "Your pants need pressing," she said, dismissing him before turning back to me. "Come along. Do you think the body will keep in this heat? Perhaps you would like to join it?"

"Yes, sister."

"I am not your sister! God help the poor devil who would be related to you. If I were her, I would pay to be orphaned completely from the family."

"Wait just a second," said the other soldier, who'd been quiet until now. He got up from his table and walked over to me. Then he lifted the hat off my head. "Look at him. Look."

"What are we looking at?" said the other Cuban.

Red slipped her hand toward her back, reaching for her gun, sure that I had been spotted as an imposter. But I could tell where the soldier was going, and shook my head ever so slightly to warn her off. The soldier walked over and pointed at my face.

"He looks very much like the president, doesn't he? A little younger," added the soldier. "But not much."

Thanks for the compliment, kid.

The first soldier took a closer look.

"He looks as much like Castro as I look like George Bush," he said.

"Perhaps I should shoot you then and get a reward."

"Stop fooling, you asses!" Red grabbed hold of my hand. "Come on! You have work to do inside."

The soldiers didn't dare follow as Red and I walked down the hallway and turned the corner. It took only a few minutes to explore the rest of the basement. Two rooms were packed with surplus equipment, old beds, mostly, but also some medical carts and assorted machines that probably predated Batista. Another four rooms were mostly empty, with a few desks, chairs, and odd scraps of furniture piled high with dust. The mortuary was the largest of the rooms and sat at the back of the hall. A pair of rolling hospital beds stood near the center of the room. A large metal gurney stood over a large drain next to them.

"We have no corpse to wheel out," said Red, checking the refrigerator on the wall. "That may be a problem when we leave."

"I'm sure we can find one if necessary," I told her, glancing back toward the hall. "Plenty of candidates."

(III)

Now that we had the interior of the hospital mapped out and Fidel located, the next step was to wait for an opportunity to get to him. At the moment, there were too many people on his floor.

"How long can we wait?" Red asked as I began changing into the khakis.

I've waited days in a jungle for the right moment to make an ambush, but in this case the wait should only amount to a few hours.

"You bored already, Red?"

"Being this close to the bastard gives me the creeps."

"Good thing you don't look like him, huh?"

While we were mapping out the interior of the hospital, Mongoose settled into position to watch the outside. We'd found an apartment building roof nearly a half mile away with a view of the checkpoint at the driveway, about half of the front of the building and all of the side.

"Bunch of VIP cars coming up the driveway," he told us when we checked in with him. "Guards just waving them through. Armored car sitting tight. Everybody seems pretty nonchalant."

"They've been doing this for a while," I told him. "That's exactly what we want."

"What are you going to do if he dies while you're in there?"

"Take his place."

"Heh. What's the first thing you do? Free rum for anyone over the age of twenty-one?"

"It'd be a start."

Mongoose wasn't the only one who was fantasizing about Fidel's death. After helping me apply my makeup, Red stepped back and got a good look at me.

"You look just like him," she said. "Just like the bastard."

"Thank you."

"Why is he still alive, Dick?"

"Good genes, I guess." I shrugged.

"No. Why the hell didn't we kill him? The CIA—why didn't they do it?"

"They tried."

"Not very hard. You know they didn't try very hard at all. They could have gotten him if they wanted to. They should have. You know how many lives he's ruined?"

I really didn't have an answer for her. The attempts by the CIA had come very early on in his reign. As part of the settlement of the Cuban missile crisis, the U.S. had privately agreed not to invade the island and, at least from what I've seen and heard, not to kill Fidel. But after Oswald killed Kennedy, all bets should have been off. You don't have to believe that Castro actually sent Oswald on the mission, or even that he had anything to do with it. The assassination provided the perfect excuse to liquidate Castro. The Soviets would never have dared to bring their missiles back on the island. Countless Cubans would have been better off.

Was there a conspiracy? Is there any truth to the theories that someone inside the U.S. government made a deal with Fidel to get Kennedy, and in exchange laid off the dictator?

I'm not the one with the answers, only the questions.

But Red had the biggest question of all, at least for me.

"What if we kill him, Dick?" asked Red. "What if you slit his throat when we go up there. Once he tells you where the other DVD is, and what his surprise is."

"That's not in the mission statement."

Red frowned. For a moment—but only a moment—she looked just like Trace.

"This isn't personal," I told her. "This is a job. Killing Fidel is not part of it."

"What if it's by accident?"

"There's no such thing as accidents."

"Murphy might do it. He's been known to show up at just the wrong time. Who will care?" she continued. "It's not like we're agents of the government. We're not breaking any law against assassination."

"We'd be breaking the law of unintended consequences," I told her. "And we're not going to do it."

Killing Fidel before we knew where the last disc was would be worse than foolish for many reasons, not the least of which was the fact that it would mean our mission would fail. But Fidel's death would also unleash whatever deathbed surprise he had planned, something the country clearly wasn't ready to deal with.

Even if neither of those were factors, however, killing Fidel might do the near impossible: make him a martyr and hero. Our travels around the country had shown that he was a lot less than that now. Cuba's future depended on her people's ability to get beyond Fidel and the past; martyring the son of a bitch would make that many times harder than it was already going to be.

Not that I wouldn't have enjoyed squeezing his neck until his eyeballs popped out of their sockets.

I started to explain all this to Red, but stopped as I saw her eyes moving past my head and over my shoulder. I turned, and saw one of the guards standing in the doorway.

"Mr. President!" he said, catching a glimpse of my face. He stuttered, and started to back out.

"Halt!" I commanded in the sharpest Spanish I could conjure. "Come here."

Face white, he gulped and walked toward me, AK47 at his side. He started to mumble something: an apology or a question, though a prayer would have been most appropriate—but Red slammed the side of her pistol into his head. People usually don't collapse like a house of cards, but this soldier did, falling almost straight down and flopping arms and legs on the floor. Red gave him a sharp kick on the back of the head, smashing his forehead against the concrete with enough force to shatter his skull.

It didn't make a lot of sound, but I thought it might alert his partner. Grabbing my blackjack from my nearest bag, I ran over to the door and waited for him to come in.

Five minutes later, I was still waiting. In the meantime, Red had trussed the unconscious soldier, put a gag around his mouth, and hoisted him to a gurney.

I love strong women.

"Go call his friend inside," I told her. "No use taking the chance he'll phone upstairs for help."

Red nodded, fixed her uniform, then went out into the hall.

"We need help back here," she told the soldier. "The undertaker passed out."

"You're a nurse."

"Yes, but I can't lift him to the table. And your friend isn't strong enough, either. He said he needed you."

"Probably he's too lazy," said the soldier, who nonetheless seemed happy to show off. He practically swaggered down the hall behind Red, body swaying as he walked.

Which was convenient. I've always found moving targets easier to hit.

Mongoose kept tabs on the VIP visitors, watching who left the hospital and letting us know as Fidel's guest queue wound down. I lay back on the gurney, waiting for the last one to leave so Red could wheel me up and we could get the op moving.

Maybe we could take out Fidel, I thought. Maybe there was a way to make it work, damn the risk of a boomerang.

While my mind was chewing that big sucker over, something of much more immediate concern popped into my head.

The credit card.

Red looked over at me. "Dick?"

I sat up.

"Give me the sat phone. I need to call Danny."

Doc and Trace were just sitting down to dinner with MacKenzie when Doc's sat phone rang. Not wanting to talk in front of MacKenzie for obvious reasons, he glanced at the phone screen and announced that his wife was calling.

MacKenzie looked relieved.

Excusing himself, he made his way out of the room and then out of the building through a side door, looking for a spot where he could talk.

"Where are you?" asked Danny when he called him back. "You're not at the airport, are you?"

"I'm outside the restaurant. What's up?"

"Don't use those plane tickets. The credit card that was used to reserve the car that Dick and Red trashed was the same used for your flight. I'm trying to get new reservations now but it's not easy. Supposedly all the flights are booked—when the hell did Cuba become so popular?"

Actually, the link was slightly more complicated—Sean had reserved the car with a card issued from a Canadian bank to one of our dummy corporations, Planet Documentary Media. We hadn't used the same card for Trace and Doc's tickets—but the corporation had one other credit card account, a Visa card that, yes, was the one we used to pay for Trace and Doc's connections in and out of Havana.

It hadn't clicked until I was lying on the gurney, thinking of killing Fidel. The mind works in mysterious ways, but at least it works.

"Are they on to us?" Doc asked Danny.

"Probably not. But—better safe than sorry. Get the hell out while the getting's good. Take the helo if you have to. Or go to ground. Your call."

I'd released Doc and Trace from backing me up; Danny was telling him to use his best judgment to get the hell out. Doc thought about it for a few moments, then decided the situation wasn't dire. He hadn't gotten any indication from MacKenzie that the Cubans were on to him. She'd been no more or less standoffish than she had the day after her drunken fiasco. He decided that if they had made the connection, the Cubans surely would have questioned them by now—if they bothered to ask questions before locking them up. The most prudent thing to do was to hang out and do nothing to alert MacKenzie. There'd be time to decide what to do after dinner. They could take an alternate flight if Danny got one, or go to the airport and get the waiting helicopter and use it to escape. In the meantime, they'd still be available if I needed backup.

Back to the table, Doc watched MacKenzie carefully, trying to see some hint of what she might be thinking. At the same time, he waited for an excuse to get Trace alone and tell her what was up.

As soon as Mongoose gave us the heads-up that Fidel's last visitor had gone, I lay back on the gurney, pulled the covers up over my beard, and turned my head to the side. I was wearing a cap over my head and a surgical mask: I was saving my good looks for Fidel.

"You should lose some weight, Dick," snapped Red as she pushed the bed toward the elevator.

"You'd do better if you took the brake off."

"Ha, ha."

She pressed the button for the top floor. We had the elevator to ourselves, but not for long. Two doctors got in on the second floor, talking about a baseball game they'd seen a few nights before. Red had fixed her hair, but her top was still strategically arranged, and I doubt they even noticed I was in the car.

They got out one floor below Fidel's.

"Hold it here a minute," I told Red as the doors closed. "Let's stop at Fidel's floor and take another peek at the security layout."

"Are you sure?"

"Trade a peek for a peek," I told her.

Red flushed, but undid another button on her blouse. The elevator lurched upward to the next floor.

"Remember to keep your mouth shut," said Red.

"Thanks for the pep talk."

The elevator doors opened. We started out, then stopped abruptly as a soldier put his chest in the way of the gurney.

"What are you doing?" he demanded.

"I'm bringing a patient," said Red.

"Not on this floor."

"No?"

Red glanced to her left, acting confused. More strategically, she gave the soldier a nice glimpse of cleavage.

"I do have the wrong floor, don't I?" she said, backing into the elevator. "This isn't the sixth, is it? How did the elevator stop here? It's not supposed to. I definitely pressed six."

The soldier stared so intensely at her I could feel the heat until the doors closed.

"No line," reported Red. "There are only two guards now on the door. A couple back by the nurses' station and one at the elevator we just opened."

A different nurse had come on duty since Red had visited last. This one wasn't quite as matronly, but she was bored, and came over as soon as Red wheeled me from the elevator.

"Sssh. He's sleeping," Red told her, pushing the gurney past.

"But—"

The nurse stopped midsentence. She had caught a glimpse of my face; even with the mask, I looked like Fidel.

"Is it—? Is it—? Is it—?" she stuttered.

Red nodded. "It's too noisy downstairs with the visitors. He needs rest. You're to say nothing. No calls. Do nothing unusual. Nothing—or it will be both our heads, I'm sure."

"Yes, yes, of course," said the nurse.

"He's to be left entirely alone," said Red, pushing me to the room opposite the stairs at the far end of the hall. "Is this room ready?"

"Of course. All the rooms are always ready for patients."

The nurse went down the hall and opened the room on the left. Red

247

pushed me in. They spent a few minutes tidying up, then Red convinced the duty nurse to go back to her post.

"She's gone," Red whispered finally.

I got up and smoothed my khakis and put on the campaign hat.

"Very scary." Red shook her head. "Give me a minute to talk to the duty nurse. Then I'll go to the cafeteria and get a plate for the soldiers on Fidel's floor. It may take a while."

"The Revolution has forever to evolve," I said.

"It's a good thing I know who you really are," said Red. "Or I'd shoot you."

Was I a little nervous?

Hell no. Little doesn't *begin* to cover it. The butterflies in my stomach were the size of linebackers. The water poured out of my sweat glands as ferociously as the Niagara River over the falls in early April.

My plan was audacious, aggressive, and over the top. *Way* over the top.

My kind of plan. No one in their right mind would expect someone to sneak into the hospital and pretend to be Fidel Castro. Which made it the most obvious thing for me to do.

A minute or so later, I heard Red laugh. That was my signal—I opened the door and ducked quickly across the hall to the stairs. I slipped into the stairwell, then down the steps, moving as quietly as I could and barely breathing. The hypo with Fidel's truth serum was in my pants pocket; my PK was in the holster at my right.

The door to the stairs was at the far end of the corridor, two rooms beyond Fidel's. I sat down on the third step and waited.

It took Red nearly a half hour to find the cafeteria, get some food, and return. There's no trouble with waiting except for the waiting . . . and the thinking, and stomach juices that go with it. I tried not to think and willed my stomach to stop grumbling. No yoga master breathed deeper or more slowly than I did, sitting on those steps.

And then suddenly I heard a woman's voice in the hall—Red's.

Laughing, she said, "Come now, eat something," loud enough for me to hear.

It was my cue. I rose, took one last slow breath, and stepped out into the hallway.

(IV)

First step — through the door.

Second step — in the middle of the hall. Two soldiers, twenty feet away, leaning over a tray of treats Red had just brought.

Leering over a treat Red had just brought.

Third step — Fidel's door.

And in.

My heart rate must have increased a hundred beats with every step.

And then I was there. Door closed behind me. Just me and the hemisphere's greatest Cold War villain, lying on the bed.

Mouth open. Snoring.

Kind of anticlimactic, actually. A letdown.

He looked pathetically weak up close. His skin was even paler than in the videos of the press conference I'd studied. His lips were parched and looked like brittle plastic. His breathing was labored. He wasn't hooked up to any machines, but there was a sick smell in the room, more like decay than medicine.

If I had come to kill him, I might have thought twice about it.

Nah.

I would have offed him in a heartbeat. Which would have been pretty quick, since mine was still pumping a million miles a minute.

I glanced around the room. The lamp had been turned low, but there was plenty of light to see. I pulled open the top drawer of the bureau opposite the bed. It was filled with pajamas.

The next drawer down had an old accordion file bound with a piece of elastic, the sort of thing an accountant or bookkeeper sometimes uses to keep records together. I almost passed it by, then decided I should check it out.

A DVD sat at the side, next to a folder of yellowed clippings from *The New York Times*. The words "last broadcast" were written in Spanish on the cover.

[V]

I know what you're thinking:

Did you remember to take the DVD with you, Dick, just in case something like this happened?

I may not be a Boy Scout, but I do like their motto: Be Prepared.

And I like this motto even better: Better to be lucky than good.

But I said it was *a* DVD, not necessarily *the* DVD. The only way to be sure it was the right DVD was to play it.

You'd think the richest man in Cuba could afford a DVD setup, and you'd be right. He had one right by his bed. I tiptoed over to it, turned it on, and replaced the disc that had been sitting inside.

(*The Greatest Moments in Yankee Baseball History.* I kid you not. Maybe there is something to the Red Sox claim that they're the Evil Empire.)

The television came on, the scene exactly the same as the one I had filmed a few weeks before.

The only problem was that Fidel was apparently hard of hearing, and had left the volume of his television on high. The set blared for a moment before I had a chance to kill the power.

Behind me, Fidel stirred.

"Who are you?" he said grumpily

I turned slowly and gave him my best Fidel glare. He practically jumped back in the bed.

"You look like you saw a ghost," I told him. I spoke in English.

"*Q-q-qué?*"

"I'm here to answer your questions," I said, sticking to English. He used Spanish.

"My questions?"

I nodded solemnly.

"Are you me?" he asked. "Is this a dream? Why are you speaking English?"

"I don't speak any language," I said. "My thoughts are your thoughts."

"I'm dead?" He looked like he was going to cry.

I didn't answer. He reached over to touch me, then suddenly grabbed my shirt.

"You are me," he said. "I am dead. Or I'm dreaming. I must be dreaming. This is a dream. This is a dream, isn't it?"

Again, I didn't answer.

"Did they die? Did it work?" he said. "My plan. Did the Yankees all die?"

"Your plan was flawed," I told him. "The plan . . . it was hardly worth the name."

"What?"

"What were you thinking? To kill all the Americans."

"You're just a nightmare," he said. "Or a trick—something my enemies sent. Guard! Guar . . . ddddd . . ."

As we'd been talking, I'd slipped the needle from my pocket and brought it close to his arm. As soon as he started looking belligerent, I stabbed him.

The drug worked quicker than I thought.

It was also more potent.

"What was the plan?" I asked.

"Ggggg . . ."

"The plan. What were you doing to the Americans?"

"G . . ."

Fidel smiled—then his eyes rolled to the back of his head, and he fell back on the pillow.

I could fill five pages with the curses that came from my mouth over the next three or four minutes as I tried to revive him.

I would have tried longer, except that I heard a key turning in the door.

Fidel undoubtedly had the biggest room in the hospital, but it was still pretty small. The closet was nothing more than pressboard partition with a curtain over it. It was too small to hide me. The bathroom was nearly as cramped, but at least it had a door that went all the way to the floor. I stepped back into it, squeezing into the corner as a nurse and doctor came in, with Red at their heels.

"This door was not to be locked," said the doctor.

"The president must have locked it himself," said the nurse.

"He is not to lock it," said the doctor. "Do you understand?"

"You tell him. I have a family to consider."

I held my breath. Red stood near the bathroom; she'd figured out where I was hiding and planned on running interference if it came to that.

But if it did come to that, we'd both be doing more running than interfering.

The nurse took out an infrared thermometer and checked Fidel's temperature while the doctor wrapped a blood pressure cuff around *el Jefe*'s arm. His temperature was normal; his blood pressure a little low, probably because of my injection.

Apparently Fidel had been suffering from high blood pressure, because the doctor took the reading twice. Then he told the nurse excitedly that the new drugs were working miracles; the president's blood pressure was now within normal limits, maybe even a little low.

"I'll have to show José," he said, and he hurried out of the room.

The nurse tucked Fidel in, then left.

"Dick?" whispered Red.

"Go," I told her. "I'll meet you downstairs."

The other nurse poked her head back into the room.

"I'm coming," said Red, leaving quickly and closing the door behind her.

I went back over to Fidel.

"Wake up and tell me what you did to the Americans, you bastard." I shook him, but he didn't stir. "Come on. What do you have planned? What is it?"

The doctor took far less time than I thought he would, and the only warning I had that he was coming was the scratch of his shoes on the floor right outside the door. I was just stepping into the bathroom when he and his colleague came in.

The other man didn't seem particularly impressed. A sedative, he said, could have produced the same result. The first doctor admitted this was true, but swore that none had been administered.

"I think you are mistaken," said the second doctor.

"Are you calling me a liar?"

"A mistake is not a lie. A mistake is simply an error."

"I shouldn't have showed you anything. I was going to share credit. Now I'll take it all."

"You're an ass," said the second doctor. He stepped over to the bathroom, flipping on the light switch as he started to enter.

"You're calling me an ass? Do so to my face."

The other doctor stopped about three feet from me, if that.

"Come on, you," said the first doctor. "What is it you are saying?"

The second doctor spun around and faced him.

"I think that a mistake is different from a lie. I don't think you are a liar."

"Hmmm."

"You should record the results. I will witness it."

"We should have two witnesses."

"Get another while I take a leak."

I had my pistol ready to pop him. That was the easy part; from there I'd have to wing it.

"I wouldn't use the president's bathroom," said the first. "It's unprofessional. And if he wakes . . ."

"Yes, true. True."

With that, they both left.

My colon could have used a bit of relief by then as well, but there was no time for anything but getting the hell out of there.

If the soldiers were looking in my direction—if they were even still out there—I have no idea. All I know is I stepped lively, with great purpose, as I strode from Fidel's room to the staircase. I hustled up the steps, then caught my breath.

From here, everything would be easy. I'd return to the room, change into my undertaker's uniform, then meet Red in the basement. The only unsettled question was which of the soldiers to wheel out as a corpse.

I'd had an incredible string of good luck—and as I said, it's better to be lucky than good.

But as I put my hand to the door, Mr. Murphy decided that string had run out.

"The president has been kidnapped!" screamed the duty nurse, running into the hall. "The president has been kidnapped! Call the soldiers! Call the guards!"

(VI)

I grabbed for the door, trying to pull it open and get out in the hall and tell them I'd been sleepwalking or something. But Murphy had greased the doorknob and my fingers slipped off.

Maybe it was my own sweat. In any event, by the time I finally *did* grab the damn thing, an alarm was sounding through the hospital.

A door in the stairwell somewhere below me opened and feet started double-timing upward. I stepped out into the hall. I couldn't see the duty nurse, but I could hear her screaming hysterically into the phone at the nurses' station, saying *el Jefe* had been kidnapped.

Using either the stairs or the elevator was now out of the question, certainly the way I was dressed. I slipped back into the room where Red had wheeled me, and saw that the nurse had pulled the sheet off the bed, taking the clothes I'd hid there, as evidence I guess.

There was no sense staying here, but I couldn't use the elevator or the stairs. I slipped into the room on the right side of the hall, opposite the one where I'd been, and pulled out the sat phone.

Red answered on the second ring.

"Yes?"

"I'm on the top floor, in the room opposite the one you left me in."

"I'll be right there."

"No. Don't do that. Get out of the hospital."

"What?"

"Leave. Call Danny and see where Trace and Doc are. If they're still in-country, I may need them to get the helicopter and pick me up on the roof."

"Dick—"

"Move, Red. I don't want to go out that way, but I will if I have to. You get the hell out."

She didn't answer for so long I thought the phone had died. "OK," she said finally. Her tone made it clear that leaving was the last thing she wanted to do.

"*Do it.*"

"All right. I'm going."

———

I knew from the satellite photos that there was a little shedlike entrance to the roof, but I wasn't sure how to get to it. The stairwell had ended at that level, and the location seemed wrong for it to be the other staircase. Getting there would be too risky now anyway.

Which left climbing out the window and playing Spiderman, a character I've always admired, even if he is a little emo as the kids would put it.

There was a good chance climbing wouldn't be necessary.

Actually, it wasn't likely it would go that far. I expected that after security raced around like chickens with their heads cut off for a few minutes, logic would set in. A team would respond to Fidel's floor, where they would find *el Jefe* sleeping like a sedated baby. Shortly after that, they would venture upstairs to the nurse who had sounded the alarm. She would tell her story. If it weren't for the bed and the clothes she'd found, the story would be dismissed outright. It still might be. But it was more likely that the security people would start looking for Red, which was why I'd told her to get the hell out of there.

They'd be looking for me as well. But inside the building, not outside.

I opened the window and looked around. The roof soffit was about twenty inches above the top of the window, and there wasn't much of an overhang; I could open the window from the top and climb up without a problem. Except for a narrow crown that ran around the perimeter, the roof was flat. I figured I'd be able to hang back down and close the window.

I opened the window, pulled myself up, and then hoisted myself to the roof. Turning around, I leaned back and tried to pull the window closed.

My fingers were about two inches short. As I squirreled around to lean a little farther down, the light came on in the room.

Back at the restaurant, Doc was polishing off the last of a cherry brandy-filled pineapple for dessert. He still hadn't found a chance to tell Trace about the credit card. Nor had he been able to detect anything in Mac-Kenzie's manner that told him she was on to them.

The others had stuck to coffee. MacKenzie had mentioned that she would drive them to the airport if they wanted. Doc didn't want, and decided that it might be easier to get rid of her if he suggested leaving right away. They'd be there so early she wouldn't feel obligated to hang around.

He looked at his watch, then wondered aloud if they ought to leave.

"You have four hours," said MacKenzie, putting her hand on his lightly. "Don't worry."

"They said we should be there at least three hours ahead. I have a lot of gear I have to get through Customs. It's always a pain."

"I'll whisk you right through."

She smiled at him. And the way she did that—sexy, but not quite—convinced him it was time to go.

Past time.

"OK, if you think it's fine," said Doc.

He reached his left hand out to get his wineglass, and knocked over his water in the process, sending it over Trace's lap.

She jumped up. Sensing he'd done it deliberately, she'd backed from the table.

"I'm sorry, I'm sorry," said Doc. He turned toward her and mouthed the words "time to go."

"Damn. You're a klutz."

"I'm sorry."

"I'll go change in the women's room," said Trace.

"Jeez, I'm really sorry." Doc rose, positioning himself so MacKenzie wouldn't be able to see Trace when she walked into the hallway for the ladies' room. When Trace didn't return, he'd suggest MacKenzie find out if something was wrong. Then he'd hightail it out as well.

But things never got that far.

"I'm so sorry your dress is wet," said MacKenzie, rising herself. "These men will help you find a place to dry it."

As she said that, four waiters closed in from the kitchen.

They were dressed as waiters. But of course they weren't really waiters.

"They have some questions for you," added MacKenzie. "I would strongly suggest you answer them expeditiously."

The maître d' came over and unbuttoned his jacket, showing Trace he had a gun. That was unnecessary, however—the Cuban nearest her was already pointing a rather large pistol at her face.

"What is this?" said Doc.

"There was a disturbance in town involving revolutionaries and thieves," said MacKenzie. "*You* have an alibi. That alibi is going to drive you directly to the airport."

Doc started to protest, but MacKenzie cut him off.

"You don't have an option. You can thank me in a different lifetime."

Doc, glancing toward the pistol she had removed from her purse, decided to take her word for it.

(VII)

Back when I was a wee rogue, Dr. Norman Vincent Peale developed a series of ideas that he summarized with a slogan called "the power of positive thinking." It combined prayer, unbridled optimism, and old-fashioned good luck to suggest that you can influence events by thinking positively about them.

I've always believed more in acting than wishing, but I can tell you that no one tried positive thinking any harder than I did as I dangled from the hospital roof while the hospital security types inspected the room I'd just left. The words formed in capital letters in my brain:

YOU ARE POSITIVELY, ABSOLUTELY NOT GOING TO COME TO THE WINDOW.

YOU ARE NOT GOING TO NOTICE IT IS OPEN. YOU ARE NOT GOING TO LOOK UPWARD.

It worked for Norman Vincent Peale. It didn't work for me.

"Look, the window is open," I heard one of the men say.

I pulled myself back with the best upside-down reverse crunch I could manage. My form may have been off, but I did pull back from the edge before the Cuban got to the window. I held my breath, listening.

"You don't think he went out there, do you?" said someone in the room. "*El Jefe* could not have climbed down. He's an old man."

"I would not underestimate him. He is capable of great things."

The men argued a bit, then closed the window.

Goat fuck aborted. Maybe there is power in positive thinking after all.

I scrambled to my feet and surveyed the roof. The small little shed I'd seen in the satellite photos was a few feet off center. It had a wooden door that looked as if it had been last painted by the conquistadors. The door itself was locked, but with a quick tap on the upper panel I got my fist through it and opened it from the inside.

I took two steps, ready to bound down the stairs to the basement. My first step was a good, galloping step, full of spring and vigor. My second step was just as strong, bouncing off the thick riser. My third step was light and airy.

Good for a cake, ice cream maybe, even a drink.

Not for a step. I found myself falling—not down a staircase, but the elevator shaft.

Out of the goat fuck and into the fubar.

The elevator in the shaft I'd just jumped down turned out to be only one floor away from the roof, a lousy twelve feet that I could have jumped with my eyes closed, though as it happened I kept them open.

That was the good news. The bad news was that I had no idea of how far it was, and had no way of preparing for the impact beyond murmuring a few favorite curse words to myself.

I also hit the cable about a third of the way down.

I rebounded off the thick wire and slammed my head onto the side of the shaft, while my back slapped onto the roof of the car. Dazed doesn't begin to describe what I felt.

I'm guessing that the elevator was empty, because I had to have made enough noise to wake up the dead. I was practically dead myself. I have no idea how long I stayed there. Probably I was out for just a few seconds, but if you say days I couldn't argue. When I finally pulled myself together and sat up, I couldn't see. My first thought was that I was blind. I blinked a few times before I realized it was just too dark to see anything.

Maybe if you fall onto elevators a lot you begin to know your way around them in the pitch-black, but my experience set was sorely lacking. I crawled all around the top, feeling with my hands to see if there was a trapdoor or an opening into the car, but there wasn't. Finally I worked my way around the wall of the shaft, feeling until I found a work ladder embedded in the side. It was too tight to squeeze down past the car, so I went back up to the roof.

Things had quieted down a bit, but the hospital was still in a lockdown. A pair of uniformed officers walked along the driveway, looking toward the security fence at the edge of the property. It was a perfunctory search, but it was a search nonetheless. Even if video cameras hadn't been guarding the base of the building, there was no way I was getting out by climbing down the side and going over the wall.

I was considering going back down into the elevator shaft to see if there was a hidden door somewhere when I heard the heavy beat of a helicopter. I turned to the east and saw a small helo with a searchlight blinking below its nose.

Danny or Red had gotten to Trace, I thought. Five minutes and I'd be out of here. Two hours from now, I'd be sitting on the beach in Miami, nursing my wounds under the care of the good Dr. Bombay.

The helo bore straight in on me. I put up my arms and started to wave. I can't remember being happier to see a helicopter in my life. I realized I'd gone way too far in Cuba, pushing things that even I shouldn't have pushed. I'd learned my lesson: no more impersonating scumbags from now on. The only bastard I was going to resemble was myself.

I waved my hands as the helicopter approached. The sun had just set, and the helo was more a shadow than an aircraft.

Then, as it loomed into view, I realized it was a Russian-made Mil Mi-8.

A very nice helicopter. But not the one we'd leased.

The Cuban air force insignia on the side was a dead giveaway. And if that wasn't enough, the man with the assault rifle leaning out of the cockpit surely would have been.

PART THREE
PANIC AND PANDEMIC

Nobuddy ever fergits where he buried a hatchet.

—KIN HUBBARD, *ABE MARTIN'S BROADCAST*, 1930

[1]

I don't know why the helicopter had been sent for sure, though I'm guessing that it was part of the general alert initiated by the nurse's panic. It is possible, though, that the helo was on some sort of training mission and the pilot diverted when he saw what looked like Fidel Castro jumping up and down on the roof.

As soon as I realized the helicopter wasn't friendly, I ducked down, steeling myself for a command performance as *el Jefe*. As soon as they landed, I would tell them a coup was under way, and have them take me to the airport.

Probably, that wouldn't have worked. It wasn't much of a plan, though it was *a* plan, which is better than *no* plan. But as it turned out, I didn't get a chance to try it.

As soon as she hung up the phone, Red had burned the rubber off her soft-soled shoes getting out of the hospital. It helped that she was on the first floor, near reception; she ran to the door, calling to the guards that there was an emergency—and kept running after they went past. She walked swiftly down past the front gate. The guards started to detain her, but she pointed to the nearby bus and cried that it was hers, and if she didn't make it her walk home would take hours. One of the men, chivalrous as all Cubans, waved her through.

The other, not to be outdone, yelled at the bus driver and had him stop and wait for her.

Red was just going to the door of the bus when she spotted an illegal taxi a few yards down the street. She practically threw herself on its hood hailing it, then had the driver take her to the airport.

Mongoose was still outside the hospital at this point, not sure exactly what was going on. Red called him on the sat phone and told him that she was on her way to the airport and to meet her there. Rather than calling Danny—who was in Jamaica, after all—she tried calling Trace and Doc herself from the cab, but got no response. So she called the company we had leased the helicopter from and told them that she was on her way for the tour.

"Tonight, senora?" asked the man who answered the phone.

"Right now."

There was a pause.

"I was told the aircraft would be ready at all times," she said. "And of course, there will be a tip for all involved. A good tip. In euros, if you wish."

Money talks as loudly in Cuba as anywhere else, and whatever further objections the man who answered the phone had, they went unmentioned.

Red knew that as soon as she showed up, the pilot would assume that she was trying to escape Cuba, and that he would most likely refuse to fly. So she had her gun in her purse, ready to pull out when the taxi drove up to the hangar where the chopper was sitting. A broad-shouldered man in a light blue shirt and chino pants was standing near the helo and came over as she got out.

"You're the one who wants the tour?" he asked.

"Yes."

"A nurse?"

He gave her a suspicious glance, then walked toward the chopper. Red followed quickly. Mongoose hadn't arrived yet, but she decided not to wait.

"You had better buckle up," the pilot told her as she got into the cockpit.

"Yes."

"Where do you want to go?"

"Over the city."

"And the beach?"

"We can go near the beach."

The pilot started the engines. He didn't appear to be armed, but it was possible he had a gun strapped below the seat.

He hadn't mentioned money, and he was certainly very calm. Red decided there was a fifty-fifty chance he was just playing her along, and intended on taking her to the nearest police station. There was only one way to find out: as soon as they were airborne, Red took her wad of euros from the bag.

"I want to fly over the Malecón, over this address," she said, giving the address of the hospital.

"That's restricted airspace."

"We'll only be there for a moment."

"It's restricted. We'll be in serious trouble if we're seen."

"We won't get in trouble," she told him, starting to count the bills in her hand. By the time she reached ten—she was counting hundred euro notes—she had counted out more money than he had seen in a lifetime.

She kept counting.

"What was the address again?" said the pilot when she reached one hundred.

The Cuban air force helicopter circled above me slowly, then began to settle toward the roof. I put my arm over my head to shield some of the grit and ran to the spot where he was coming down. I planned to jump into the doorway at the side and immediately launch into my Fidel routine. But just as the helo got close, it suddenly lurched away.

I turned toward the door over the elevator shaft, expecting that the security people had finally made it to the roof. But there was no one there. I turned back around and saw a second helicopter coming in from the direction of the airport, skimming in low over the city.

More cautious this time, I pulled out my sat phone and quick-dialed Trace's number. There was no answer. I edged toward the elevator shaft, waiting—if it started to fire, I'd leap back inside.

The helo came right over the edge of the building, almost leaning on the roof. Red was in the cockpit on the right, waving frantically. I grabbed at the door handle, threw it back on its rails, and then dove inside. The helo pitched forward, slamming the door closed behind me. Before I could pull myself back upright, we were out over the beach.

"Now," said Red in Spanish to the pilot. "We need you to take us east." She was thinking of one of our backup escape boats near Matanzas.[29]

"You don't want to go to Miami?" said the pilot.

"Miami would be fine," I told him, coming into the cockpit.

"I think the men in the helicopter that is following us would object," said Red. "I called them off by saying we were with the security service. If we go north, they'll realize something's up."

The helicopter that had circled the building above me was about a half mile away, on our left side, to the southwest as we flew in a slow loop above the city.

"Can we outrun them?" I asked the pilot.

---

[29] Forgive me for being vague; it was located near the house of a friend of a friend.

"Probably not."

"Let's try it anyway," I told him.

"I think we should improve the odds," said the pilot. "There is a case in the rear near the bulkhead that contains a grenade launcher."

I reached down and opened up the long flat case. A Russian RPG-7 sat inside. I pulled it out and began assembling it.

"Do you know how to use it?" shouted the pilot, leaning the helicopter northward.

"I've tried my luck with one or two in the past."

"Good."

I first saw the RPG-7 in Vietnam, where the VC and regulars used it as an antitank and anti-everything weapon. It's point and fire, so simple even a terrorist can shoot it, and they do. The rocket-propelled grenade it launches is more on a par with a bazooka shell than a regular grenade. It can penetrate armor, though by now most modern tanks have little to fear from it.

Helicopters and light trucks are a different story. In Iraq, RPGs have taken out Hummers and a number of helicopters, including Apaches.

Still, hitting a moving helicopter is not especially easy when you're in a moving helicopter yourself. I waited as our pilot dropped his speed, letting the other chopper pull up alongside. As it drew parallel, I threw the door open. But instead of firing I fell backward, pushed by the strong wind current. Cursing, I rolled to my side and brought the rocket launcher to bear from the other side of the cabin.

In an instant, I saw the puzzled face of the other aircraft's pilot. I braced my left foot against the seat, then fired point-blank at the Plexiglas in front of him.

I missed.

But not by enough to matter. The missile shot into the fuselage directly behind and a little above my aim point, striking the bottom of the engine. So instead of killing the pilot and copilot outright, they had a few seconds to consider their sins before meeting their maker. The helicopter blossomed into a red fireball, keeling over to the left away from us as we changed course for due north.

"We have just enough fuel for Miami," said the pilot after I buttoned the chopper back up. "We will have to fly low, but I believe we will make it. My name is Perez. I have been waiting for this day since you reserved the helicopter. And many years before that."

There were five minutes there where I felt really good. Maybe even ten. I was banged up all to hell, but I'd managed to switch the DVDs, and spent face time with Fidel to boot. I'd taken ridiculous risks and come out without a scratch.

Lots of bruises.

But as I leaned back in the seat, the euphoria of escaping alive began to wear off. I still didn't know what Fidel's surprise was. And that had been one of the main reasons to take all those risks in the first place.

The pilot kept us at low altitude, the throttle jammed against the last detent. The Cuban air force supposedly scrambled some planes after us, but we never saw them. A U.S. Coast Guard patrol plane picked us up on its radar when we were about ten minutes from U.S. airspace and began hailing us. We had to sweat it out for a few minutes, not daring to identify ourselves just in case we were being trailed by Cuban MiGs, which have been known to relish taking on unarmed aircraft. Then finally the pilot acknowledged the coast guard's call, popped us up, and declared our peaceful intentions. I got on the radio and asked to speak to a Homeland Security supervisor I knew. He wasn't available, but the name-dropping had the proper effect, and within a few minutes we had an escort to Homestead Air Force base. Two F-16 Falcon fighters came out to meet us. Our pilot would have done a barrel roll if I'd let him.

And if he'd had any fuel in the tank. We made the last ten miles on fumes and varnish.

I haven't had a chance to mention what happened to Mongoose, whom you last saw on his way to the airport, sent there by Red.

He arrived at the hangar area just in time to see the helicopter Red had hired take off. After a sufficient amount of cursing, he followed a prebriefed backup plan and went over to the terminal building, where he called Danny for instructions. By this time, Danny had Junior at the ready back in the States, and our resident computer geek hacked into the airline reservation system and planted a couple of emergency tickets, using backup IDs.

See why he's behind the lines?

No, neither does he.

Trace and Doc, meanwhile, had failed to check back in after Danny's warning to Doc, and in fact Danny wasn't sure what was going on until Doc landed in Mexico. He'd immediately gotten on the phone to Danny, who called me while I was trying to explain to an air force intel type at Homestead why I couldn't talk to him without shooting him first.

Danny went to work shoring up Trace's cover story, and even put in a fake call from Canada to the Cuban information ministry as Trace's boss. In the meantime, I went outside and called Ken, my favorite Christian in Action. It took nearly a half hour of diddling with various assistants and desk people before I finally managed to get through to him.

He wasn't exactly the overjoyed, fun-loving admiral I'd come to know and loathe.

"Where are you, Dick?" he asked. There was an accusatory tone in his voice, as if he were saying something closer to *What the hell are you up to?* Or probably more accurately, *How am I going to cover up my butt this time?*

"I need a plane and some support for an operation in Cuba," I told him. "One of my people is there."

"You've been *very* busy."

"I need a plane."

"Dick, where are you?"

"I need a plane."

"We'll get your person out, don't worry. Where are you? We need to talk in person."

"I need a plane."

"My aide here says you're at Homestead in Florida? I'll be there in a few hours."

He hung up. I'd gone back outside so the air farcers couldn't hear me, and when I looked around I realized there were plenty of planes nearby. Knowing the air force, it would probably be months before they realized one was gone.

I didn't steal one. There were several reasons. Probably the most important was Danny's call a few seconds after I got off with the admiral. He'd been monitoring the Cuban defense radios and had just heard a broadcast declaring that there had been an attempt on Castro's life.

"They're at high alert," said Danny. "I think it's about your high tea with the fearless leader. They mentioned the helicopter. It sounds like all hell is breaking loose."

"Anything on Trace?"

"No. But listen, Junior has been looking at that hard drive and he wants to talk to you."

"Put him on."

"I have a draft of Raul's acceptance speech," said Junior. "He's being elected president next week."

"There's a shock. I never would have expected it."

"Is that sarcasm, Dick?"

Why is it that nerd types never understand concepts like irony, sarcasm, and humor?

"What do you think, Junior?"

"Um, I don't know." And not knowing, though probably suspecting the joke was on him, he changed the subject abruptly. "I also have a draft of his speech after his brother dies. He's talking about a pretty big disaster to hit the U.S. Our economy's going to be fucked for twenty years."

"He used the word 'fucked'?"

"I'm still working on my Spanish, but it was in that ballpark."

"Have you seen the satellite photos of the Colombian border?"

I'm not sure what I expected Ken Jones to say when he arrived, but I know it wasn't that. And I wasn't in much of a mood for surprises or left turns.

"I have a person stuck in Havana, and you're worried about drug smuggling?" I answered.

"This has nothing to do with drugs, Dick. Except maybe the ones Hugo Chavez is using."

The admiral nodded at the aide who'd come with him. The aide pulled up the narrow briefcase he'd brought and opened it on the table. We'd been given a ready room on the base for our meeting. The two bodyguards the admiral had brought with him—nothing I said, I'm sure—were outside the door keeping curious air farcers at bay.

In my experience, curious and air farce are pretty much a contradiction in terms, but I digress.

"This is what the border of the two countries looked like a month

273

ago," said the aide. I didn't quite catch his name; it might have been Needleneck.

He laid out a series of satellite photos of Venezuela's Apure region, the country's western midsection. (Draw a line between Caracas and Bogotá; split the difference and you're in Apure.) It's your typical semi-penetrable jungle, punctuated by numerous streams and wetlands.

"Now look at these," said Needleneck.

The photos were of the same area, but now the highways were lined with troop trucks.

"Someone's going hunting," I said, stating the obvious.

"Chavez is trying to get Colombia to stop going after FARC," said the admiral. "Their campaign against the guerrillas is getting a little too successful for him."

FARC is the Spanish abbreviation for the Revolutionary Armed Forces of Colombia, your basic nutso-commie group of crazies who have been disrupting Colombia for roughly two decades now. They support their mayhem and random acts of violence by dealing drugs, kidnapping, and whatever other illegal activities happen to strike their fancy. Just the sort of thugs Chavez would champion.

I'll spare you the South American politics. I should mention, though, that FARC has traditionally operated on the *other* side of Colombia near Ecuador, and that Chavez would later claim he had sent the troops to the border because the Colombians had gone into Ecuador where the tangos were holed up. If you're trying to squeeze logic out of that, don't bother. The point Ken and his physique-challenged aide were trying to make was: Chavez was up to bad things.

And where did we come into the picture?

In two places. The first was Raul's hard drive.

"The hard disk you stole from Raul's computer contains some e-mail messages from Chavez about the troop movements, apparently notes that he's hoping Raul will incorporate into speeches backing the mobilization," explained Needleneck. "Chavez is looking for a specific provocation before ordering his troops in."

"We oughta hope he follows through," I said. "Colombia can be in Caracas inside a week."

The Venezuelan army numbers maybe thirty-four thousand men. They have about eighty AMX 30 tanks, which are decent second-rank main battle tanks. More impressive are the Sukhois[30] they've been buying lately to replace the F-16s they can't fly because they've run out of spare parts.

Pretty good by Latin American standards. But not quite good enough if you're comparing them to Colombia. There the army numbers over a hundred thousand, with another hundred thousand or more in the reserves. And these guys have experience fighting in the jungle, battling narco-terrorists a hell of a lot more committed to their own ideals—and money—than the Venezuelan army is to Chavez.

Colombia doesn't have anything like the AMX, but they do have a bunch of Bradley Fighting Vehicles and lighter vehicles suited to jungle and mountain warfare. They have a dozen or so Kfir fighters, which are Israeli-made knockoffs of the Mirage III: slight advantage to Venezuela, but only slight. They have a *lot* of artillery and, oh yeah, American advisors with access to considerable intelligence and logistics resources.

"I don't think either side would win in a war," said Needleneck.

"They will if we help," I told him.

Needleneck glanced at his boss.

"I'm glad you feel that way, Dick," said Ken, dropping the other shoe.

"I'm not going to Colombia, or Venezuela. I'm getting Trace Dahlgren out of Cuba. And then Red Cell International is going to spend some of that money you owe the company on a very nice, all-expenses-paid vacation for its key stockholder."

"We'll take care of Ms. Dahlgren," said Needleneck. "We're already making inquiries through our Canadian friends."

I know he meant that to sound encouraging, but given the Christians in Action record in Cuba, it was anything but.

"I can handle it myself," I told him. "You've got other problems to worry about. This thing with Venezuela, Fidel's surprise—"

"Dick, you don't want to go back to Cuba yourself," said Ken. "Haven't you seen the bulletin?"

I shook my head. Needleneck opened his briefcase and pulled out two more pieces of paper, hard copies of electronic bulletins that had been issued to every police and army unit in the country. Page one had a

---

[30] I'm not allowed to tell you how many they have. But then again I got the number from Ken, so it's probably not accurate anyway.

picture of yours truly in a hospital corridor, along with Red. Page two had a description of our terrorist movement, which had nearly killed *el Jefe* before being foiled by the brave members of the security forces.

There was one encouraging note: Trace wasn't mentioned. The Cubans hadn't connected her with any of this. Though of course that wouldn't stop them from doing so in the future.

With or without evidence.

"Did you manufacture this, Ken? Because it wasn't on the hard drive."

"It's legitimate," said Needleneck. "We have our sources."

"I'm not going to Colombia," I told them. "My job is finished. The DVDs were switched, and you got a bonus."

"Colombia's not the real target," said the admiral. "Panama is."

Needleneck's briefcase opened again, and I was treated to another set of satellite photos, this time of the ocean.

Empty ocean, at least as far as I could see.

"What am I looking at?" I asked finally.

"Periscopes. Here, here, and here," announced Needleneck, pointing at the pages, a note of triumph in his voice. "Chinese periscopes," added the admiral. "Three submarines, filled with troops."

Before we go any further, a history lesson for the grasshopper at the back of the class with a confused look on his face.

Most Americans remember, vaguely I'd guess, that the U.S. built the Panama Canal in the early twentieth century. It opened in 1914. For the next eighty-five years, we protected it, keeping it open to international shipping. Yes, partly for our benefit—the canal made it much cheaper to ship goods from the eastern U.S. to the western coast and beyond—but the rest of the world did pretty well with it, too.

We gave it "back" to the Panamanians in 1999, under an agreement Jimmy Carter had worked out when his psychoanalyst told him to get in touch with his inner Santa Claus. Carter was another favorite bubblehead of mine—Academy grad and nuclear submariner, he was smarter than shit but like many submariners he lived in his own world under the sea, or wherever . . .

I'd guess that most Americans probably think that giving the canal "back" to the Panamanians meant that *Panama* would take over the operation and benefit from the trade and traffic it generated. But what *really* happened was that Panamanian officials turned around and cut deals with foreign companies to run the canal.

And guess where those foreign companies call home.

The U.S.A.?

Bzzzzz. I thought you were sleeping, grasshopper.

The Chinese now control most of the key ports in the canal. The true communists of the twenty-first century don't bother taking things over at the point of a rifle; they just plunk down money for it. It's much cheaper, faster, and the only downside is that you have to host the Olympics every twenty years or so.

Back in the day, the U.S. had a permanent SpecWar detachment in the Canal Zone providing training for waterway protection, harbor security, and riverine warfare. I didn't personally work with them, and my connection since has been limited, with an exception we'll get into shortly. I do enjoy regular reports on the money-laundering operations by the Chinese and Russians, courtesy of a former Soviet operative there, if only for entertainment value.

Needleneck spent the next twenty minutes delivering a briefing on the Chinese military buildup over the past decade or so, concentrating largely on submarines. Some of what he said is common knowledge and not classified, including the general identity of the three Chinese submarines allegedly in the photo he showed me.

They were Chinese Type 039 Song-class boats, homegrown attack submarines propelled by diesel engines and capable of launching cruise missiles. Their presence that far from Chinese waters surprised many analysts, since diesel boats didn't have long-range capabilities. (That must be why German U-boats never sailed off the American coast during World War II, and American submarines never choked up Japanese trade. Oh, wait a minute . . .)

The discussion of the submarines and the rest of the Chinese navy was fascinating, but didn't have much to do really with our story. More germane was an ancient merchant ship—ironically of Panamanian registry—that had rendezvoused with the submarines roughly twelve hours before. The ship had left Cuba five days before, taking a very leisurely pace as it sailed through the canal.

Its cargo was described as tools and machinery.

Since when does Cuba *export* tools and machinery?

It doesn't.

It exports cigars, a bit of sugar if the harvest is good . . . and armed mercenaries, which it did often to Africa and places like Grenada during the latter stages of the Cold War. Now, according to the Christians in Action, they'd decided to stay at home and train others.

Venezuelans, in this case.

Their target was a port installation run by Hutchinson Ports—a Chinese company—at Cristobal on the eastern end of the Panama Canal. According to the admiral, they were now aboard the Chinese subs.

Huh?

The Chinese were helping attack their own installations?

Huh?

Say again: *Huh?*

I love conspiracy theories as much as anyone, but by this time my head was spinning. I couldn't see why the Chinese would be transporting saboteurs targeting a port run by a *Chinese* company. And outside of general principles, I couldn't understand why the Venezuelans were involved, or what this had to do with the border of Colombia.

I *could* see the profit motive for Cuba, I understood the import of the evidence on Raul's hard drive, but I couldn't quite fathom all of the connections. And having had more experience with the CIA than I'm comfortable admitting, even under oath, I was somewhat skeptical, even when they showed me encrypted and coded radio transmissions cinching the connections.

I turned to Ken.

"What exactly is it that's going on?" I asked. "Just give me a two-minute no-shitter."

"The Venezuelans—disguised as Colombian terrorists—are going to stage a takeover," said Ken. "Chavez is going to send a force to help subdue them. The Chinese will use this as a pretense to move troops into their facilities in the Canal Zone. There'll be escalation from there."

"The Chinese want to take over the canal," added Needleneck. "It'll reduce their shipping costs to Europe dramatically, giving them inroads to the one major market they don't control right now. Chavez wants to help, partly to cement a new oil deal, and partly because he figures that anything that will hurt the U.S. is good for him. Cuba's involved because of the cash and because Fidel and Raul see this as the ultimate fuck you to the U.S. You saw what Fidel said in his tape. This is it."

Whoa, Nellie. Stop the tape right there.

This was what Ken thought was Fidel's big surprise?

"That was supposed to happen after he died," I pointed out. "He's not dead yet. He's getting there, but very slowly."

Needleneck shrugged. "The doctors turned out to be a little better than he thought. Finally, a real Cuban medical miracle."

I knew they were wrong. Oh, I'm sure that in a general way, Fidel and his bro were convinced that anything that screwed us was good for the world, and vice versa. I could see them giving the OK to train the men. They needed the cash, and weren't in much of a position to deny Venezuela anything—if Chavez stopped supplying cheap Venezuelan oil to the island, they'd be right back where they were at the end of the Soviet Union.

But I'd heard Raul ranting about Chavez, and knew from our tête-à-tête that Fidel wasn't crazy about him, either. Fidel wasn't about to outsource his revenge. Besides, this was too small from his point of view to satisfy his rage. If his history showed anything, it was that he thought big. Megalomaniacs usually do.

"We need you to work with the Panamanians to cut this off," said Ken. "We need some cover here—the U.S. can't just barge in. But if you said you had information, and then volunteered to help the Panamanian Public Force,[31] they'd go for it in a heartbeat."

"It has to be launched quickly—the assault is set for tomorrow night," said Needleneck.

"We'll provide assistance," said Ken. "All we need from you is political cover—the usual ability to say we're arm's length from the situation. You understand."

Sure. When the shit hits the fan, it flies all over Dick, not everybody else.

"Tell the Panamanians you uncovered the plot in Cuba," added Ken. "That will cut off any questions about our involvement."

"The Cubans already know you were in Cuba," added Needleneck. "They've connected you with the attack. They're preparing a formal protest to the UN."

---

[31] Panama's national police, which handles most defense duties. I'll explain later.

"It mentions me by name?"

I looked at Ken. He nodded solemnly.

Needleneck opened the briefcase once more and produced yet another intercepted Cuban document. I was, in fact, named as the suspected force behind the raid, hired by the U.S. government.

I was completely flattered. And I was pissed. Linking my name to the operation put Trace in even more danger. Now if the Cubans figured out who she was, they'd be sure to grant her permanent residency in one of their jails . . . if not cemeteries.

"How much help did the Cubans have deciding I was involved?" I asked Ken.

"We're going to help you get your girl out," he answered, ducking the question. "We're working with the Canadians. You have nothing to worry about as far as that's concerned. Her identity will be protected. We'll get her out. That's a personal guarantee. Me to you."

"Great," I said, getting up.

"Great as in, you're going to help?" asked Needleneck.

"Great as in, don't do me any favors."

"You're not being cooperative here, Dick," said Ken.

I imagine he said some other things as well, but I didn't stick around to hear them.

(III)

The first order of business was to find out where Trace was.

We started with the assumption that she would be taken to Villa Marista, the state security headquarters in Havana, where she'd be questioned and probably tortured while the authorities decided whether to a) shoot her full of Thorazine and send her to the political wing at Mazorra for electroshock therapy, or b) just shoot her.

How long she would be kept there was anyone and everyone's guess; the average of the many sources we consulted seemed to be about a week and a half.

Danny hopped on a plane to Miami to press our friends there for contacts and additional information. Meanwhile, I needed to get some people into Havana ASAP. Mongoose hadn't landed in Toronto yet; Sean was in Europe and out of commission as far as this operation was concerned. Red, Doc, and I were "burned," likely to be arrested if not shot as soon as we were spotted. The only shooters I had who were immediately available were Shotgun and Junior. Shotgun didn't speak particularly good Spanish and Junior's didn't sound very Cuban. And neither knew his way around Havana.

Not that either of them would let that stand in the way of helping Trace.

"Kick ass, Dick. When's the plane?" asked Shotgun.

"There's a flight from Miami to Mexico that you can take if you get to the airport in an hour," I told him. "We'll get someone from Homeland Security to walk you to the gate."

"Kick ass."

"You're going as a Canadian tourist."

"I are Canadian, eh?"

"Just don't stop at every snack bar and fast-food shop on the way."

"Kick ass."

Junior needed even less encouragement. He'd just gotten off a plane in Jamaica when I got ahold of him. We booked him on a flight and then into a hotel as a doctor from Belgium involved in an international exchange.

"Belgium?" he asked. "Why not Spain?"

"Because your Spanish sounds like you picked it up in Des Moines," I told him. "Just go there and keep your mouth shut. Take two of the sat phones that look like cell phones. Just two; if they see more than that they'll either get greedy or suspicious. We'll call with more instructions."

"On my way."

With Red now known to the Cubans, I reached outside of Red Cell International for a fresh face. The face I had in mind was fresh, but not particularly young—Edward "Crusty" Lopez had blown out more than sixty candles at his last birthday party.

How many more is a closely guarded secret, known only to those at the party. But I wouldn't trust Crusty to have used the right number anyway.

Crusty is a friend and associate of Doc's from back in the day—not quite from when the navy was still using sails, but close. A chief petty officer when he retired, Crusty was never a SEAL or a frogman. He was a samurai in the fine art of procurement, however, one of Doc's inspirations, a recommendation all to itself.

Most important, Crusty could speak Cuban Spanish like a native. His parents and a number of other relatives had come from Cuba during Batista's reign. They weren't fooled when Fidel came to power, and fled, mostly to America. A few hardy souls remained, including an uncle whom Crusty had visited two years before.

While he's in good shape for his age—still runs about two miles a day, not counting what he spends chasing women—Crusty was not only too old to be a shooter but had never trained as one besides. But he could handle a weapon, and was more than willing to help out. Danny had already used him in Miami to gather information, and when I called to ask if he'd be willing to visit his sick (and nonexistent) aunt in Havana, he said his bags were already packed.

The rest of us—myself, Doc, Red, and Mongoose when he landed—headed back to Jamaica to regroup and plan our next move.

I caught an hour nap waiting for our plane to take off in Miami, and snoozed for another hour on the way down to Jamaica. I wasn't exactly fresh as a baby when I woke—I ached in ten million places—but my brain cells were working again. And by the time I landed, I realized that our original premise could very well be wrong.

The Cubans were talking to Trace because they suspected she might be somehow involved in the death of a black-market thug. That could mean that she wasn't at Villa Marista at all—the regular police would be the ones interested. The distinction was important, and went beyond where she might be held—the Cuban authorities have traditionally been easier on common criminals than they have been on political prisoners.

Security is also less substantial. I feel pretty confident that Red Cell International can get into any installation, including Fort Knox, but even so, slipping in and out of a police station, even in Havana, would be orders of magnitude easier than worming our way into Marista.

"We're still going to need muscle," said Doc when we started looking over the street maps and satellite photos of the various police buildings in the city. "We need more people on the street, more backups, more safe houses. We need fresh faces. And serious firepower if Murphy shows up."

"Not necessarily," I said. "All we need is to have them look the other way. We have to give them something to do. Something big."

"What are we going to do? Relaunch the Bay of Pigs?"

Not a terrible idea, if done right, and against a smarter target. But I had something much simpler in mind.

"We'll just kill Fidel."

I wasn't really going to kill Fidel. What I had in mind was simply broadcasting the fact that he was dead on the national Cuban television station. Within minutes the police would be responding to spontaneous outpourings of joy or sorrow—take your pick—and getting Trace out of the police station would be easy. And as easy as taking over the police station would be compared to taking over the home of Cuba's political police, the television station would be a hundred times easier. Cameramen tend to carry less guns than patrolmen.

Still, Doc was right. We needed manpower to deal with any possible contingency. And we needed it right away, if not sooner.

That was one of the reasons I called Ken to say I'd help him save Panama from the Chinese. The other was that I wanted to see if the Canadians would tell him where Trace was, since they wouldn't tell me.

"The Canadians are very antsy about being involved in any of this, Dick," said Ken when I called.

"I'm still waiting for you to tell me something I don't know."

"I can try, but no promises."

By contrast, I was more than willing to promise: I'd do nothing until I had the information.

There was grumbling. Ken told me I drove a hard bargain. He used colorful navy language to do it.

"Sweet talk isn't going to change my mind," I told him.

Two hours later, Ken called and told me Trace was a "guest" of the Cuban government in a small detective bureau just outside Havana.

I caught a flight to Panama forty minutes later.

(IV)

At that very moment, Trace Dahlgren was reveling in the storied hospitality of the Cuban police, criminal investigation section. Immediately after her detainment,[32] Trace was taken to a local police station and searched. Her personal belongings, including her satellite phone, were confiscated. She was taken into a back room and searched by a pair of older Cuban women armed with latex gloves. It was a full inspection, and while the women didn't rough her up, it was neither pleasant nor gentle.

The matrons declined to give her her clothes back. Instead, Trace was handed a blue cotton work gown and some slippers and brought upstairs to a very cold interrogation room. There she was met by a frumpy detective in his mid-fifties who began by asking her to recount everything she had done since landing in Havana.

He wasn't Sherlock Holmes, nor did he look all that interested in being there, so Trace played the role she figured he expected to see: a dazed and confused documentary producer who had no idea what she had gotten herself involved in. When he started questioning her about her credit cards, Trace immediately realized that they were somehow involved and became both vague and overly helpful, supplying details designed to make her look like a financial ditz.

The Cuban detective didn't waterboard her or beat the soles of her feet. He did take down everything she said, writing it out in Spanish and working very slowly.

He also asked her to repeat the entire narrative four times.

By the fourth time she was getting testy. She knew it was part of a plan—the more someone tells a story, the larger the chance that discrepancies will creep in. Trace wasn't too worried about being tripped up. Not only did she shorten the narrative each time around, but everything she said was true—she just left out the good parts of her visit. But Trace *hates* wasting time, and she had to fight against her natural inclination to deck the son of a bitch.

---

[32] The lawyers say we mustn't use the word "arrest" since she was never actually arrested or charged with a crime. By that quaint notion, a good portion of the men and women in Cuban jails haven't been arrested, either. Clearly, they're there for the parties.

Finally around three in the morning she was shown to a cell in the basement and told she could sleep for a few hours.

"I want my clothes back," she demanded. "And turn out the damn light."

She did get her clothes back, but the light remained on. Someone came with breakfast at six the next morning. Breakfast was cold, watered-down coffee and a piece of bread so old it could have been baked by Columbus.

Trace demanded to see the Canadian ambassador. The man who took her tray said nothing. When no one appeared after an hour or so, she began repeating her request with shouts loud enough to rumble the walls. No one answered. In fact, for several hours the Cubans seemed to have completely forgotten about her. No lunch came, and there was no interrogation. Finally, around three or four—she had to guess at the time, since the authorities still had her watch—one of the policewomen who had searched her the night before came down to the cell, threw her shoes in, and told her to get her "fat ass" off the cot and follow her.

Trace Dahlgren has many assets, but a fat ass isn't one of them. Still, she tried to stay in character, giving a fake quiver as she put her shoes on and followed the Cuban up the stairs. The policewoman had violated an important tenet of prisoner handling—never turn your back on the person you're escorting—but Trace thought it was possible she was being released and decided not to jump her. That proved to be a good decision, not because the Canadian ambassador was waiting upstairs—he wasn't—but because there were six men with AK47s between her and the door.

Another four were waiting to pack her into the back of a van. Once safely locked in, she was driven to San Miguel del Padrón, the section of Havana where the detectives responsible for "economic criminals" had their headquarters.

The detectives had a serious problem. Their comments during the interrogation made it clear to Trace that they didn't particularly like our friend José Martí, whose real name turned out to be José Martinez. But the ersatz Martí had probably been paying them off, and no one likes losing a source of easy income, especially in a place like Cuba. Meanwhile, his rivals were almost certainly paying the cops under the table as well. Their continuing to do so depended very much on their staying out of jail. Which wouldn't happen if they were implicated in his death or any of the crimes that led up to it.

So at first blush, the arrival of a foreigner on whom everything could be blamed was perfect. The detectives didn't even need to question her—they decided they would make up what they wanted and then forge her signature to a confession. She wasn't even worth torturing.

But the attack on Fidel complicated matters. Before the detectives could pull everything in line, an order came from above to find the connection between the Martí incident and the attack on Fidel. The detectives "knew"—or thought they knew—that there was no connection. But that wasn't going to be good enough for their boss, who saw this as an opportunity to outshine his opposite number in the political police, who were conducting their own inquiry.

Their dilemma was reflected in the questions they asked Trace when she arrived.

How long have you hated Fidel Castro?

How much did the Yankee imperialists pay you to kill him?

Who were the Cubans who were going to help you escape?

Trace kept her head and stayed to her original script, acting bewildered and confused. The detectives hounded her with questions for about an hour and a half before giving up, just in time for happy hour.

Junior had never been to Havana, so he spent the first several hours after landing there orienting himself to all the tourist highlights: every jail and police station within twenty miles of the center of town. By early afternoon, he had a reasonable understanding of the city's layout . . . and the police precincts that went with them. We still hadn't gotten word on where Trace was, so he turned his energies to procuring bicycles and motorbikes and stashing them around the city. Then he went back to his hotel to wait for Shotgun and Crusty.

Crusty didn't get his nickname because he likes thick Italian bread. Rumor has it that even in his youth he was a cranky son of a bitch, and his mood hasn't aged gracefully. He can charm the pants—literally—off women when he wants, but cross him and you'll be grabbing for an asbestos bodysuit.

There's only one thing worse—being late when you're meeting him.

Shotgun and Crusty were supposed to meet at the Havana airport, near the large bank of doors leading to the parking lot and street. According to their planes' schedules, Shotgun should have arrived about ten minutes ahead of him. But Shotgun's plane was delayed by mechanical troubles, and by the time he finally got to Havana, Crusty had been waiting nearly ninety minutes. He'd never met Shotgun before, but we'd e-mailed him a couple of photos before he left Miami, and Shotgun is not exactly hard to pick out in a crowd.

"Where the hell have you been?" growled Crusty as Shotgun sauntered through the small crowd. "And what the hell are you eating?"

"Have you seen your aunt?" said Shotgun, using the code phrase we'd settled on so he could identify Crusty.

"Fuck my aunt. You know I've been waiting here for almost two hours?"

Shotgun started to laugh.

"What are you laughing at? And what the hell are you eating?"

"Crusty, right?"

"What are you eating?"

"Oreos. Want one?"

"What the hell would I want an Oreo for? You know what those things do to your digestive system? You want me to go irregular?"

"How's your aunt?" said Shotgun, which was the backup question.

"She's a dried-up old bitch. How's yours?"

"Bakes a hell of a cheesecake," said Shotgun. "Want to share a cab?"

"They're all thieves," said Crusty, starting for the door. "This place is worse than New York."

Crusty haggled with the drivers until he found one willing to take them for half the going rate. But he didn't haggle at the illegal hotel he'd picked rooms at—the proprietress was a curvaceous fifty-some widower who looked at least ten years younger.

At six, Crusty and Shotgun rendezvoused with Junior at a small restaurant in the old section of Havana. They were all together when I called them with the information about where Trace was.

"I want you to watch the place," I told Junior. "Get a feel for who comes in and out, the routines, you know the drill. If Trace is moved, I want you guys to follow her. And we'll need transport to the southern part of the island, and a couple of backups."

"Got it, boss."

"You're just gathering intelligence," I emphasized. "The whole team will be in tomorrow night. Be ready to move."

Pretty clear, right? No ambiguity in those instructions.

I wasn't in the restaurant with them, and none of them have been particularly candid about what happened after Junior killed the talk button on his phone. So I don't know exactly what happened when. But I do know there was a conversation, and I'm guessing it went something like this:

> JUNIOR: I know that place. It's tiny. There are two floors and a basement.
> SHOTGUN: Is there a fast-food place nearby?
> JUNIOR: We can get her out ourselves. Why wait for Dick?
> CRUSTY: There's no reason at all. All officers think they're God's gift on earth. Everyone knows chiefs *really* run the navy.
> SHOTGUN: I'll do it if there's a place I can get some Twinkies on the way.

There may have been more to it than that. *Maybe* Crusty acted as the voice of reason, trying to talk them out of doing anything rash, suggesting that they wait until I was there. It's possible Shotgun wanted cupcakes instead of Twinkies.

Whatever exactly they said, by 6:30 they were on their way to spring Trace out of jail.

Their intentions were honorable, even admirable. But so are the paving stones on the road to hell.

(V)

I landed in Panama City about 3:00 P.M. The embassy sent over a marine in plainclothes to act as my driver. So much for any chance of acting below the radar.

Those of you following along at home probably think that Ken made such a big deal out of getting a "nongovernment" person in to help the Panamanians as part of the gum-ba-mint's general reflex toward outsourcing dirty-hands jobs. I know that's what I thought. But the reasoning turned out to be more complicated.

Or maybe a lot simpler. Because as the marine drove me to an industrial park outside Panama City, I realized that the operation had all the makings of a goat fuck. Not just a plain vanilla goat fuck, but a truly royal goat fuck, with bows, ribbons, and a fifty-piece brass band.

Make that *60 Minutes*, congressional commissions, and general shoe stomping at the United Nations.

The surefire sign was a big-ass Cadillac with American flags on the fenders. The ambassador himself was involved in the "project."

Wait, I'm libeling the wrong person. The *deputy* ambassador was calling the shots.

In the interests of brevity, I will spare you the well-deserved diatribe against the rolled-cuff denizens of Foggy Bottom. I will also admit, for the purposes of the legal deposition, that there are *some* hardworking, right-minded people in the State Department.

Two at last count, but one was nearing retirement age.

The deputy ambassador in question—we'll call him Deputy Dog—was a sawed-off runt of a man in his mid-forties who thought of himself as a combination of Napoleon and Henry Kissinger. He spoke with a European accent, though he'd been born and raised in the Midwest. Even the sane states produce nut jobs every so often.

Deputy Dog strode across the large hallway at the front of the building as I entered. I put my hand out to shake. He put his on his hips.

"You're Mar-chinko?" he asked. He came to about my chest.

"That's Marcinko."

"You're an expert?"

"I've been around."

He frowned, turned on his heel, and walked back across the room toward the open door at the far end. I turned to the marine and told him to grab a beer.

"I don't drink, sir."

"We'll work on that later," I told him. "For now, go relax and wait outside."

"Sir, yes, sir."

Don't you love them when they're young and corruptible?

The room Deputy Dog had disappeared into was a quasi-command center, complete with laptops, top-shelf communications gear, and more maps than Rand McNally prints in a year. Three or four dozen Panamanians, half in civvies, half in national police uniforms, scurried back and forth looking important, but probably doing about as much work as your typical Can't-Cunt's aide back at our Pentagon.

At the center of the room sat a table with a massive map of eastern Panama. Little plastic markers held various positions around the table.

Deputy Dog was restaging D-day.

Or at least he thought he was. He called the group to order, introduced me to his Panamanian "staff," then proceeded to give a pep talk about how freedom, justice, and the American way hung in the balance.

Fortunately it was in English, so it's possible a few of the Panamanians missed the nuances.

In my younger days, when I was bold and reckless, I would have sat and listened to maybe ten minutes of the speech before interrupting. Now I'm older and wiser, calmer, and even Zen-like in patience. I stopped Deputy Dog no more than sixty seconds after he started.

"Let's cut all the bullshit here and tell what you're planning," I said. "And you can do it in Spanish. I understand enough to get the highlights."

The Panamanians brightened. Deputy Dog reddened.

"I'm afraid you don't understand the situation here, Marcinko," he blustered. Still in English.

"I understand it real well. That's your problem."

And with that, I went out to find my marine and the hotel.

Deputy Dog would have been just as happy if I'd gone back to the airport and returned to Jamaica. But that wasn't my intent. I'd come to give the Chinese a kick in the pants, and I fully intended to do so.

The Panamanians would work out fine, as long as they didn't have to deal with Deputy Dog. And I'd already figured out how to work around him.

When I entered the room, I recognized an old friend of mine, Gabriel Aznar. If I understood Deputy Dog's accent, the gray-haired Aznar had recently been appointed head of the Panama Public Force's counterterror group.

"Gab" Aznar was a member of Panama's special forces units before we went down and kicked out Noriega; I believe he'd even been in the States to train with some SEAL units. But I didn't meet him until years later, when I was a civilian again.

Red Cell International undertook some contract work for a shipping company that made it expedient to deal with the Panamanian authorities. By that time, Panama had abolished its military, handing over most of its function to the national police force, aka the Panama Public Force. Aznar had been effectively demoted back down to lieutenant, despite his experience and seniority.

Luckily for all concerned, especially myself, the section he was posted to just happened to have jurisdiction over a small portion of the canal. I was able to provide Aznar with information that yielded a major arrest aboard a ship transiting the canal. The arrest led to the collapse of a fairly large drug operation run by Colombian terrorists, a win-win for all involved, especially Aznar, whose career was put back on the fast track.

Oh, it also greatly benefited my clients, but I see no harm in that.

Was Aznar grateful? To *moi?*

Let's just say anytime we're out for dinner or drinks, he buys.

I'd winked at him just before walking out on Deputy Dog. He winked back.

I called Danny from the car and asked him to run down Aznar's contact information. Then I leaned over the seat and told the marine to take me to the Dorado Hotel.

"But, sir, you're registered at the Bristol."

"That's why we're going to Dorado."

I gave him directions. The Bristol is a top-notch hotel in Panama City, a chic, high-profile place for chic, high-profile travelers. The Dorado is a cheap hotel catering exclusively to Panamanians, about the last place anyone would expect to find an American. The AC rarely works, the cable is nonexistent, and if you asked about room service the front desk would question your sanity. But to find a place farther below the radar you'd have to visit a cemetery.

Danny called back with the information on how to contact Aznar a half hour later. I called one of his aides at headquarters, gave him my sat phone number, and then went out shopping. He called me as I was counting out the change for a few energy bars.

"That was some show," Aznar told me. "The deputy ambassador has been fuming ever since."

I arranged to meet Aznar in an hour, then went about my chores. He was waiting for me at his headquarters, a bottle of Bombay Sapphire on the conference-room table when I arrived.

We exchanged toasts for a while. Then I suggested we go someplace more secure.

Aznar blinked a few times.

"We scan this place for bugs every day," he said.

I put down my drink and walked over to the big clock on the wall. It was a battery-operated job, the sort you can pick up at Wal-Mart for $9.99, or in China for half that. I flipped it over, pulled out the battery, and tossed it to him.

"Look at that very closely. I'll be outside, waiting."[33]

The plan Deputy Dog had outlined involved half the Panamanian Public Force and the better part of a Marine Expeditionary Unit. It called for a coordinated attack on land and from the air. It might have worked once in a million years.

"Don't you think this is overkill for a dozen attackers?" I asked Aznar, after he sketched it out for me.

"Of course." Aznar shrugged. "It's not my plan. It's the minister's."

"Did you tell him it stinks?"

Aznar smiled. That wasn't the way things were done in Panama, even after Noriega.

"First of all, I'll go out on a limb here and tell you the marines aren't coming," I said. "I'm all the help you're getting."

"That ought to be more than enough."

I smiled at him, then helped myself to the Sapphire.

---

[33] The bug was in the battery. I hadn't scanned it; I simply got lucky, recognizing the clock right away from my previous travels in China.

They beat me with it once; ain't gonna happen again.

(1)

According to the CIA's intelligence—admittedly a contradiction in terms—the Venezuelan-Chinese plan called for the submarines to bring the raiding party close to the mouth of the canal. The fake guerrillas would take over a ship that was just entering the canal and proceed to Cristobal. There they would take hostages and seize control of the Gatun Locks about five miles farther west. A hostage crisis would ensue.

The Chinese would use diplomatic pressure and the threat to close down operations at the canal to keep the Panamanians from doing anything rash like rescuing them or calling the U.S. in to do the dirty work. As the crisis grew to a fever pitch, Chavez would present himself as a negotiator. The hostages would be freed and everything would be hunky-dory.

What would happen to the guerrillas?

Most likely they were considered not just expendable but nonreturnable. It was *possible* that a deal would be arranged to bring them back to Venezuela and somehow manage to escape. But my feeling was that they were going to be shot at the end of the crisis. They were just too much a liability to have around.

I suspected that the "hostages" who would be taken were really members of the Chinese Red Army, and the simplest damn solution to the entire affair would be to blow both them and the tangos up. But of course then every talking head from Beijing to Washington would be crying on TV about the innocent slaughter. So the only alternative was to stop the operation in its tracks.

I saw two possibilities, not counting Deputy Dog's plan. The first was to give them a real surprise when they hit the dock—replace the Chinese who were there with our guys. Then when they came expecting to tiptoe in with a nudge and a wink, we'd kick them in the balls.

This would have been my preferred method had Deputy Dog not been involved. The Panamanians would have been fighting on their own home turf, from easy to defend positions, with tactical as well as strategic surprise on their side. We could also surround the enemy without too much difficulty, taking over the ship ourselves as soon as they were headed toward shore.

But Deputy Dog's plan called for a force to engage the guerrillas in the canal itself, before they landed. We'd never get a chance to launch our surprise. Even if Deputy Dog's overly complicated plan worked—complete with feints, encirclements, an aerial invasion, and probably a refreshment stand, all presumably while television cameras were rolling—stopping the ship in the canal was a major risk. Deputy Dog had chosen to make his assault at a very narrow spot right near a lock. If the guerrillas sank the ship, removing the wreckage would take weeks if not months. And the political fallout would be the same.

So the best alternative was behind door number two: get them while they were still on the submarine.

Which explained what Aznar and I were doing packed into two small fishing vessels twenty miles off the Panamanian coast at nine-thirty that night.

Our navy had been tracking the Chinese submarine at long-range with the help of a Navy Orion antisubmarine warfare (ASW) aircraft and a robotic underwater device that is controlled by a mother submarine[34] for at least a week. Now as we were being rocked by a suddenly roiled ocean, a petty officer aboard the Orion passed a long pinpoint location on where the Chinese boat was.

You're probably thinking that, given all the high-tech doodads at our disposal, intercepting the submarine was easy. But the little boat Aznar was able to commandeer couldn't go very fast; twenty-four knots with the wind at its back was probably its top speed. This was in sharp contrast to the Chinese submarine, which was doing close to thirty knots and could go even higher.

We also didn't want to make it obvious to whoever was working the sonar on the Chinese boat that we were following them. In fact, we wanted to seem like we were hardworking Panamanian fishermen, out after dark hauling in our daily bread.

The Atlantic didn't cooperate. The sea that had looked so calm from Fidel's hospital tonight swelled practically as high as that roof. The wind added a bit of cold spit, mostly in my face as I studied the waves with my night glasses.

I know what you think *I* was thinking: *Lassoing this submarine is going to be a piece of cake.*

---

[34] That's all the navy will tell me about that.

But actually, I was thinking exactly the opposite. Back in my salad days, we used to train for submarine extraction all the time. We'd stretch a line across the path of the submarine's advance. The submarine would slow its speed until it was going *just* fast enough to maintain a constant depth (and, naturally, its course). To make sure the submarine knew where we were, we'd use sonic "clackers" that allowed it to range and home in on our signal. Wham-bam-thank you, ma'am, the line would grab on the periscope (or vice versa); we'd be hauled to the conning tower, get handholds—before you knew it, we'd be basking in the sun, mission accomplished, a babe on each arm.

Well, this *is* fiction. In reality . . . we'd have only one babe apiece.

Heh.

The exercises were conducted under relatively good conditions—no one was shooting at us or the sub. Everyone was pick of the litter at what they did, and everyone—not just the SEALs, but the men aboard the submarines—was highly trained and pulling together. Even so, those exercises were difficult physically and filled with plenty of opportunity for Mr. Murphy to work his magic.

What we were trying to do here was several times harder. For one thing, the submarine wasn't going to be homing in on our signal—if things went right, they wouldn't know we were there. For another, the submarine wasn't going to be traveling at a snail's pace. For another—

Mercifully, my train of thought was interrupted by a communication from the aircraft.

"Contact is slowing," said the petty officer tracking the Chinese submarine. "Same bearing. Mile and a quarter from you. Wait—looks like he's going to spin around."

That was what we were waiting for. The submarine was doing what we call a "box square," pulling a routine maneuver to check to see if anyone had snuck onto its backside while it wasn't looking. This is somewhat more difficult than looking over your shoulder as you walk past a dark alley, but the principle is the same. To do it, the submarine would have to physically slow down—not quite stop, mind you, but the closest we were going to get.

"Get the men into the rafts!" I told Aznar.

"OK, Dick. Good hunting for us."

I moved next to the boat's captain and turned my mike back on.

"Orion, how are we doing?" I asked.

"You need two degrees starboard. You're three miles out."

We made the correction. The captain backed off the motors gently—any abrupt action now might tip the Chinese off that we were interested in something more than nocturnal flounder. At the back of the boat, Aznar and his men slipped into the rafts, drifting on the water.

"You're right on beam," said the petty officer. "Half mile."

I waited until the submarine was about two minutes away, then I turned to the boat's captain. "Exactly as we planned. No matter what happens, you hold your course. Understand?"

"*Sí.*"

"*Gracias.*"

The two divers who'd been chosen to help me were waiting at the crowded fantail of the boat. I trotted back, strapped on my oxygen tank, put on the fins, and went off the side.

It's a popular misconception that submarines sail deep beneath the ocean depths. They certainly dive deep when they have to. But a diesel submarine like the Song spends much of its time relatively close to the surface. There it can use its periscope and even raise its radio mast if it needs to.

The Chinese submarine was sailing at roughly ten meters below the waves—thirty feet. Not very deep if you're a frogman.

The water was black. The cold I'd felt on deck was even worse.

I liked that.

My two Panamanian divers were a short distance from me, swimming with small wrist lights that made it easy to spot them.

The submarine had no such lights. But it was big, dark, and created a hell of a current as it moved toward us. I signaled to the others to fan out along the nylon line we were carrying.

Our goal was simple. The periscope would snag the line and bring us alongside the submarine. We'd place some small charges on the hull, then wait until they went boom, sixty seconds later.

Actually, we wouldn't wait. We'd swim like hell, so the percussion wouldn't kill us. Even underwater, if you're too close to something that blows up, you tend not to have that problem, or any problem in the future.

But continuing with the plan: the sailors inside the submarine would hear the explosions and say, "What the fuck?"

In Chinese, of course.

If we did it right, it would sound as if there had been a malfunction in the main ballast tank. The submarine commander, trying to avert a massive catastrophe, would surface for an inspection. Then we'd have real fun.

Assuming we did it right. If we didn't, we'd be swimming in the ocean picking our toes for two or three hours. More motivation than I needed.

The way I had calculated it, we should have jumped into the water no more than 150 feet from its bow as it came toward us. It should have practically hit me in the face within thirty seconds of my entering the water.

But it didn't. Not at thirty seconds, not at sixty, not at 120.

I was beginning to smell FUBAR. Had our line missed? Had the submarine veered starboard or port? Had it dived below us?

Was the mistake ours? Were we too high or low?

I checked the depth meter. I was at precisely the depth the Orion had told me the submarine was sailing at. We'd been at the right heading. *Where the hell is the damn thing?*

I swam a little left, and then a little right. I didn't want to go up too much farther than I was, and going deeper didn't make much sense, either.

Damn Chinese. Can't they get anything right?

I'd just about sworn off lo mein for the rest of my life when I felt my midsection try to leave my body. For a split second, I didn't know what the hell had happened—then I realized the line had snagged the submarine.

In the next second, a huge black shadow appeared behind me, so close I could *almost* reach out and touch it.

Almost. Because along with the shadow was a serious eddy of water that pushed me to the side. Fighting it was like trying to swim up Niagara Falls.

I'm a strong swimmer—stronger than you, I'm willing to bet—but even I was like a minnow against this tide. I put my head down and paddled ferociously, losing ground. Then suddenly the current reversed direction and I was sucked directly toward the black hull. I landed hard against the vents on the free-flooding cavity, the ridge that runs along the upper hull of the boat to allow it to sink below the waves.

At least I think that's where I hit. I slammed against the submarine so sharply that I was dazed for a few seconds. Luckily for me I hit my head, so no real damage could occur.

Somehow—probably out of unconscious desperation—I grabbed one of the gates.

We'd actually caught a break, because although the submarine had been traveling fast relative to us, it was barely moving in relation to everything else. It had stopped dead in the water, possibly to make it easier for the sonar specialists to figure out what those tiny outboards above them meant.

Or maybe they'd heard the ringing in my ears.

One of my Panamanian helpers came up on my right, tapping me on the shoulder to ask if I was OK. I gave him a thumbs-up, then signaled for him to climb onto the conning tower. Once there, he set up a pair of weighted lines to make it easier to get back on the sub after the explosion. He draped the lines nearby, taking one and working himself out along it to wait for the fireworks.

(The other Panamanian had hit his head on the hull rather hard. Either just before that happened or just after, he'd released the snaps that held him to our snag line and was pushed away by the current. He ended up hundreds of yards away and was lucky to be picked up by one of the boats later on. He had a hell of a story to tell; too bad the blow against the submarine killed his memory of it. Apparently not blessed with a Neanderthal skullplate like yours truly, he suffered a hell of a hangover.)

I opened my rubber sack and took out my explosive charges. I rigged them on a pair of suction cups—crude contraptions modeled after the devices SEALs sometimes use to board ships—set the timers, and backed away.

You're probably wondering why the charges weren't a lot larger—not just small enough to sound as if they'd come from the submarine itself (as opposed to depth charges or torpedoes, which would make it think it was under attack and therefore likely to dive to safety). You're thinking: *Hell, Dick, you've gone to all this trouble. Why not sink the damn submarine and be done with it.*

I like your thinking.

But . . .

There was the fact that officially at least neither the U.S. nor Panama was at war with China, though that wouldn't have stopped me. Sinking the submarine near the canal would potentially create the sort of traffic jam we were trying to avoid.

There was also the fact that submarine hulls are a bit harder to dissect than the outer covering of your average warship. Which doesn't mean it couldn't have been done, but the difficulty—and the pucker factor—would have been considerably higher. We're talking a lot more explosives, a lot more strategically placed. I couldn't get that big a charge on short notice if I tried.[35]

None of which should give you the idea that the charge I attached was insignificant. Which made the fact that Mr. Murphy had tangled one of the weighted lines around my leg and made it impossible for me to get away more than a little annoying.

---

[35] Which the lawyers say I didn't. For the record, the Panamanians don't have ASW equipment, and I needed something without U.S. fingerprints. I still have my regrets, whatever the suits say I should say.

(11)

While I was having fun in the water, Junior was entertaining the troops with impersonations.

As directed, Crusty, Shotgun, and Junior had located the police station where Trace was being held. They'd also done some general spade work to determine where the Canadian embassy was, just so they knew where Trace was likely to be taken once (if) she got sprung by the Canadians. It was while they were doing the latter that an "opportunity" to rescue Trace presented itself, and they took advantage of it.

No, I don't buy that version either.

I think Crusty, Shotgun, and Junior located Trace and decided they were going to get her out ASAP. I think they then went to the embassy intending to do what they ended up doing, which was following a young Canadian diplomat as he left work. The diplomat headed for a bar that catered to rich foreigners not too far from the embassy. While the diplomat was getting hammered, one or more of the boys brushed up against him in some manner . . . and the diplomat just happened to drop his ID badge and all of his identifying papers, passport and wallet, into his/their hands.

Sixty seconds later, Crusty, Junior, and Shotgun were on their way back to the police station.

The police report filed the next morning in Havana indicating that the same diplomat had been found passed out and robbed behind the bar is surely a coincidence.

It's not hard for an American to impersonate a Canadian. All you have to do is move your voice a little farther into your nose, say "eh" a lot, and adopt the air of a goofy but charming younger brother. Junior had no trouble doing all three.

The detective in charge of the station was a bit nonplussed to find that the Canadian embassy had sent over a diplomat to retrieve his "guest witness," as Trace was being called. His first line of defense was to tell Junior—in his guise as the French-speaking Canadian ambassador's aide, Monsieur Depoise—that he had no idea whom he might be talking about.

Junior dealt with that problem with a quick two-step—he produced a photocopy of Trace's Canadian passport, and then suggested that a call to the Interior Ministry would jolt the detective's memory.

"If this is an internal matter, then I am sure I cannot deal with it myself," insisted the detective.

"Perhaps you should call your superior," suggested Junior. "Then you will find that I am not lying."

"I know you are not lying," insisted the detective, who knew better than to insult a foreign official without being told by his superiors that he could do so. "There is no need for verification."

Suggesting that the detective call his boss wasn't a bluff on Junior's part. Outside, Crusty had tapped into the telephone lines. Crusty planned to tell the police officer to do whatever the idiotic Canadian wanted. But the detective never picked up the phone. He just simply played the role of all good career officers everywhere, first feigning ignorance, and then simply refusing, as agreeably as possible, to act.

"You can at *least* let me see her," said Junior. "Give me a few moments with her, eh."

"I can't do that. No." The detective shook his head. "If she were here, which she is not, I couldn't."

"Well if she's not here, then I wouldn't be seeing her if I saw her, would I?"

The police officer smiled. "Now I am confused. My English . . . not very good."

"I am new at the embassy," said Junior, trying another tact. "I don't want to do the wrong thing."

"No, no, of course not." The detective, sensing that his pest would soon be gone, became polite and even accommodating.

"I don't really have much experience," added Junior. "Sometimes there is a fee involved, eh?"

The detective squinted slightly.

"A user fee?" added Junior.

"Are you suggesting a bribe?"

"No, of course not. As I said, I don't know the protocol. There would be a bill for the prisoner's food, maybe your time—"

"Senor, the Cuban police are not corrupt."

"Of course not."

"I will show you where she is. You may not speak to her," said the detective abruptly. "This way, you can tell your boss that she is all right and in good spirits."

"Thank you," said Junior.

He started around the counter. The detective headed him off.

"There are substantial fees for any guest we detain," said the Cuban. "There is a great cost to the state."

Junior nodded. The detective suggested that a hundred dollars Canadian would be a good down payment. Junior—with the hint of a wince—said he would make sure the government paid as soon as he saw the prisoner.

"The fee is generally paid in cash," said the detective.

"Eh? Once I see the prisoner, I'm sure it could be arranged."

"You have the fee on you?"

Junior retrieved his wallet. As it happened, Monsieur Depoise had had 103 Canadian dollars when he misplaced his wallet.

"Only just," said Junior.

The detective smiled and held out his hand. Junior put the wallet back in his pocket.

"I think this sort of fee is payable on the other end of the transaction," he told the detective.

The detective sighed, but after a moment led Junior through the back to a staircase leading upstairs.

Outside, Crusty and Shotgun followed Junior's progress with the help of a bug Junior had smuggled into the country and had activated in his pocket. From watching the building as well as listening in, they calculated that there were no more than five, and probably only two or three, policemen on duty. Getting Trace out would be easier than any of the PT routines she typically started the day with.

Shotgun went to arrange the vehicles for their escape while Crusty stayed near the telephone pole near the rear of the building, monitoring the bug and waiting in case there was a phone call. Crusty heard Junior go up the steps, admiring the large—and empty—room just off the landing that served as a common office for the detectives. He heard Junior greet another officer, who was in a smaller room to the right as he went down the hall.

"Love the paint scheme in that little room," said Junior.

"It's gray," said the policeman.

"We Canadians love gray," said Junior. "Reminds us of winter. That room's about the size of a bathroom back home. You only have the one guy assigned there?"

And finally, he heard Junior ask his guide if he was sure that the "guest" couldn't see or hear them through the two-way glass.

"Impossible," said the detective.

"You think you need the chains?"

"Standard procedure, senor."

"What if there's a fire? Where do you keep the keys?"

The detective patted his pocket.

"Now you see she is alive and in good health," he said. "You can tell your superiors."

"I would like to talk to her."

"No. No."

Junior didn't bother arguing anymore. Not only did he know that there were only two men in the entire building, but he also realized that the detective was not carrying anything larger than a hideaway pistol, if at that.

He looked for a chance as the detective led him back downstairs. But the Cuban had suddenly become wary, and rather than drawing close when he took out his wallet, he went back behind the counter to the desk where he'd been when Junior arrived.

"The fee should be left in the tray," he said, almost as an afterthought.

"Almost" being the key word.

"Are you sure you don't want to count it?" asked Junior.

"I trust the Canadian government."

There was no sense making the man more suspicious. Junior left the money in the basket. He also left the bug, attaching it below the counter, figuring that it might provide useful intelligence for his return.

Outside, Crusty peered around the corner of the building as he heard a car drive up. It was a Toyota Landcruiser, less than a year old. As soon as he spotted it, a familiar sense of déjà-fucking-vu flooded into his gut.

Mr. Murphy had just arrived in the guise of the Canadian special affairs attaché.

307

(III)

Untying a tangle of knots requires two things one rarely finds while topside on a rapidly submerging submarine—time and patience.

The timer on the explosives was preset to sixty seconds; I'd already used about fifteen of them setting it, pushing away, and dangling like a cooked goose from a Chinese butcher's display. My only option was to cut the line and float free.

I took out my Panamanian diving knife—my custom Strider was back in Jamaica—and started hacking through the line.

It didn't want to give. On TV, lines always snap at the sight of the blade. In real life, the strands hang together like glue paper sticking to the back of a rat scurrying through an alley.

I had a lot of sympathy for the rat until the blade finally made it through the last of the nylon-titanium thread. I shot backward so quickly that at first I thought the bomb had exploded. When I realized it hadn't, I pushed down toward the hull of the sub, hoping to find a handhold or something to grab on to so I'd be sure to be on top of the submarine when it surfaced.

I didn't hear the explosion, or even feel it. I did notice a sudden surge of bubbles from the bow area as I grabbed one of the protrusions[36] that ran along the stern hull near the openings for the missiles. I assumed that was the bang, and I held on tight, expecting that we'd surface any moment.

We didn't. As a matter of fact, nothing happened for what seemed like an eternity. I was considering jumping up and down on the god-damn sub when it finally began moving.

Downward.

Damn Chinese. I should have known you can always count on them to do things ass backward.

I pounded on the hull of the sub, though I doubt they heard much of the sound, since it was covered with acoustic tiles.

What they undoubtedly did hear was the detonation of a backup

---

[36] There are various pieces of metal welded or bolted to the hull of most submarines. One of our technical consultants believes I hooked on to one of the "spikes" that is normally used in port for a kind of wire fence topside, but that would mean one of the sailors forgot to stow it. Could be. All I know is it was attached to the submarine.

charge my Panamanian friend had been carrying in his rubberized ruck. As soon as the sub started downward, he pulled himself up the line to the conning tower, set the timer, and then worked himself back out. Damn smart kid. If he ever decides to come to El Norte, there'll be a job waiting for him at Red Cell.

This bang did the trick. The Chinese captain, his career no doubt flashing in front of his eyes, decided to stop screwing around and ordered an immediate emergency blow—your basic crash dive in reverse. The submarine did a kind of a U-turn in the water, and shot up toward and through the surface like a bronco busting out of the chute at a Friday night rodeo.

I went flying as well, tumbling off the hull like a flea off a dog that's just jumped into a bathtub. I shot into the air, then hit the water on my back so hard I thought I'd landed on a sidewalk. But I'll say one thing for Murphy: he gives as well as takes. He popped me up about ten yards from the raft with Aznar, the leader of the Panamanian assault team.

There was a full moon that night, or they might have run over me rather than picking me up. As it was, the Panamanians barely stopped to get me aboard before racing to join the rest of the team on the hull of the Chinese submarine.

Mongoose was already there. In fact, he and two Panamanian friends were standing right over the hatchway as the Chinese broke the lock and came up for a breath of fresh air.

Zap-boom-pop—Chinaman number one over the side.

Zap-boom-pop—Chinaman number two over the side.

Zap-boom–rip-pop—I think Mongoose broke Chinaman number three's neck.

By the time I reached the submarine, Mongoose had already taken out the topside security team, eliminating the initial resistance. He and his two shadows, along with three other Panamanians from the first raft to hit the sub, then descended through the sail into the control room, where they effectively took over the ship.

Did I mention the tear gas?

Following the general principle of better-safe-than-sorry, the Panamanians dropped a few tear-gas canisters down the open hatch. That made things easy inside, adding to the utter chaos the Chinese had to deal with. The boarding team wore gas masks, but those of us topside generally chose not to don them.

Mistake. Almost instantaneously, the gas began to waft upward. So there were quite a few red eyes on deck when the first of the Chinese prisoners, including the submarine's executive officer, came up.

The executive officer was pulled unceremoniously and placed, not too gently, against the side of the conning tower.

"You speak Spanish?" I asked in my best impression of a Panamanian.

He replied in Chinese, asking for a towel for his eyes. I understood it, but not very well.

"How about English?" I said. "You speak that."

"English—yes. Towel for eyes."

I whistled for Aznar, who found the officer a hankie. By this time, several other sailors had been sent up the ladder, including a young junior lieutenant—the equivalent of an ensign in our navy—who was having a hard time breathing because of the gas. He coughed and bent over, hands clutched to his chest.

Who says we don't take humanitarian concerns into account during wartime?

"Search the bastard," I barked after I kicked him in the gut.

Why'd I hit him? Because the junior lieutenant had a pistol under his shirt, which he was trying to pull out. Obviously he was bucking for the fast track to commodore.

He got a bath for his trouble. The pistol went in after him. I would have kept it as a souvenir but it was a Type 77 and I've already got a couple.

Downstairs, the submarine's captain and Mongoose were having a bit of a language problem: the captain didn't understand that none of the languages Mongoose understands, including English, include the word "no."

"You're going the hell up the ladder." Mongoose was using Spanish—we were all Panamanians, remember. He'd had to take his gas mask off to make himself heard. The submarine's environmental system had filtered some of the fumes away by now, but there was still more than enough gas to irritate his eyes.

"Up. Up. Up." Mongoose gestured when the captain didn't respond. "You go up."

"I stay with my crew," said the captain.

Actually, I'm only guessing at what the sub commander said, because he was speaking in Chinese, a language that Mongoose has only the most theoretical understanding of. The captain continued, probably pointing out that they were in international waters and this takeover violated about fifty international laws. He also seemed to strongly suspect that Mongoose and the Panamanians, despite their Spanish and nondescript uniforms,[37] were American. Finally, he said something along the lines of "Shoot me here."

Or at least that's what Mongoose thought.

"I *will* shoot you here." Mongoose demonstrated his willingness to do so by holding a pistol to the captain's head.

Give the submarine commander credit—he blinked, but probably only because tears were still streaming out of his eyes from the gas. He wouldn't budge.

Meanwhile, I was getting a little impatient topside. Half my body was bruised, and the other half was shivering.

"What the hell is the hold up down there?" I yelled down. "Bring the captain up. Now! *Breathing.* Not too many bruises."

Best to be specific, especially where Mongoose is concerned.

Mongoose snapped to, grabbing the captain in a bear hug and then shoving him up the ladder. One of the Panamanians took him and passed him along. In short order the captain was deposited on the deck like a mail sack filled with overdue bills.

I helped him to his feet and told him in Mandarin that he was in a world of trouble.

He replied with a few choice naval terms.

"You're going to cooperate," I told him in pigeon Chinese. "Or your submarine is going to be sunk."

My translation of his response was imperfect, but it did involve a reference to my ancestors, none of whom he seemed to consider honorable. I grabbed him by the front of his uniform and pressed him against the side of the tower.

"You speak Spanish?" I asked.

He said in Chinese that he didn't understand me.

"Then I'll use English." I gave it my best south of the border spin. "I want the Venezuelans. They come with me. Or I sink your submarine. Which is it?"

---

[37] Mysteriously, all identifying insignia seemed to have been removed.

He blinked, then nodded.

Eighteen Venezuelans, stripped to the waist, hands high, filed up the ladder a short time later. One by one we searched them, then passed them down to the rafts.

It took us about a half hour to get all of the Venezuelans off. By that time, the Chinese crew was starting to rally from their surprise, and even though I had their captain with me, I didn't trust that they'd remain passive for very much longer.

But I couldn't resist the temptation of having a look around the control room before shoving off. Taking the rungs by two, I went down and had a good look. Mongoose had taken pictures of everything he could see in the control room, the sonar station nearby, and a space that turned out to be the com area though it didn't seem manned. It was a real Kodak moment—even if the camera he was using was a Chinese-made model.

There's irony in that, but I don't think the Chinese Navy would really appreciate it.

(IV)

There's a coda to the story:

As we were leaving, an American destroyer that had been part of the surveillance team thirty-five miles to the north hove into view, every light aboard blazing. The skipper must have opened the engines and thrown everything that could burn into the turbines to make the speed. In any event, he bore down on the sub, then broadcast a message over the radio and through his loudspeakers:

"Unidentified vessel. You appear to be under attack by pirates. Do you request assistance?"

The Chinese captain politely declined.

"Are you crying, buddy?" asked the navy captain.

The response was in Mandarin, but I think you can figure out what it meant.

The Venezuelan would-be commandos were a pretty sorry lot. At least half of them got seasick during the hour and a half raft trip back to land. All were pretty damn cold when we landed, in no shape to take control of anything.

Aznar, on the other hand, was in an excellent mood. This operation was sure to get him serious recognition from the government—a promotion in rank, and very possibly future consideration as one of the Public Force's bright young (or not quite so young) leaders.

Which made this an excellent time to tell him why I'd come.

"One of my people is stranded in Cuba," I told him after he'd secured his prisoners. "I need to mount an operation there and I need some help. People I can count on."

"Cuba?"

"What I need are shooters with experience, who speak Spanish, but are not necessarily guys who are *currently* in uniform," I told him. "I could use retired guys, or . . ."

"Men who are on leave."

"Exactly."

"Yes." He turned around. "I would say a good number of these men here are probably due for a few days of rest."

"Paid rest," I added. "If a dozen of your finest can meet me in Panama City tomorrow, I'll be sure to show them a good time."

"They'll be there, Dick. You can count on it."

Deputy Dog—remember him?

The deputy ambassador began foaming at the mouth when he discovered that I had pulled the rug out from under him. He commandeered a Panamanian Public Force helicopter and flew out to Fort Sherman, where Aznar had put in.

Fort Sherman was built in the early twentieth century out on Toro Point on the north side of the canal. Besides protecting the canal, it was the U.S. Army's jungle warfare training ground, and quite a large number of Central and South American troops learned the basics of jungle fighting there. We gave it over to the Panamanians in 1999, along with its brother on the opposite coast, Fort Amador.

The Panamanians have made such great use of the property that most of it is now under the control of Mother Nature, the most ferocious landlord of all.

(Following along at home? Up-to-date maps may not list it. Look for Shelter Bay Marina, which is what they call the big cement pier. It's across the way from Colón.)

Mongoose and I were enjoying a few cold Balboas—the local beer—with the Panamanian ops guys when Deputy Dog arrived. The prisoners were sitting at the far end of the dock area, awaiting the helicopters Aznar had called in. Aznar himself had already taken the leader and his two lieutenants for interrogation.

I didn't go along myself; my stomach is delicate, you understand.

"You fucking son of a bitch," said Deputy Dog, stomping toward me. "You're going to jail for this."

"Hey, skip, someone's looking for you," said Mongoose, smirking behind his beer.

"You violated—you ruined—you screwed up—our plan—"

"Your plan sucked," I told him. "And is now obsolete. The Venezuelans are over there. They've already confessed. The Chinese submarine is limping home. My bet is it'll take the longest way around possible."

Deputy Dog said a few other things, but they were drowned out by the arriving helicopters. Finally he stomped off in the direction of the prisoners.

"Time to go, Mongoose," I said as the drum of arriving Hueys filled the air.

Mongoose scooped up a couple of bottles for the road. "We're riding with the prisoners, skipper?"

"Hell, no. Deputy Dog's going to want to do that. We're taking his helo."

And we did, all the way back to Panama City.

[V]

By now you're probably wondering what happened to Junior, whom we left standing in the foyer of the small Cuban detective bureau just as the real Canadian representative walked through the door.

The Canadian, a tallish fellow named Paulson with thick glasses and a Toronto accent, sauntered down the hall, announcing in a loud voice that he was from the Canadian embassy and wanted to speak to the person in charge.

Junior had two choices. He could have made a dash for it, running past the Canadian into the street, where Shotgun and Crusty would help mount a counterattack. Or he could stay and try to bullshit his way out the door.

There's a time for running and there's a time for bullshitting. Being inexperienced, Junior didn't recognize the difference, and chose the latter.

"They sent you, too?" he said, approaching Paulson.

"And you are?"

"Monsieur Depoise. I just arrived yesterday and here I am. Just threw me into it."

"What section do you work in?"

"Passports," said Junior cheerfully. "Why they sent me here is baffling."

"I have a writ for the filmmaker's release," said Paulson, reaching into his pocket.

"Great." Junior turned and pointed toward the Cuban detective, who'd been taking all this in. "She's upstairs. I'll go get her."

"Not so quickly, I think," said the Cuban. "Let me see your credentials again."

"Sure," said Junior. He turned to Paulson. "I already paid the document fee, so you don't have to worry about that. I guess I should have gotten a receipt though."

"What fee?" asked Paulson. "And who exactly are you?"

Things would have undoubtedly gone farther downhill from there had the proceedings not been interrupted by a hundred plus decibel crack of an exploding grenade—the report of a flash-bang tossed through a window into the reception room by Crusty. At nearly the same instant, Shotgun came barreling through the front door, an AK47 in his hands.

Junior dove on Paulson and threw him to the ground. The detective was nowhere near as quick. Shotgun, operating in shoot-first, ask-questions-never mode, put three bullets in the Cuban's chest before he could grab his service revolver from his nearby desk.

Junior's eardrums were reverberating with the shock of the explosion, so he didn't hear Shotgun yelling to him to go out and get the car started. Instead, he scrambled to his feet and grabbed the detective's pistol from the open drawer. Still stunned, he took a few deep breaths, then ran up the stairs, a few giant steps behind Shotgun.

"I'm in here!" yelled Trace from the cell at the end of the hall.

Shotgun ran straight to the door, found it locked, and yelled at Trace to back away. He put a bullet point-blank into the keyhole and kicked the door into two distinct and splintered halves.

In his haste, Shotgun had missed the detective Junior had seen upstairs earlier. As Junior reached the landing, the Cuban came out of his office, pistol raised. Junior fired several times. His first bullet hit the floor; his second grazed the detective's chest. The third, rising with Junior's unsteady arm, got him square in the side of the head.

Shotgun was standing at the end of the hall, AK47[38] ready to take out the detective.

"Hey, thanks, little buddy," he told Junior, then went back to rescuing Trace.

Junior didn't hear him. His ears were still ringing with the blast downstairs, but the reason was more psychological than physical. He stopped running and stood in the corridor, staring at the blood as it spurted out from the dead Cuban's head. It looked black rather than red, much darker than he would have expected.

It was the first time Junior had killed someone.

I'm not going to wax poetic about dead bodies, or what it's like the first time you actually kill someone. To be honest, mostly you're in a situation where you don't have the luxury of thinking about what the hell you've done. And in those rare instances, like this one, where a few milliseconds are available, reactions are all different. You can't make a blanket statement about someone getting all choked up — or the opposite,

---

[38] They were using the weapons we'd left behind earlier, in case you're wondering.

laughing about how mashed the person's brains were. I've seen both reactions.

My philosophy comes down to this: being dead sucks. Much better to be on the other side of the gun.

"We getting the hell out of here, or what?" demanded Trace, coming out into the hall.

"Nice bracelets you got on your feet," said Shotgun.

"Where the hell are the keys?" she asked. "Junior? *Junior?*"

He turned around slowly.

"Do you know where the keys are to these leg irons?"

"Downstairs."

Paulson had gotten to his feet in the hallway. As soon as he saw Shotgun, however, he dove back to the ground, expecting to be shot.

"Who's he?" said Trace. She stopped and grabbed Junior, shouting the question, then repeating the words slowly so he could read her lips.

"Canadian," said Junior, retrieving the keys from the dead detective's pocket.

If that bothered him, he never said.

"We gotta take him to the embassy or they'll think he did it," said Trace. Freed of her restraints, she strode to Paulson and grabbed him by the scruff of the neck, then spun him up over her shoulder. Her first step was shaky, but she quickly found her balance and carried him outside.

Crusty had brought the car around.

"I hope none of you have blood on you," he told them as they got in. "I'm sure the rental people will charge extra."

Among the goodies Junior had smuggled into Cuba was a new Belgian passport for Trace. After dumping Paulson off at a bus stop—taking him to the embassy would have been too dangerous—they got rid of the car, then headed to a backup hotel where we'd reserved a safe room. Phase one of the operation over, Shotgun and Junior hit the bar for a quick dose of bruise-killer. Trace went to shower.

When Trace came down a few hours later, her hair was close-cropped and blond. She wore a tracksuit purchased from the foreign store across the street. And her English had a decidedly French accent.

Not sure where she picked that up.

"I'm ready for a Kodak moment," she told Junior.

They went back upstairs. Once upon a time, passports were relatively easy to forge. Now—they're still relatively easy to forge, if you know what you're doing, and if you have a program on your computer and special paper that helps you do it.

Trace stood up against the wall. Junior took her photo and inserted it into the blank spot in the program template.

"You look good as a blonde," he told her.

Trace frowned at him, without bothering to look at the image.

All that remained was finding a printer. (The paper needed to be printed by a color laser, and it hadn't been practical to try and get that into Cuba in their luggage.) In any other city, they would have their choice of dozens of Kinko's and computer cafés. This being Havana, however, their options were more limited. The hotel had a small business center for use by foreigners only, but it was after-hours and the place was closed.

"Maybe we can get someone to open the place up for us," said Junior as they stood outside the door.

"Let me take a look at it." Trace glanced around, then walked to the door. She had lost her lock picks along with all of the rest of her gear and clothes, but the lock was about as sophisticated as most locks back home.

Which meant it was easy pickings.

Trace turned to Junior and uttered the words that strike fear in the heart of every married man.

"Lend me your credit card," she told him.

Not being married, Junior complied.

Trace slid the card into the doorjamb, leaned slightly on the knob, and opened the door.

"Go," she told Junior after waiting a moment to make sure no alarms would sound. "Keep the lights off."

"You mean, work in the dark?"

"The bogeymen won't get you. I promise."

Junior slipped inside. The room was divided by a series of carpet-covered partitions, which provided a modicum of privacy for each station—a nice touch, considering that software on each computer would record everything that was typed. But Junior didn't need a computer.

A networked laser printer sat at the rear of the room. He found it, unplugged it from the network, and fired up his laptop. Two minutes later, the passport blank was fed out of the top of the printer.

Where it promptly jammed, about three-quarters of the way out.

"Someone's coming!" hissed Trace outside about three seconds after Junior figured out how to open the printer.

He pushed it closed, then slipped behind it in the corner as the lights turned on. A vacuum cleaner started to hum.

Thirty seconds later, the vacuum cleaner abruptly shut off. Junior heard the male cleaner curse in a loud, gruff voice. Then he heard Trace asking if someone could help her get into her room.

Trace was speaking Spanish, but her accent was entirely her in her hips. The janitor quickly volunteered, and they left the room together.

This was Junior's cue to get the hell out of there as well, but he couldn't do that without the passport page. The printer refused to let go until, out of desperation, Junior sent another page through, forcing the page out. It was a little smudged, but it was clearly the best he was going to do. Junior grabbed it and got out.

On his way back to Trace's room, he passed the janitor in the hall, staring at the cord to his vacuum cleaner, which had inexplicably frayed. There were sweat rings under the man's armpits, and he looked as if he'd just run a marathon.

With the passport ready, Trace, et al., headed for the airport. Danny, meanwhile, was prevailing on our Christians in Action contacts to set up four plane tickets—to where didn't matter, as long as they were out of Cuba.

They were still waiting to hear where they were each headed when they realized the red lights in front of the airport were blocking the entrance to the terminal.

"Shit," muttered Trace.

"Think they're looking for us?" asked Junior.

"Maybe, but it's too late to turn back now," said Crusty. "Just play it smooth."

He drove right up to the roadblock and began demanding in curse-salted Spanish to be let through. The policeman simply waved at him, telling him to turn around.

"No flights, no flights," said the man.

The Cubans, following a plan laid out by Chavez, had shut down the airport in connection with the canal plot, not realizing that it had been foiled. The runways stayed empty until the next morning at ten, when a plane from Venezuela landed. They later claimed that nothing had happened. The several hundred passengers whose flights had been canceled obviously were hallucinating, since according to the Cubans those planes had in fact landed or taken off.

Trace and the others didn't know this at the time. Danny had no information either. The logical conclusion was that the airport had been closed because the detectives' bodies had been found. Thinking they were only a few steps ahead of the authorities, they drove back into the city, got rid of the car, and made their way to a bus station.

It was only then that they decided to call me and tell me what the hell was going on.

If I'd been able to get my boot through the phone I would have given them all a good piece of shoe leather.

"This is what happens when you do an op without thinking it through," I told Junior.

"You always say, seize the day."

"You seize it, not screw it up."

Trace grabbed the phone from him.

"Why are you balling Matthew out?" she asked. "I could have rotted in Fidel's jails. Why don't you thank him for rescuing me?"

"I'll thank him when I see him," I said. "After I kick him in the butt. Now how the hell are you going to get off the island?"

"We'll go south and hook up with the backup boat," she said.

The Cubans had already increased their naval patrols following my recent adventures with Fidel, so escaping by water wasn't going to be as easy as Trace thought. And in any event, we had to arrange for the boat to rendezvous off the Cuban coast, something it was now too late to do. So I told her to hole up for the night, and the next day.

"You want us to spend another twenty-four hours here?"

"Work on your tan," I told her.

I hung up before she could object.

(1)

The fat lady had not yet sung, as Yogi Berra would put it, but she was in the wings, ready to take center stage. Getting Trace and the boys out of Cuba was going to be even easier than I thought—there was no need now for the Panamanian muscle I'd just recruited. They could use one of the backup boats, or steal one; we'd get Paul M. W. Smith and his refurbished PBM flying boat—just now back in service—to pick them up and bring them home.

And yet . . .

A familiar feeling of déjà this-ain't-over vu snuck up my spine as Doc and I conducted our personal mission debrief at the bar in the Panama Queen hotel. It was well past three in the morning. The bartender had gone home, leaving us in the trusted hands of Dr. Bombay, whose contribution to the proceedings was invaluable. But even with his guidance, I knew we had a lot more work to do.

Ken, of course, was ecstatically happy. Not only had the Chinese and Venezuelans been busted, not only had we gained a wealth of intelligence on a heretofore top-secret submarine, but the State Department had been kicked in the gonads.

I'm guessing that was worth more to him than everything else, but who am I to say?

As far as I knew, Ken and his cohorts remained convinced that the canal was Fidel's master plan for revenge. They were wrong, clearly. As nasty as it would have been, it didn't meet Fidel's requirements for dealing the capitalist pigs a death blow that had his signature on it. Too subtle for an old commie.

Back in the sixties when he allowed Khrushchev to locate his ballistic missiles on the island, Fidel had been thinking of Armageddon. He'd only want more now.

"If he put a nuke in the canal, that I could understand," I told Doc as we reached round thirteen in our personal debrief. "But there was no nuke on that ship."

"The Chinese wouldn't have let that happen," said Doc. "Too much money to be made."

I sipped my drink. Fidel wasn't beyond using a nuke, and it was reasonable to think that he had enough connections among hardliners in Russia to find someone willing to sell him one. Maybe he'd managed to scrape together enough cash to buy it.

But Putin wouldn't let that happen. He might want to tweak the U.S., but if a Russian A-bomb turned an American city into ashes, the Europeans buying his natural gas would get very, very nervous. Anything that hurt his gas and oil sales would hurt the Russian economy, threaten his leadership, and dent his personal pension plan.

Maybe he didn't buy it from Russia. Pakistan, India—anyone with the capacity to make a weapon could "lose" it as well.

"Hard to imagine that we wouldn't have heard any rumors about that," said Doc. "Maybe not out of Cuba, but certainly on the seller's end. Besides, if something like that was for sale, don't you think the crazy Saudi would have outbid him? Bin Laden's richer than Fidel by far. He could buy Cuba twenty times over."

"True."

"Junior's coming along," said Doc, sensing that we'd already kicked the subject to death. "Really bucking for a place in the field."

"Yeah."

"Why don't you like him, Dick?"

"Who says I don't like him?"

"You don't use him."

"He's in Cuba, isn't he?"

"Yeah."

"Then I'm using him, ain't I?"

"I guess." Doc studied his glass for a second, then emptied in a gulp, ice and all. He spent the next minute or so grinding the ice cubes into tiny shards, savoring the cold. "You have been kind of tough on him."

"If you think I've been tough on him, just wait. I'm betting springing Trace was his idea."

"That's a bad thing?"

"It was reckless."

"They got her out." Doc leaned over the bar and scooped his glass into the bin of ice. He swirled the glass, settling the ice, then filled it to the rim with gin.

"They were lucky they got her out," I said. "It could just as easily have gone the other way."

"Luck is a matter of perspective," said Doc. "Somebody once told me, a good shooter makes his own luck. He trains, he prepares the mission, he executes."

I hate it when someone uses my words against me.

"I like the kid," added Doc, hoisting his glass. "Reminds me of another young and rash SOB I knew back in my early days in the navy."

"Clearly you hung around with the wrong kind."

"Still do," he said. "Still do."

Actually, if we'd known what Junior was about to do next, even Doc would have been angry with him.

After they got themselves sorted and settled following the escape, Crusty took them east of Havana where a trusted cousin lived in a small village.[39] Though surprised to see him and the other three unexpected guests, the cousin invited them in and gave them something to eat. The appearance of distant relatives out of the blue was not without precedence, either in Crusty's family or for most of the island's residents, especially when the family had "lost" members to emigration over the years. Cubans as a general rule are generous hosts, and it would be a rare family that didn't welcome even the blackest sheep for a short stay.

Of course, Crusty didn't tell the cousin what was going on, only that he'd come to the island to see a great-aunt on his mother's side (the opposite branch of the family from the cousin, so cross-verification wasn't a problem) and then decided to visit some of the other relatives while there was still time. He introduced Trace as a "friend," adding just enough winks to piss Trace off. Shotgun and Junior were passed off as friends who'd wanted to see the country, and whose presence was not necessarily legal (from the U.S.'s point of view), a common enough occurrence in Cuba that it aroused no undue suspicion.

What it did do was invite a lecture from the cousin, who interpreted the statement as meaning they were left-leaning Americans interested in the "Cuban miracle." Shotgun and Junior were treated to a discourse on the realities of that miracle, including a catalog of every hardship the cousin's family had ever endured, starting with the confiscation of their

[39] Since naming the actual village might jeopardize Crusty's relatives, we'll leave the name out in this account.

property and ending with a chronic toilet paper shortage, both of which seemed to provoke equal outrage in the cousin.

Junior was bored and went off in a corner to play with his laptop. (The beta version of the new *Rogue Warrior*™ game, in case you're interested.) Shotgun, on the other hand, was the perfect audience. He kept smiling and nodding while pulling the occasional bit of snack food from his pocket.

In the morning, Crusty's cousin went off to work at a local farm. Trace decided to scout the village. She wasn't just doing sightseeing—our stashed boat was more than a hundred miles away, and it would be easier to simply steal one here. She took Shotgun with her, leaving Junior and Crusty to get some sleep.

Junior napped for an hour or two, but nerves eventually got the better of him, and he got up to do some work. After making sure they were alone in the house, he fired up his laptop.

The night before, he'd played games. Now he felt as if he ought to be working. Connecting to the Internet via the satellite modem, he called up Google Earth and surveyed the general area. Then he ran down the news, both in Cuba and the rest of the world. Then finally, bored but feeling that he ought to be productive, he tapped into the Rogue Manor network back home and reviewed the files that were on Raul's hard drive.

Pornography filled about half of the drive. Most of the text documents were endlessly boring speeches, including the one that had helped alert the CIA to the canal conspiracy. The other files were e-mails and various odds and ends in different formats that Junior had a hard time deciphering. His Spanish had improved considerably over the past few days, but there were still vast gaps in his vocabulary and comprehension. He spent more than twenty minutes puzzling over a file that turned out to be a simple Excel spreadsheet listing restaurant bills, apparently some sort of expense voucher.

Junior was just starting on a new file when he smelled Crusty's cigarette smoke wafting into the room, a kind of early warning that the former chief petty officer was on his way.

"Computers cause cancer," said Crusty, leaning over Junior's shoulder.

"Like cigarettes?"

"At my age, tobacco's good for you," said Crusty, taking the pack from his pocket. "And sterility. You got that thing two inches from your balls."

Junior didn't think Crusty's medical advice could be trusted. Still, he shifted around and put the laptop on the seat of the chair next to him.

"Help me with some of these, would you?" he said. "I can't figure out what they mean."

"What do I look like?" Crusty scowled. The correct answer would be: a crazed armadillo. He took a slow drag from his cigarette, then waved his hand, shooing a nonexistent fly. "You think I'm a computer gizmo guy?"

"They're some sort of memos or something in Spanish. This one's about serum or something."

Junior held the laptop screen for him. Crusty stuffed the cigarette in his mouth, folded his arms, then leaned so close to the screen Junior thought he was trying to put his head through it.

"Inoculations," said Crusty. "This is a list of inoculations. People getting shots, and where. Shot shots. Not bullet shots."

"Yeah, I got that," said Junior, pulling the computer back. That jogged his memory about a memo on the drive directing "recipient" to proceed to the Assembly for inoculation. He began searching for it.

"These are big shits, you know," added Crusty.

"Big who?"

"Big shits. That's the mayor of Havana. That's the party secretary. That's—"

"Do these words tell you what the disease is?" asked Junior. He'd selected a different memo, and held up the computer again.

"Hmmmph," said Crusty when he finished reading it.

"Well?"

"They're to report to the Assembly building this week for an immunization. This is a reference here to Fidel's death."

"I saw that."

"It hasn't happened. But they mentioned it. Which is strange. Here, give me this damn thing."

Crusty took the laptop and read the memo. Despite his hostile attitude toward computers, he actually seemed to know his way around them pretty well. He brought up a number of different memos and read through them quickly.

"They're not supposed to go into the area around Vianna Norte before getting the shots," said Crusty finally.

"Why not?"

"Beats the hell out of me. Maybe so they don't pick up the disease."

"Vianna Norte?"

"Never heard of it."

"It's the name of the place where the inoculation is being shipped from," said Junior. He got up, then took the computer back. "Here's the memo about when it's arriving—from Vianna Norte. That must be where the lab is."

"And all the sick people," said Crusty.

Junior didn't pay attention. He was already trying to locate Vianna Norte on Google Earth.

II

I woke in Panama City to the buzz of my sat phone. Pulling it from the side table, I flicked it on, held it to my ear, and heard Ken Jones tell me I was a genius.

A chill shot up my spine.

"What do you want now, Ken?"

"You're a genius, Dick. And a true American hero."

Damn, I thought to myself. *The day hasn't even started yet and here it's all shot to hell.*

Ken had taken to heart what I'd said about Fidel wanting something more apocalyptic to go out on. He'd put several analytical teams to work assessing the situation and reviewing spy data. Somewhere between wearing out their erasers and playing wastepaper basketball, they'd come up with a new theory not all that far from the one Doc and I had kicked around during our bar debrief: Fidel was going to nuke New York.

Or some other East Coast city. Most likely New York. Maybe.

Unlike us, the analysts (presumably) hadn't been drinking when they contemplated this, and so they were able to arrive at a conclusion that never occurred to us: the Cubans hadn't bought a bomb. The Soviets had left it behind in 1962.

"I doubt that's possible, Ken."

"That was my reaction, too." Ken's voice was in its aw-shucks mode, the sort he uses when he doesn't want someone to know that he knows that he's the smartest person in the world. It's meant to seem self-depreciating, though of course it's actually the opposite.

"No one stood on Cuban soil and counted the warheads going in," said Ken. "Or the missiles. It's been buried in a cave there all this time."

"Which cave?"

"I don't know which cave. That's immaterial," said Ken. "It's not there anymore."

"Where is it?"

There was plenty of sarcasm in my voice, believe me, but it went right over Ken's head.

"The Cubans sent a merchant ship out from one of their western ports two days ago, when it looked like Fidel was going to finally die. They haven't called it back yet. We think that's the ship where the bomb is."

The ship in question, *Cuba Libre*, had had a somewhat checkered history as a Soviet merchant ship during the 1970s and '80s. Though not quite old enough to have been involved in the Cuban Missile Crisis itself, it had shipped regularly back and forth between Russia and Cuba, bringing the socialist haven bourgeoisie supplies like wheat and rice that the workers' paradise couldn't grow or buy on its own.

At some point, the Russians had turned the ship itself over to Cuba, perhaps as a partial payment for the services of Cuba's army in Angola, where the ship made a few stops during Cuba's nonimperialistic imperialism foray there. It had plied the Caribbean waters for a few years, allegedly transporting fruit and vegetables, though the CIA files showed its services had been retained by at least two companies that had ties to drug dealers in Panama. For the past six or seven years, it had sat at anchor, rotting away—until six months ago, when spy satellite photos showed that it had suddenly been refurbished and painted.

Cuba Libre wasn't a warship, just a plain jane merchant vessel, and there had been no reason to keep too close an eye on it. Work had been finished a few months back, but the ship had stayed at its moorings east of Havana, according to the various satellite and other reconnaissance data.

Until the other day.

"Where's it going?" I finally asked the admiral.

"Not clear."

"Stop it and find out."

"I'm glad you feel that way."

Used to be, there was a suspicious merchant ship on the seven seas, the navy—any navy, not just ours—stopped it, got the captain and the papers, and found out what the hell the story was.

Oh, but gentle reader, that was before the days of twenty-four-hour news channels and wall-to-wall political correctness. Murderers aren't criminals anymore; they're people with inappropriate attitudes toward social norms. A gun dealer who sells weapons to a terrorist group is an entrepreneur. North Korean vessels loaded with missiles for Syria aren't a threat to world peace; they're a vital cog in world trade.

Stopping a vessel because it happened to be Cuban had apparently become a crime on par with destroying the habitat of the wild Philadelphia spotted frog. The navy could only board the ship if there was a real reason to do so.

"Why don't you tell the IRS that they didn't file all of their required tax forms," I told the admiral. "They'll stop them in a flash."

"Be serious, Dick."

Here's what the admiral meant by "be serious": he wanted yours truly to board the ship and find out what the hell was aboard it. I would do this under cover of darkness, of course, with absolutely no commission from the U.S. government, and no connection thereto.

Unless, of course, I found something. Then the entire Atlantic fleet, waiting just over the horizon, would zoom in on the ship and blow it out of the water.

Whether or not I got off first, I suspected.

"I have two men I want you to take with you," added the admiral as he finished outlining his plan. "They're experts in nuclear weapons. They'll be able to tell you the most likely hiding places. And if you find a bomb, they should be able to diffuse it without it blowing up."

Did he say "should"?

Yes, though he skipped over it very quickly. That's not the sort of sentence where I like to see qualifiers.

"I still have people I have to get out of Cuba," I told him.

"I thought you said that was under control."

"It is under control. That's why I have to get them out."

"Dick, let me take care of that for you."

I laughed.

"I'll take care of my people, you take care of the *Libre Cuba* or *Cuba Libre* or whatever they're calling that floating typhoid trap."

"Dick, your country is calling you."

Ken Jones as Uncle Sam.

Frightening.

"Just have the navy stop the damn ship and be done with it," I told him. "The hell with political correctness. Get one of the SEAL teams—"

"You of all people should know the bullshit I have to put up with, Dick. You know what kind of hell will break loose if we're wrong."

"You can be wrong, Ken? Really?"

The admiral sighed. It sounded staged.

"That ship is sailing in the general direction of New York, Dick. Don't you have relatives there?"

"It's sailing or drifting?"

"I find your humor in the face of this potential disaster highly inappropriate."

"Some people might call what you're asking me to do piracy."

"I'd call it a smart business decision to remain one of our prime contractors."

Yes, I agreed. No, I wasn't entirely convinced that Fidel had sat on a nuke for nearly fifty years, then loaded it into a dilapidated tub and set it off for New York.

But hell, Fidel *was* up to something big. And after everything Fidel and I meant to each other, I couldn't let him get away with this.

Besides, when was the last time I turned down a chance to board a ship at sea?

Back in Cuba, Junior had convinced Crusty that they should ride to Vianna Norte and visit the lab where the inoculations were being prepared, and see what they could see. He didn't use advanced psychology or emotional blackmail or tug on Crusty's patriotic strings—the plain truth was that Crusty was bored. As I'm sure Junior was.

Trace and Shotgun were still out taking a look at the town. So Crusty and Junior hopped in the car and headed toward Vianna Norte.

The town was a speck on the map all the way on the northern side of Cuba. If there'd been good roads in that direction, it would have been about an hour and a half drive, if you obeyed the speed limit. It actually took closer to two and a half. Not much happened on the way. Crusty and Junior went through two apparently impromptu checkpoints manned by local policemen. Their passports showed they were well-off Europeans, a fact reinforced by the rental car, which very few Cubans would own.

It probably didn't hurt that upon handing over their documents, Junior added five convertible pesos to each passport. The cops waved them through without so much as a lecture about the need to wear seat belts—something Crusty refused to do because he felt it hurt his digestion.

("At my age," he says, "I wouldn't mind taking a flight through the windshield. A different way to go out.")

As I've said before, Cuba's a beautiful place, and the scenery was enough to keep Crusty, who was driving, from complaining too much as they drove. But about five miles outside of Vianna Norte, things started to change. Junior noticed that the buildings they were passing were empty and that a number had even been bulldozed. Given Cuba's perpetual housing shortage, this was unusual. No replacements were nearby, either, at least not that they could see. Even the large billboards that you see everywhere in Cuba proclaiming the greatness of the socialistic state were missing.

Two miles from where the map indicated Vianna Norte lay, Junior spotted a pair of towers flanking the roadway ahead. At first glance, they looked as if they were water towers. But as he looked around at the empty land he realized there would be no need for storage tanks here.

"I think we're being watched," he told Crusty.

"Maybe I should stop and moon 'em."

They were just coming up a shallow rise; as they reached the peak, Junior spotted a flashing light in the middle of the road ahead.

"Another roadblock," Junior told him.

"Really? It looked like a merry-go-round."

"I'm running out of five-peso notes."

"Then we'll tell them we gave at the office."

As they drew closer, Junior sensed that five pesos wasn't going to cover it.

"Troop truck behind them," he told Crusty. "Quarter mile away. And there's an armored car or something. There's a dip in the road; I can't see."

"Two dips in the road," said Crusty, slowing as two men got out of the car and began walking toward them.

Crusty rolled down the window, preparing what would have been, for him, a friendly greeting—which meant he planned on holding the usual curse words as he asked what the hell they were up to. But the man who came around to the driver's side of the car didn't give him a chance to speak.

"Out of the car," he demanded.

The other man came around to Junior's side and said the same thing.

"Now just a minute," said Crusty, fingering the pesos Junior had just handed him. "I have our passports."

"I'm not interested in your passports," said the man, pulling a revolver from his belt and pointing it at Crusty's head.

III

If there is one thing you could say about Crusty, it's that he knows his revolvers.

"Smith & Wesson, Model 19 Combat Magnum with K-Target frame," he mumbled as he got out of the car. "Four-inch barrel. Which would make it one of the very original models."

Not quite the gun aficionado, the details were lost on Junior, who in any event was looking at a more pedestrian though just as deadly Beretta automatic. Both men got out of the car slowly, hands high. They were prompted to turn around, and one by one searched, none too gently. Though the first man had claimed they weren't interested in their passports, their wallets and documents were confiscated and then inspected.

"You are Spanish?" asked the police officer who did the frisking.

"I'm from Barcelona," said Crusty. "He's Belgian."

"How come you speak like a Cuban?"

"I have family here."

"Where?"

Crusty named a town about ten miles away. It wasn't just to give them an alibi to be on the road; he wasn't about to point the Cuban authorities toward his real relatives.

"And why are you on this road?"

"Driving to my family."

"And you?"

Junior pretended not to understand what he said.

"He's a friend of my son's," said Crusty. "He's a doctor and may want to invest in a business here. A cigar factory."

The officer scowled.

"You can't get there from here."

"Why not?" asked Crusty.

"You came from Havana?"

"We were in Colon, looking for an old friend."

"Who?"

"Juan Gonzalez. He wasn't there."

The man walked to the other side of the car.

"You are a doctor?" he asked Junior.

Junior pretended not to understand. Crusty translated into pigeon French, and Junior nodded.

"A doctor, and you want to invest in cigars?"

"They're good for your health," said Crusty quickly. "Everyone knows that."

The Cuban frowned, then walked back to the car blocking the road to use his radio.

"Maybe they want a bribe," whispered Junior.

"They can scratch my ass if that's what they're after."

The officer finished his conversation and strode back.

"You take the car," he told the other Cuban. "I'll take them."

"What?" demanded Crusty.

"No more out of you, old man. Both of you are coming with me, under suspicion of being spies."

Under any other circumstances, Crusty would have complied. But the Cuban had used the magic words "old man."

It was one thing for Crusty to talk about his age, and quite another for someone else to.

"Who are you talking to?" Crusty demanded.

"You, old man." The Cuban thrust the Magnum toward his head. "You're older than all of us combined."

"And you're stupider than all of us combined."

"Stupid." The Cuban extended his gun. His finger was already on the trigger. "Stupid? The only stupid one I see here is you, you ignorant ancient skunk."

"That's because you can't look in a mirror."

"If you don't get in that car—"

The Cuban never finished what he was going to say. Crusty had leapt from his feet, twisted in the air, and delivered a flying kick to his arm.

Besides being a terminal crank, Crusty is a sixth-degree black belt in karate. He'd probably be higher ranked, but he has trouble finding sparring partners who don't mind listening to his complaints while he throws them to the mat.

The gun went flying. The Cuban, relatively large, staggered back. He got his balance just in time to receive another kick, this one to the head à la Bruce Lee. Blood spurted all over the place as he recoiled to the ground.

"You got blood on my Keds," complained Crusty. And he started kicking the downed Cuban in earnest.

As Crusty hit his Cuban, Junior tried bowling over the one near him. Unfortunately, the man outweighed him by a good hundred pounds at least, and Junior bounced back against the car.

Luckily for Junior, the Cuban had put his pistol back in his holster. As he reached for it, Junior threw himself against his legs, tackling him.

The gun went off as they fell. Junior felt himself go slightly faint. Sure that he was dead, he decided to go out with a flourish, pushing hard into the Cuban's midsection and pummeling anything he could reach. He kicked and scratched and pounded, eyes closed. He felt sure that when he opened them St. Peter would be standing above, shaking his head.

But it wasn't St. Peter he saw when he opened his eyes—it was Crusty, who'd run over and demonstrated some more of his kicking techniques, rendering this Cuban unconscious as well.

"Let's go, come on," said Crusty, but Junior couldn't hear him—the gun blast had temporarily deafened him.

"In the car. Come on," said Crusty, pushing Junior into the vehicle as he grabbed the Beretta that had fallen nearby.

Junior's hearing started to return after they'd gone a mile. No one had started to follow them yet, but that was just a matter of time.

"Pull over near that tobacco barn," he told Junior.

"This is no time to take a leak," said Crusty.

"I don't have to pee. I want to hide the car here."

"What the hell do you want to do then? Walk back?"

"Crawl if I have to. I want to get a look at what they were guarding, don't you think?"

"Waste of time. They were probably looking to kidnap us."

"No, they accused us of being spies."

"What do you expect them to say?"

"They were only being nasty until you said I was a doctor," said Junior. "That scared them. Something really interesting must be going on down there."

The first Trace knew of any of this was when Junior called her on the sat phone shortly after he'd hidden the car inside the barn. She responded like the calm, cool leader she is.

"You stupid idiot, Junior. What the hell were you thinking?"

"There's something going on down here, Trace. Something very strange."

"Something strange is going to be going on in your backside if you're not up here when Dick comes to pick us up."

"What time is the pickup?"

"We haven't arranged it yet."

"We'll be back in time."

"How are you going to do that? Are you going to walk?"

"If we have to."

"Don't go anywhere until I get back to you," said Trace. "You hear me?"

"I hear you."

Note that he didn't say he was listening, much less that he would do what she said.

About two minutes after Junior got off the sat phone with Trace, two troop trucks sped past the barn, obviously thinking they had fled down the road.

"Think they'll be back?" Junior asked.

"The question isn't whether," said Crusty. "The question is when."

Junior wanted to circle around to Vianna Norte, and suggested that they walk behind the building as a start. It wasn't a bad idea, Crusty told him, but it was also the first thing the soldiers would think of if they came back and found the car. It was smarter to cross the road and go from there. As an extra bonus, that direction was north and would take them closer to the coast—an important consideration should the soldiers not get tired of looking for them before dark.

The problem was that there was almost no cover in that direction. The ground looked as if it had been parched clean.

Junior trotted for the first half mile. Crusty . . . Crusty walked. And not particularly fast. Junior kept circling back, urging him to hurry.

"At my age, hurrying is only helping the undertaker," he growled.

Junior scouted ahead, then came back, repeating this for the next half mile or so. The ground remained parched as far as he could see.

Finally he heard a vehicle in the distance. He ran to Crusty, and got him to flatten himself on the ground while the car passed, driving in the direction the troop trucks had taken. Junior didn't get a good look, but he thought it was the car that had blocked the road earlier.

"Let's go, let's go," he told Crusty.

"It took me long enough to get down here," answered Crusty. "I might as well enjoy it for a while."

"Come on, before they come back."

"Kids. Always in a goddamn hurry."

Crusty rose and, despite his complaints, moved forward at a somewhat quicker pace. Once again, Junior went and scouted ahead, trotting toward a rise about a half mile off.

He crawled the last hundred yards, but instead of finding more troops or a lookout tower, all he saw was the start of a jungle. The first twenty yards or so were sparse, with bushes scattered amid a few trees. But fifty yards in it was almost impenetrable. He pushed his way in a hundred yards or so; when he didn't see anything except for trees and brush, he went back and found Crusty, who was just reaching the tree line.

"We can use the jungle for cover and get close to Vianna Norte," Junior told him. "Then when it's time to bug out, we can slip north to the coast. It can't be more than a mile or so."

"Humph," said Crusty.

"If you don't want to come, I'll go myself."

"I don't want to come," said Crusty. "But I am, aren't I?"

It took Junior and Crusty nearly an hour to make their way through the belt of thick vegetation that Junior had found. Eventually, the trees and brush thinned out to the point where it was easy to move. Using the sun as a guide, they began moving northeast, aiming to cut around and approach Vianna Norte from the north. Twice they nearly tripped over buried foundation stones, the apparent remains of small buildings, probably houses, that had been leveled years before. The uniform thickness of the trees told Junior that the area had been cleared until perhaps fifteen or twenty years before; he wondered why the jungle had been allowed to take it back over.

"Maybe one of Fidel's mistresses liked the color green," snapped Crusty when he asked.

"The area where we were, that was cleared much more recently," said Junior. "It looks like it was bulldozed pretty recently."

"Maybe one of Fidel's mistresses liked the color gray."

"Maybe it was farm fields," said Junior, answering his own question. "And they razed it, so no one could hide near the road."

Crusty grunted, about as close to a compliment as he ever got.

After another hour of walking, they were surprised to hear the sound of the surf. They made their way through the trees and found themselves on a bluff overlooking the sea. The waves crashed roughly against the rocks below.

Crusty studied the rocks and the bend in the coastline, trying to orient himself. According to the map, Vianna Norte was about a mile from the water; they'd been two miles or so west of it when they were stopped.

"We came a little too far toward north," he said finally. "Vianna Norte should be east of us about two miles."

"Two miles is nothing."

"For you, maybe. Don't forget we have to go back."

"Worst case, they can pick us up here," said Junior. "Besides, what else do we have to do?"

"If I'd known there was going to be this much goddamn walking involved, I would have stayed home," said Crusty, falling in behind him.

Crusty's estimate of the distance to Vianna Norte was off by nearly a mile, but well before they reached its outskirts they ran into a tall chain-link fence.

This wasn't the leftover remains of some long-abandoned rich man's estate; it was shiny and new, not more than a few months old, if that.

It was also topped with barbed wire.

Crusty probably wouldn't have wanted to climb the fence anyway, but the wire at the top made him positively stubborn when Junior suggested it. Finally, Junior agreed that they should look for an easier place to get through "before doing anything too optimistically strenuous," as Crusty put it. So they started walking along it to the south.

Before they'd gone more than a hundred yards, they found a spot where a large tree had crashed into the fence. Most of the chain-link section was still intact, but the trunk held down the barbed wire. Junior pulled himself up and hopped over, trotting back toward the north. Grumbling and cursing beneath his breath, Crusty followed.

They hadn't gone very far when Junior spotted another fence paralleling the first. A little farther on, he spotted a squat brick building set into the side of a hill. He worked his way up the fence line in the direction of the ocean, until he found a better view of the building.

"Looks like a hospital," Junior told Crusty when he finally caught up to him. "But with all these fences, maybe it's a prison."

"Same thing," said Crusty.

It can be hard for the uninformed to distinguish between hospitals and prisons in Cuba, at least from the outside, since many mental hospitals are actually prisons. But this facility was fairly unique, as Junior saw when he climbed a tree several yards behind the fence and got a good look at the grounds. There was a wide, deep dent in the coastline directly in front of the building. And in the middle of the dent was a marina.

A very large marina, in fact. There were at least a hundred boats moored near the rocks. They were skiffs and pleasure boats, a few small cabin cruisers and powered whaleboats. Maybe a third had canvas coverings; the others were completely open. Not one looked to be more than a few months old.

"Well, there's how we're getting off the island," said Crusty. "Assuming we can find one with gas."

"Why the hell do you think they're there in the first place?" said Junior. "If this place is a prison or even a hospital, why would they have a marina? With brand-new boats?"

Even Crusty couldn't supply an answer to that, sarcastic or otherwise.

They moved down the fence line closer to the water. There was a single guard post on the northwest corner of the compound where they were, but it was easily avoided by moving farther west. The boats themselves were unguarded; it wouldn't be very hard to swim out and take one. The only question was whether they would have any fuel, but as Crusty pointed out, the boats couldn't have floated there by themselves; there must at least be fumes in the tanks.

As far as Junior could tell, there was no one guarding them, though they were visible from the shore and the building. Once night fell, however, there'd be little trouble escaping detection.

Trace and Shotgun located a boat that would be easy to "borrow" for the evening, and then as a bonus spotted two unattended motorbikes in a yard on the outskirts of the village. A bit of Red's concern for Cubans had rubbed off on Trace, giving her slight pangs of conscience as she confiscated the bikes and took them to a hiding place off the road, but she allayed them by leaving convertible and real pesos worth several times the bikes' value in their place.

Trace and Shotgun were on their way back to Crusty's cousin's house when Junior called her to tell her where they were.

"Can't you sit still for five minutes?" she said. "I told you not to move."

More than a little of the kettle calling the pot black, but Junior didn't rise to the bait.

"You wouldn't believe what we found."

"Sit tight," Trace told him when he finished describing the compound. "I'll be over in an hour."

"It's at least two hours away, Trace, and there's a checkpoint at—"

"Just sit tight. Don't move. All right?"

"But—"

"Just sit tight."

Kind of wonder why she bothered saying that even once, don't you?

[IV]

The U.S. government played absolutely no role in my sudden interest in *Cuba Libre,* and had nothing to do with my getting up to the ship. At no point in the proceedings was there any connection, official or otherwise, between myself and the U.S. government or its various agencies. I received no cooperation nor direction, and had no communication with any branch of the service or any member of the U.S. military or Homeland Security during the operation. I acted entirely on my own, as a concerned citizen of the world, under the various sections of maritime law that permit, or may not permit, the casual inspection in transit or not in transit of materials or goods by an interested or uninterested citizen acting under the charter of the United Nations. I take full responsibility for myself, my actions, my thoughts and curse words, forever and ever, amen.

Now that the lawyers are happy . . .

A CIA Gulfstream picked Mongoose, Doc, and me up in Panama City a short while after I got off the phone with Ken. It flew us to an undisclosed location—that would be Tyndale Air Force Base, Florida—where we were met by a Navy P-3C Orion outfitted for support duties. (The aircraft was attached to a Patrol Squadron Special Project Unit, but wasn't a spy plane itself, I don't think.) The Orion flew us up to Naval Air Station Jacksonville, where we were met by a Grumman C-2A Greyhound.

Grasshopper? You have a question?

Yes, the Greyhound is a carrier-based aircraft responsible for delivering things like the mail and DVDs to aircraft carriers.

Consider us the mail.

The Greyhound took us to an undisclosed aircraft carrier—which would be CVN-69, the USS *Dwight D. Eisenhower,* affectionately known as *Ike* to the six thousand or so sailors who call it home—sailing off the East Coast. A lieutenant with an oversized security detail in tow met us maybe three seconds after we rebounded against the arrestor cable and quick-stepped us to an SH-3 Sea King idling on the deck nearby. The Sea King lifted off as soon as Doc was in the cabin—leaving Mongoose and me to throw ourselves through the helo's open door, barely getting inside. A burly petty officer grabbed Mongoose by the back of the shirt and hauled him in; I had to fend for myself, jerking my feet up and in just as one of the crewmen slammed the door shut.

Not that they were in a hurry or anything.

The helo took us to the *Wasp*, an assault ship sailing roughly a hundred miles northeast of the *Ike*.

The *Wasp* and her sister ships look very much like aircraft carriers looked during World War II. Straight flight deck, little island off to the side, and enough firepower to give a fleet of battlewagons agita. But the *Wasp*'s main purpose was to support amphibious operations, hostile and otherwise.[40] In function at least, the *Wasp* is more closely related to the landing ships that brought men into Okinawa and Iwo Jima rather than the carriers that launched the planes to cover them.

The *Wasp* can carry about thirty-eight Harrier jump jets, those fancy but dangerous fighters that can take off and land like pogo sticks, straight up. In this case, the *Wasp* was carrying only helicopters, but that wasn't a knock. The choppers were a mix of AH-1 Whiskey Cobras—mean-ass gunships whose ancestors first flew in Vietnam—and MH-53Es, another aircraft whose roots go back to the days of Cream, Credence, and cratering hootches in Southeast Asia. The marines use the MH-53E "Sea Dragon" as the heavy lifters during assault operations. When the neighbors get rowdy, these are the choppers you call in.[41]

We were met on the *Wasp* by a lieutenant from Naval Intelligence, a very serious fellow who had the eyes of a mole and cheeks that looked as if they'd been drilled into his face. He snapped off a salute—better safe than sorry, maybe—then introduced us to a CIA officer named Laundry (really), a guy in his mid-fifties who seemed to be straining to smile. Laundry, of course, wasn't identified as a CIA officer, but he had the Langley bob and weave as he walked; my guess is that he worked paramilitary out in the sticks for quite a while before coming back to HQ and carrying water and other things for the operations directorate. There was a whiff of longing in his voice when he spoke, as if he was thinking, *Damn, I wish I were going on this operation*, though maybe he just had to visit the head real bad.

---

[40] Yes, there *are* nonhostile amphibious operations. These ships, their crews, and the marines working with them have an enviable record of helping people out after natural disasters, such as tsunamis in Southeast Asia.

[41] There may have been some Seahawks and other types below decks, but we didn't see them.

Laundry and Intelligence took us to a small cabin in the belly of the beast where our two nongovernment government assets were already waiting. One was a nervous, cocker-spaniel type, who'd clearly been drinking espresso all day from his water dish. Thin as a rail and at least six-five, he practically bounced out of the chair when we came in. Pumping my hand profusely, he swore allegiance to the bitter end.

I told him I appreciated the sentiment, but doubted it would come to that.

He said I should call him Frenchman. I'm not sure how he picked that handle, and frankly I was afraid to ask. He looked more Greek than French, and his accent was southern U.S.

Frenchman carried two small instruments, both of which would have looked right at home on Mr. Spock's belt in the first season of *Star Trek*. One was about the size of a PDA, or personal digital assistant, the geeky mini-computers engineers are always tapping love notes on in meetings. His gizmo was apparently able to analyze different types of radiation, sniffing isotopes, or something along those lines as they floated in the air. The other device looked like a small flashlight with three antennalike prongs on the end. He was even more cagey about what this one did, saying only that it "worked along the same lines" as the other.

The other technical expert was huddled inside the hood of his blue sweatshirt, hunkered over a cup of coffee as if he were out in the frosty tundra, rather than in a space where the temperature had to be pushing eighty degrees. When I extended my hand he put up his.

"These have to stay clean," he said.

His name was Win, and Laundry introduced him as the bomb defuser, supposedly one of the top guys in the world when it came to analyzing and turning off the intricate systems that make nukes go boom. So I thought the comment about keeping his hands clean meant that he had to keep his fingers nimble and flexed, kind of like a concert pianist thoroughly paranoid about his hands. But as I found out, Win meant clean literally. The only thing he was paranoid about were germs, and at several inappropriate points over the next few hours he delivered impromptu lectures on the number of a variety of microscopic creatures that roamed various surfaces around him.

Intelligence gave us a brief on the position of the Cuban ship. Laundry provided photos and schematics of the layout, along with some guesses about where a warhead would be kept. Then Frenchman and Win took over, telling me how they could detect a nuke, how much time they'd need to diffuse it, and some other related tidbits.

"There's only so much we can be sure of until we get onto the ship itself," said Frenchman, hopping back and forth. "We need to be very, very close to the device. Real close."

"I'll get you there," I said.

"Um, I should mention one thing," he added.

"Yeah?"

"I can't swim."

"Not at all?"

He shook his head.

"I'll bet you'll swim if we toss you into the water," said Mongoose.

'Goose smiled, but Frenchman didn't smile back.

Except for the fresh coat of paint, *Cuba Libre* looked like any of the gray commercial trawlers you've seen in scratchy photos from the 1970s. The superstructure was toward the stern. A pair of booms dominated the deck.

Mongoose and I both studied the photos carefully. There were no trailing lines, nor any signs of conveniently sloppy seamanship. The hatches to the cargo holds were battened down, and if there were crew members aboard—and presumably there were—none had shown himself when the planes were nearby.

There didn't look to be any fixed guns anywhere. Small weapons, of course, could be anywhere. The ship was traveling very slowly; Naval Intelligence said it moved no faster than four knots during the day, and usually cut that to two at night.

My favorite means of boarding a ship is across the gangway, preferably under my own power after a nice long liberty. If that can't be arranged, I'm not particular.

Our options were severely limited in this case. Flying in aboard a helicopter was out of the question. Not only was the navy not about to lend us one, but the CIA wanted our inspection to be as secret as possible. Ideally we would get on and off without being seen, heard, or dreamed of.

Climbing aboard from a rigid boat would have been the next best option, but our party was so small that any serious opposition would jeopardize the mission.

That left only one real possibility. We had to be invited aboard.

We spent the next few hours getting some food and rest. Mongoose wanted to go down to one of the shipboard gyms and work out a little; Naval Intelligence arranged that for him. Because of security precautions, he had to clear not just the gym but the passageways and every space where he went, trying to avoid unnecessary contact.

That was probably just as well, given Mongoose's fondness for marines. He'd spent some of his best moments in the service beating the hell out of them.

I checked in with Danny, who'd set everything up for a midnight pickup on Cuba. Trace had told him what was going on with Junior, et al., but the version I got was short on those details. It sounded like everything there was under control and our people would be home soon.

Famous last words.

(V)

Our operation on the *Cuba Libre*, in time stamp style. Just remember real life doesn't quite move in such neat increments:

2010: That's ten past 8:00 P.M. in civilian time.

Mongoose, Frenchman, Win, and I changed into civilian clothes, the sort of thing weekend warriors might wear while fishing. Doc, who was acting as our mission coordinator and interfacing with Naval Intelligence and the rest of the navy and CIA *ass*-ets, briefed the helo crew on our plan and worked out various contingency plans in case the shit hit the fan.

2012: Escorted by two marines on security detail who had orders to shoot anyone who got in our way, Mongoose, Frenchman, Win, and I trotted across the deck to a waiting Sikorsky MH-53E. The whole ship seemed to shake as the aircraft's rotors began spinning. Doc went over the emergency procedures with us, checked our gear, and gave us the thumbs-up. Then he went forward and squeezed into a jump seat not far from the two pilots.

2013: We were airborne. Frenchman practically rebounded off the ceiling of the helo, unable to control his adrenaline rush. Win pulled the hood of his sweatshirt—he'd insisted on wearing it, arguing it was typical civilian gear—so far over his head he looked like a gnome.

2020: The crew chief reported that everything was "copacetic." I took that to mean things were on schedule.

2045: Frenchman announced he had to pee. The crew chief offered him two options—he could open the hatch and piss out the door as we flew, or he could use the yellow jug strapped to the spar. Frenchman decided he'd hold it in.

2103: Doc came back and told us we were five minutes from drop. Since our gear was pretty minimal—besides our clothes, Mongoose and I carried survival knives and a pair of high-tech miniature satellite radios, courtesy of the CIA—it didn't take long to look it over and get ready. Mongoose inflated a raft on the deck of the helo.

2107: The chopper lurched sharply to the right and descended toward the waves. It had skimmed so close to the water that the landing gear would have been wet had it been extended.

The crew chief looked at us, then barked a warning that he was opening the ramp at the stern. Frenchman suddenly looked seasick. Win tightened the drawstrings on his hood even tighter.

"Into the raft," I told them.

Frenchman sprawled forward, tumbling into the small craft. Win sat down calmly, then scrunched himself up to avoid being touched by the rest of us, whose germs could not be trusted.

2108: The rear ramp of the helicopter slammed open. Wind, dust, and a fine mist of water flew around us. I grabbed the line on the gunwale and hunkered down as the raft slid aft toward the waves. My stomach lagged a few yards behind as we plummeted into the water — think Six Flags Water Park, without the stiff entry fee and the overpriced burgers.

Wha-lal-lop!! Our bow shot below the waves, and the fine mist I'd felt on the way out turned into a deluge. We spun sharply to port. We didn't take on water — there wasn't any more room, as we were already under the waves.

The downdraft from the blades of the helo pushed us down farther, the aircraft pounding the air furiously as she pulled away. Veering east and out of sight, the chopper sent a hurricane-force wind into us, whipping the raft like a leaf caught in a drain.

Frenchman began puking.

2110: Mongoose and I succeeded in stabilizing the vessel. We'd lost one of the paddles overboard and Mongoose found it necessary to paddle with his bare hands. We were still underwater.

"Bail!" I told the others. I added several expletives to emphasize the importance of my order.

"If you're going to puke," Mongoose added, "do it overboard."

Frenchman took Mongoose's advice to heart. Win pulled out one of the collapsible pails — think reinforced plastic bags — and went to work. Sensing progress, I unlashed the small outboard from the side and began setting it up on the transom at the stern.

2115: We were under way, headed toward the course the *Cuba Libre* was taking. Doc checked in.

"You havin' fun yet?" he asked.

"Real fuckin' funny," answered Mongoose, who was handling our satellite link. "You and fuckin' Shotgun fuckin' belong fuckin' together."

"The f-word frequency is up," said Doc cheerfully. "You must be doing well."

2125: The bottom of the raft, though slick, was no longer filled with water. My GPS reading had us dead-on course for the *Cuba Libre*, just over the horizon. Doc, who was watching a radar plot supplied from a JSTAR's aircraft, confirmed that we were on course for an intercept. I leaned on the throttle of the tiny outboard.

2140: I steered directly toward the bow of the *Cuba Libre* in view, still maybe two miles off. The boat had minimal navigational lights, not spots or even a work light on deck, but it stood out pretty well in the darkness, a big looming shadow that says, *Come to papa.*

2150: We got ready to look like shipwrecked pleasure boaters who have been lost at sea for several days. Mongoose messed up his hair—hard to tell given it's about a half inch long—and threw salt water into his eyes, rubbing them harshly to irritate them. I channeled my inner wildebeest. Frenchman, soaked with vomit and still hanging on the gunwale, didn't have to act and wasn't going to invite very close inspection anyhow.

Win, I'm not sure about. He hadn't said a peep since we boarded the helicopter.

With the ship getting closer and closer, I secured the engine, then dumped it below the water. I pushed our weighted waterproof gear bag gently over the side as well. I'd cut both loose when I was sure we were going to be picked up.

If the ship were to pass us by—not out of the realm of possibilities—then we would haul the engine and bag back aboard and use the boarding suction cups and lines to get aboard. Assuming we were close enough, assuming the engine worked, etc., etc.

Harder than trying to shit into a test tube, you say?

You may be right.

2155: Mongoose fired a flare. There was no acknowledgment from the ship.

2157: Mongoose fired another flare. We followed with a hearty round of cursing as the bastards still didn't respond.

2159: Yet another flare. We were so close that we could fire point-blank and hit the bow.

I began sizing up the ship for boarding.

Suction cups are about the worst way to get aboard a vessel, with the possible exception of dropping from ten thousand feet without benefit of a parachute.

No, I take that back—they're definitely the worst. At least if you're falling you know your agony will soon be over.

2200: A light appeared on the port side.

"Looks like they're manning a boat," said Mongoose.

I waited until the boat was in the water to cut the lines to the engine and extra gear. We were past the point of no return.

2210: Two crewmen came out to rescue us. They seemed extremely reluctant to take us back, circling several times before approaching. Even then, they looked us over pretty well before bringing us aboard their whaleboat. Frenchman's limp body finally convinced them we were legit.

A rope ladder was lowered as we approached the *Cuba Libre*. Mongoose pretended to slip as he went and fell into the water. The rest of us remained prostrate in the rescue boat.

If we'd been out in the water for two days without food and very little water—our cover story, remember—we wouldn't have the energy to run up the rungs. Besides, the weaker we seemed, the more at ease the crew would be. And we needed them at ease.

Finally, they rigged a line and began pulling us up.

2230: Hauled up on deck, we were surrounded by six sailors with AK47s.

Things were looking up.

2240: While we were waiting for a doctor, Frenchman told me he'd lost one of his isotope detectors somewhere along the way.

No fear, he said. He could do the job *almost* as well with the one he had left.

2242: A seaman brought dry clothes. Despite our protests, we had to change on deck. We weren't objecting out of modesty—though in Win's case he probably really was worried about the random germs he kept mentioning. With no place for Frenchman to hide his radiation detector, the Cuban sailors saw and confiscated it at gunpoint. It was the one that looks like a PDA, and that's what he claimed it was.

"What do we do?" Frenchman whispered to me.

"We'll use our eyes. Shouldn't take more than a week."

Somewhat less important than the detector, the Cubans also confiscated our radios. These—supplied by the CIA—were designed to look like iPod Shuffles, the small clip-on MP3 players that are about half the size of a matchbook.

The sailor took all of our wet clothes—except for Win's sweatshirt, which he insisted on keeping and wearing over the new shirt the Cubans supplied.

While we were dressing, a man came to look us over. He appeared to be a *real* doctor, with a stethoscope and one of those fancy little lights that doctors like to use on your eyes right before they hand you the bill.

What is a real doctor doing on the ship? I wondered.

I didn't get a chance to ask. The doctor looked us over, said something to the mate in charge, then walked away. We sat on the deck, freezing our butts off, for more than a half hour. Mongoose and Frenchman both asked for a blanket, but the mate in charge of us didn't answer. Finally, a seaman came up with a bucket of lukewarm soup. The taste was somewhere between black bean and brown dishwater. We pretended we were starving and lapped it up.

2320: We were led below to what turned out to be one of the cargo holds. It was empty.

One of the sailors stood guard outside the door.

2321: Mongoose and I began examining the cargo space, looking for an alternative way out. It turned out to be a very large rectangular box, with two doors in the bulkhead facing the bow. That included the one we came in through. Both were locked. The hatchway at the top, which Mongoose reached via welded rungs that ran up the starboard side of the hold, was closed and apparently locked. After about five minutes, Mongoose declared it couldn't be opened from inside.

The deck we were sitting on was made of grating; we could see through it to the space below. Mongoose suggested that it was rigged to allow for the decking to be removed, making the hold deeper. Sure enough, there were bolts holding the decking to long I-beams running across the space. Win dug a small knife from his sweatshirt pocket that he managed to conceal and we used it as a tool. The first bolt took more than ten minutes to remove, but everything was easy from there.

2338: I was just about to slip through the grate when the door to the hold was unlocked. I replaced the grate as quietly and quickly as I could, while the others shielded me from view.

The mate who'd been in charge of us above entered.

"You will come with me," he said, using English.

"Now what, Dick?" whispered Mongoose as we filed out.

I was about to tell him that we'd grab him and just leave him in the hold when I saw two other sailors, both with AK47s, in the passageway outside.

"Bide your time," I told him.

I was half expecting more guards to be waiting farther down in the passage, but there were none. As we walked toward the ladder at the far end, I glanced at Mongoose. He nodded almost imperceptibly.

2342: As we started up the ladder, Mongoose drew even with the lead guard, who was walking about three paces behind the mate in charge. I had the sailor acting as rear guard. But I couldn't get close—the slower I walked, the more he lollygagged.

I was about to reach down and pretend I had to tie my shoe when Mongoose made his move. I spun and threw myself at the sailor behind me. He was a good twenty years younger and thirty pounds heavier than I was, but I had surprise on my side. He fell back to the deck, his AK47 flying from his hands. I reached the rifle first but the Cuban sailor managed to grab the stock before I could pull it to my chest. He levered it away, then made the mistake of looking at the gun rather than me. I let go and punched him in the face.

It had no effect.

Another punch. Two.

He pulled the gun up and tried to smash the stock into the back of my head.

The fourth punch was the charm. He rolled to the side, still holding the rifle but dazed. I kicked him in the seat of his intelligence, pulled the gun from his grip, and rolled to my feet, huffing a hell of a lot more than I'd care to admit.

Mongoose, meanwhile, had grabbed the other man's rifle and was squatting with it near the ladder.

Unfortunately, our impromptu plan failed to account for all contingencies. One specifically presented a problem:

The mate who'd come to get us had pulled a pistol from his pocket and held it at Frenchman's head. He told us to drop the guns or he would fire.

2353: Mongoose asked me what I thought we should do.

I shrugged.

"As soon as he fires, he's mine," I said, raising my rifle.

I greatly preferred that Frenchman *not* be shot, since he was the only one among us who knew how to work the radiation detector. I watched the mate for a few seconds, waiting for him to tire and lower his gun.

Suddenly something flew across the narrow passageway. The mate jerked back, his gun lowered. I tapped my trigger and the gun roared, the report echoing loudly off the metal bulkhead of the passageway.

I'd aimed for his temple but in the dim light and all, I missed.

I hit his sideburn and ear instead.

"God, he's dirty," said Win, pulling his knife from the Cuban's neck.

0002: We made our way up the bridge and took the captain prisoner. Unfortunately, he wasn't particularly cooperative and it took a few blows from the butt end of Mongoose's rifle to convince him not to alert the rest of the crew.

Frenchman and I went in search of his radiation detector with the help of the ship's second mate. The mate was cowed by the rifles, but the look in his eye made it clear he would bolt at the earliest opportunity.

Frenchman didn't look too much better. His hands were shaking when he took the detector off the desk in the captain's cabin.

"Here we go," he said, pressing the button at the bottom.

The instrument didn't light up. He switched it on and off several times, shook it, and then tapped it hard against the cabin bulkhead.

It lit up. I grabbed our radios and ran back to give one to Mongoose.

0015: Frenchman and I were down in Cargo Hold Number 3, working our way around the perimeter. So far, our inspection had been a bust.

Mongoose called me on the radio. There was trouble up on the bridge. Two sailors apparently coming on duty sensed something was wrong and turned around before Mongoose or Win could stop them.

0018: The sailors aboard ship began to rebel. Mongoose and Win barricaded themselves on the bridge.

"We're not going to be able to hold out too much longer up here, Dick," Mongoose told me over the radio. "Time to abandon ship."

I was about to tell him to go ahead when I saw shadows approaching around the corner of the far passage. There were three sailors, all with rifles.

Things are about to get a little more interesting, I thought to myself.

Then the shooting began.

[VI]

We'd worked out a plan with the navy to back us up. If they didn't hear from us by 0100—one in the morning—they'd fly a helicopter overhead, claiming to be answering the distress call from the raft and looking for us.

But 0100 was a good 0030 away.

Our only option was to fight it out.

Bullets whipped across the narrow passageway, puncturing the pre-Glasnost Russian steel as if it were Swiss cheese. Fortunately, the Cuban sailors were shooting like sailors—they either stuck their weapons around the corner and fired blind, or shot without turning the corner at all. So while the passageway was filled with smoke and my eardrums were numb, none of the bullets hit me or Frenchman, who'd collapsed onto the deck at the first bark of the guns.

I moved up the side of the passage, pressing so hard against the bulkhead that I probably put a crease in it. When a rifle barrel poked around the corner, I reached out, grabbed it, and pulled.

Its owner sprawled past me, landing facedown as his rifle flew a few yards beyond him. I slapped the butt of my gun against his head, stunning him into unconsciousness, then went to one knee, waiting for his companions. When they didn't come, I curled myself around the weapon and threw myself into the elbow of the passage, gun aimed in their direction, trigger depressed maybe nine-tenths of the way.

The passage was empty. They'd run away.

"Frenchman, grab that rifle. The coast is clear," I shouted.

He ran forward.

"There's no bomb in this ship, Dick. We've been through the superstructure, the hold, all these cargo bays. There's no bomb."

"You're positive?"

"Every place we've been. There's no place else."

"The crew quarters."

"How could they put a bomb in the crew quarters? That'd be insane."

As opposed to hiding a nuke and then sailing it toward New York in the first place? If that's the measure of sanity . . .

"Come on," I told Frenchman. "The crew's quarters will be this way."

Things were getting hairy up on the bridge. Mongoose had secured both doors, but the sailors had taken some furniture or something and were using it as a battering ram against the one at the port side. The bulkhead shook every time they hit it.

"Ain't gonna last," said Win grimly.

"You an expert on doors, too?"

"I'm a materials engineer. I'm telling you it won't last."

Mongoose went to the other side of the bridge and cracked open the door, then quickly shut it as he caught a glimpse of someone in the corridor. But he was too late—three or four Cubans sprang against it. Pushed back, he tried to raise his gun but couldn't as the sailors rushed inside.

Win sprayed the entire bunch with his rifle. Somehow he managed to miss Mongoose—whether by luck or aim, it wasn't clear. The sailors rebounded back into the passage, trailing blood. Mongoose threw himself against the door and secured it.

"We gotta get out," said Win.

"Top of the bridge."

"How?"

Mongoose turned, and in the same motion swung his assault rifle like a bat through the glass over the helmsman's station. The window panel that covered the front of the bridge shattered, falling in shards on the instruments and deck. Leaning forward, Mongoose grabbed hold of the thick furring where the glass had been, tore it and the remaining shards down, then pulled himself through. He clambered on top of the bridge compartment and leaned back down.

"Let's go," he told Win.

A narrow catwalk was mounted aft of the bridge. Mongoose jumped over the rail and ran a few feet down the port side. A survival raft was lashed to the top of the superstructure, secured against the forward part of the funnel. He clambered up and undid two of the cable ties, then reached inside and grabbed the flare pack.

"Fire some of these," he told Win, jumping back down. "Shoot 'em in the direction of the fleet."

"They're almost in the bridge."

"Just fire the flares."

Win did as he was told. Mongoose called me on the radio and told me what was happening.

"We may have to jump into the water," he said.

"Go. The navy'll be here soon. As long as you have the radio, they'll find you."

"Yeah."

Just for the record, that wasn't the most confident "yeah" I'd ever heard.

The Cubans with the makeshift battering ram gave it one last college try and pushed their way onto the bridge, spraying their AK47s as they went. Win dropped to the deck and fired the last flare through the open windshield. There was a thud, then a flash and red sparkle.

"We're going off the side!" yelled Mongoose. He leapt up and pulled the raft clear of its last restraints, then threw it toward the water. "Jump as far as you can."

"Yeah," said Win, pulling his sweatshirt hood over his head before taking a running start toward the rail.

The ship's crew had rallied for the assault on the bridge, leaving the crew spaces vacant for Frenchman and me. This wasn't a big ship; there were no more than two dozen men aboard, if that.

So why had the galley been turned into a sick bay, complete with a full suite of medical machines and a dozen cots?

It was a very odd arrangement, so strange that I started checking under the cots and then pulling open the cabinets and lockers at the far end, trying to figure out what the hell the Cubans were up to.

"There's no bomb in here, Dick," said Frenchman. "Not even a watch with painted-on radium."

I grunted, barely aware of what he was saying as I tried to make sense of what I was seeing. A row of refrigerators sat near the head. They were small fridges, the sort you find in dorm rooms. Except these were chained shut.

A few well-placed rounds from the AK took care of the chain. I pulled the door on the first one open and knelt down. Trays of sealed test tubes filled the interior.

"You got any idea what this shit is?" I asked Frenchman.

"It ain't nuclear material," he said, holding the detector toward it. "We better get the hell out of here."

I grabbed two test tubes and led him back out into the passageway. As I started up the ladder, I spotted someone ducking into one of the cabins beyond us. I launched myself after him, throwing myself against the door as he tried to close it. I wedged my foot into the space, forgetting I was barefoot.

The pain was all the motivation I needed. I bulled my way into the cabin, bowling over the man who'd tried holding me out. It was the doctor.

I had a few questions for him, but this wasn't the time or place to ask them.

"You're coming with me, Doc," I told him. Before he could protest, I smacked the side of his head with the rifle butt. "Take two aspirin and call me in the morning, right?"

I scooped him over my shoulder and went out to find Frenchman waiting in the passage.

"Which way?" he asked.

"The way you're pointing."

"Up?"

"Better than down."

We went up the ladder to the main deck, then found a door to the gangway along the side of the ship. While Frenchman raced forward with his detector, still not willing to admit there was no bomb, I looked for a lifeboat or some other way for us to get off the ship and get away in one piece.

The boat that had been used to get us was sitting on its davit, the cover still off. I dumped the doctor inside as Frenchman ran toward me.

"Nothing!" he yelled. "Nothing. Damn!"

I wasn't sure why he was running until a muzzle flashed far behind him. Two sailors up near the bow had spotted him and were firing at him. I shot through the magazine; I may or may not have hit them, but they stopped firing.

But Frenchman was lying on the deck.

"Damn," he mumbled.

That was the last thing he said, in this world anyway.

Mongoose swam for the raft, which was floating upside down about a dozen yards from the ship.

Win hit the water much harder than he expected, and between the shock and cold, his head was scrambled. He fought his way to the surface, but once there had no idea where he was. He stroked frantically, furiously attacking the waves, but he wasn't nearly the swimmer Mongoose was, and found it difficult to make much progress. In less than a minute, he was exhausted and began sinking under the water.

He fought desperately at first, but he was so tired that his arms felt like drain pipes filled with cement. The fatigue grew exponentially, until he was seized by an overwhelming need to sleep. His eyes had been closed practically since he hit the water. Now the rest of his body began to relax, giving up.

He was slipping downward when Mongoose spotted him a few feet from the raft. He spun around, tugging the raft with him for a stroke or two before letting go as Win sank. He caught him and hauled him back.

Right about then, the sailors who'd made it off the bridge without being burned spotted the raft and began firing at it. Mongoose didn't realize this; all he knew was that the raft was sliding away from him. As he swam after it, something hit him on the back—a pebble, he thought, not bothering to ask himself who would be throwing rocks in the middle of the ocean.

He took a few more strokes toward the raft when a light went off in that dark skull of his and he realized the sailors were shooting at the raft. With Win hanging on his left side, he began pulling in the opposite direction. But he didn't realize that he'd been hit by a bullet until his right arm locked up. His right trapezius muscle had been torn, the rest of the muscles in his arm and shoulder couldn't handle the load anymore.

"Shit," he mumbled, treading water with his feet. "Damn navy is never around when you need it."

I tossed Frenchman's limp body into the boat and began lowering us toward the water. The craft went down at a snail's pace. Any second I expected one of the Cubans to run up and plaster me. But they didn't.

The only one who seemed interested in me at all was Murphy, who managed to mangle either the line or the davit mechanism so that the boat stopped cockeyed five feet above the water. I didn't even notice at first; I kept tugging, thinking I was going down. Finally realizing I was stuck, I reached upward to put my weight into a heavy tug—just in time for Murphy to undo whatever he had done and send the boat crashing down into the water.

Give the Russians their due—whatever trees they'd made the old lifeboat from were as tough as the best iron. The staves bent and groaned, but didn't break. I fell against the outboard at the fantail, knocking the world sideways for a few moments.

The merchant ship had been moving all this time, so when I finally cleared my head and got up to start the outboard, it was a good fifty yards beyond me. The sailors who'd been shooting at Mongoose's raft spotted me and turned their attentions and bullets in my direction, firing from the rail at the stern of the ship. I couldn't hear their gunfire over the motor or the sea, but their muzzle flashes were plenty obvious.

I reached to scoop up my gun and return fire, but I'd lost it going down. It probably wouldn't have mattered much—I'd lost the spare magazine I'd had as well and was out of bullets. I stayed down, turning the tiller so the boat moved away from the Cuban vessel. Finally, with my head a little clearer, I saw that there were no more flashes along the rail of the *Cuba Libre*, which by now was about a quarter mile away.

I turned back in the direction where I thought Mongoose would be. It was too dark to see anything, and the motor was so loud my head was vibrating. I turned it off, then cupped my hands over my mouth and started yelling.

"Mongoose! Mongoose, you jackass! Where the hell are you?"

"Jackass my butt," came the answer.

"That's right," I said. "You do have the butt of a jackass. Now tell me where the hell you are or I'll make you swim all the way back to Norfolk."

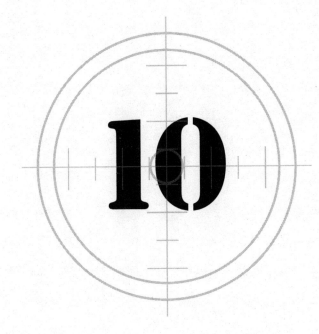

The navy helicopters found us about a half hour later. By that time, I'd bandaged Mongoose's shoulder and Win had regained enough of his strength to lecture me about the dangers of touching raw blood. The Cuban doctor I'd taken with me was still out cold.

One of the Seahawks dipped down close and sent a basket for my passengers. I went up last. The *Cuba Libre* was a mile or so away, black smoke still trailing from the bridge. Even so, I half expected it to launch an antiair missile in our direction.

"Come on," growled Doc as I twisted upward in the wind. "Get in here so we can get the hell home."

He helped me into the cabin. I gave him a quick brain dump on our search and our guest.

"Give my friend there something to keep him sleeping until we're back aboard the *Wasp*," I told the corpsman.

"Morphine's good for that," he said, digging into his bag.

Mongoose got his own dose. The bullet that hit him had had the good sense to go straight through his shoulder and come out the other side. This was a lot better than many of the alternatives, though I can't say that Mongoose appreciated that. He sat back against the hull of the helo, trying to slow his breathing as his wound was cleaned. As the morphine took hold, he starting humming a song his Filipino grandmother had taught him when he was little.

Win sat on the bench. Yes, he was wearing his sweatshirt. Yes, it was pulled down over his head. And yes, it was sopping wet. But what the hell, everybody has to be sentimental about something.

Frenchman had been hit in the heart, the head, and the neck; take your pick on which bullet killed him.

Every time another soldier goes down, you think of the ones who've gone before.

And their families. Especially in this case. Frenchman wasn't a shooter or an ops guy or anything like that; his wife and kids, if they had any, probably didn't even know he was working for the company. It would all seem very unfair. And it was.

He'd done an important job for his country, but the odds were that no one who was close to him would ever know that.

Instead of flying us to the *Wasp*, the helicopter brought us to a navy command ship. The CIA officer who'd helped plan our visit was waiting. So was Ken.

"Dick, what the hell happened?" demanded Ken as I walked across the deck from the chopper. "Was there a nuke or not?"

Two seamen carrying Frenchman on a stretcher passed. Ken didn't even glance at him.

"No nuke," I told him. I kept walking. My clothes were still wet and I wanted to get the hell out of them. I also wanted to check on Trace and the others; by my reckoning they should have been scoping out the bar action in Miami by now.

"Wait—who the hell is that?" the admiral asked, pointing to the stretcher taking the Cuban from the helo.

"That ship had a sickbay better equipped than the one aboard this ship. A dozen beds at least. And the latest med gear. And these, in a re-frigerator."

I handed over the test tubes I'd retrieved.

"He's some sort of doctor," I said. "I figured we'd want to know why."

"What the hell is this stuff?" asked Ken, looking at the vials.

"Damned if I know. Here's a question for you: is there any Bombay Sapphire aboard this ship?"

(11)

Junior had told Trace that he would sit tight, but the odds of that happening were about the same as Fidel having a deathbed conversion to capitalism, and Trace knew it.

"We need the bikes," she told Shotgun, turning back for them.

"Hot dog," he said. "I'll race ya."

Junior did actually *try* to sit tight . . . for about ten seconds. Then curiosity got the better of him and he started looking for a way to get past the inner fence and take a look inside the compound.

He didn't have to look very far. There was a narrow trail about thirty yards from the bluff where he and Crusty were hiding. The trail led from a part of the beach that couldn't be seen from the compound or marina to a hole under the fence. The trail was undoubtedly used by workers sneaking away for trysts or the usual recreational activities.

(Are you following this at all, grasshopper? There are two sets of fences, an inner one and an outer one. Junior and Crusty are inside the outer one, and outside the inner one. Though not for long in Junior's case.)

Junior had no trouble slipping under the links. The woods were still relatively thick, and once he was off the trail a few feet he had trouble even spotting it. He made his way back in the direction of the building they'd seen earlier, stopping every thirty seconds or so to make sure he wasn't being watched.

It took him over a half hour to get close enough to the building to survey it. By now the sun had started to set. This provided him with more cover, but it also made it harder for him to see where he was going, and he walked straight into a triple-strand barbed-wire fence about eight feet high and black, about ten yards from the building.

(That's the third fence set, if you're keeping track. Glad someone is.)

The barbed wire ripped up his clothes and put a gash into his thigh, but the most severe injury was to his pride. But that was a good thing—it reminded him that he hadn't been watching what he was doing carefully enough. He untangled himself, then pried the strands apart and slipped past.

A four-foot chain-link fence (number four) ran across the grounds, marking off a lawn area from the trees. The building had a half-dozen spotlights near the roof, but they were widely spaced and it wasn't hard to pick out a path through the shadows. Junior made his way to a side door, but sensing that it would be attached to an alarm, began looking for another way in.

Around the corner he came upon a window cracked open at the bottom. The curtains were drawn and the room was dark. He slipped his fingers in and pried it upward. Then, after leaning halfway in and listening to make sure no one was there, he wiggled through, climbing onto the floor as quietly as he could.

It took a few seconds for his eyes to adjust to the dim light in the room. The air had a bleached scent to it, as if he were in a laundry. But the room was a regular office, with two metal desks and several filing cabinets. Junior went to the door and listened for a while without hearing anything. Then he went back to the desks and began going through them.

The few papers he found had to do with supplies. The file cabinets were stuffed with files, each with handwritten notes and sheet upon sheet of documentation. While he had a workable knowledge of Spanish, he couldn't decipher the handwriting. He took two of the files at random, folded them, and stuffed them in his waistband under his shirt.

A lab coat hung at the back of the door. Junior took it, then cracked open the door.

He could feel his heart pounding in his throat as he peeked out. He suddenly froze, unable to move. He'd lost his nerve.

For a few seconds, Junior considered backing out—moving quietly to the window, and going back to Crusty. But then he asked himself, *What would Dad do?*

Junior managed a breath, then stepped out into the hall.

Like hell.

I would've gotten my butt out of there pronto and done as I was told.

Past history and all evidence to the contrary notwithstanding.

Junior—Matthew—was raised by a single mother in suburban Virginia. There'd never been a father around. He'd been an extremely bright kid in very difficult circumstances. For most of his life, his mom worked two jobs.

When he was little, she got a night job, arranging her schedule so she would get back in time to wake him up and get him ready for school before going to bed. When he returned from school, she'd be there as well, ready to supervise his homework.

By the time he was in fifth grade, Junior was what they called a "latch-key kid"—he let himself into the house when he got home, called his mom, then did his homework and other chores. Now, most kids—myself included—would have gotten into plenty of trouble under that sort of arrangement, but Matthew was different. He had a tremendous sense of responsibility, not to mention love for his mom, and instead of cutting class left and right or sneaking off with friends after school, he hit the books, read a lot, taught himself computer programming and a million other things.

I don't mean that he never got into any trouble, but his name was known in the principal's office for achievement, not misbehavior, and the only reason the local cops knew him was that his mother worked as an assistant dispatcher part-time Saturdays to make some extra money.

But growing up without a father wasn't easy. When he was five or six, Matthew asked his mother where his dad was, then who he was. She gave him various stories, not exactly lies, but not exactly the full truth, either. She told him his father was in the navy, away on a dangerous mission, and that maybe someday he would return. Then for a while she claimed that he'd been wounded, and might never come back. And then after that, when he was ten or eleven, she confessed that she didn't know where his father had gone.

Somewhere around his sixteenth birthday, she told him I was his dad. Actually, he guessed it based on different things she said and hints she dropped over the years. Before telling him he was right, she made him promise that he would not try to contact me.

I had no idea I even had a son—or if he was it. As I've said, the circumstances make it possible . . . but this is about Matt, not me.

When his mom died, Matthew felt relieved from his promise. Still, it took him roughly two years to get in touch with me, working his way slowly by befriending Shunt and some other mutual acquaintances. It wasn't until we'd both gone through North Korean hell together that he got up the courage to tell me who he was. He felt that having survived that first op, he'd proven he was related, not to me so much as to himself.

That's why he wanted to be a shooter, part of the action side of the operation. He wanted to prove himself to himself. And then to his dad.

I guess most men are like that. We need to show ourselves as well as others we belong. The impulse can lead us to achieve great things. But it can also make us a little reckless.

All right. Maybe I would have gone into the hall myself.

But that's just me.

The corridor was empty. Junior walked swiftly to the end, where a set of double doors led to a staircase up and down. He chose the ones leading downward, and soon found himself in a maze of laboratories. A few had people working inside them, but by moving swiftly past the doors he managed to avoid being stopped or perhaps even being seen.

Junior found an empty room at the end of the hall. Binocular-style microscopes were lined up on three benches near the middle of the room. Petri dishes were stacked in an incubator against one wall. The dishes were labeled with letters and numbers that gave no clue about what experiments might be conducted here. There were no logs or computers anywhere to tell him.

Maybe if Junior had studied biology rather than computer science, he would have been able to figure things out. But instead he took two Petri dishes from the middle of one of the stacks and put them in his pocket. He went back to the stairway and tiptoed all the way up to the third floor, which was the top of the building.

This floor was very different than either the basement or the floor where he'd come in; it looked like a traditional hospital or nursing home, though there was no nurses' station in the middle. Patient rooms lined the hallway, which led to a large common room at the far end. All were empty. The place was definitely lived in, however. Though the rooms were generally neat, some of the beds were messed up, and there were books and magazines on the night tables, and clothes in the closets.

In the third or fourth room, Junior picked up one of the books on a side table. He stared at it for a moment, knowing something was unusual about it but not quite able to figure it out. Then it dawned on him—it was in English. So were all the other books there.

It was the same way in the next room. The four paperbacks on the nightstand were all American paperbacks. There was also a small Spanish-English dictionary at the side of the pile.

Junior took a mental inventory of everything else in the room: suitcases, shoes, a pair of sweaters. Then he tried to note what he *didn't* see: no clothes in the drawers, no newspapers, no private papers, no clipboards or folders with patient data.

Survey complete, he left the room and went to its neighbor. But before he could do little more than confirm that all the books here were in English, he heard voices in the hall. The people who lived here were returning from wherever they'd been.

Junior took a deep breath, then tilted his head slightly, and walked swiftly from the room. He turned right, in the direction of the common room.

It was the wrong way to turn—he thought the residents would be coming up from the stairs at the opposite end of the hall, but it turned out that there was another set of stairs in an alcove at the side of the common room that he had missed earlier. It was too late to turn back, so he strode with his head down, walking against the flow.

The people passing him ignored him, or at least didn't stop him. Junior, his heart thumping so loud he swore it was bouncing off the floor and walls, made his way through the common room and into the alcove at the side. He grabbed the door from someone, nodded purposefully, then trotted down the steps.

On the second floor he was caught in a flood of people, apparently returning to their rooms from dinner there. Nodding and smiling, Junior waded through them, pushing gently until he was able to get through. He reached the first floor and went out of the stairwell, walking past an assembly room and down the hall. The room he'd come in through was near the very end of the hall; all he had to do was get into it, then go out the window.

Junior was about six feet from the door when a female voice behind him ordered him to stop. He ignored her, pretending he didn't hear. As he heard her walking swiftly down the hall behind him, he considered whether to just make a run for it but decided that was too risky; he could make it out of the building but she would undoubtedly set up an alarm and he would never make it past all those fences.

The woman called to him sharply. He turned around, expecting a nurse, but saw instead a security officer, who already had her hand on the holster at her hip. She was maybe three feet away.

"*Sí?*" said Junior.

"What are you doing?" asked the officer.

"Working," said Junior. He had to stick to one word responses so his accent and limited vocabulary wouldn't give him away.

"You should be at dinner with the rest of the staff."

Junior shrugged.

"Why aren't you upstairs at dinner? Are you sick?"

"Not hungry."

She looked at him suspiciously.

"You don't have your ID," she said.

Junior made a show of patting his chest.

"I'll get it," he said, turning away.

The officer grabbed his shoulder.

"You don't look familiar," said the officer.

Junior realized he had pushed things as far as he possibly could. There was only one thing left—push some more.

So he pushed the security guard. Then swooped over her and grabbed her gun. She bit and clawed at him; Junior gave her a kick, whipped the pistol in her direction once or twice, then ran into the room he'd used to enter, escaping out the window.

It took nearly two hours for Trace and Shotgun to get north. By now Danny had been able to get a rough fix on where the facility was, and gave them a good set of directions tracing the route Junior and Crusty had taken. He also scrambled M.W. and his trusty PBM flying boat; M.W. headed north with Red in case a rescue at sea was needed.

Trace and Shotgun ducked the checkpoints easily enough, but found that the roads near where Junior and Crusty had been chased were now completely blocked to all traffic. They detoured through a pair of empty fields, cut back to the west, then found another road heading along the coast.

"You know what's the matter with Cuba?" Shotgun asked after they stopped outside the facility's perimeter, near the water where they were supposed to meet the others. "They don't have any 7-Elevens."

"So if there were 7-Elevens in Cuba, it'd be perfect?" snapped Trace.

She began climbing up a rockslide to get on the high ground over the water.

"Close to it. Imagine having a Slurpie right now? Or a Ring Ding."

"Heaven."

"You got that right." Shotgun heard no sarcasm in Trace's voice. After all, he was talking about junk food, not something to joke about. "I'd settle for some Oreo cookies."

"You don't have any in those pockets of yours?"

"Had the last one an hour ago. I'm down to Fig Newtons. This is hardship, man. Real hardship."

Junior made it to the woods, but just barely. Thirty seconds later, two guards armed with shotguns came out to look for him. They passed him by, hustling down the path. Junior thought of trying to follow and maybe tackle one of them, but then thought better of it.

A good thing—a few seconds later, more guards came out, running down the trail with some sort of supervisor. (Unlike the others, he was wearing a white shirt rather than khaki.) He told them they were looking for a patient disguised as a lab worker, and they should consider him armed and dangerous.

"You will simply kill him," said the Cuban. "Don't hesitate. And do not touch the body, or especially the blood. Take no chances."

Junior slipped a little deeper into the shadows, then pulled out his sat phone and called Crusty.

"Where the hell are you?" snapped Crusty when he answered his phone.

"There's a bunch of security people coming your way," Junior told him. "Get out of there."

Junior gave Crusty a few more details about what he had seen, then told him he thought he'd be able to slip out through the marina. It'd be easier than going through the woods, since the guards were concentrating their search there.

"I'll check back with you in an hour."

"Don't get lost."

Junior pulled off the lab coat, figuring it would be a beacon to the guards. Then he took off his shirt and turned it inside out, hoping the coagulated blood left from the Cuban they'd killed earlier might seem slightly less conspicuous. But it was a false hope, and finally Junior decided that wearing the lab coat made more sense—especially if he went back inside the facility.

Why back inside?

Junior realized the Cuban security force had responded to the alert the way most security forces would: they sent out search parties, which would deplete their regular force and patrols. Those search parties would pursue their subject—and leave the building itself wide open.

There was no one at the door to the hospital, or in the hallway. He walked in the direction of the marina, hoping that he would find a set of doors that would take him out there. He did—but just outside of them he saw a security guard with her back to him. She was short, with longish curly black hair and a pronounced curve at the hips. It was the guard he'd wrestled with earlier.

He swung around and ducked into the nearest office.

A clerk or a secretary was sitting at a desk behind a reception counter. The counter was so high that only the very top of her head was visible.

"About time," she said, practically jumping up. "I'm starving."

Junior bit the side of his tongue and hoped his heart was still somewhere in his chest.

"Where's Ernesto?" said the woman, coming out from around the counter.

"Sick." Junior fell back on his one-word Spanish.

"I'll bet. What a phony." The woman lowered her gaze to his pants, catching sight of the blood and a rip from the fence. "What happened to you?"

"Uh—"

"You had a smoke outside, didn't you? That's why you're late."

She came closer and touched his leg; he stepped back immediately.

"I wasn't going to hurt you. You should have that fixed."

Before he could say anything, she added, "Oh, don't worry, I won't tell on you. But don't expect me back right away, either. One favor deserves another. And don't let the director see your coat dirty like that. He'll fire you. Which would serve you right."

She stomped off to eat.

Junior glanced around the office, looking for another lab coat but couldn't spot any. Finally he sat at the desk where the woman had been.

She'd been playing computer solitaire. Not very well.

Junior knew he had to get the hell out of there, but he wasn't sure exactly what to do. The only thing he could think of was to shoot the guard—he had her gun, after all—and then make a break for it. But he was afraid that the noise would bring too many other guards.

He was also queasy about killing someone else, especially a woman. Doing it while he was involved in a struggle, with no choice, seemed somehow different than planning it.

He fiddled with the computer as he tried thinking of an alternative. Besides the solitaire game, two programs were running. One was a text messaging system used by facility personnel to communicate; little different than the corporate text message systems Junior had seen before, it had a small window with a few buttons governing how the messages were disseminated. The other program was Microsoft Word for Windows, the ubiquitous word processor.

The MS Word screen was blank. Thinking he might find some useful intelligence, Junior went through the open file menu and began scrolling through the list of documents. They were all letters from the director to different personnel at the facility. He opened the first on the list, the most recent document that had been created.

It said personnel were not supposed to sneak out for cigarettes "or other activities" while on duty and would be severely disciplined if they did.

Junior looked at a few more of the memos, his natural curiosity taking over despite the danger he was in. He found his way into the computer folder where various operational memos were stored. He opened a few, reading a few sentences to see if he could get the gist, and then moved on. The administrator seemed to be a punctilious asshole, micromanaging every aspect of the employees' work habits.

And then Junior came to a memo that addressed Fidel's death, and procedures to be taken when that occurred.

It had been written several days before, apparently right after Fidel had been hospitalized. It was a long, detailed list, filled with instructions on where people were to report and what alerts would be sounded.

Junior couldn't understand everything, but it was clear that Fidel's death would set in motion a detailed response at the facility—a response big enough, he thought, to make it easy for him to escape.

According to the plan, the alert would begin with a text message through the system: *El Comandante en Jefe has passed on.*

Easy enough to initiate, he thought.

Junior slipped the mouse to the bottom of the screen, bringing the text message system up.

Had he given the matter a little more thought, he might have realized that putting the facility on a special alert wasn't the best idea. True, it might divert a guard or two—at first. But that long and detailed a list should have made it clear that anyone out of place would arouse suspicion. And that was the last thing Junior wanted.

But Junior didn't give it any thought. He pulled up the program, typed in the words that appeared in the memo, and sent it as a "broadcast all" message. Then he typed the double confirmation—also outlined in the memo—and sent that as well.

He rose and scrambled from the desk. Before he reached the door, a siren began wailing so loud his eardrums nearly split. As he covered his ears, two Cubans raced past him into the office. He put his head down, stepped out into the hall, and turned toward the door.

Which was being locked off by a pair of security gates, inside and out.

While Junior was wandering through the Cuban lab/hospital, Crusty retreated farther into the jungle. Guessing that the security guards would search the area near the trail first, he tried tracking to a point where he could slide under or climb over the outer fence without too much trouble. But by now it was too dark to see easily, and he had to move slowly—so slowly, in fact, that he was soon overtaken by the guards. Fortunately, they had as much trouble with the vegetation and darkness as he had, and despite their flashlights passed within a few feet without seeing him.

On the other side of the fence, Trace and Shotgun saw the flashlights poking through the trees. They took up a position near the spot where Crusty and Junior had first gone in, then waited as the guards made their way to the fence. The Cuban soldiers hesitated for only a few seconds before slipping through.

"You have the one on the left," Trace told Shotgun as the men started past. She leapt up, ran two steps, and launched herself at the back of the lead Cuban.

Trace's forearm hit the back of his head with a satisfying crunch. He fell forward at an angle, his legs buckling. Trace grabbed at his side but lost her balance; both of them tumbled down a narrow rock-filled slope, just missing several boulders. She scrambled to her feet, then kicked the Cuban in the face. Dropping her knee into his back, she pulled the gun from his holster, but by now he'd lost the will to fight and lay prostrate on the ground.

Shotgun had taken a less showy route, grabbing his soldier from behind and squeezing.

Very hard. The man coughed, struggled, coughed again, then lost consciousness. Shotgun disarmed him, and with the handcuffs he was carrying in his belt secured him to a tree three or four yards from the trail.

"More coming," said Shotgun when Trace ran over to him, pointing to the flickering flashlights back up near the fence.

Junior found himself in the middle of a human tsunami. People seemed to have materialized in the middle of the hall. They rushed past, grim looks on their faces. Two or three of the women had tears rolling down their cheeks.

"Everyone, to their stations. Everyone, to their stations. You will do your duty," said a voice over the loudspeaker.

Junior realized that if he stayed where he was, eventually he would be questioned and probably discovered as an imposter. So he chose someone to follow and started walking down the hall.

He made it to the door of the room he'd come in through without being stopped. Pushing inside, though, he found himself face-to-face with a pair of startled secretaries.

"Wrong room," muttered Junior, retreating back to the hall.

The hall was still filled. He went to the stairs and began trotting upward. He got to the third floor, but then stopped near the door, unsure what to do.

Footsteps in the stairwell below pushed him back into action. Junior grabbed the door handle and strode out as purposefully as he could into the corridor.

There were only three or four people in the hall, each scurrying to rooms farther down. Junior took a quick right into the first room he came to. The occupant who slept in the bed closest to the door was in the bathroom; the other stood dressing behind the curtain that divided the room.

A sweater and robe sat at the foot of the nearby bed. Junior grabbed the sweater and robe, deciding to pass himself off as a patient while he looked for another way out. He threw off the lab coat and pulled on the sweater, donning the robe as he strolled down the hall toward the common room.

It was empty. He went over to the windows, looking for a fire escape. He'd just pulled back the curtains when a loud voice startled him.

"What are you doing out here?" asked a woman behind him.

Junior turned. A male and female nurse stood in the alcove that led to the other stairs. The male nurse had a tray in his hand, stacked with medicines. Both wore surgical masks and rubber gloves.

"I, uh—"

"You're ready?" asked the woman.

"Yes," said Junior.

"Roll up your sleeve."

When Junior didn't respond—he didn't understand her Spanish—the nurse walked to him and rolled the coat and sweater out of the way.

"Don't be a sissy," she said. "It won't hurt at all."

The male nurse came over with his tray. Junior started to pull his arm away, but the woman's grip was firm.

"It's not going to hurt, my God," she told him. "You won't feel a thing."

The needle went in. Junior winced, hamming up his reaction for her benefit. By now, two other patients had appeared.

"Go get your bag," said the male nurse. "Then come back and wait. And why are you wearing the robe? You are not a patient anymore. Remember that. You've been cured. This last shot makes you strong. Enjoy your freedom."

Junior walked slowly from the room. Other patients were coming down the hall in ones and twos. Each carried a suitcase. They were quiet, but most were smiling. Junior nodded; they nodded back.

A security guard had appeared at the end of the hall, making it impossible for Junior to use the stairs. He ducked into an empty room at the right, then went to the windows at the far side, thinking he might be able to escape that way. All but a small panel of the windows was fixed in place. Even if he could have squeezed through it—dubious, he thought—he'd have to jump the three stories to the ground.

His only choice was to stay with the patients until some other opportunity presented itself. He still had his sat phone. He took it out and called Crusty.

Crusty, still ducking the second wave of security guards, answered the phone with a hushed but still cranky, "What?"

"I'm in the hospital," said Junior. "There's been an alert that Fidel died. I'm not sure how long it will take for me to get out."

"You need help?"

"No. I just have to lay low for a bit."

"Right."

Junior checked the closet, wondering if there might be a spare suitcase or something else he could use to blend in. But it was empty.

There was a sharp rap on the door. It swung open and the nurse who'd administered the shot entered, followed by a soldier.

"Come on. Let's go," said the nurse. "What are you doing?"

"I—"

"Where's your bag?"

"I—uh—"

"Just come on," said the guard sharply.

Junior walked out into the hall, following the nurse back to the common room. All of the patients were there, talking among themselves. The buzz disoriented him for a moment; then he realized they were all using English.

The nurse clapped her hands.

"As soon as there's confirmation," she said in Spanish, "you can board the boats. As soon as there's confirmation."

"Sister, we should be using English only," said one of the patients.

"Yes, yes, you're right. English from this point only."

Now what have I gotten myself into, Junior wondered.

Trace and Shotgun had barely dispatched the first set of guards when the flashlights of the second wave appeared near the fence. They hunkered down, ready to ambush the newcomers.

But the guards never reached the fence. One of their radios cackled, and they were summoned back to their stations inside the facility.

Trace took out her sat phone and called Crusty.

"Where the hell are you?"

"Sitting in a pile of sticker bushes, wondering why the hell I agreed to do this."

"Where are you in relation to the fence?"

"How the hell do I know?"

"I'm glad you're so cheerful."

Crusty's response was unprintable, even for me. Trace and Shotgun went through the fence, then followed Crusty's insults to his hiding spot.

Earlier, Danny had dialed into the assets my CIA honcho buddy Ken had promised, asking for some help. It seemed to him that the request had been directed to the round file until one of our com lines suddenly lit with a call from someone in Maryland.

Probably just a coincidence, but that does happen to be the state where No Such Agency is located. Or would be located if it existed.

"Someone inside the facility you asked us to watch is trying to call out," said a man with a machinelike voice. "Would you like us to let it go through?"

"Can we answer it and pretend to be whoever it is they think it is?"

The man took a second to untangle Danny's garbled syntax, then said he could, and left Danny on the line as the call proceeded. Danny could hear the conversation and speak to his NSA contact, but the people on the line couldn't hear him.

"*Sí?*" said a female voice on the NSA side.

"This is Facility B. Is the situation genuine?"

"The situation?"

The NSA operator didn't know what the caller was talking about, but Danny did.

"Tell them yes. Tell them yes."

"Genuine," said the NSA operator.

"Proceeding," said the caller from the facility, who then promptly hung up.

Up in the ward room, Junior listened to the conversations around him, trying to tease out what was going on without having to ask and give himself away. But the clues were contradictory. People talked about feeling good, seeing old friends, relaxing, checking into a real hospital—and they did it in mostly heavily accented English, even harder to understand than Spanish.

Finally a staff member emerged from the alcove and consulted with the female nurse. She nodded, then clapped her hands.

"Listen, everyone! Listen!" she said. "We have confirmation! We will board the boats immediately."

"Fidel is dead," said one of the men.

There was a hush, and then a loud shout.

"Fidel is dead! Board the boats to America!"

[IV]

The captain of the navy ship where Mongoose, Doc, and I had been delivered was old school—he had a full selection of health elixirs in his cabin, including Bombay Sapphire.

Obviously, the man should be promoted to admiral posthaste.

He treated us to a toast in the wardroom, then led us to one of the command ship's secure spaces so I could brief Ken, Laundry, some other analysts, and a flock of Naval Intelligence types and other assorted hangers-on on what had transpired on the ship.

I brought the bottle with me, of course.

When I was done talking, Ken nodded to Laundry, who gave a quick and rather subdued overview of what had happened after we left the ship. The vessel had radioed Havana and said it had been attacked by American agents—so much for Ken's insistence on using a third party to preserve deniability. Several men had been killed; at least two others were believed to have gone overboard, including the doctor.

"They asked for further instructions," said Laundry. "They were told to proceed as planned to New York."

"Obviously, you didn't do a good enough job searching, Dick," said Ken. "Now we're back at square one. We'll have to stop the damn ship ourselves."

"Hey listen, Admiral, that's bullshit," said Mongoose, standing up. "We went through that whole fuckin' ship—there wasn't no bomb there, believe me. If Dick couldn't find it, it wasn't there."

"Your loyalty is admirable," said Ken. I think he meant that to be an insult. "Understandable. All right. I want a workable plan to stop the ship within the hour. Dismissed."

"Still thinks he's in the navy," whispered Doc, sitting next to me.

I didn't hear him. My thoughts were elsewhere.

"I'm surprised you let us down," said Ken, walking over as the others shuffled out. "But I guess it was inevitable. You're not perfect."

He sounded almost relieved, as if he had been betting against me all along, and was now finally pleased that I had "failed."

"How big is the sick bay on this ship?" I asked him. "How many beds? A hundred?"

"God, Dick, I don't know. We'd have to—"

"On most merchant vessels, sick bay is a closet; you're lucky if there's aspirin in stock. But theirs was a floating hospital. Test tubes, everything."

"What are you getting at?"

"The person we should be talking to is the doctor," I told him.

"Granted. But—"

I got up. "He'll know whether there was a bomb aboard the ship. And I have my own questions for him."

"You can't ask them. The cover story is, you and the others died at sea. He's the only survivor."

"Why the hell do we need a cover story? At this point."

"Dick, the cover story is the whole reason you're here. *Capisce?*"

That's Italian for, *Do you understand, or do I have to break your knee-caps?*

"Then I guess my work here is done," I said, standing up. "I'd like to get some rest."

"Very good," said Ken.

Three guesses where I headed. The first two don't count.

The doctor was guarded by a pair of plainclothes CIA paramilitary types as well as two of the ship's marines, all of them standing at drill-sergeant attention in the passage outside sick bay. This actually made it easier for me to get in—I nodded to the Christians in Action, who nodded back and stepped aside. The marines, seeing that it was OK with the spooks, didn't say boo.

The doctor was sitting up, but he was still pretty out of it from the drugs we'd given him in the helicopter. I grabbed a chair and sat next to him, asking in Spanish how he was doing.

He had a little trouble focusing. When he managed it, however, he jerked back.

"I'm not going to harm you," I told him. "What's your name?"

He didn't answer.

"My name's Dick Marcinko," I told him. "What's yours?"

Still no answer.

"I can call you asshole, if you want," I said, switching to English.

"Spencer Rodriguez," he answered.

"Good." I didn't believe him, of course—how many Cubans have you ever met with the first name of Spencer? But even a lie was better than silence. "Why were you aboard that ship? Were there many sick men?"

I asked in Spanish. He didn't answer. I tried the question again, speaking much more slowly, just in case my pronunciation was the problem. But he sat stone-faced.

I tried in English. He still didn't answer.

"You are a doctor, right? A real doctor? Not a fake."

"I am a physician, as educated as any American."

"What was in the test tubes?" I asked. "There were test tubes in those refrigerators in the sick bay. What were they for?"

No answer.

"Was it poison?" I asked.

Nothing. But I realized the way to get him to talk was to make him angry, or question him in a way that pricked his ego.

"You were going to hurt people?" I said. "As a doctor, you're sworn not to, right?"

He seemed on the verge of saying something, but held it in.

"An American doctor wouldn't hurt anyone."

"Phhhew."

"So was that medicine? To help people?"

He pressed his lips together.

"No. It was a kind of poison, wasn't it?" I said as everything slammed together in my head. "You're going to infect the crew with some sort of disease. It's biological warfare."

The doctor put his teeth against his lower lip, then clamped his mouth shut.

I went to find the admiral.

Back at the hospital, Junior joined the line of men going down the steps. He was still unclear about what was going on.

Tables had been set up near the landing at the bottom of the stairs. The men and their bags were being searched by security people and staffers, all of whom were wearing surgical masks and gloves as the people upstairs had.

Junior still had the pistol and his sat phone. Knowing either might give him away, he looked around for a place to hide them. He got rid of the gun by pretending to tie his shoe near the base of the stairs, then slipping it under the open tread. But the line began moving before he could get rid of the phone. Desperate, he pushed against the man who had just surged in front of him, slipping it into the compartment on his bag.

A routine had been established at the tables. A man would give over his suitcase, then hold out his arms to be searched. Once that was done, he was led toward the wall, where someone with a camera snapped his photo. A minute or two later, he was handed an American passport.

Or what looked like an American passport. Junior guessed they were bogus, since the people here hardly looked like consular types.

At least not American. Clearly they must work for the government somehow. They looked sad, grim, as if carrying out their duty. But what was it, exactly? If they all thought that Fidel was dead, why hand out American passports? The staff hadn't cheered upstairs; it was the patients who were happy. They were still happy now, buzzing with excitement.

The man in front of him had reached the guard and held his arms out, waiting to be searched.

"What is this?" asked the official at the desk. He pulled the sat phone from the outer pocket of the man's suitcase. "Where did you get this?"

"I never saw it," protested the man.

The guard next to him smacked him across the face. "Liar! Against the wall!"

The man, his face white, tears streaming from his eyes, began to protest. The guard took out his pistol.

"Against the wall!"

"I did nothing."

A loud pop reverberated through the vestibule. The Cuban collapsed to the floor, a bullet hole in his forehead.

"Take him away," the guard told an aide. He turned back to Junior. "Next. Empty your pockets."

M.W. and Red had completed the circuitous route from Jamaica and were closing in on the hospital. Worried about his last encounter, M.W. had equipped the plane with more antennas, newer radio frequency scanners, and a more powerful ECM jammer obtained from the Russian black market via an Israeli who owed him serious favors. The Russian electronic-countermeasures suite was arguably as good as anything the U.S. had, outside of dedicated ECM aircraft; no radar would be able to see him once he flipped his fuzz switch, though the fact that the ECMs were on would tell them he was there.

The jammer wasn't selective; it worked on all electronic devices. M.W. and Danny had discussed the possibility of using it to jam the local communications if things got hot, and now that the aircraft was within range, Danny asked M.W. to block the radios the Cuban security people were using.

Reluctantly—as I said, jamming the signals would make it obvious *someone* was around—M.W. agreed.

"Look at all these damn boats," said Red, using the night glasses to survey the marina. "There have to be a couple of hundred. More."

"What the hell are they doing out here?" said M.W. "This isn't a tourist area. From what Danny told us, the place is a mental institution—a prison. Right?"

"Get closer."

Red watched as two launch-type boats pulled from the pier, then began treading slowly toward the boats at the far end of the complex.

"They're leaving now that Fidel's dead," she said. "That makes no sense. Now's the time people should stay. With Fidel gone, Cuba can breathe again."

"They only think he's dead," M.W. reminded her.

"The Cubans think he's dead. And they're letting them go."

"Doesn't make sense."

"Maybe it does," said Red, reaching toward the com panel. "How do I dial Dick's sat phone?"

Junior felt as if he were in a trance. Whatever he'd felt earlier when he'd shot his first man up close in the head, he felt ten times worse now. The Cuban had been killed because of him.

A shooter has to get past moments like that, or else he's no good to anyone.

Or worse, he's dead.

The fact that he'd been dreaming about being a shooter since he was a kid, and even more than that, his need to prove himself to me, really hurt him then. He was faced with the reality of what that all meant, and it paralyzed him—he literally walked stiff-legged to the desk, mechanically holding out his hands, then going and getting his photo taken, following the guards' directions like a mindless drone without comment.

But on the other hand, the shock may have helped him get past the security people. His reaction was just the sort of reaction they expected from a scared shitless patient—even if he was a good ten or twenty years younger than everybody else in line. And he wasn't the only one who was shocked—everyone up close, guards included, seemed a little dazed. No one bothered to ask why he didn't have a suitcase, or ask anything at all.

People think courage means you're not scared. Hell no. Everybody gets scared somewhere along the line. The important thing is what you do, what you manage to do, when you *are* scared.

What Junior did was this:

Passport in hand, eyes so glassy that everything around him was a blur, he walked out the now open door, passed by several security people and hospital staffers, and went down to the piers. He was in a boat before he knew it, heading out in the middle of a boatlift that rivaled Dunkirk in size, and had the potential of Hiroshima in impact.

[V]

Y ou have to analyze those vials," I told Ken when I found him. "And you have to press that doctor to find out what the hell is going on. He knows. He'll talk, if you put the screws to him."

"You're not talking about torture, are you, Dick?"

This isn't the time or place for a long discussion on "interviewing" techniques, what works and what doesn't, where something is appropriate and how far you can pressure someone before anything they say becomes bullshit. The point here is that Ken—the number two man at the CIA—wouldn't make a move without calling in his team of lawyers to paper him with excuses, or whatever fancy bureaucratic word he'd substitute if he was writing this.

You can complain all you want about the government's hiring "mercenaries" and handing terrorists over to third-world countries, but it's happening because people don't have the balls to stand up and say, "This is a hard omelet we're making here, and in the process there are going to be some eggshells on the floor."

No, we don't have to throw out the Constitution. What we have to do is stop letting hissy fits over pseudo issues get in the way of good judgment.

How did George Washington deal with Major André after he 'facilitated' Benedict Arnold's desertion?[42] There's your role model.

I didn't give that lecture in the operations center of the ship. What I said was, "Let me talk to him."

"He's in my custody right now, Dick," answered Ken. "I'm here. I can't just let it happen."

"Right."

I took a step back, gave the most proper salute I could summon—they would have been proud of me back in boot camp—and turned on my heel. Then I marched double-time to the wardroom where the CIA officer I'd handed the test tubes over to was having a cup of coffee. I told him I needed one of the test tubes.

---

[42] He was hanged.

They don't teach that in school anymore, do they? That's half the problem right there.

He didn't argue. Might have been the four-letter verbs I used.

I was on my way back up to do a little show and tell with the doctor when my sat phone rang. It was Red.

She hadn't quite connected the dots, but I had. I changed direction again, returning to Ken.

"A few hundred prisoners escaping Cuba at the same time, when obviously the government knows about it," I told him. "Castro's revenge."

"Biological warfare, Dick?"

"It's easier to do than a nuke."

It didn't take long for Ken to confirm that there were boats moving out from Cuba; already there had been a report from a navy surveillance plane of an unusual number of small craft in the waters east of Havana. The coast guard, navy, Immigration all scrambled to deal with the exodus.

"We'll turn them back," said Ken.

"That may be a problem," said one of the analysts. "The Cubans have put a couple of their own vessels out from Havana. They may want to keep them from returning."

"Then we'll sink every boat if we have to."

I had only one problem with that—Junior was almost surely on one of those boats.

Probably, if I'd asked, Ken would have lent me the Seahawk that had brought me to the ship so I could get down to Cuba and find out what was going on.

But he was busy, so I didn't bother asking.

"We need to get south in a hurry," I told the pilot when I rounded him up belowdecks.

We were airborne in thirty seconds.

[VI]

Junior didn't speak when he got on the boat. Two Cubans were already aboard. Obviously excited about getting away, they took almost no notice of him as he sat on the bench at the back of the open cabin. The night had turned chilly—it was now under fifty degrees—but neither seemed to mind.

A handful of the boats had radios, but most, including Junior's, did not. There were no supplies on board, not even a candy bar. There were life rings, but no other equipment beyond the simple instruments at the helm.

The engine made a dull, even purr as it came to life. One of the Cubans cast off, and the boat began making its way out of the marina. A dozen other boats did so at roughly the same time. Two or three dozen others were already out ahead of them; another two or three dozen would come right behind.

The breeze off the ocean smacked Junior's face. Gradually, he started to come back to his senses. There wasn't a Eureka moment; God didn't reach down and tap him on the shoulder, and nothing in his imagination shook him and told him to get ahold of himself. But at some point, he did.

He got up from the bench where he'd been sitting and walked over to the man at the wheel.

"Where are we going?" he asked in English.

The man looked at him for a moment, then laughed uproariously.

"To freedom! Fidel is dead," said the Cuban. His English was heavily accented.

"Why did we wait until he died?"

"It was promised to us that we would be free." The Cuban looked at him more carefully than before. "What happened to you? You don't remember?"

"How wouldn't he know this?" asked the other. Then, in a more ominous tone, he told Junior that he didn't recognize him.

"I came just today. To the hospital," said Junior.

"Hospital. Right," said the first man. He turned to the other and said something in Spanish. They both laughed.

"Your English is very good," said the first Cuban.

"I'm an American," Junior confessed.

The man smirked. He didn't believe Junior, or thought he was just getting into the spirit of his new land.

"Why did they give us shots?" Junior asked. "Before we left?"

"Inoculations."

"Against measles," added the other man. "Everyone in America has measles. We have to be very careful."

"But I had a shot for that when I was a kid."

"So did everyone," agreed the first man. "But the Americans don't. This is a booster, to protect us."

Junior knew that Americans didn't have the measles—the disease had practically been eradicated a generation or two before. So why would they need a booster?

Obviously, they didn't. Either this was some sort of ridiculous Cuban paranoia, or something else was going on.

Part of Junior's brain was still frozen by the brutal killing of the innocent man in line, and his role in it. But the rest was working fine, and began agitating for some sort of logical answer to the question of what was going on. He thought of what he'd seen in the basement, thought of all the people with masks.

"We were poisoned," he realized finally. "They gave us some sort of disease, which we're going to spread as soon as we get to America."

The Cubans looked at him as if he were crazy.

"We can't go on," he said, grabbing for the wheel.

The boat veered hard to port. The Cuban who'd been at the wheel lost his balance and fell to the deck. But the other man, heftier, landed a haymaker on the side of Junior's head.

Junior fell to the deck. He froze for a second. But this time, underneath the thick layer of ice a volcano exploded. He threw himself back in the direction of the punch, landing full on the Cuban. How many blows he struck—three, four, twenty—he couldn't say later. But however many it was, the other Cuban fell dazed on the deck.

The other man had risen and grabbed the helm again. He tried to fend Junior off, but he had no chance. A pop to the nose and a hard smash to his cheek took the Cuban down.

Junior grabbed the wheel. He started to spin it toward land, then realized that everyone in the flotilla was infected; just turning his little boat around would have almost no effect. He had to get everyone to turn back.

He steered back toward the front of the pack and put his hand on the throttle, jamming it wide open.

Most times, the easiest way to figure out what's going on is to ask someone. And since the patients had gone, the only people left to ask were the staff.

With the patients gone, the security staff stood down from alert, leaving only a small token guard. There was one person near the rear of the building; it took Trace all of perhaps two seconds to knock him out using one of her karate moves.

By then, Shotgun was already through the door and into the administration office, the same one where Junior had sent the message that launched a thousand boats.[43] The administrator was in his inner office on the phone. Shotgun, with his usual sensitivity to good manners, knocked and then entered.

Or maybe he knocked after he entered. The fact is he did knock, even if it was on the side of the administrator's head.

And with the barrel of his pistol.

"Hang up," said Shotgun.

Crusty, coming in with Trace, repeated the words in Spanish. Trace didn't bother translating—realizing actions spoke louder than words, she pulled the phone off the desk, tearing out the cord.

"What the hell is this?" asked the administrator.

He tried to stand. Shotgun pushed him down in his seat.

"Is Castro dead or not?" blubbered the man. "What is going on?"

"What is going on?" asked Trace. "Where are the boats going?"

Crusty began talking to him. The administrator—the word he used in Spanish technically means president, but administrator seems more appropriate—was a bit reluctant to be candid, but the barrel of Shotgun's pistol persuaded him to be loquacious. He said that the operation had been set in motion erroneously, but after checking with his superiors via radio—which had been mysteriously jammed until just a few minutes ago—the decision had been made to let it proceed.

---

[43] That's a botched homage to Homer for all you literary types.

In dribs and drabs, he explained the mission—the prisoners were being allowed to escape to America.

"Why?" asked Crusty.

No amount of prompting from Shotgun would convince him to say anything else.

Trace, wanting to make sure that Junior had in fact left on a boat, took a quick tour of the facility while they were talking. She walked down the hall, sidearm tucked close to her body. Three or four of the offices were still occupied, the workers clearing up whatever paperwork the launch of the operation required. But they were very relaxed, and if they noticed the strange woman passing their doors, they didn't sound any alarms.

The second floor of the facility was similar to the floor that Junior had been on, with a large common room at the far end. When she got there, Trace noticed that a tray of hypodermic needles had been left on one of the tables, along with some gloves and masks. There was no serum, but she took a few of the setups with her before going up to the third floor. When she didn't find anyone there, she returned to the administrator's office.

The administrator looked a little worse for wear, but refused to talk.

Until Trace took the needle from her pocket and approached him with it.

Then they couldn't get him to stop screaming.

(VII)

When the Seahawk took off from the command ship, we were roughly 120 miles north of Cuba. The Seahawk is many things, but fast is not among them. Even with a tail wind, no cargo, and a minimal crew, the helo had trouble making 150 knots.

You can do the math if you want. As far as I was concerned, each mile seemed to take an entire year.

We were roughly halfway there when Trace called in from Cuba. Threatened with being "inoculated" himself, the director had told her exactly what was going on.

"They've been working on a strain of Ebola. It's a virus that causes hemorrhagic fever," she explained. "The symptoms won't appear until seventy-two hours after inoculation. By then, it's too late."

Hemorrhagic fever isn't a common disease in the Western world, and that's a damn good thing. Go to the Sudan or Zaire, and you'll find a different story. The illness starts with a fever and, usually, diarrhea. There are cramps, vomiting—your typical flulike array of symptoms.

But within a few hours, it starts getting worse. A day or two later, and the fever's higher. By that time there's little hope that you can do anything except let it run its course. At least half the people who get it die from it, and once it starts spreading, it's pretty hard to deal with. There are no known cures to the natural strains of the disease, and quarantining sick populations seems to be the only answer.

Nature has its own way of dealing with it in Africa. The disease spreads very quickly in villages that are small and isolated. Once sick, the people tend to move around even less. They all die in a week or so, limiting the spread of the disease.

Put it in a developed country, where people move around a lot . . . different story. Except for the death part.

"Ask him about the ship," I told Trace. "What are they planning? Another way to infect people?"

I took the test tube from my pocket. Suddenly it seemed a hell of a lot more fragile than it had before.

"He says he doesn't know anything about a ship," reported Trace.

"Are you sure?" I asked.

She didn't answer.

"Trace?"

I heard the sound of gunfire in the background, then the phone fell to the ground and the line went dead.

Trace had been interrupted by a pair of security guards, who'd come up to the reception area to get their overtime chits signed. Finding the facility's administrator being questioned by a bunch of gringos was about the last thing they expected.

For a second or two, everyone froze. Surprisingly, it was Crusty who made the first move.

"Can't you see we're busy?" he growled.

He emphasized his annoyance by taking the heavy ashtray from the edge of the administrator's desk and flinging it like a Frisbee at the first guard's head. He hit him squarely, and the man fell straight back.

His comrade, however, did what security guards are supposed to do—he pulled his gun out to fire.

He was a little too late. Shotgun put two bullets through his temple before he could raise it to aim.

The shots alerted one of the Cubans' comrades in the hall, he charged in and got off a burst before Shotgun dispensed him as well. Meanwhile, someone sounded an alarm down the hall.

"Out the window," said Trace.

"I ain't going out no goddamn window," said Crusty. "It's undignified."

"You want to be dignified, or you want to be alive?" asked Shotgun.

"Both."

"We'll dress you in a tux when we stuff you into your coffin," Trace told him. Then she grabbed the hospital administrator, threw him over her back, and led them out.

The Cuban must have weighed close to two hundred pounds, but Trace kept pace with the others as they ran around the rear lawn toward the dock. A motorized whaleboat was tied up at the near end, and they jumped in. Trace dumped the administrator and grabbed the wheel. The engine seemed to start even before she touched the panel; maybe it was as anxious as anyone to get the hell out from under Fidel's thumb.

"Well, you could at least wait for me to cast off, damn it," growled Crusty as the boat strained its lines. He undid them, then went to leap in—and missed.

Shotgun hauled him up with one hand, depositing him with very little dignity on the deck. Spitting out water, Crusty rose.

"I can tell you ain't never been in the navy, girlie," he sputtered. "Order of the day is to wait for your goddamn crew before shoving off."

"Keep your head down," she warned as bullets began flying from the docks. "You better pray those assholes are terrible shots."

"Screw prayer," said Crusty. He reached down and took the pistol from her belt. "The Lord helps he who helps himself."

And with that, the chief plugged the two soldiers on the dock who were shooting at them.

(VIII)

A few miles to the northwest, Junior had his throttle nailed to the max, racing toward the head of the flotilla. The moon had fought its way through the cloud cover, and he could now see fairly well, at least well enough to make out where the other boats were.

He still didn't have a radio, or even a firm plan on what he was going to do. He only knew that he was going to somehow get the boats to turn around.

Nearing the lead vessels, he spotted a boat two or three times the size of the others to his east. This was one of the Cuban patrol boats that had come out to escort the smaller craft in the direction of Miami.

Junior didn't know that. He just figured that something that big would have a radio and a PA system that he could use to communicate to the others. He pointed his bow in the patrol boat's direction, nearly swamping his own craft with the sudden turn.

Roughly sixty seconds later, Junior was close enough to see one of the crewmen on the patrol boat watching him from behind the large tube of one of the missile launchers. The man did nothing as he approached, apparently unsure what was going on. Finally, with Junior twenty yards away, the man turned and ran toward the wheelhouse, apparently to alert his skipper.

Junior backed off the throttle, but his timing was poor and his seamanship worse. He surged sideways toward the patrol boat, no longer under control. Junior braced himself as the port side of his little cruiser smacked up against the side of the large navy vessel. The impact shook him, but he managed to throw himself onto the other boat, grabbing one of the metal bracing wires near the mortar and dangling over the side as the craft separated.

Jolted by the impact of the collision, the two crewmen fell to the deck. Then they scrambled to get away from the crazy man who'd just jumped aboard their ship—the crews had been warned that the patients on the small boats were highly contagious.

As warships go, the Cuban Osa patrols boats aren't very ferocious. They're notoriously unstable in heavy seas and have engines crankier than a '68 Olds Vista Cruiser. The missiles on most if not all of Cuba's

versions have been taken off the boats because of various problems associated with them, though in this case the launch tubes were left in place.

Still, they're not small craft—they displace over two hundred tons
when fully loaded, measure over thirty-eight meters from stem to stern,
and are manned by a crew of four officers and two dozen men. So Junior
wasn't exactly trying to take over a rowboat here.

The first sailor he saw who didn't run from him was a man near the
AA gun at the fantail. He also had been dazed by the collision, and didn't
react in any way until Junior started punching him. He flailed back
desperately until Junior connected with a roundhouse to the chin. At
that point he disintegrated, collapsing near the gun and then sliding
off the patrol boat as it pitched in the water.

Hunting for a weapon, Junior settled for a large wrench from a tool
locker near the gun mount, then ran toward the superstructure. A sailor
saw him coming and retreated, battening down the hatches as he went.
When he found the portal locked, Junior began battering it with his
wrench. He made such a racket that he didn't hear the first few rounds
being fired at him from the base of the radar mast. Finally realizing he
was being shot at, he ducked down, hugging the deck as he tried to work
his way around the port side of the boat and find another way inside. The
helmsman, possibly hoping to knock him off or else still trying to gain
control after the collision with the cabin cruiser, weaved back and forth,
making it hard for Junior to get anywhere.

"Ebola?" said Ken when I told him what Trace had found.

"Yes."

"Those boats have to be sunk. Have to be."

I agreed—even though I knew that Junior must be on one of them.

Ken told the ship's captain that he needed a direct line to the aircraft
carrier we'd visited earlier. I was about to hang up when he came back on
the line.

"Dick, are you still there?"

"Yes, sir, I am."

"You have people in the flotilla?"

"More than that," I told him. "My son's there."

"I'm sorry, Dick. I'm very, very sorry."

He hung up. I turned to the pilot.

"We need to go a hell of a lot faster than this," I said.

"Cuban patrol boat is dead ahead, a hundred yards," said the pilot, pointing.

"We need to be over it. Now."

Junior clawed his way past the forward missile launcher, heading toward the door that sat directly below the bridge. This, too, had been locked down; frustrated, he climbed up on the ladder next to it and tried breaking the oblong porthole of the ship's command center with his wrench. Even if he'd succeeded, he wouldn't have been able to get in because the space was so small, but he was desperate and angry and not thinking straight. He cracked the glass on the first blow, but otherwise did no damage; on his fourth or fifth shot he lost his balance, and with the ship turning hard to port, slid across below the rail and fell into the sea.

There was no way I could see him fall—we were at least fifty yards away, and even with the boat's nav lights on most of the deck remained in shadow—but I sensed immediately that someone had gone over, and that it was Junior.

Call it a father's intuition.

I leaned forward against the windscreen.

"What's that in the water, starboard side of the boat?" I yelled at the pilot. I was wearing a headset, but my voice was loud enough that he could have heard me without it.

The pilot banked and scanned the water with his Gen 3 night-vision glasses.

"Man overboard," he said finally. He was a hell of a lot calmer than I was.

"We're getting him."

"Sir?"

"Only one of my people would be crazy enough to try to take over a ship like that single-handedly," I told him. "We have to get him."

"I was only going to ask if you knew how to work the winch, sir."

I didn't, but the directions were fairly obvious—the arrow pointing down means down, right?

The problem was, I couldn't see anyone in the water. I leaned out the open doorway, willing whoever it was to appear.

Hell, not whoever. I knew it was Junior. Don't ask me how, but I knew.

"Matthew! Matthew Fuck-ing Loring!" I shouted. Sometimes you have to use tough love to get results. "Get your ass out where I can see it or I'm jumping in after you!"

Nothing.

Jumping in wasn't an option—with no one inside, I'd have to climb up the rescue line. But I told myself that if he didn't appear in five seconds, I would.

"Matthew!!!"

One second. Two seconds.

The helo fluttered back and forth. The patrol boat had twisted back north and was moving away.

"Matthew! Time to go!"

Four seconds.

"Swing down as low as you can," I yelled to the pilot.

Five seconds.

I'm not sure if he heard me, let alone whether he tried to warn me not to jump, which he claims he did. But if he did say something, I didn't hear it—I was already out the door.

Aboard the PBM flying boat, M.W. was getting nervous.

"That helo is too damn close to that missile boat," he told Danny. "The patrol boat carries shoulder-launched antiair missiles."

"The navy knows what it's doing," answered Red.

"Bullshit on that. Get on the radio and tell him to get the hell out of there."

Before Red could answer, the infrared launch detector aboard the flying boat began to bleat. There was a missile in the air.

The only thing I could see was the dark sheet of water that surged over my body as I hit the water. I pushed my feet together as I plunged downward, got my arms up, and did my best mermaid routine as the ocean trumped gravity and my momentum died. Kicking upward, I broke through the water, I felt a surge of adrenaline.

Then I felt a shock.

Damn, that water was cold.

"Junior!" I yelled, turning around. "I know you're in here somewhere! Where'd you go?"

I saw a reddish spark on the missile boat, and thought it was an illumination flare being fired. Behind me, the helo tucked hard on its rotor—it looked as if it were flying sideways—shot off a bunch of countermeasure flares and did a strange-ass dance in the air. By the time what I was seeing sank in, the helo had managed to duck the Cuban SA-7 that had been launched almost point-blank in its direction. (Probably a good thing, actually. The seeker in the shoulder-launched missile needs a few seconds to find its target, and by the time it was ready to rock the only thing in front of it were the decoys.)

The warhead blew up almost directly above me with the loud pop of a dozen July Fourth fireworks. I dropped below the surface for a few seconds, hoping to avoid any shrapnel. When I broke back to the surface, the night glowed orange-red, thanks to the decoy flares. They weren't quite as bright as an LUU-2 illumination "log," but they gave me more than enough light to see around me in the water. I started yelling for Junior again as I searched.

Finally I felt something bump against my back.

My first thought wasn't a happy one. I spun around, grabbing at the shadow, fearing I was too late, that he'd been killed somehow.

The son of a bitch smiled at me. He yelled something that I couldn't hear. He yelled again, and I realized the exploding missile had popped my ears out temporarily.

"What—took—you—so—long?" said Junior, slowly mouthing and shouting the words.

"You're in a whole shitload of trouble, kid," I yelled back.

He grinned. Probably he said something like, "So what else is new?"

"You all right?" I asked.

He grinned again.

"Better than you, old man."

I didn't hear that, or I would have smacked him so hard his teeth would have ended up in his rump.

I looked around, getting my bearings. The helicopter had banked east. Obviously we were going to have to find another way home.

"Let's swim for one of those boats," I said, starting out. "Pick the nearest one."

The crew on the Cuban patrol boat had recovered from their near infection experience with Junior and were now responding to the developing situation the way a professional navy should. Though they'd missed the helicopter, they had chased it from the area without its harming any of the small boats they were charged with protecting.

Now their radar showed there was a second aircraft in the vicinity—the Martin PBM.

As soon as M.W. saw the launch warning, he started a series of evasive maneuvers—pilot language for flying like a maniac. He ducked two missiles with the help of his decoy flares, and threw his fuzz busters back on, hoping to jam anything more ambitious.

The ECMs scrambled the radar aboard both Cuban ships, knocking out the targeting gear on the antiaircraft guns. But the weapons could be manually aimed, and a low and slow target like the PBM brought out the best in the gun crews. Bullets began puncturing the hull of the boat as M.W. swung away from a second volley of surface-to-air missiles. He turned the plane hard on its wing, almost directly into a barrage from the second patrol boat, which was a bit farther north.

"We gotta get the hell out of here," said M.W., trying to find some part of the sky that wasn't full of lead. "Hang on."

"How do I work the loudspeaker?" asked Red.

"What the hell are you talking about?"

"The loudspeaker. You said you had one, right? When you were showing me the gear."

"Yeah, but—"

"How do I use it?"

"You don't. We're getting the hell out of here."

A few weeks before, Red would have made an appeal to M.W.'s patriotism. But her time with us—Trace especially—had shown her how to quickly size up a person and appeal to them properly.

"Dick will double your fee," she said.

"Where do you want me to fly?"

Trace saw the flares of the rocket launches from the motorized whaleboat she and the others had commandeered. Realizing the helicopter was under fire, she maneuvered the boat in that direction, expecting that she would be needed to pick up survivors.

Murphy directed the prow of her boat directly in our path. He also threw the shadows so that it was impossible to see us.

By now the flares had all died and the ocean around was just a dark collection of shadows and blackness. My ears were still shot, and with all the strum and drum neither Junior nor I realized the whaleboat was bearing down on us. When it was maybe ten feet away, I looked over my shoulder, saw the dark shadow.

"Down!" I yelled, reaching toward Junior to throw him under the water as I dove. But he was a foot or so too far away, and I missed him. The whaleboat drove on, oblivious. I dove downward, but Junior hadn't heard my warning. The whaleboat smacked his arm and side, spinning him around. Stunned, he floundered in the water, then began to sink.

Trace, Shotgun, and Crusty immediately hove to, stopping the engine and turning the boat back in our direction.

When I saw Junior floating in the water, my first thought was that he'd been clipped by the propellers that had missed me. I closed my eyes, and stroked toward him. I purposely avoided his arms or legs, ducking my shoulder down and then came up in his chest, trying to act like a giant life preserver.

Shotgun fished us out, depositing both of us together on the bottom of the boat with a crash that nearly swamped it.

Crusty expressed his joy at seeing us with his usual aplomb:

"What the goddamn hell are you doing swimming around in the dark?"

At least my hearing had returned. I got to my knees, and saw that Junior had all his limbs. His senses were a different story. But he was breathing. I left him with Crusty and went over to Trace, who was still at the wheel.

"We have to get away from the flotilla," I told her. "The fleet's going to blow it up."

"Where do you want me to go?"

"Just turn around," I said.

"We're going to let the navy blow all these people up?" said Trace.

"You got a better idea?"

"There has to be one."

I took her sat phone—mine was in the drink somewhere—and dialed Ken.

"Dick, where the hell are you?" he thundered as soon as he picked up.

"I'm with the Cubans. We need to get these boats—"

403

"It's out of my hands, Dick," he said, cutting me off. "The president wants them sunk. The Harriers are on the way. You get the hell away from them. Give me something to identify your boat."

Before I could think of how to answer, a siren sounded overhead. Then a woman's voice began speaking in Spanish.

"Fellow Cubans! Now is the hour of opportunity! With Fidel out of the way, it is time to retake Havana! Change course for the west! It is time to return our homeland to the people!"

It was Red, broadcasting over the PA system M.W. used to lead parades and jolly boaters on pleasant afternoons.

The only effect the speech had at first was to concentrate the antiaircraft fire from the patrol boats. The PBM zipped downward, then banked behind the flotilla as Red continued to broadcast.

"They'll be shot down!" said Trace.

"Don't worry about them—they'll fend for themselves," I told her. "Turn us west, and head toward land."

"But—"

"The other boats will follow. Shotgun, fire that pistol. Get their attention."

I could hear the jets approaching. Something flared from one of the patrol boats. Then a Roman candle erupted from the other one.

One of the Harriers had hit it with an air-to-surface missile.

"Hoo-rah!" yelled Shotgun.

"Don't cheer too loudly," said Crusty. "We're next."

"Hey look," said Trace, glancing behind her. "The Cubans are following us. The boats are following us."

Up in the plane, Red continued to broadcast.

"Hold on, hold on," said M.W., "we're getting something in from the navy."

He killed the PA so he could listen in. The lead Harrier pilot told him, somewhat politely, to get the hell out of the way so he could blow the boats to smithereens.

"Negative, negative!" shouted M.W. "We have people on those boats. Navy people," he added, thinking this might convince the aviator.

It had about as much effect as pissing in the wind.

"Sorry, sir. I have my orders. Now get out of the way."

By ones, twos, and threes, the Cuban boats began following us in the direction of Havana. But I knew it was only a matter of time before the Harriers would decide to press their attack.

I hadn't killed my connection to Ken. I raised the phone to my ear, trying to come up with some way to talk him into stopping the assault.

"The boats are following us," I told him. "They're going to Cuba."

"I don't care, Dick," he said. "Truthfully, if there was an epidemic there, it'd be devastating. The only humane thing we can do is kill them now, before they infect the island."

"The Cubans have an antidote," said Junior. His voice sounded like the rasp of a rusty saw. "They ordered an antidote brought to the capital. It's in the memos on the hard drive. That's how I knew where to go."

"Ken. There's an antidote in Havana," I said. "An antidote. Let them land. Take out the gunboats and any defenses so they can get there, but let them land. The Cubans can deal with it. These people don't have to die."

Doc was in the command center with Ken and the navy commanders, screaming at them to get the Harriers called off. One of the Harrier pilots called in for directions on what to do about the PBM, and then reported that the flotilla appeared to be heading for Havana.

Ken told the attack force to hold off the attack until he contacted the president.

A pair of Harriers streaked overhead, banking around as they surveyed the ragtag fleet that was now headed toward Havana.

"They're not firing," said Trace. "He stopped them."

For about two seconds there, I felt good, as if we'd adverted a major catastrophe.

And we had. Maybe. If Junior was right.

One person would know—the hospital administrator lying in the stern of the boat, hands and feet bound by strips of cotton from Shotgun's shirt.

I went over and pulled him up by the neck.

"Tell me about the disease," I said to him. "What's the cure?"

"I know nothing."

"Tell me, or you're going over the side."

He began crying, insisting that he knew nothing.

"I don't know anything about the drugs. The doctors. It was all the doctors. They worked on it for ten years, perfecting it."

"Is there an antidote?"

"I think—yes, but I don't know."

"Take us back to the hospital," I told Trace.

"They're not there. They've left."

"Where are they?"

"Havana. I don't know. Anywhere. They've been gone for the last nine or ten months. The project had become mature they said."

Mature as in ready to be launched.

"Give me their names," I told him.

The fourth one was Spencer Rodriguez.

"Spencer?" said Crusty. "That's a strange name for a Cuban."

"His parents were English."

"Did you say *Spencer* Rodriguez?" I asked.

"Yes."

I pulled out my sat phone and called Ken.

"Can you get a helo to pick us up?" I asked. "We need a ride back north."

(IX)

The Seahawk that grabbed us was the same one that had deposited me earlier; he'd been orbiting to the west, waiting to see if he was needed before returning to his ship.

With no crew aboard, the pilot had to hold the aircraft just a few inches above the waves. Despite the fact that Murphy was blowing as hard as possible in our direction, the pilot did a great job getting the helo close enough for us to get in. With Shotgun's help, I pushed Junior in, then hopped in myself.

Murphy didn't want to let me go. He sent a gust of wind that swiped the chopper sideways, then just for giggles picked it up a dozen feet in an instant. I held on to the side of the door, managing to pull myself up just as the aircraft tucked forward. Hopping up, I slammed the door closed; within seconds we were hustling our way back toward the command ship.

The Seahawk had flown to the very edge of its operating range, and the pilot spent most of the flight back fretting over his fuel supply. He was probably about ten seconds from telling me to get ready for a rough landing in the drink when the blinking beacon of the command ship came into view. We touched down with little more than vapor in the tanks. But that was just fine with me.

Junior was pretty woozy. I helped him out of the chopper, carrying him in my arms as a pair of seamen and a marine rushed forward to help.

"We have to get him to sick bay," I told them. "Show me the way."

"We can help, sir."

"Just show me the way."

One of the seamen hopped to and led me into the ship, treading through the passages to the sick bay. The CIA guards there gave me a nasty look, but let me pass when they saw the kid in my arms.

Dr. Rodriguez was in the same bed where I'd left him.

"Well, Spencer, we meet again," I said as I entered. "I brought you a patient."

The Cuban looked up from the gurney, puzzled.

"I need a hypo," I told the nearby corpsman. "A needle."

He hesitated, glancing in the direction of a set of drawers. I put Junior down on the gurney next to the doctor, then went to the drawer and took out a needle. Reaching into my pocket, I retrieved the small test tube I'd taken earlier.

The top of the tube was made of thick glass and had been melted on. The damn thing was tough—I couldn't get the top off, and even a couple of raps against the nearby counter failed to either crack it or get it loose. Finally I grabbed a nearby plastic cup, put the tube inside, and smashed it open with the butt of my knife.

"What the hell are you doing?" asked the corpsman.

I ignored him, filling the hypo and then going over to the doctor.

"That's one of your victims," I told him, pointing at Junior. "How do we cure him?"

"Dick—don't!"

Someone had fetched Ken. He was standing in the doorway.

"Matthew here is infected with Ebola. I'd advise everyone to clear out," I said.

The corpsman's eyes grew wide and he moved away.

"Dick, if you infect the doctor, you'll be arrested for murder."

"That's not what this is about," I told him. "We're in this together, my son and I."

I plunged the needle into my arm.

Junior blinked at me.

"Dad?"

I turned to the doctor. "How do we find a cure?"

"You just . . . took it," said the doctor. "The test tubes aboard our ship—they're the antidote. For our people at the UN."

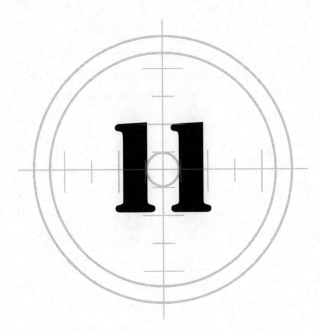

(1)

A couple of things happened in pretty quick succession: Ken sent someone to get the other test tube I'd brought to the ship, orders were sent to seize the Cuban merchant vessel, and a seaman was dispatched to find that bottle of Bombay Sapphire I'd left behind earlier.

Down near Cuba, the PBM landed in the water and picked up Trace and the others. They were a few minutes out of Miami when I got ahold of Red and told her what had happened.

"Have the Cubans turn north," I said. "If they go to Havana, they'll die in seventy-two hours. There were plenty of test tubes aboard the merchant ship to save them."

"Thank you, Dick." Red practically kissed me over the phone.

There wasn't enough in the test tubes, as it turned out. And the Cuban flotilla never actually made it that far north. The navy intercepted them. The terms of my nondisclosure with the government following the mission prevent me from telling you that American doctors were able to clone the cure and inoculate all of the Cubans, who were then brought into America in small groups so as not to alert the media what was going on. The sailors aboard the command ship received the same treatment, though they were never fully informed of what was going on. They did, however, receive an extra two weeks of liberty when the ship returned to port, and I'd guess that most of them would feel that was a more than square deal.

Oh, was I not supposed to say that?

Tear out this page and burn it. Or eat it. Whatever works for you.

Most of what I *can* say, you already know.

Shortly after we wrapped up, Raul Castro formally took over for his brother and instituted what he called reforms. Among them: "ordinary" Cubans can now use cell phones, even if they can't actually afford them, and can shop in places where they can't afford to shop.

Come to think of it, the place sounds more like America every day.

Our new president has made some gestures toward better relations. It's now easier for Cuban-Americans with family there to visit and send money. Will that help them in the long run? The answer, as they say, is above my pay grade.

As of this writing, Fidel hasn't died. If you don't think that he's still in charge in Cuba . . . I have a very nice bridge I'd like to sell you.

What will happen in Cuba in the long run isn't clear. I know what I hope will happen. I'm betting you do, too.

Red, Shotgun, Mongoose, Trace, Doc, Danny, Sean, about a dozen people who were important behind the scenes but didn't do anything to blow their cover and make the book—they're all still with me. Crazy assholes.

Junior spent about a week in the hospital, recovering not so much from the Ebola but from the battering he'd taken during the operation. He was chomping at the bit to get out several days before the doctors released him.

I spent that week dictating this account. We've spoken just about every day since then, but we still haven't talked over the father-son thing.

Maybe we will, sometime soon. The important thing is, I know how I feel about him, and he knows it, too.

Can't ask much more from a pair of warriors, Rogue or otherwise.